THE SACRIFICE ZONE

Also by Roger S. Gottlieb

Morality and the Environmental Crisis
Political and Spiritual: Essays on Religion, Environment, Disability, and Justice
Spirituality: What it Is and Why it Matters
Engaging Voices: Tales of Morality and Meaning in an Age of Global Warming
A Greener Faith: Religious Environmentalism and our Planet's Future
Joining Hands: Religion and Politics Together for Social Change
A Spirituality of Resistance: Finding a Peaceful Heart and Protecting the Earth
Marxism 1844-1990: Origins, Betrayal, Rebirth
History and Subjectivity: The Transformation of Marxist Theory

Together in
the struggle.
My best to you.

THE SACRIFICE ZONE

A NOVEL

Roger S. Gottlieb

atmosphere press

Published by Atmosphere Press

Cover design by Nick Courtright
Cover photo by Roger S. Gottlieb

The Sacrifice Zone
2020, Roger S. Gottlieb

10 9 8 7 6 5 4 3 2 1

atmospherepress.com

Contents

PART V

To Miriam
For your wisdom
Thank you

And (once again)—
To the Earth
Without whom this book
could never have been written

"Sacrifice Zone":

a place so polluted it can never be cleaned up

Present as Prologue

The five days off had been wonderful for Sarah. Though she made a point of going into some kind of wilderness at least three times a year, it always felt like it had been too long since the last trip. In the spring she had been to the Utah canyon lands, barely escaping a flash flood in a narrow slot by climbing up to a six-inch ledge and holding on for dear life as the immense force of liberated water streamed past for two hours. It had scared the hell out of her, but the purple and yellow wildflowers blooming in the desert, and the way the light created strange patterns on the water, colored by the sandstone and the glowing twilight sky, made it more than worth it.

This time she'd hiked a mild thirty-six miles in five days, hitting the ridges for the autumn views from the Presidential range of New Hampshire's White Mountains in the day and walking back down below the tree line to sleep in her cozy little tent. Together her gear made around thirty-five pounds, enough to give her a slight burning sensation between her shoulder blades, as if someone were pushing tiny needles into her skin. Her arches cried out for ice at the end of the day and the muscles in her ass complained that her pack straps had been too loose and her back hadn't carried nearly enough weight. Halfway up a three-hour climb, balancing on a series of medium size boulders damp from the rain, she would occasionally wonder why in hell she was doing this if she didn't have to.

But she knew. On the third morning the shockingly cold clear air invited her eyes to open by themselves, without the grogginess that often afflicted her in the city. The whispers and rustlings as forest twilight turned to night made her feel safe and loved, like being at a family reunion with people who actually cared about her. On other trips she'd watched mountain goats finding their way down near ninety degree slopes in the Weminuche Wilderness; heard a coyote howling his joy at being who he was after she'd crossed a pass at twelve-five on the Continental Divide; seen a perfect Harlequin duck, with its chaotic white and black and brown markings, floating on a perfectly still lake up against the sheer face of a mountain in Glacier Park, with a waterfall leaping sixty feet down the cliffs into the water as a mist cleared.

She paused at the overlook, pretty much the last place she'd get a vista before entering into the first stunted and then gradually larger pine and birch and maple forests. Taking off her pack and sitting on a large round rock, she gazed long and hard, taking in the brightly colored trees stretching far into the distance, the mammoth hulk of Mount Washington to the north, the smaller ridges of mountains spreading out to the west. She marveled at how much of New England's woods had returned, even though this meant that the destructive agriculture and manufacturing had just moved south, or to places like Guatemala and Bangladesh. A lot of the scars on the land that the hardy pioneer stock of the eighteenth and nineteenth centuries had made were overgrown by small, but flourishing, woods. If they could recover here, maybe the black marks being made today, and which would, she knew, be made for a lot of tomorrows, could be overgrown as well.

She bowed her head slightly to the sky, the colored leaves ("Who thought of this leaves changing colors business?" she laughed to herself. "My compliments to the designer!"), and the two hawks riding the thermals. Then she shouldered her pack, relishing its lightness with all the food gone and the way even a few days seemed to strengthen her upper body, and headed down the trail. Down to the car, back to Jamaica Plain, and to the work, the all-important work. She laughed out loud, feeling with pleasure the crunch of her thick soled, worn hiking boots against the stones, carefully stepping over the roots and gently, almost dancing, past the muddiest bits and the treacherous wet leaves on top of slippery small logs on the trail.

Hours later, nearly back to the flat that would lead to the trailhead, the sound of a stream fifty yards to the side playing with the last of the season's bird calls, she heard a weak voice. "Help, please, help" filtered through the trees. Dropping her pack, she ran down a well-worn spur trial to see a man sprawled on the ground, pain set in his lips and eyes, clutching at his left knee with both hands. He had ruffled gray hair, a scruffy beard, new looking equipment and clothes, and seemed to be holding back tears with each jerky breath.

What was this?

PART I

Chapter 1
Daniel

Daniel kept shifting his wineglass from one hand to the other and back. He pretended to study the framed photos of desert sunsets and the watercolors of tropical flowers, and he tried to interest himself in what people were saying. On the surface, he hoped, he was just another mild-mannered, jolly party guest. One more politely smiling spouse at the same old holiday get-together for the folks from Amy's office.

He nodded to Phyllis, slender and well preserved at fifty-four, wearing elegant slacks, a gold beaded blouse and a lilac batik scarf, talking about the failure of the Democratic Party to do anything serious for the white working class. There was Cal, aiming for the neo-hippy look in a black Indian styled tunic, studying the appetizers, perennially aggrieved about immigration reform. Sylvie had a Black Lives Matter button conspicuously pinned to her large, multi-handled leather handbag. And Abe, the senior partner, who often made it clear he didn't buy all this exercise-health-perfect-diet-purity crap, contentedly worked on his third scotch and his fourth smoked salmon and brie.

Daniel knew what good people they were, at least as good as he was. Together they all hated Donald Trump and Fox News, sympathized with the downtrodden and, like Amy, spent a fair amount of time helping folks who were far too poor to get decent attorneys. They lamented the changing climate and then got on with their lives.

And it was all he could do not to start screaming at them about what growing their coffee did to the hillsides. And the children forced to pick it. And what it cost in greenhouse gases to transport it from Kenya or Sumatra.

When he went into the beautifully decorated kitchen—with its obligatory granite countertops, oversized Sub-Zero gleaming stainless fridge and stove, view of the open floor plan and adjoining family room littered with toys for his hosts' far above average children—he noticed the recycling bins. Thick sky-blue plastic, slightly worn around the handles, half full of empty wine bottles, finished cans of artichoke hearts, and used tin foil. They just made him feel worse. How much more was there in this house, in all the houses, that wouldn't get recycled? And besides, he knew all too well that recycling was a sham, that staggering amounts of energy were used to produce what got recycled, and package it, and ship it, and melt it all down to start again.

The party was well catered—tiny appetizers of avocado and prosciutto, curried carrots glazed with honey, crisp crackers covered in flax seeds, turkey slices and spiced chicken wings; then a whole ham surrounded by three different potato dishes, pilaf, and a mountainous salad; even blackened tofu for anyone who had doubts about meat. There was enough liquor to drown a college fraternity, and desserts that would cure any latent problems with low cholesterol. It was a beautiful spread, decorated with slender crystal vases filled with bouquets of irises and lilies. But as Daniel munched on the few clearly vegan choices and sipped what he hoped was organic rosé, he saw the long check out rows of all the supermarkets, both the endlessly inviting overpriced ones that called themselves 'natural' and the huge warehouse-style ones for regular people staffed by underpaid, sullen minorities. And then he saw all the stores, in all the countries. And he cringed inside.

Byron and Steven, with whom they occasionally socialized, drifted over. They were a strangely similar couple, both tall and thin, both wearing wire rimmed glasses and neatly pressed open neck tailored shirts. Both spoke in hushed tones, conveying studious, serious attentiveness, a tone that helped them get anguish-filled divorce cases or the task of defending reckless teenage sons of wealthy families who'd had a little too much to drink before driving. Byron asked Daniel about his teaching, and Steven inquired after Sharon's health. They were pleasant and well-intentioned, but Daniel could see Byron's hand fiddling with his watchband as he waited for Daniel's reply, and Steven barely let Daniel finish his usual "Yes, Sharon's doing fine, at least seems to be, thanks" before he nodded, smiled, nodded and excused himself to get another glass of white.

They needn't have worried. He would behave. Not raise his voice, pound on a handy table, and accuse all of them, including himself, of the unforgivable crime of which they were all a part.

For he had promised Amy. She'd asked, practically begged: "Daniel, *please*, not again, o.k.? You know what I mean. Just enjoy Ralph's food, and the lovely house Beth has decorated so nicely, and don't, *don't*. And if you could, please Danny, put on something other than. That." She gestured at the wrinkled and stained jeans, the pullover Greenpeace sweatshirt that had, after far too many late nights of research fueled by chocolate covered peanuts, grown tight around the inevitable mid-fifties male pot belly. So he'd brushed what was left of his thin and graying hair, trimmed his unruly beard and mustache, and switched the jeans for gray khakis with a slightly elastic waist and one of the blue dress shirts he hardly ever used.

"Oh, much better, thank you, thank you," said Amy,

reaching up to stroke his face in a gesture that made him feel both loved and small, like a child. "Danny, I'm really worried about you. You know how I feel," (and indeed she recycled, and never forgot to bring cloth shopping bags to the supermarket), "but it won't do any good to get crazy about it."

He loved her, there was no doubt about that. And he was deeply grateful that she had forgiven him, far more than he'd forgiven himself. He admired her intelligence and how, as a hardworking liberal lawyer, she'd saved more than a few people from unjust prison terms. Yet as much as she cared about "the rights of the oppressed," and she'd smile at the corny phrase even as she used it, she could leave it alone when the day was done. She'd put on sweatpants and an old t-shirt, make herself a giant bowl of popcorn, watch some disease of the week movie on cable, cry a few tears as a mother saw her son die or some middle aged professional woman give up her career to care for her mom with Alzheimer's, and then go to bed happy.

He couldn't leave it alone. Or go to bed happy. Ever since they finally understood what had happened to Sharon—actually, what he had done—he'd become obsessed. Monomaniacal. Insufferable. There were the times he stared into his computer screen feeling like the mercury residues were entering his lungs with every breath; the dying fish from the polluted rivers in Chile were covering the surface of the nearby pond. He felt his heart wrenching in his chest, a pressure on his eyes, a sadness so heavy he wasn't sure if he could lift his body out of the chair. But he wouldn't share those moments with anyone, and could only tolerate them for a few minutes before he switched websites, did some more research, and felt the comforting flow of anger once again.

When an acquaintance said, "Daniel, you're becoming a real drag," he smiled and agreed. Then his smile faded, his voice rose, his finger pointed. "If you want to see a real drag, check out the effects from uranium mining on some native reservation in Utah, where the cancer rate is eighteen times the national average."

Yet there was still a part of him that didn't want to make Amy unhappy, or more unhappy than he'd made her already. She looked forward to these parties, and he didn't want to spoil it. So he gave a brief smile, leaned over to kiss her cheek, and walked back to his tiny writing room to collect his wallet and keys. But quietly enough so that she wouldn't hear him, or at least so he thought, he whispered furiously to himself, "Who's crazy? The guy on the Titanic who runs around telling people they've hit an iceberg? Or the people who keep on playing bridge and waltzing to the string quartet?" He could see how trite the analogy was. But that really wasn't the point, was it?

So he'd come to the party. And so far had kept the peace.

Until Sally came over. Sally whom they'd known for years, who'd baked them lasagnas after Sharon was born, who'd divorced her husband years ago and flowered into a national spokesperson against capital punishment. Sally who seemed to never miss a hot yoga class, forget a friend's birthday, or gain an ounce in twenty years; and who seemed to think it was her God-given responsibility to cheer up anyone who looked down at the mouth.

Which certainly meant, at this relentlessly cheerful party of relentlessly good people, Daniel. So Sally came over, with her perfect black slacks and dark green silk blouse, some kind of brightly colored vest with tiny mirrors on it, a necklace of honey hued Moroccan amber and neatly trimmed jet black hair framing her flawless complexion, clear blue eyes and shortened nose.

Daniel nodded a wary hello and tried, with little success, to smile. Given what was going on in the world, what was the point of all this perfection?

"Just the man I need," Sally said, with a pseudo-conspiratorial wink. "Amy's told us about how you're really into the environment." Daniel resisted the emotional recoil that sought to make his mouth turn down and a curse come out of his mouth.

"Into it, yeah that's me. Of course, you could say we are all really *into it* all the time, right?" His forced chuckle fooled no one, and he knew it.

"So," said Sally, sounding a little confused by Daniel's poorly hidden hostility but not one to be put off that easily, "I thought since you're all for nature, you might give me a little tip about where to go snorkeling and see the coral reefs. There're so many places, but I thought, Daniel, maybe he's been, maybe he knows. So, nature boy," she smiled at her own charming silliness, "got any tips?"

He could see she was trying and deserved a polite brush off. He knew Amy was listening to see if he would do what he'd promised. But the words just wouldn't come. If only Sally hadn't made her little 'nature boy' comment, as if any of them weren't part of this vast and mysterious thing, even as they were doing it in. And then, with the finality of a door slamming shut or a window being violently smashed, he didn't care.

"Snorkeling. Coral reefs? Here's the thing," his false jollity and the mean edge to the smiley tone made her head, which had been leaning in for the presumed intimacy, snap back. "The thing is. The thing is," he repeated, then paused, using an old professorial trick to get the undergraduates to wait for the punch line, "the coral reefs are dying, bleaching white. Go to Australia, St. John, Belize. Go anywhere. Thirty, forty, some places fifty percent or more. And the fish: angelfish, puffer fish, the ones that look like boxes and the ones with snouts like swordfish. Getting wiped out because they can't feed on the coral. So if a funeral is your idea of a great vacation, check it out."

"How awful. But, why?" asked Sally; and it was hard to tell if she was upset by what he was saying—or upset that he hadn't played along with her generous attempt to engage him in light party talk.

"Ocean temperature too warm from global warming. Seawater too acidic from, oops, there it is again, global warming. Sewage from the hotels from all the folks who want to, you know, snorkel and see coral reefs." He mimicked her tone, not much but just enough so that she felt the contempt. "Why? Because of us."

Sally pressed her lips together, tilted her head to one side. She was, it was quite clear, considering what she'd heard. Daniel knew what was next.

"Terrible, just terrible. It must be so upsetting." Daniel recognized the strategy. First you empathize, then offer the fix. "But there must be people working to help, yes? Groups, like, I don't know their names, but so many of them ask for contributions and have ads on TV. I mean that French guy, Cousteau and, what is it? Oh yes, Greenpeace. Right?"

"Yeah, sure," answered Daniel. "Good folks. Doing their best. But it doesn't come close." Sally had unconsciously moved further back and now he leaned in, fixing her blue eyes with his own watery brown. "Look Sally, imagine you're attacked by something big and mad—like a pit bull defending its owner or a wolf whose pups you've come too near. And they rip into your thigh, from here," he tapped his leg near his hip, then just above his knee, "down to here. And someone wants to help." His voice was rising, and he knew it, and didn't care. "Really help, you know. And they offer you, you see," almost shouting now, "They offer you a band-aid, for that huge gaping wound that's bleeding you out." Down to almost a whisper. "A band-aid."

The party had hushed and he immediately felt like a fool, and knew how angry Amy would be, because, after all, he'd promised. But he couldn't help it.

***

For a while he'd wanted to be a great novelist. And write he did. A long, tedious saga about his emotionally distant father, depressed mother, and Alzheimer's afflicted grandfather. His first sexual experiences had figured prominently, and so had his love-hate relationship with his graduate school mentor—a man universally recognized by himself as one of America's greatest writers.

It had turned out to be a carbon copy of dozens, if not hundreds, of similar novels by smart, untalented English grad students. Everyone else who looked at it, from the agents and big publishers who turned him down to the critics, almost all of whom didn't bother but when they did noted a few good scenes in which the hero was in the woods, or the beach, or just strolling about a city park, but dismissed him as "derivative, tediously familiar, and very far from the cutting edge." The general public passed him by on the way to mild-mannered erotica for middle-aged women, sword and sorcery sagas that went on for thousands of pages, sweet—and thankfully short—spiritual memoirs, and stories about India or Rio or turn of the century Paris.

The biggest surprise was that after a while he saw it too. And it was kind of a relief. All those years of thinking he had to write something great, and almost but not quite concealing from himself the deeper knowledge that he simply didn't have it in him.

So he wrote some articles on other people's books, became review editor of what another colleague called a "very good second rate journal," got tenure, and tried to communicate a little bit of what he loved about Tolstoy and Conrad to his students. He could have grown old with some grace, watched his daughter finish college and move on with her life, maybe give him grandchildren or maybe not. Even being a public interest lawyer, Amy made enough money for them to be comfortable, to have decent cars and the occasional self-indulgent vacation in the Caribbean or Tuscany. They shared childcare when Sharon was younger, and worries about her when she became a teenager. He'd have retired, maybe developed his gardening and written some poetry, grown old, and died.

But something happened.

Chapter 2
Daniel

There was only the faintest glimmer of light in the eastern sky, but the local robins and cardinals were singing anyway. They flitted from tree to tree in the orchard, hoping to find a careless insect, or a particularly tender piece of grass, or a twig shaped just right for their nests. From the small farm at the other end of the narrow country lane, a rooster crowed, feeling, no doubt, that if he was up everyone else should be too. Daniel shifted his weight on the thin, lumpy mattress which barely protected him from the plain wooden floor of the little room he and Amy were sharing for the weekend. Then he stretched out his legs, pointed his heels, and hoped that by pulling on his spine he could lessen a particularly thick morning fog.

"No," he thought, "not right. Just focus on what is here, no judgment, no striving for something different." If he was tired, just investigate the fatigue and take it for what it was, without wanting it to be something else. Such wanting was the root of suffering. To overcome suffering, all that was necessary was to accept it, without judgment. "Don't even accept it," The Teacher had said. "To say you accept it is to suggest that you might reject it. But how can we reject what is? Just let it be, and let yourself be."

"Let it be, let it be, let it be," Daniel whispered to himself, waiting for a little of the promised detachment to kick in. But it wouldn't. Not for him. His half-shut eyes that wanted to close, the pressure behind his forehead, the way his legs felt almost too weak to stand, the jolt of cold dawn air on his neck and his nipples—these were what they were and no matter what The Teacher said, he wanted them to be different.

He pulled on a black sweatshirt over the tattered white t-shirt he'd slept in, slipped on an old pair of sandals and shuffled to the communal bathroom, averting his eyes from the other students in the hallway. "Do not engage with the other students during your time here," The Teacher had instructed them. "This is not a social scene, but a time when all the games your ego plays are stopped. This is no time to be cute or charming or smart or nice. It is not time to be anything or anyone. If you have questions you can ask me during the dharma talks every day between one and one forty-five. The rest of the time, silence. No media of any kind, certainly,"—she had paused, looked each of them directly in the eyes—"no phones. Just yourself. No escape."

From the bathroom, Daniel hurried to the meditation hall, hoping to get there a few minutes before five so that he could stretch his back and thighs before the first session began. Each practice was an hour—and there were ten of them during each day. The rest of the time was spent in labor—in the kitchen, the gardens, the tool shed—making the Buddhist Center of Pomfret, Vermont run smoothly. He and Amy had paid $400 for the privilege of three days of silence, bad vegetarian food, and sleeping on a lousy mattress without a pillow. "In our tradition," The Teacher had said softly, "we do not eat meat or sweets, watch television—or use pillows. Luxury and attachment go together, like the horse and the cart."

It was six minutes to the hour when he got to the hall—wooden floors and a high arched ceiling with thick wooden beams running its length. In the corner was a pile of round zafus—meditation pillows of faded blue and red and black, well-worn from thousands of hours of pressure from hundreds of plump and boney and muscular asses all connected to people who thought that watching their minds in silence would ease their pain. Along the sides of the hall were a few Tibetan thangkas, painted silk images of the saints and sages of Buddhism. One, Samantamukha Avalokiteshvara, represented compassion. Daniel wasn't sure how five heads of blue and red and yellow, above a graceful torso from which four arms extended on each side, would take away his suffering, but he liked the lotus blossom the saint stood on, and the puffy white clouds that framed her downcast eyes and gentle expression.

"Like, dislike, like, dislike." On and on his mind went. And that was the problem. The Teacher had been clear—"Let it all be. Let yourself be." Daniel was not unfamiliar with the basic Buddhist mantra: *because we want, life is suffering; so stop wanting*. And even if he didn't believe it, he'd promised Amy, really promised this time, to try. If this didn't work—well, his marriage had been headed on a long downward spiral for some time now, and it wasn't likely to come up. Unless he could relax? Chill? Take it all in stride? Trust someone to make it better?

There you go again, he inwardly chastised himself. Try, for Amy. For Sharon. For your marriage. Just look at the damn painting, and the beams, and the stars through the dirty windows, and huge yellow candles on the altar and incense holders covered with ash and the single huge picture of Buddha looking down with detachment and wisdom and God knows what else. Just look and don't notice the wrinkles in the fabric, the black stain, the.

Then The Teacher's voice again: "No judgement, no preferences. Let everything be. Let yourself be."

But he couldn't. The meditation sessions were agony, even

though The Teacher had, with what might or might not have been a little grimace of judgment, made it clear he could use one of the rickety straight-backed wooden chairs at the ends of the hall rather than sit cross legged on a meditation pillow. And the daily instruction sessions—"dharma talks" they were called here—left him alternately bored and irritated.

"Why," he'd asked the first afternoon, "why is being here"—he gestured at the small teaching room where other students sat on cushions and he and Amy sank back awkwardly on an ancient, frayed and tilted green couch, "better than being anywhere else? And why is meditating better than not meditating."

"Better?" The Teacher had seemed just slightly amused, "who said better?"

"But then why should I do it?"

The Teacher's mouth turned up slightly, her pale face, narrow lips, slender nose, tilted slightly to the side, as if to bring her ear close to Daniel's mouth and hear him more clearly. Then she straightened, returned her lips to their usual inexpressive straight line. "I do not believe in 'should,' for 'should' tells us to be something different. I believe we should let ourselves be."

"But," interrupted Daniel, who had a good four reasons as to why this made no sense.

"But," The Teacher continued, her even tone never altering, her complete lack of response to his interruption more effective than any raised tone or rebuke, "While I have not said you should, I do not believe you, or anyone else, will live a life of contentment unless you come to know your own mind, and that requires meditation. So that we learn to recognize the mind's tricks and lies: the vast promises it offers and how little it can deliver on those promises."

Not so subtly Amy elbowed Daniel, demanding silence. This was not, he could hear her voice, yet another place for a rant about dead lakes and the carcinogens in the blood of newborn babies. This was a place to calm down, to lower the noise in his head that he compulsively shared with everyone.

***

Amy had sat down with him in the living room, reaching over to take his hand for the first physical contact they'd had in a long time. Her voice was subdued, even. This was way beyond shouting, and he knew it. "This is it, Daniel," she told him. "I cannot live with you like this. Ether this works or." She couldn't finish the thought. But they both knew what it was. "I thought maybe Dr. Emerson would help, but you wouldn't listen to him either."

"But, I'm right!" Daniel yelled so loud that Amy's eyes widened with her own anger – anger stoked by the steadily gathering storm of Daniel's near screaming about air pollution in Los Angeles and lowered sperm counts from toxins in toothbrushes. Of Daniel alienating every friend they had and too many family dinners ruined by impromptu lectures about lead in inner city drinking water or the rights of chickens. Of Amy biting her lip, offering consolation even though it had been his fault, not hers. Of trying to change the subject, act interested, be sympathetic. Of Sharon storming off to her room, hands covering her ears, screaming at her father to "Give it a rest, Dad. It's bad enough what happened to me. We've heard it all before!"

That time, as Sharon stormed out, Daniel's voice had dropped to a whisper. He tried to call her back, but only a stuttered mumble came out. His chin fell onto his chest, a slight tremble ran through his hands. What had he done? Why had he done it? To Sharon, whom he adored, the light of his life. Before he had failed her with what he hadn't taken care of; and now by inflicting bitter stories of polluted beaches and dying species. These stories, too, were a kind of poison. Why couldn't he stop?

He wanted to tell her, her and Amy, whom he loved so much. He wanted to tell them that it was because he loved them so much that he had to do this work, take in all the details—like the lead in the air in Manila from the old taxis, poisoning kids like Sharon but who could never go to the great doctors they had here. That he couldn't bear the thought of Sharon growing older in a world wracked by storms and droughts, with ever fewer birds in spring. And that when he looked at Amy, or felt her breasts press against his chest, the sweetness of her flesh made him think not of caresses and sex but of the way pesticides caused the plague of breast cancer in women.

But when he tried to talk about the love, and the deep, unending fear, it just came out as rage and bitterness. That was the best he could do. That—and the reading, and thinking, and broadcasting what he learned in any way that he could think of.

Amy raised her voice, pointed a finger at his face, demanding he be different. "Do you want to be married or to be right? I want my life back. My life that you have stolen, yes, *stolen*, with this endless crusade. We are here, all of us," she gestured to the two of them, to Sharon's room, to the tree lined street outside on which families and joggers and old ladies with their dogs walked toward the nearby pond, "and you act like we and everything else are already gone."

***

It was Sunday at one, time of the program's last Dharma talk. The Teacher sat on the slightly raised platform at the front of the room, her legs gracefully arranged in a full lotus, her right leg on top of her left, the back of her right hand gracefully resting in her left palm, her arms fully relaxed in the middle of her body.

She was a gaunt woman who must, Daniel thought, have had a full head of hair like everyone one else at some point. But now her scalp was shaved bare. The skin was taut between her temples and jaw, as if it might snap at any moment, exposing the hard, uncompromising bones beneath. Any soft, unnecessary flesh that might have made breasts or a plump ass was long gone. Dark brown eyes looked carefully at each person, her mouth moved only to speak and her lips almost never expressed either appreciation or displeasure.

"And this is why we say the 'middle way.' Do not deny your basic needs for food or shelter or companionship. And do not indulge them. Do not cling to your appearance, to your possessions, to your career, to your..." she hesitated for moment, and seemed perhaps to have given out a barely perceptible sigh, "family. Live with what is, with what you are, with how you and the world are connected, and always changing. Notice how your mind creates the reality around you. The purer the mind, the purer the reality. If you purify your mind through meditation, through self-knowledge, you will know reality for what it is: a series of moments, each one leading to the next. That is why everything that lives will pass away. Each moment is like a death—and a birth. So. This is what is. Let it be."

Daniel raised his hand, and next to him on the old couch he could feel Amy's body stiffen, hear her rapid intake of breath. The Teacher nodded in his direction.

"I'm trying to understand."

She cut him off. "Perhaps you do not need to try. Simply let the words be," she rotated her right hand so that the palm faced the ceiling, then tilted it slightly towards him, invitingly, "and whatever happens will happen. With understanding, or without. The words are there, as are you. The trying is an extra effort. Do you want to make it?"

"No. Look, I'm sorry."

"There is no need to be."

"No!" Shouting now. Heedless of Amy's hand gripping his knee with increasing force. "I'm trying to understand what all this *means*," he raised both hands and rotated them in quick circles. "This place and these pictures on the wall and the candles and..." his voice a little lower, for there was still some part of him that had no wish to be any nastier than necessary, "you. But surely you know what is going on." He pointed with two fingers toward the window, the woods and fields outside the building, the entire world beyond.

"Look," he started again, and perhaps there were tears in his eyes and his voice was moist, but he was talking fast. "I had a friend, known him for years, lost touch because I thought his wife was boring. Then she died, young, really young, from breast cancer. Turns out she was a really special person, did work for battered women while raising four kids, treasured by everyone who knew her. So I drove six hours to the funeral, listened to all these people, hundreds of them, talking about 'Leah was such a wonderful person' and 'What a tragedy.'" And I wanted to scream, fought the words down so hard I thought my throat would snap. I wanted to say to them all," his voice raised again, he stood without realizing it, and he moved his head from side to side, looking at The Teacher, and the other students, and Amy and the trees outside the window: "It's not a tragedy. It's murder. You think it was her damn genes? Or bad luck? What do you think is in the water? The food? The air? Don't you know? And if you do know, why don't you say something?"

He looked around, saw that he was standing, and realized he'd been nearly screaming. Now, voice so low they have to strain to hear him, "Do you want me to let that be? Just get to know my mind while that is happening?" His mouth twisted down, his eyes squinted, tears flowed from his eyes and his hands clenched. There was confusion in his voice, a hunger to escape that which he knew to be inescapable. "Really, is that what you are saying?"

The Teacher waited, spoke calmly. His outbursts did not seem to have registered. "Your outrage and your fear are burdens. Do you wish to carry them?"

Daniel's head snapped up. He stared at The Teacher, eyes wide, studying the woman's face as if to see into her soul as deeply as he could. And then he looked away. The tension left his body. His voice cleared; all sound of tears was gone. It was over. He had tried with this woman. As he had tried with Amy. He couldn't try anymore.

He squeezed Amy's hand once; was it a goodbye? Then he stood, and spoke quietly, the grief and anger were gone, replaced by a cold, uncaring distance.

"It's not about what I want. There's something else here. Something much bigger."

He looked down at Amy. "I'll be waiting in the car."

***

The Teacher was silent. Calm. Unmoved. This display, the ego's desperate need for flight when it is challenged, she had seen countless times. A fantasy of changing others, of making them better—how it grips you and won't let go, and leads to nothing—all too familiar. She nodded to him, neither encouraging nor irritated. "We will be here," she added, "if you see things differently in the future."

***

They no longer sat on the couch together, watched old movies before bed, or talked about the news. Communication had dried up like a once bubbling stream after a drought. "Pick up Sharon at three." "The refrigerator needs to be fixed." "Please pay the electric bill." Daniel had an old single mattress laid out in his small study. They hadn't slept in the same bed for months. And now they no longer ate together. If Daniel walked into a room, Amy would stare at him, layers of hurt, anger, and deep confusion in her eyes. And he'd walk out.

Then, on a rainy Saturday morning when Sharon was away on a school trip, Amy asked Daniel to come into the living room. He was more disheveled than usual, beard untrimmed, his wrinkled and not particularly clean flannel shirt half in and half out of his sweatpants. What now? he wondered. And was pretty sure he knew. Still, his eyes widened in fear and expectation, seeing a vastly different future than anything he'd expected, clouded over with fear.

Her tone was even, as if reading from a book that she would soon close, whose plot had ended badly, but in which she no longer had any emotional investment. "This is no life. Not for me. Not for Sharon. She's nearly fifteen, and we will have to work out where she stays until she goes to college. But we need some relief."

"Relief?" his voice cracked, as he moved back to the familiar terrain of anger, and of a desperate need for someone, for *her*, to understand. "Ask the people who..."

"NO!" she stopped him. Then, with less force, "Don't bother." He silenced himself, wondering for a moment if there was any way not to fall into the dark hole that was opening up under his feet. But, as it always did when his own suffering arose, he moved outward, and could see only the endless suffering of the forests, the dolphins, the coughing children. Compared to all that, what did his loneliness matter—meals eaten alone, no one to listen to his ever more frequent nightmares, or even to share some brief pleasure about seeing a pretty cloud in the sky. He would be alone; it would hurt. But so what? It was just pain, and so small in the scheme of things he couldn't let it move him.

Amy reached out to touch his face, then pulled her hand back. She stood, stepped away, fixed her eyes on his. "I love you, Danny, and I always will. But I won't live in a non-stop funeral, not when there's so much life left. In me, and in the world."

Later, when he thought about it, he missed her terribly. But he didn't think about it too often. There were too many other things on his mind.

Chapter 3
Anne

When she talked, her hands moved slowly, rising and falling with her deliberate, measured speech. Palms up, she would lift her hands almost to her shoulders as she talked of familiar Buddhist virtues: awareness, detachment, compassion. And then they would turn over and gently sink down as she pointed out the inevitable suffering that came from clinging, dislike, and ignorance. Her low, even tones were not so much soothing as expressionless. You could read anything you wanted into them, but there wasn't much there—except the simple ideas which she believed had saved her, and she was sure could save anyone else. Do not seek, do not avoid, know your own mind so that you do not deceive yourself. Be kind without attachment to anyone else's happiness. Do not resist fatigue or pain or frustration. Do not want something different than what is. Such wanting is the root of suffering.

Her office was a study in understatement. An old wooden desk that might have come when the property was first acquired, left over from the small private school that had gone bankrupt in the 1950s, sat in the corner. In front of the desk there was a simple armless wooden chair. A small laptop sat in the center of the desk, and folders neatly marked stood in metal racks on one side. The walls were bare except for one picture of a Buddha statue, and under it, printed in large, round letters, the Four Noble Truths: *life is suffering, suffering is caused by desire, desire can be overcome, by the 8-fold path.* A small bookcase, filled with compilations of sutras and commentary from India, Tibet, China, and Burma rested unevenly against the wall, the bottom of one of its legs having worn down. There was no further decoration, and the only other furniture was a second wooden chair, also armless, placed by the side of the door.

Show time, she thinks, preparing for the daily question session, tightening a wrinkled tunic around her waist with an old cloth belt, slipping her feet into sandals so worn they seemed more like cardboard than the wood they'd started out as, briefly wondering yet again if the absence of a mirror indicated real modesty or just a flair for exaggerated self-denial. The middle way, Buddha had taught, the middle way, no extremes. But who could know what an extreme was anymore? Go into the drug store and they had twenty-three different types of shampoo and two million apps for the cell phone that she needed to keep in touch with the people who made donations to the Center. But she'd tossed the mirror out years ago, thinking that the less she noticed how she looked the less other people, namely her students, would too. Was she right? Or did they just notice that she looked like shit?

There it was, again, the ego that never ends. She almost laughed out loud, then patted herself soothingly on her chest, just above her tiny breasts, and finally gently caressed the top of her shaven head. And then, with a harshly different emotional tone, the interior words: *Time to do your wise teacher imitation.* Once again, she wondered if she would ever let go of her silent, private cynicism, the posture of doubt and denial she never shared with anyone and that years ago she'd named The Voice.

Never! My only rebellion. Haven't I done everything else? Celibacy and poverty, non-violence and kindness to animals and to depressed middle-class women who came to complain about their failed love affairs or problems getting pregnant. And to those who came because their children were drug addicts, they had breast cancer, their fathers had raped them for years, or their husbands were screwing their best friends.

She didn't have sex with her students the way many other teachers did. Didn't indulge in writing the same book six times in a row and getting a "following." Had given up coffee, alcohol, sugar, and meat, even though she occasionally had dreams about bacon cheeseburgers. She was kind to the volunteers who helped out, took almost no money for herself, walked when she could rather than driving, kept her heat at sixty-two degrees during the brutal winter and never, ever used air conditioning.

But to give up the little voice that would mock herself, the teachings she lived by, and all the seekers who brought their desperation to her door? *Lovely clothes you're wearing, another thrift store special*? as she pulled on faded corduroys and a threadbare flannel shirt with a slight rip at the elbow and two missing buttons. *Is that what you're doing*? it would whisper, as she instructed a student in how to watch the breath and let thoughts come and go. Then it would laugh. And in the privacy of her office she, too, would laugh, thinking of the images of the laughing Buddha, of the jokes contained in Zen teaching riddles. And once in a great while, as a quiver spread from her lower back to her shoulders and then her gut, she would hear The Voice, and hear own laughter, and wonder to whom they belonged.

Lately The Voice had been more active, a nasty tone coloring its usual mild irony. She had noticed, with a glimmer of interest and a touch of distaste, this spiteful turn of her own inner mockery. Interrupting her meditation, even once trying to crowd out her own voice during a Dharma talk, seeking to defile her deliberate, undeniable truth.

It was a fairly typical group at the center this weekend. A few middle-aged women facing divorce or dying parents. Two millennials who'd been on anti-depressants for years and were trying to replace Wellbutrin with meditation. A smiling, genial, grandmother who'd learned meditation at her progressive church, and who kept sighing, with a small smile, at how easily her mind wandered.

And then there was Daniel—angry at the world and covering over what she could easily see was anger at himself. The way he kept biting his lip, clenching his hands, and then slumping into a poorly hidden despair. And his wife, checking him out with hidden glances, her own mouth occasionally turning down in exasperation, or worse, when he asked The Teacher a hostile question.

His agenda was clear: save the world, make it all better, while not knowing anything about his own mind. She could see that without a very long practice he would go nowhere, just alienate his wife, make himself miserable, frighten everyone he talked to, and never gain the basic insight: you couldn't change others, you could only change yourself. If you did that, if you cured your obsessions and desperation and crippling fears, then others might learn something from what you had done and undertake the journey themselves. That was what she had accomplished. That was why she was The Teacher. Easy? Surely not. And she had the scars to prove it. But it was the only way. Only when countless people undertook that difficult, painful journey would the world not be ruled by fear and greed and rage. Only then.

As the session wound down, Daniel started in once again. Telling a long story about a friend's wife dying of cancer. Looking alternately lost and angry, angry and lost. Unimpressed and unmoved she watched him lose control, yell at her, make a fuss, tell her she didn't understand. To her faint satisfaction she managed to get the last word, spoiling his grand exit, his drama filled stand-against-the abyss, with her firm, unarguably authoritative, “We will be here if you see things differently in the future.”

***

And yet that night, once again, she couldn’t sleep. She would focus on her breath and view reality simply as a temporary constellation of what Buddhist philosophy called *skandas*: the heaps of sensations and beliefs, emotions and desires and physical forms that made up the illusion people trapped in ignorance and illusion called “self.” She would observe how when she thought of Daniel the muscles in her upper back would tighten, and she would feel a burning desire to lecture him on the futility of his anger and self-importance. But then, as she simply experienced the back spasms, without judgment or resistance, they would gradually subside; and so would the desire. This was a mental process she had mastered years ago.

But The Voice, louder than ever and increasingly insistent, kept interrupting. *Back spasms?* And it would laugh. *You got a lot bigger problems than your back.* She would answer with the teaching: firm, gentle, unalterable, dissolving the Voice into a collection of cynical, angry beliefs, and perhaps some unresolved fears or guilt from her now distant past—plus some indigestion. Then it would dissipate, like smoke from a small campfire doused by a steady downpour.

But the flames she thought extinguished would rise again. *You really think there’s nothing to be done?* And so they wrestled, the teaching and The Voice, each seeking victory in a battle she’d thought long ended.

Once she had taken this life to heart, she did not expect happiness. Indeed, the very idea of happiness made her vaguely uneasy, and if it had ever arrived, she would have felt like the host of a small family gathering if perfect strangers walked in and asked for a drink. But calm, acceptance, above all equanimity. Were these not guaranteed by the teaching? The inevitable fruit of a life of moderate asceticism, attention to duty, and endless hours of meditation?

Yet as the days and weeks after her encounter with Daniel passed, much of what she'd mastered seemed to slip away. She would open her eyes ten minutes into what was to be an hour of personal meditation, get up and walk outside into the surrounding woods. There she would pick up fallen oak branches from the forest floor and slam them into tree trunks, or throw stones across the nearby meadow, once wrenching a muscle in her shoulder with the force of her throw.

She had trained her mind like the most obsessive triathlete trained her body, but now it rebelled. Endlessly, to no purpose, it poured over her past. What had gone wrong with Lily? Why did nothing ever work? What were Joffrey's last months like, as he succumbed to a vicious, fast-moving pancreatic cancer during her third year in California? Or Patricia's, after the stroke? She had ignored their illnesses and their funerals, never returned to the house on the hill. Stayed away, even though her plain brown shirt would be wet with tears after each meditation session, and even though she had dreams of their shrill voices and their tormented faces and The Voice would ask, *What are you doing?*

Was she losing it because of what she had seen Daniel go through? Because she had to watch him throw away what he had to try to make people behave differently, because he thought he could lessen the pain. Who was she to make such a harsh, uncompassionate judgment? Daniel had his path; he would have to face the truth of life. Why was she so angry with him?

For angry she was. She had unbidden fantasies of grabbing his shirt, shoving her face up against his, and shouting: "Don't you see what a waste this is? You can't help people." And occasionally the anger would leak over. She got impatient with Lyrna, the soft-spoken volunteer who had been doing unpaid labor for months just for the privilege of being at the center. "No, not at all," The Teacher had said in a clipped, stern tone of obvious impatience and negative judgement, "by now you should know how the room is to look," when some of the meditation cushions were askew in the main hall, and two chairs had not been properly placed against the far wall. She saw Lyrna's face turn white, her eyes hug the floor, and heard a mumbled "I am so sorry, Teacher," as she ran to make things right.

What are you doing? The Voice whispered. *Do you have any idea?*

And then the rage would subside and she would sit, staring out the single, unwashed, dusty window in her office, not really seeing the trees or the sky. Of course there were environmental problems, global warming and the rest. What could be wrong about doing a little bit to help? And why was she angry at him for leaving early—it was obvious he needed weeks, months, years of her teaching. *A great loss, no doubt,* mocked The Voice.

What was anger but fear and vulnerability hidden, covered over by enough energy to make you feel less alone and afraid? But what did *she* have to be afraid of? After all, the key, the heart of The Teaching, was that her *self,* this icon that virtually everyone carried around, bowed down to, and was willing to do unspeakable things to protect and enhance, this *thing* that people everywhere made such a fuss about—this was just an illusion, something thrown up by the heaps. To be taken no more seriously than the image on the screen in a movie theater—crack the lens on the projector, turn on the lights, cut the wires to the twenty-seven overpowering speakers—and all the drama would fade away.

But it didn't. *What have you done?* The Voice repeated,

until the backs of her hands were raw as she scratched them with her own nails, usually trimmed and now far too long. If the self was nothing, an emptiness, what could threaten it? Why—underneath her simple brown tunic, the plain white t-shirt she wore for modesty over her miniscule breasts, her skin that she washed when it needed to be washed and almost never touched otherwise, beneath the muscles and ribs, why did her heart—the heart she'd turned her back on so many years ago—hurt?

And then there was something else, something trivial, even nonsensical, but in a way more deeply unsettling.

She wanted some ease, and she wanted some pleasure. Nothing big, like illicit sex with a good-looking student. Nothing expensive, like the kind of house she'd grown up in. Just a pillow when she slept to support her neck; a meditation cushion, quite small really, to make the long sessions less uncomfortable and ease her no longer young hips and knees. A heavy fleece sweater to put on first thing in the morning when the inside thermometer read under sixty degrees and the chill seemed to penetrate her skinny body from all sides. Things she had cautioned against, and forbidden herself and others, for years.

But most of all, and this was truly bizarre—she wanted sweets. She had intense images of imported Belgian chocolate, the kind that came in flat boxes with each piece—caramel, covered almond, nougat center, and best of all, the rectangular cubes with three different colors of chocolate in neat slabs—nestling in ribbed brown paper cups. She could see them, lying on the coffee table in the house on the hill, gifts from grateful European investors who had made out quite well in one of Joffrey's schemes. Wrapped in gold paper, with the name of a European capital embossed in raised letters, and the legend "chocolatiers to the crown" on the sides. Huge boxes, with over a hundred pieces insides, just waiting for the eager fingers of the family, as they all—Lily and Joffrey, Patricia and Anne—gorged themselves.

Chapter 4
Daniel and Sarah

The trail down the mountain was the usual mix of roots and rocks that make backpacking in New England a constant threat of stumbles, sprained ankles, and wrenched knees. Now, after a day of drenching rain, there was also mud, slippery leaves, and the danger that a large rock might turn almost as slick as old ice.

But Daniel didn't mind. He was happy to be in the stunted pine forests just off the ridge of New Hampshire's Presidential Range. The sun was finally out, the sky a brilliant mid-Fall blue, and the early October colors he'd glimpsed before he left the high ridge had sweetened his soul for a few minutes. Yesterday he'd walked a trail from Mizpah Spring Hut to Lake of the Clouds, catching a few spectacular glimpses of entire birch and maple forests in yellow and orange and red, spreading out on either side for dozens of miles. Then the mist had rolled in, and slowly turned to a steady soaking drizzle. It had been slow going, five miles up to the last shelter before the steep ascent to the top of Mt. Washington and another five back, and even though this was a high ridge trail, with often sheer grades on either side, the ridge itself often went steeply up and steeply down. The light day pack he carried weighed only a few pounds, but the rough surface took a toll on his toes and knees, and twice he'd let his attention wander to thoughts of what acid rain was doing to the high forests of this region, and he'd slipped and fallen.

After ten miles of this, he was more than ready to be back in the "hut" at Mizpah Spring. It might be called a hut, but it was really a solid, two-story building with a large hall for dining, a highly equipped kitchen, and several rooms packed with bunk beds to allow backpackers to walk in the mountains without food or tents. The price of admission was steep, but the food—all of it packed in by ferociously fit twenty somethings who thought little of carrying eighty-pound packs up the rugged three miles from the nearest trailhead parking lot—was remarkably good. Fresh vegetables for a large tossed salad, baked chicken in a sweet and sour sauce, apple pies, fresh bread.

He had desperately needed to get away. That's what he had said to himself. That's what Amy, now three years amicably divorced, had said. That's even what Sharon, who had recovered quicker than they'd dared hope, had told him. She had seen the dark circles under his eyes, the pallor of his skin from so rarely going out to the pond to look at the seagulls or the sky changing color in the evening, and heard the slight stutter in his voice. "Dad, you're just making yourself crazy. You love it so much, go take a look at it before it's all gone." Then she'd hugged him, and smiled in such a tender way he thought he might melt onto the floor, and added: "You do so much for all the trees and things, maybe you could let them do something for you."

He'd protested, and delayed, and told them he got plenty of nature just looking at the birch tree that had grown, all these years, from a twelve-foot sapling to forty-foot giant that had to be trimmed so it didn't drop branches on his neighbor's roof. And there were always meetings, and emails to newspapers and political figures, and information to keep track of and collate and share on the website he'd created, a site some people actually thought was worth something. He had an intuitive knack for seeing patterns, sensing connections, and often knowing earlier than most where the next crisis would appear. Weeks, sometimes months, before most other people were able to connect the dots, he would post his hunches—and from time to time the larger story, the bigger publicity, would follow some time down the road. He knew that a few environmental journalists followed what he wrote, that the local people from Audubon and Sierra Club were interested. He served a function: small, he knew. Not nearly enough—nothing ever was—but some miniscule but real part of what so desperately needed to be done.

A few people in the department had not been pleased, when he shifted to "Literature and the Environment" and "Environmental Non-fiction," thinking he should continue to teach the same old Melville, Hemingway, and Woolf, but he had stared them down at a department meeting, asking them if they knew about the staggering rates of asthma from bus and truck emissions in the inner city neighborhood less than a mile from their urban campus.

But it was taking its toll. Too often he would stare at the statistics on the computer screen, fight to keep himself from screaming at people who didn't see things his way. When Amy had left, it seemed to make things simpler for a while. And they fought less. But late nights of work had begun to feel unbearably lonely. Maybe, if he got away, something would change.

He bought some hiking gear, made reservations for two nights of lodging, dinner and breakfast at one of the AMC huts, studied maps and saw that he'd have fairly short hikes in and out, and a long ridge walk with just day gear in the middle. If the weather was nice, he'd get the foliage at its peak. That, as people always said, would be something. He almost backed out at the last minute, noticing a small but persistent set of stories about strange rashes among fishermen in North Carolina, rashes that didn't look like the usual poison oak or insect bites. He could smell something coming out of there, something in the river he'd bet.

But in the end he forced himself to hit the 'shut down' button on his computer, took the four environmental magazines he had on his 'to read' list out of his day pack, promised himself he'd work even harder after a little break, and off he went.

Daniel was no mountain man, no intrepid explorer, but he had been camping a few times with friends in college, who had taught him the basics of simple map reading, fire building and tent assembly. And the hut system in the Whites made things a lot simpler. He needed lunch food and trail snacks, rain gear and a small pack, toiletries, and decent boots—and these days that stuff could be had, incredibly light and waterproof and nice looking, at any number of camping stores. He found it more than a little ironic that to go back into nature he had to stock up on things like *Gore-Tex*, *vibram*, and *microfiber*, products of incredibly sophisticated technological development. But he also knew he wasn't about to walk the one hundred and seventy miles to the trail, or hunt a deer and make shoes and a warm coat out of his hide. He was part of the system. And no matter how much he hated it, and no matter that he no longer ate food from animals, and drove as little as he could, and bought organic food, he still plugged into the same old power grid.

The biggest problem, he realized fifteen minutes in, was how out of shape he was. The first quarter mile had been gentle, almost completely flat. At the base of the mountain range the colors were brilliant, and a ten-foot-wide shallow stream made a soothing burble to accompany bird calls and rustling leaves. The weather was mild, even a little humid, and Daniel was overdressed in his soft-shell pants with several zippered pockets, long sleeve high-tech shirt and windbreaker. But soon the brook turned into a series of marvelous waterfalls cascading over white and gray rocks, with autumn colored leaves swirling in back currents and collecting along the sides of sticks. The trail changed too, suddenly going almost straight up. The close-packed dirt gave way to exposed roots and sharp rocks.

Soon Daniel was passed by laughing high school students, trail runners who could somehow jog uphill, and then a family with two infants in child carriers and a six-year-old. Then he was on his own: heart pounding, muscles in his thighs grasping with every large step as he tried to force his way up the steep grade. His shirt, breathable as it was, soon filled with sweat, and, much more annoyingly, sweat poured off his forehead and into his eyes, making him squint, and itch, and have to stop to take off his glasses to wipe his eyes. And each time he stopped, it was harder to get going again. But he wasn't going to rest. It was only two and a half miles up to the ridge. Two and a half miles, that was nothing. What was he, an old woman? A cripple? This was just a walk up a hill for God's sake.

But where had this ridiculous macho streak come from? He was an intellectual in his fifties, not some REI jock. But even while he smiled at his foolishness, he wouldn't give it up.

Suddenly something broke free inside. A howling livid rage at all the polluters, meat packers, defenders of cancer-causing chemicals, and politicians who didn't care as long as the donations kept rolling in. The anger fueled his steps. His heart subsided, now strong but steady. His thigh muscles didn't ache so much. He figured out how to keep walking while he wiped his eyes. The freshly-made oxygen from the forest filled his nostrils, the trickle and tinkle of water from the brook his ears. Even with all his newly purchased fancy equipment, he was part of the forest, of the mountain, of the earth. There were no people around, but he was not alone. And he realized, for a few small minutes, that even late at night staring at the terrible numbers, he wasn't alone then either.

At the top of the ridge, where the entry trail intersected the long ridge line that would lead north to Mt. Washington and south to the hut, there was an overlook. "My, oh my," he whispered to himself, as he emerged from the wind-stunted pines onto a large flat rock. The sharp hillside swept down and away, the turned leaves of the forest created a vista of red and yellow and orange. Far below was the road he'd driven in on and then another range of small mountains. To his right was the bulk of Mt. Washington, 6000 feet of dark rock, the strength of ancient stone. And beyond it, all the sky and the clouds and the sun, and a few of what looked like hawks, gliding with the thermals, serrated wings spiking into the sky. It all seemed to so full of promise, of an essential goodness of which he couldn't ever consider himself worthy. It had been given to him, to everyone, and they were destroying it.

On the third morning, on his way back down to his car, his mind started to fill with everything he needed to do. That problem in North Carolina was top of the list. Was it some factory dumping something toxic? Something that went into the fish? Could it be emissions making a strange funneled pattern because of the temperature of the water in the river? Did he have contacts in the area he could email? Maybe just post it as a question on his website instead of acting like he knew something, when he surely didn't. He was rejoining the stream now, at a point where a dramatic thirty-foot waterfall sheltered fifty feet off the trail. From there it was only another quarter mile straight down on the still slippery roots and rocks, and then back to the flat and his car and then work, the all-important work. He had had his rest, his brief respite. Enough was enough. His deep pleasure in where he had been was real, but it didn't matter. Any more than the pain in his legs when he walked or how alone he felt at the end of each day.

***

He had been calling out, weakly because of the pain, for some time. Then a woman ran over to him, squatting down by his side and putting a hand on his shoulder. "Knee?"

"Yes, big time. Clumsy jerk," Daniel pointed to a patch of mud with a long boot skid in it, "Slipped. Boots tangled. Couldn't go all the way down. All my weight." He gestured with his chin to his left knee.

"You want me to have a look? I'm not a doctor, but I've been around a few injuries in my time." He saw a reassuring smile. "Of course if it's broken, there's nothing I can do except walk to the car and get help." He nodded, the fear in his face mixed with relief that he wasn't alone anymore.

"O.k., let's have a look." She started to pull up the pants leg and he yelped. "That bad?" "No, sorry. I'm just scared shitless."

"Oh, it's probably just a sprain or a strain. And someday I'll have to get somebody to tell me what the difference is. Know what I mean?" She laughed. And Daniel, despite his pain and fear, laughed along with her. "Don't worry, happens all the time. I was up at the base of Washington and didn't see some leftover ice. Down I went, feeling like fool, and my ankle..." She pattered on, all the time slowly inching the pants leg until his knee was in view. The kneecap was about an inch to the left of the bone.

"I think, can't be sure, but it looks like a dislocation. Hurts like hell, I know. But not too big a deal—I mean compared to complex fractures or getting a tree branch deep in your eye. Have to get the cap back. The pain will be there for a while, but it should get a lot better when we do that."

Daniel peered at her, scared, unsure. Short brown hair, clear blue eyes, small mouth that held a comforting smile, a small body that moved with confidence and grace. Should he wait for a doctor to somehow arrive on the scene? Question her at length to see if she knew what the hell she was talking about?

Fuck that, he thought. It hurt too much to wait. And besides, there was something about her that he trusted. She didn't seem to be trying to prove anything, or want anything. And her concern didn't mask any fear.

"What do we do?"

"I don't do much," she smiled wider. "It's all you big guy." Despite his pain he chuckled at the silly phrase, then grimaced as the movement shook his tortured knee. "You need to straighten that knee as fast as you can. Just stick out your leg real quick and hold it there for a slow count of five. Sharp pain as the cap scrapes back across the cartilage. But then it will be back where it should be, or at least a lot closer. It'll still hurt like hell, but that will be an improvement, right?"

"Right, got it, straighten and hold."

"I'm with you. Don't worry." She shifted her weight up towards his head. Placed her right hand on his brow and her left on top of his thigh. In a vastly different situation, he realized quickly, it might have been a sexual gesture. His mind raced through sexual fantasies of this lovely woman who was standing in as a healer, his own folly of thinking that anyone this much younger and together could ever be interested in him, and the insanity of thinking about any of this when he could barely move for the pain.

"O.k., o.k." He took a long breath, then another. "Now," he yelled. A fresh bolt of pain ripped through his knee, like nothing so much as a set of small blades being dragged across the inside of a bone.

Through his panted gasps he heard her counting. "1, 2, 3,

hold it, 4, 5. Relax." He let the extended leg sink back. Like magic, the pain, still awful, was now manageable. She'd cured him. Appeared out of nowhere and made things hard but tolerable, not anything he couldn't live with.

He saw her smile down at him, and felt a brief flash of pleasure, as if he'd aced a tough exam and the teacher was pleased.

"Daniel Aiken," he said, extending a hand, "Can't thank you enough."

"Sarah Carson," she answered, shaking his hand, adding, "We can't go on meeting like this," and laughed again. Despite the pain, he laughed as well.

"Look," she said, "You can wait here while I see if I can get some more people to help stretcher you out. I can drive to the AMC center, about ten miles, and maybe get an EMT. On the other hand, take a look." She pointed skyward, and he saw that the morning's blue had given way to dark and threatening clouds. "It might come down, hard. You can never tell in the Whites."

"I get it. I can try to walk the last bit to my car. It'll feel lousy, but I can drive back to Boston and let them do whatever they do in an ER. At least they can give me some crutches. But I can't get down the trail by myself. Can you help?"

"Sure. Just hold on a sec." Sarah jogged back to her pack and took out the little first aid kit. Rummaging through the tweezers, travel scissors, and antibiotic ointment, there was a long cloth bandage and some ibuprofen. "Take the pills, they'll help with the pain and the swelling, a bit anyway. And let's wrap that knee." Daniel closed his eyes and bit his lip. Suddenly, he didn't want to seem weak in front of this woman. Most of the time his masculinity seemed like an old school sports uniform, something that maybe used to fit him, but just gathered dust in the closet, and wouldn't work for what his aging body had become in any case. But there was something compellingly attractive about her, something beyond her obvious kindness and good humor and carefree confidence.

His knee wrapped, one arm around Sarah's shoulders and the other supported by one of her hiking poles, Daniel made his way down the trail. "Slow and easy," Sarah kept saying, "No rush here. Just be on the trail. Sorry about the pain."

"I must weigh a ton, how are you managing?" he panted, straining to keep his left foot off the ground. Any touch of weight was just short of excruciating.

"Piece of cake. In fact, reminds me of a time," and she launched into a mildly amusing story about her own knee dislocation, a narrative involving a poorly tied shoelace, an ill-fitting boot, overturned lentil soup, and an irritated moose.

By the time they got to the trailhead, she had spun out the story, and told it with such an understated, self-deprecating wit that Daniel had hardly noticed the last few hundred yards. He groaned himself into his car while Sarah went back up the trail for the two packs.

When she returned his pack, she stood next to his car, talking through the open window, her hand resting on his shoulder. "Can you do this? It's three hours or more back to Boston." He saw her looking him over, clearly concerned about his welfare. It had been so long since anyone had physically touched him, he almost started to cry, fantasizing about crawling into the back seat of her car and letting her decide what would happen next.

"Yeah, I'll be all right. The pills helped. And no matter what, I've got to sit somewhere. Might as well sit in this car and get home."

Sarah hemmed and hawed, told him she wasn't sure, and finally said:

"O.k., but I'll be right behind. If you start to conk out or lose focus or the pain gets too bad, we'll figure something out."

"You're an angel," he said with a half-joking tone, but

reached out to touch her hand to let her know he meant it.

"This angel wants her charge back in his house in one piece. Let's go." She put her hand on top of his, let it linger for a moment longer than a handshake or a simple farewell. And then walked back to her car.

Chapter 5
Daniel and Sarah

After they'd said goodbye at the local hospital, they'd exchanged numbers, and when he felt like a human being again, he called and begged her to let him at least buy her dinner to show his appreciation. To his surprise, she'd accepted.

Daniel did his best to make himself presentable, not quite knowing what to expect and what this meant, only that he had been distracted all day knowing that he would see her again. Feeling his heart beat a drumroll in his chest and watching his hand shake a bit as he thought of walking into the restaurant, seeing her at a table, and probably stuttering over his "hellos" and "how are yous." Then he would softly curse himself for a fool. He tried on and discarded the Indian style tunic that hadn't worked for twenty years, studied an old black sweater and found a stain on the back, and finally settled on a gray tailored shirt, to go with his gray slacks, and at the last minute added a sport jacket. "Aging professorial chic," he muttered to himself, glancing at his reflection in the mirror before leaving. "And please, God, let me not act like a jerk in front of this woman." But he knew he probably would.

Trying to strengthen his knee and cut down on petrochemical consumption, he walked slowly down Centre Street, the heart of Jamaica Plain. On Boston's south side, it was often described as a "mixed" neighborhood. This meant, he supposed, that the heavy-set close-cropped butch-looking dyke could hold hands with her lipstick lesbian girlfriend with minimum paranoia; that nobody minded the old fashioned synagogue that had taken up residence on one of the richest streets, turning a living room into an old fashioned place of worship whose rabbi, a kind and learned man, jogged around the pond wearing a belt that held two small water bottles; that people had all sorts of dogs; that at the main pharmacy almost none of the employees had English as their first language; that one bedroom condos were going for 400k only a few blocks from one of the most drug-ridden, gang-dominated housing projects in the city; and that in summer a white-haired man with a long beard did yoga on his second story porch, listening to Mahler and Mozart on a little portable music system. It was the perfect place, he'd often thought, for a misfit like himself. People here obsessed about all sorts of things, and his monomaniacal environmental lunacy was just one more case in point.

As he studied the shop windows, he felt once again that the street looked like it had been assembled from sets for at least three different movies. There was the romantic comedy where thirty something's strained love affairs came and went in small, hip, ethnic restaurants—that was the movie for the sushi place, the Indian place, and the one that served six different kinds of crepes. Then there was the nostalgic for the fifties flick, in which people went to Sal's barber shop and George's Shoes, where the samples in the window were covered with brown paper at night to keep their shine. And then there was the depressing documentary about modern urban blight, where the recently abandoned gas station, the second hand clothing store, and the dirty luncheonette would have been right at home.

"And which movie for me?" he wondered, "where does a

gray, bitter-but-really-scared, fifty-four-year-old English professor, waiting to get older and grayer, who's lost hope in the human future, find a place?"

"God help me, in my own messed up brain," and he laughed out loud, then laughed again because a woman in a three hundred dollar Marmot windbreaker, pushing a baby stroller that looked technically sophisticated enough to double as a lunar landing module, shot a quick nervous look in his direction. He really didn't care if people thought him strange. And it wasn't his own life that bothered him: the brown aging spots on the back of his hands, the way his right heel gave a painful jab first thing every morning, or how half the time, even when he thought he should, he couldn't get it up. No, it was the world that made him cry his eyes out, spit and snot dripping into his beard, his eyes flooded with the salt water of a tortured, useless grief.

Daniel still limped a bit, but when he saw her at the table of the Kashmir House restaurant, smiling in greeting, he straightened up and tried to look strong. And he hoped that whatever happened he wouldn't start yelling at her about three billion fewer birds in North America or how the snow on top of Mt. Everest was too polluted to drink.

***

Sarah had been glad when he called. She was between projects and, unusual for her, found herself a little at a loss to fill her time, even a little lonely. There was always the weekly yoga class, running the pond and the dirt trail through the narrow strip of woods that separated Boston and Brookline, keeping up with the almost always dispiriting environmental news, not to mention rape, starving children, global fascism, and ethnic murders. "But is that enough?" she laughed to herself. So a dinner out might be something different, something nice.

And there was something about him that attracted her. A kindness in his eyes, a willingness to laugh through his pain, and a vulnerability he hadn't hid. On a whim she looked him up on the internet: "Daniel Aiken, Jamaica Plain." Then she saw his website, and then she understood.

She opted for her usual dress up, a process she enjoyed even though it didn't happen too often. The skinny jeans she'd bought ten years ago still fit, the light blue sweater wasn't too tight, but not too loose either, and the small butterfly shaped brooch with a spherical emerald in each eye picked up the colors of her own eyes, and those of the matching earrings. The jewelry had come from her mother, a graduation gift, and one of the last things her mother had been able to give her before an unexpected stroke had taken away most of her mind, her ability to walk, and, soon after, her will to live.

***

They sat at a small table towards the rear, a silenced large TV screen dominating one corner, a small ornate bar with a surprisingly good selection of vodkas and whiskeys the other side. Only a handful of tables were occupied on this weekday evening.

"How's the knee?" Sarah asked. "Looked like you were moving pretty good when you came over."

"Thanks to you, and a lot of Advil, I can walk almost as well as a ninety-year-old." They shared a laugh, while Daniel furiously searched his mind for memories of how to make charming small talk with a woman that you thought looked incredible but to whom you had no right to be attracted.

He saw Sarah studying his face, her eyes alive and seeming to carry a hidden intimacy. What was she thinking?

"So, Daniel, it turns out we're in the same business."

"What? You teach literature?"

"No, comrade," she laughs, "Saving the world. I looked you up after we agreed to eat. Wanted to make sure you hadn't committed too many axe murders or sold too many women into slavery. Found your website, the stuff you've studied and put together. It's very good."

He looked at her, his eyes widening. "But what's this got to do with you?"

"I run a small, one-woman clearing house for people involved in grass roots environmental campaigns. I hook up the local activists with experts, the experts with local activists, the few decent lawmakers with the people who know what the laws should be, the people getting poisoned with anyone who can help."

"How," he stumbled over the words, "how do you do this?"

"You mean who pays the rent?" she picked up the poppadum, gently breaking it and took a small bite. "Pretty good, check it out."

Daniel leaned forward. Was this some kind of joke?

"It's just me, supported by a few grants from grateful people, and one *really* rich guy who wrote me into his will with no strings attached and then conveniently died (not to worry, he was eighty-nine). I don't have the big guns of Sierra or Audubon, but I don't have their overhead, their publicity problems, or the tightrope between big donations and decent policies." She smiled at his shock, then surprise, then delight.

Daniel felt his nervousness turn into something else: a sense that by some miracle this graceful, smiling woman lived in the exact same world of politicians ignoring lead in the water of minority communities and an ocean that would soon have more plastic than fish. His mind froze, jammed like a computer with too many inputs at the exact same moment. He simply looked at her, smiling with every ounce of his being, and put his hand over his heart.

"Tell me," he asked, his voice eager, almost childlike, "tell me, oh, I don't know, tell me something."

"Not much going on right now," she began. "But the last one was something. Fracking, a little town in Western Pennsylvania, just a few thousand farmers and little store owners and garage mechanics and old ladies and schoolteachers. You know about fracking, right?"

He nodded, thinking of the enormous machines, flames coming out of water faucets because gas and chemicals had polluted wells, drilling noise that never stopped, ground that shook from impact, livestock that sickened and died, a rash of earthquakes, and leaked methane that was worse than CO_2 for the climate.

"Bad stuff," she went on, "for sure. But the companies have," she paused, made her eyes large and staring, and slowly spread her hands wider and wider, "so. Much. Money! And there it was. Neighbor against neighbor, 'you polluting bitch' and 'you enviro lunatic,' fistfights in the local bar. Family members secretly going to lawyers to see who had the right to sign the land away. One side couldn't understand how anyone could bring in the stink and noise and chemicals. The others, who can blame them?—needed money for college, grandma's medical expenses, or a car that wasn't held together with hope and duct tape."

"Fools," said Daniel, "some pretty little town. How could they?"

Sarah looked at him. Didn't respond. Then took a sip of her Indian lager and another bite of alu paratha.

"So. What next?" Daniel asked impatiently.

Sarah smiled. "You really want to know?" she teased, watching his expectancy grow. "Most people would be about ready to discuss just about anything else by now."

"Not me. I'm all ears. What the hell did you do?"

"Turned out a local lawyer had moved there to be in the country and get away from chemicals in the city. And the city she'd left was this one, and she knew me, not much, but enough, in college. She brought me in on the case.

"First thing was talk to some community leaders. That means the three Christian clergy in town. But I didn't go straight to them. I went to people they'd trust. A Bishop for the priest, the central council of Methodists, and some of the environmental Evangelicals for the Baptists. I reminded *them* of all the proclamations their groups had made about environmental issues. Stewards of the earth, make nature the sister of humanity, need to protect children. Then I had *them* contact the locals and put in the word—a lot of clergy on the ground haven't a clue about the changes in religious thinking—and about me. *Then* I met with them, and gave them the facts about fracking, and very gently reminded them what religious activists had done in the past about slavery, war, and segregation.

"A few Sunday sermons later and it wasn't mom and apple pie plus money versus tree-hugging hippies anymore. It was complicated. And when it's complicated people start to think. And ask questions. And then we win. Sixty three percent of the town voted against letting it happen. Just one little town, I know, but God it feels good to win one."

"Damn those gas companies," he said quietly. "Damn them."

"Yeah, for sure," she answered. "But those folks, you talk to them. God, they're kind of lost. Chasing some big payoff that never comes, enough money to make up for what they never feel they have." Daniel looked up from his vegetable biryani. Was that all she would say about the fossil fuel megaliths who were destroying the climate, poisoning the water, and paying off politicians?

She called the waiter over for another beer. "And I understand how ripped off the ones who lost the vote felt. You know—you live in this little place where real money is always somewhere else. You see a chance to get something—fifty thousand, maybe a hundred, maybe more. And all you have to do is sign a piece of paper. There it is, right in front of your nose. And then it's gone—sacrificed to some god you don't believe in called the environment. Brutal." When the lager was brought, she poured half in Daniel's glass. "Still, the town did the right thing. So: let's have a little toast to the right kind of sacrifice."

Chapter 6
Anne

The house, everyone agreed, was magnificent. Set at the end of a steep two-hundred-yard driveway off a small winding road in northwest Framingham, Massachusetts, a mixed suburb with most of its middle- and upper-class homes on its outer edges, a few intense miles of malls and shops along Route 9 through its middle, and a dark and depressed southern section of cheap stores, a large women's prison, basements for AA meetings, and shabby apartments for a surprising variety of legal and illegal immigrants. The distance by road from the prison to the Sattvic home was perhaps five miles, but in money, class, ease, and beauty, it was the other side of the moon. Close to the top of the highest hill within fifty miles of Boston's west side, the windows and sliders commanded a view that stretched to downtown Boston and the Blue Hills. Each morning the sky turned the usual sunrise colors, there was a sizable pool for hot summer afternoons, and the finely tailored lawn, cared for by small army of constantly changing illegal Mexicans and Brazilians under the close watch of an American-owned landscaping service, ran directly into a three-hundred-acre nature preserve. Anne had once seen nearly a dozen deer come out of the woods on a January dusk, their sharp hooves making crisp sounds as they went through the thin ice covering the snow on their lawn.

It was often, as a friend of Anne's from the other side of Route 9 once giggled, "scary quiet." At least that's the way it was when she was a young child. Later, no matter how much sunshine flooded through the huge plate glass sliding doors, no matter the value of the art displayed in cleverly situated niches in the wall, the fine quality of the china and flatware and top-drawer copper bottomed pots and the designer labels of Anne's mother's wardrobe in her walk-through cedar lined closets, it turned loud and dark.

Her father Joffrey had begun with a slight inheritance from his father, owner of a small-town bank that got eaten, to his financial benefit, by Chase Manhattan. Joffrey had looked hard at the culture, the country, other people with money and the people who wanted money, and saw that real estate in ski areas was going to explode over the next twenty years. And explode it did. Areas like Killington and Okemo in Vermont, Loon in New Hampshire, even Telluride in Colorado—where Joffrey's success in New England made him the only non-westerner invited to invest—were expanding. People who could afford a condo or second home just for skiing often didn't care about the details, walking in with so much money that half the time they didn't need a mortgage to buy something for several hundred thousand dollars or more. So Joffrey bought up old properties near the mountains, turned meadows and forests into places with names like Alpen Meadows and Jackson Gore, and then put up hotels, vacation homes, and a few hundred condos, with the occasional slope-side restaurant thrown in. Where there had been deer and raccoons and even the rare shy bear, there were now streets, driveways, pools to attract the summer crowd, and for the lucky few, the ability to ski from "Your front door to a diamond trail, halfway up the mountain. Don't drive home, take the ski lift!"

Because of Joffrey, useless brush and pine needles and

muddy ponds would become beautiful vacation homes, cute condos for successful single men, lushly carpeted McMansions for people who wanted to ski with their children, all of them at once, and the grandchildren and maybe even a few cousins as well.

"I am," he said late one evening after hours of work, a few drinks and some sex, "like a magician." He laughed, spilling a little of his last brandy of the night. "Or even a second-rate god. In the Bible, God just says 'Let there be'—and from nothing, there's the world." His wife nodded, her head movement encouraging, her face unmoved. "When I say 'Let there be houses with big wooden decks with a view of the mountain's east side so close you can almost tell what the skiers are wearing,' it might not be from nothing, but pretty close." He carefully put the empty glass on the night table, laid his head on the pillow and lapsed almost immediately into a deep, dreamless sleep.

***

Patricia came from an elite Maryland family whose contacts had just started to evaporate when the later generations couldn't hold on to the money the earlier ones had made. She and Joffrey met at a party in New Haven, where Joffrey was majoring in economics at Yale and she had been bused in from Connecticut College. Unromantic and committed to a future life of money, love wasn't particularly important to either of them. But, and they were each a little shocked at how much it took them out of their usually level-headed calculation of future earnings and investments, sex was. Patricia sensed that her slender, pastel, willowy beauty made Joffrey nearly desperate to both arouse and ravish her. And she would reward him with muffled screams of pleasure. To her own surprise, Patricia wanted to be ravished—ordered, pushed into position, entered without hesitation or asking of permission. And she wanted to be anonymous, as if this really weren't her, and then she could take his penis in her mouth, submit to anal sex, and do anything else Joffrey wanted to do with—well, not her, but whoever this person was whose body gave her so much pleasure.

The intensity lasted nearly a year, and that was enough for the two of them. With a degree of cold-blooded calculation that only astonished either of them because it was so unusual in other people, they agreed to marry, use her family name and his ambition and skill and moderate inheritance to make a home, a family, and hopefully a small fortune.

***

The pregnancy was brutal. Patricia lost count of how often she threw up. And there were headaches, fatigue, and back spasms. As her desire for sex simply evaporated, she saw Joffrey not as the conquering hero of the bedroom but a clueless, pawing bother. Her swollen belly didn't turn him off—it just raised the ante on her vulnerability, a quality that seemed to make him want her even more.

"Are you crazy," she would hiss, five months pregnant, when he would try to arouse her by touching her now much more substantial breasts and her painfully sensitive nipples. "I can't keep a sandwich down, I've barely slept all week, my legs hurt, my back hurts, my head is splitting, and you want *sex*?"

Joffrey would limp off, muttering under his breath. He would never yell, pound his fist, or slap her face. Or screw around. He was, Patricia knew, bound by a whole set of rules that defined his manhood. He might drive a hard bargain, expect to be catered to by his wife, or have a cruel verbal streak, but he wouldn't bribe a city official, get divorced, or hit her. To Joffrey acting that like that signified weakness, and he could never be weak.

So he would leave her alone, retreat to the brandy and a new project, some Swiss themed condos near Killington. She could trust that he would take care of the business and the money. She was left to manage her discomfort, her bad moods, and her pregnancy by herself.

To complete the awful pregnancy, Patricia went through a draining thirty-six hours of labor. She, who always submitted to the expertise of professionals like her obstetrician, had an overriding fear of Cesareans, having lost a friend to one. So she struggled with false labor, things heating up and then, unaccountably, slowing down. At the very end she closed her eyes, begging every God she didn't believe in for help. And when that didn't work, she simply gave up all thought, willed her body and the child to work together, and made it happen. And out came Lily, who opened her eyes briefly—quite strangely seeming to see what was around her—and then closed her eyes and started to scream.

She didn't seem to stop, except for brief periods of sleep and while she was actually feeding, for a good deal of the next two years. They heard that the Chinese had a centuries old term for the "hundred-day cry," which was, for Lily, more like the hundred-week.

Patricia, exhausted from the pregnancy and the sleepless labor, was glad to have her out, but took weeks to feel well enough to really attend to her in any way. Early bonding between mother and child? Not very much or not enough. That was the opinion of the psychiatrist Patricia consulted many years later.

"I'm sorry, Joffrey," she would say when she hadn't arranged a particularly elegant dinner after he returned from a business trip, or picked up the dry cleaning with his best monogrammed shirts. "I'm not right, since the birth. My body. It's just not the same. And with Lily crying at night I'm tired all the time."

Her voice trailed off as he simply stared at her. She knew what he was thinking, he'd said it often enough. This was just weakness, women's weakness. He did his work. She should do hers. With all the help his money bought her, it wasn't that much now, was it? Sometimes Patricia thought there was a hint of fear in his face when she told him how bad she felt. As if maybe he thought he was supposed to make her better and hadn't the faintest idea how. But it would soon pass, and be replaced by hostility and faint mockery.

Trapped in the big house, without intimate friends or family to call on, helped by maids and babysitters but feeling increasingly inadequate, Patricia fell into a moderate depression. She still dressed impeccably, put her attention on losing the weight the pregnancy had put on, but constantly felt defeated by a child who almost never seemed pleased. Joffrey escaped into his work, his major bond to Patricia defeated by her fatigue, residual physical pain, and dark mood, repeatedly making it clear that all this was Patricia's responsibility.

By Lily's second birthday whatever digestive or neurological growing pains had tormented her had dissipated. If she tended towards the shy side, if she learned to read a little later than other kids, if once in a while she would become completely fixated by fear or desire—a terror of moths, a desperate attachment to one particular t-shirt which she wore to shreds, a burning hatred of a girl who'd been a casual playmate for months—well, Patricia told herself, all kids were a little strange. If the day care center or the school or the pediatrician didn't think there was anything wrong, then there wasn't. This stunning house was filled with the best that money could buy. Last year they had vacationed in the South of France and this year in a spectacular, secluded, and very exclusive resort in the British Virgin Islands. Patricia had a few interests—new exhibits at the Fine Arts Museum in Boston, a bridge circle that had formed out of the wealthier families in the neighborhood. If Joffrey wasn't around very much, if Lily wasn't the world's most affectionate child, well, such things couldn't be helped.

And yet. And yet. It wasn't just that Lily rarely hugged or kissed her mother, or told her—or anyone else—that she loved them. It was that she seemed to be carrying some basic darkness of mood, a disconnection from the world that made no sense in a young child. "It sounds silly," Patricia told her mother, during one of their infrequent check-in phone visits. "But it's like she never really got here. No, that's not it. It's like she just doesn't belong. Not with the other kids she knows, with me or Joffrey, with anyone. She just stares at us during dinner. Oh, she eats, but she almost never says she likes what we give her, no matter what it is. And she plays with toys, but most of the time she doesn't care what happens to them. Unless it's one special thing, and then she goes nuts if someone else touches it."

Her mother sniffed, then sighed, then sniffed again. Dealing with problems had never been her strong suit, and anything this ephemeral just sounded like "nerves"—her all-purpose description for any difficulty that couldn't be solved by money, personal discipline, or a good white wine. "These things pass, my dear. Have no fear. In a year or two you won't even remember. Tell me again where you got that antique vase you mentioned."

So for a very long time Patricia stopped sharing her worries about Lily with anyone. But it wouldn't leave her alone. She knew something was wrong with her child. She would try to cover her fears with shopping, or supervising some new plantings along the long, twisting driveway. And then they would return in a rush, and she would obsess about Lily's last childish tantrum, or her hiddenness, or her flat affect.

One day she watched her neighbor's two children, a boy seven and a girl three and a half, playing in a huge sandbox, the boy handing little plastic shovels to his sister, making up stories about princesses living in the little sandcastle the girl built, whispering pretend secrets into her ear.

Suddenly, it was clear. Lily needed a sibling. She could see them playing on the lush swing set Lily rarely used, frolicking in the pool, watching cartoons, sharing the delights of ice cream with hot fudge. Better a sister, she was sure. The idea of a miniature replica of Joffrey was not terribly appealing. But she would take what she could get.

But how to get it? Joffrey's interest in sex was far off from what it had been. Maybe in his mind mothers and intercourse just didn't go together. She sometimes wondered if he was sleeping with other women, but she was pretty sure that infidelity didn't fit with his sense of what his 'job' was. Their lovemaking was rare at best now, a situation that satisfied her, since her mind was on Lily, and the house, and the house, and Lily.

Much worse, she could still hear Joffrey's laugh—ill-humored and bordering on cruel—when she had very lightly raised the idea of another child. "You can't handle one, and you want another? Even with all these day care places and nannies and toys and this," (he pointed towards the house, the pool, the view, things he'd certainly never had), "it seems like it's too much. One will do fine, thanks." He'd looked her straight in the face, narrowing his eyes as he did when he wanted to be sure she Got the Point!—and walked off.

Patricia knew a confrontation would get her nowhere. But she was determined, maybe more determined than she'd ever been in her life. Lily was her daughter. She needed *something*—to have someone else in what Patricia realized in her hidden despair was an exquisitely decorated, loveless house. Patricia knew she wasn't a great companion for a child.

She did what was necessary, and really did care. But childish fun had never been part of her own mother's repertoire and it wasn't part of hers. Kid's songs and dressing up dolls and reading *Goodnight Moon* for the fiftieth time—it bored her and she knew it. Worse, in thoughts she almost never let herself think, Lily's coldness and strangeness frightened her.

But how could you be scared of your own child? Wasn't that awful? If this would help them all she would gain the weight, probably tear again, do more organizing and hiring and overseeing. And she'd face Joffrey's rage and meanness and anything else he could throw at her.

But it was much easier than she expected. He came home from an extended trip. She arranged a dinner of his favorite foods, bought two bottles of phenomenally expensive wine (whose price she lied about when he asked), wore a new dress which strategically displayed the parts of her body she could tell he was still attracted to, and managed, as she served the dinner, to casually brush up against him. Her breasts would touch his back, her thigh against his arm, the neckline of her dress would casually slip a little too low and her back (which she often thought her best feature) would show through the diaphanous material.

What with the wine, the low-key come on, and Joffrey's own sense of power after a successful trip, she wasn't surprised when he took her in his arms, kissed her, and then forcefully led her to the bedroom. She did what he asked, distracted from her typical limited physical pleasure by the desperate hope that she'd get pregnant from this one time, since she wasn't sure how often she could pull this off. He controlled the encounter, as he had to if he was to "perform" (as he put it) "the way a man should." What he didn't know, what she could never, ever, tell him, besides the fact that she'd been tracking her cycle closely and knew this was as good a time as she would get, was that she'd put several strategic holes in her diaphragm, holes big enough that it was pretty much as if she were wearing nothing. And to add to her chances, she woke him in the middle of the night, complaining of a nightmare, asked him to hold her, and strategically moved against him just enough to make him feel that he'd decided to have her again, whether she wanted it or not.

And so, more or less nine months later, out came Anne. Joffrey had been stupefied by the news of a second pregnancy, computing the costs of double the child expenses, deeply offended that Patricia's birth control hadn't worked. "Oh dear, these things do happen," she'd said. "Just ask anyone," knowing well that Joffrey would never ask for information on such a topic, his squeamishness over discussing sex (as opposed to doing it) combining with a manly sense that he should know whatever he needed to know without anyone's help.

Lily, now five, seemed variously intrigued, bored, and repulsed by the whole business. She watched her mother growing larger by the month, saw a room prepared for whatever was going to come out, asked a few questions. And spent even more time alone in her room. For Patricia this second pregnancy was a revelation. The early nausea passed in a week, for several months she had more energy than she'd had in years, and she even felt enormous rushes of sexual desire. Though Joffrey wasn't much help in that department—he had now decided that that mothers and sexual partners were exclusive categories, and having sex with a pregnant woman was like sleeping with your own mother—for the first time she discovered the joys of masturbation, spending long, lazy afternoons alone in the house with nothing but her fingers and some delightfully scented massage oil for company.

As with the pregnancy, the birth itself was easy. Four hours of labor, a few minutes of pushing, and out came her second child. The completely unreligious Patricia said a brief prayer of thanks that it was a girl, held her close and felt like whatever she'd had to give up for this moment was more than worth it. She'd given Lily a playmate, a sister, whom she'd call Anne after her closest friend from school. Lily would get better, they would all get along, and the house would have some love.

PART II

Chapter 7
Daniel and Sharon

"There we were in the hospital room," Daniel told a friend later. "Sharon and me and a nurse and the ob-gyn. Four of us, easy to count. And then there were five. No one had come in the door, there weren't any windows. Where did she come from?" He thought for a second, trying to avoid the cliché but then not caring. "She's a miracle. That's all, a miracle."

Sharon was a beautiful baby, with smooth, clear skin, a surprising head of black hair, the correct number of fingers and toes, and deep blue eyes. She was an easy baby as well, miraculously sleeping a good seven hours at night almost from the first, crying only when they were too dumb to realize she needed to be held or changed or fed, grabbing onto things like his scraggly beard at two months, crawling and walking and talking and feeding herself right on time. "Diagnosis?" the pediatrician had laughed, "hot ticket."

He and Amy had adjusted well, until five months in when she'd developed severe breast infections. Her nipples too tender to nurse, exhausted from the pain and fever, she would expel her breast milk and Daniel, sleepier than he thought possible, would heed Sharon's first whimpers well past midnight, gather her in his arms, change her, microwave the little container of breast milk, switch on some bland New Age music, and sitting in near dark at the dining room table, feed her.

There was a kind of peace and fulfillment in those few moments, repeated each night for two weeks, that he'd never felt before or since. He belonged to her, without question or holding back or calculation of what he could get in return. All those years of hiding in his books, the smart kid in school who didn't have many friends, the lover of old books and poetry. The carefully acquired masculine façade of control and distance. The thoughtful husband, the competent scholar and teacher, the good citizen with a neatly trimmed front hedge. All that receded and what rushed in, like a wave in front of a sudden and violent storm driving the water higher than it had ever been, was a fierce and protective passion for this tiny being in his arms.

***

Boston is soggy after a week of rain and Sharon, now three, is bored and rambunctious, filled with energy that no amount of stories and songs and board games can satisfy. Daniel is enjoying the treasured four month academic vacation, vaguely attempting an article on Hemingway's view of empathy while being Sharon's full time Dad. Amy is in Missouri, helping her mother transition to a nursing home.

It is yet another day of sudden, soaking downpours, followed by a brutal sun which suddenly gives way to dense clouds, fog, and then more rain. But this afternoon there is a special treat. Daniel took Sharon to Richard's apartment in one of the poorer sections of nearby Cambridge. An acquaintance from graduate school, Richard has a son almost exactly Sharon's age. That has led the two of them to become far closer than they ever were in the far away time of 'b.k.'—"before kids."

The two men sat in the kitchen, sipping beer while Sharon

and Peter play "chase"—a game which involved one of them suddenly starting to run through the narrow hallways of the small apartment while screaming and laughing at top volume as the other tries to catch up. Richard and Daniel chat about kids, wives, bestselling books that are really not very good, how hard it is to work and parent at the same time, and how great it is that the kids can get a little energy out.

Just outside the entrance to the kitchen, at the end of the hallway, there is a loud slamming noise, a brief silence, and then a sharp and terrified scream from Sharon. Daniel leaps to his feet faster than he thought possible, knocking over the beer bottles. He is by her side before he realizes he has moved, cradling her in his arms, staring at a red line of blood three inches long running down her forehead, murmuring words of comfort as she howls in pain. Richard, surprisingly calm, gestures at the edge of the molding. "Must have hit that. Nothing else around here." Peter starts to whimper, scared, needing reassurance. "Just a little bang," says Richard, taking his hand. "Let's get her a band-aid, o.k. buddy?" He soon returns with a modest first-aid kit, produces a disinfectant and a large gauze pad. "Hold the pad to the cut," he tells Daniel, who shifts position so he can cradle Sharon in his left hand and try to stop the bleeding with his right.

A few minutes later the blood has almost stopped, but a three-inch gaping wound remains on Sharon's forehead. Richard suggests the nearby emergency room, a few stiches maybe, see what the doctor says. So they bundle Sharon and Peter into the car, singing songs to take the kids' minds off the blood and pain and shock.

It's surprisingly easy to see a doctor—or resident, or intern, or whatever—who announces with certainty that this will take about four stiches, don't worry, not a problem.

Daniel explains to Sharon: "They will sew up the cut, sweetie, don't you worry, I'll be here the whole time." Sharon looks up at him, eyes wide. “Will it hurt?” “They will give you a little injection for the pain, honey. It’s o.k.; I’ll be here.”

He holds Sharon’s tiny body on the operating table so that she won’t flinch against the procedure. The bright hospital lights stare down, exposing every pore in Sharon’s skin, making her squint against the glare. Daniel wants to take her into his arms, envelop her. For a moment he has a bizarre fantasy of having a womb himself, of taking her into his body so that nothing can hurt her.

The doctor raises a long bright needle, thicker than anything Daniel sees at the dentist’s for his root canals. It digs first this way and then that, spreading the Novocain through the skin so that the child will not fight against the stitches. This is the worst part, more traumatizing and painful than the blow against the molding, and Sharon howls with outrage. Daniel is completely calm—his hands holding her still; then alternately reassuring, singing to her, trying to get her attention on something else as they wait for the painkiller to work.

The stitching itself is quick, even though it takes six rather than four. Daniel focuses on the needles as he continues to sooth Sharon, willing the bright steel to be true as it punctures the beloved flesh. So frail, so small, there’s almost nothing there he thinks, as he sings yet another verse of “Inch by Inch.”

“All done,” the doctor says brightly, “here’s a sheet with instructions for bathing and disinfectant. The stiches will fall out by themselves in a week or so. Shouldn’t leave any mark, maybe just a tiny one. Kids, they holler it out, but they forget about it long before we do.”

“Thanks so much,” answers Daniel, unlimbering himself from the contorted position of both holding Sharon down and comforting her. As he stretches his arms, he is suddenly light-headed, faint, sick to his stomach, and struck with the worst headache he has ever felt. She was alive, she was alive, that was all that mattered. But my God, her blood, it's under that perfect skin, just waiting to come out. And I was right there, and I couldn't protect her.

***

For six years he had been cultivating a little piece of his yard. "Grow some vegetables for us, let Sharon have a taste of real food, right?" Amy had smiled and said if he wanted to fight the weeds and do the watering she'd help out with the eating. "But," she added, her tone surprisingly serious, "check the soil. Around here you never know about lead." He'd agreed, but then promptly forgotten. For a small city backyard, he had almost a dozen trees—Norway maple mainly, with a few oaks and one lovely birch that had been only a sapling when they'd bought the house and now brushed against the third-floor attic windows. The grassy part was lush, and the neighbors on one side had beds of lovely orange lilies and roses climbing the side of their garage and a happy little red leafed Japanese maple. Lead? Poison? Here? Not possible. This wasn't Pittsburgh or some mining town in Minnesota. This was safe.

He had a hard time with a few greedy squirrels, and some blue jays that thought by rights everything belonged to them. But he knew enough to avoid chemical pesticides and most of what he planted, except for the truly pathetic dwarf carrots, had done all right. So for years they had enjoyed food just out of the ground. Even in summers when it had been too hot or too rainy for some reason, the broccoli always did well, and Sharon had loved to run to the backyard when she came back from daycare in early September and eat it straight off the stalk.

***

Things continued in a smooth rhythm of work and family, shared child care and play dates, clothes shopping and house repairs and dental appointments. They were all healthy; they had enough money. Watching Sharon grow, day by day, year by year, was a constant, sustaining joy. But then, as she turned twelve, the smooth cover of his smoothly adjusted life ripped off like a doctor uncovering a hidden and perhaps fatal tumor beneath what seemed to be normal flesh.

It began with Sharon being, not sick exactly, but not well either. Her energy, her mood, her eating habits—not terrible, just not right. Of course, he told himself, walling off the fear, at twelve years old, preparing for the emotional assaults of middle school, her body changing every other week, trying to make the transition between loving her parents and the seemingly obligatory American adolescent renunciation of everything they stood for, it wasn't surprising that some days, a lot of days actually, she didn't seem to be herself. Of course she would be *off her game*—and he enjoyed the archaic turn of phrase—for a bit. Who wouldn't be?

But then it got worse. Where schoolwork had always varied between easy and sort of hard, now she was complaining that she just "can't do it no matter how hard I try. And it's not my fault. It isn't." And she would storm off into her room, tears flowing. Her robust appetite faded and she would pick at her food, then complain to Amy in a whisper, that "I can't go to the bathroom—I try and try, and it hurts." Amy and Daniel tried vitamin pills and patience, herbal formulas for energy and concentration, soft music to help Sharon relax and some deep tissue massage on her intestines.

For the first time in Amy's life, they seriously worried. It was such a strange collection of problems, which often varied from day to day, week to week. They both had a deep counter cultural distrust of western medicine, having heard far too many stories of unnecessary operations, drug company lies, and disastrous long-term effects from cholesterol pills and hormone therapy. So they went the alternative route. Acupuncture first, which Sharon hated, while Daniel held her hand and the doctor put needles in her ears, fingers, and abdomen. Six treatments later, no change. Perhaps a little worse. A Chinese herbalist asserted that Sharon's kidneys were too yin, that she might have congenitally deficient chi, and prescribed a foul-tasting tea that Sharon simply could not keep down. Then homeopathy, but while the tiny white pills were easy to take, they did nothing. A nutritionist banned gluten and dairy and meat and non-organic food and sugar. After a month they found Sharon with a candy bar she had begged from a friend, but she cried that she had only been able to eat half of it. At last they sent her to a child therapist, who admitted being unsure of the diagnosis and recommended twice a week sessions for six months to see what would turn up.

One night, after another round of tears, complaints of stomach pain, and utterly failed homework, Daniel and Amy stared at each across the dining room table.

"No more," said Amy, with a heavy finality that Daniel knew would be almost impossible to overcome. "We are going to see her doctor as soon as we can."

"But," he answered, his mind resisting, searching for something to say that would blot out the reality that his daughter was seriously ill, not just "going through something."

Amy looked up from her hands, her lips tightening. She had gone down the alternative road with Daniel, but he could see from her face she had moved on. "But what?"

Daniel flinched at her cold, controlled tone. At times like this he felt lost, as if the trustworthy paths that he had faithfully followed had simply petered out, leaving him adrift in a wilderness. Sharon couldn't be really sick, could she? It just. Wasn't. Possible. And then all the possibilities, possibilities he had buried under comforting banalities of "growing pains" and "emotional adjustment" and "young bodies take a while to adjust"—all rushed into his mind like water from a burst pipe. Leukemia. Brain tumor. Some structural problem in her intestines that would require surgery. Some deep mental illness. Each one had its own compelling terror. He saw his hands trembling and with a muffled curse clasped them together until they stilled.

He saw Amy looking at him coldly. She had no fear of her own anxieties, he knew, but he also knew that she was gauging his strength, wondering if he could handle what might be coming.

***

The late September sun was making vibrant sunset colors that they could just make out between their towering maple trees and his neighbor's oversized house. Amy and Sharon had returned late from the doctor's appointment, Amy indicating by wordless gestures to Daniel that nothing would be said until Sharon went to her room, which she soon did, leaving most of her salad and veggie burger untouched. As Daniel compulsively chewed on the last string bean left in the salad bowl, a bean that had come straight from their back yard, Amy began, her tone strangely hushed, "Something has happened. To Sharon. But first, I have to know: all those years ago, you did get the soil checked, for lead I mean, right?"

"No, sorry, never got around to it. But," his voice quivered slightly as he moved to the edge of his seat, trying to see past the pressure of fear that made him want to close his eyes. "What about the doctor?"

Amy swung around to face him, leaning forward in the rickety wooden dining room chair, short brown hair with streaks of gray, usually calm expression now turned to the intense anger that instantly arose when someone, anyone, threatened her child.

"I'll get to the doctor. But, the test. You told me you would."

"Yeah, I know, I should have. But this has been a residential neighborhood for almost a hundred years. What could be in the soil?"

Amy's eyes narrowed further, her tone sank to a whisper holding barely suppressed fury: "Lead, that's what. Sharon used to get a blood test every year at the doctor, and the test hurts. But she was too old for it. We thought. And she hated it. But today she had another test. And the results weren't good. She's. Been. Poisoned. That's why she is the way she is."

Daniel blinked his eyes, the panic feeling felt like a weight pushing harder and harder on his eyes, his mouth, his heart. "But. But. Isn't that for poor kids, eating paint chips or something?" He thought of the abundance of food, much organic, very little of the processed stuff containing the usual array of unpronounceable poisons that Americans seem to think are harmless and maybe even tasty, that Sharon had chosen from every day of her life. Surely, surely, lead poisoning wasn't something that could happen to this house.

"You are ignorant, Daniel, just ignorant."

"Oh, and all of a sudden you're Rachel Carson," he answered, leaning in towards her, his voice rising, hammering out the words, his face rigid with anger, his tongue tripping itself. "Sh, Sharon is sick and you're thinking about bi, broccoli? Who the hell are you to tuh tuh talk that way to me?"

Amy's eyes narrowed even further. She stood up, all five feet two of her quivering with an obvious effort not to yell. With a concentrated passion that told Daniel this wasn't going to be deflected, she spoke slowly, emphasizing each word; "This is your daughter, Daniel. And something is not right in her blood. She will have to take pills, for a long time, to get it right. Everything that's been going on with her. All of it. Could be the lead. Probably is. And we can only pray that it can be reversed.

"So do not talk to me about Rachel Carson or who the hell I am. You are a college professor, not the village idiot. Go and find out where the lead comes from. And what it can do. What you may have done. And don't talk to me until you have." She leaned forward and stared into his eyes, until he broke the contact, suddenly finding something of great interest in his left shoe.

And so he learned the history of the use of lead in paints and gasoline and, since lead was used in their drinking cups, how it might have been responsible for the madness that afflicted many Roman emperors. And that the constipation and loss of concentration, moodiness and abdominal pain, loss of appetite and energy that afflicted his daughter could all come from too much lead.

Two weeks later he stared at the wrinkled form from the state lab, the one to which he'd taken a sample of his garden's soil: "Significant amounts of lead in soil, unsafe for growing food for human consumption." When he called to double check the results, rigid with disbelief and horror, the technician explained. "All those cars, for years and years, using leaded gas. They thought the lead was good for it. They had no idea. But the exhaust goes into the air, and then settles down. Oh, don't forget houses. Outside paint has lead, paint job starts to fade and peel, then scrape, scrape, scrape—where do you think the dust from all that scraping goes?

"But it probably wasn't from your vegetables. Or not all. And some people, you know some people—who knows why?—they just seem to be a little more susceptible. Best of luck to your daughter." And he hung up.

Daniel had been standing in the living room. His knees

gave out as he sank to the carpet. Tears flooded his face, his fingers turned to claws, the nails scraping his own flesh, and pain shot through his stomach. He'd poisoned her, how much he wouldn't know for a long time. It wasn't possible. But it had happened.

An intellectual, a *professor*, and he'd known nothing. Too busy doing everything that needed doing every single day: paying bills, fixing the house, getting tenure, preparing lectures, supervising play dates, finding good books and stimulating computer programs, making arrangements for their little family vacations; getting Sharon into the right schools and the really creative summer camps. Somehow he had found time for all of that. But not for *this*. He'd been scared of lots of things for Sharon: rigid teachers, boring schools, sexism that crippled too many girls, eating disorders, abduction by strangers in a supermarket. And so far, none of them had happened.

She'd been just fine, safe, blessed.

Except she hadn't. She was ill. Because of him. He would never, *never*, forgive himself. Or all the people who had put this poison into the world and not insisted, from the first moment they knew the truth, that all of it be removed.

His tears stopped. He lay down on the carpet, curled up on his side, his hand pressed against his face. He wondered if he would ever be able to get up. Because it was worse, far worse.

Part of him *had* known. He had simply been too scared to face it. All his youthful loneliness had been assuaged, if only a little, by walks in the woods, sitting in his tree house, listening to crickets on a hot night. A few camping trips with friends in junior high school had shown him a world of night sounds, pine trees growing on almost vertical hillsides by holding on to rock with roots that made him think of his own hands or the prehensile feet of chimps, birds that called at dawn, the odd rabbit, or badger, or skunk that they stumbled across. And being outside in a full moon, so laughably, magically bright he kept holding up a book to see if could—and he could—read by it.

Along with Sharon it was *this*—the trees, the birds, the sky—that had kept him going as an adult. He'd soothed the usual pains of life, nursed the wounds of his failed novel or some aggravation at the university or his grief when his parents died within a year of each other or the way he and Amy had become so, well, *used* to each other—by taking a walk at their nearby pond. It was just a few blocks to a paved path one and half miles around, a pocket-sized island on one side, an old Elizabethan boat house on the other, with geese and ducks and sometimes swans and very rarely a heron. The birch and beech and oak trees that framed it, the turtles that would sun themselves on fallen branches, the cormorants ducking under the surface and coming up twenty feet away. All within the city limits of Boston. Hadn't that been the one soothing presence when he was sad or scared?

Did he really think these weren't under attack by acid rain and global warming and developers just itching to pave it all over and put up condos? Somewhere deep inside he had known that something was wrong, but he couldn't face it.

What had it cost him, all that fear and hiding? Those times when Amy had asked, during what could have been a shared moment of pleasure, or joy, or even grief, when she had demanded, "Daniel, where are you? It doesn't seem like you're really here. Hello? Hello?" And she'd make a joke about it, knocking on his head with her knuckles, just hard enough to cause a little pain, not much. He'd laugh in reply, reassure her, remind himself how lucky he was with her and Sharon and a nice house and a tenured position. And he'd stuff the reality back where he couldn't remember it—except, of course, he had to know where it was so he could avoid it.

He'd always been more or less sympathetic to the

environmental cause, and as a card-carrying east coast academic, he'd always voted Democrat and hoped somebody would clean things up. In Junior High School, Earth Day had meant a day off of regular classes, and much later he'd seen the frightening covers of *Time Magazine* ("Be Very Afraid!!!!"). But it never felt that close. Outside of some bad air in the summer, living in Boston was safe. And while everyone pretty much accepted how polluted the Charles River was, there didn't seem to be much happening environmentally. And if there was, surely someone else would take care of it. He had so many other things, important things, to do.

But no one had taken care of the lead in his back yard. And his daughter had been poisoned—not by some psycho who put arsenic in random Tylenol bottles or some terrorist with Anthrax, but by him, by her father.

Slowly, feeling each movement an effort, he got to his feet. No more, no more. Even if Sharon recovered, as the doctor thought she would. It didn't make any difference. He couldn't continue to hide. Whatever he thought he was protecting had put him on the road of a terrible sacrifice. Now he would give up his dreadful normality for something else.

He cleared his shelves of resources for an article on Joseph Conrad's essential loneliness to make room for a whole new set of books. If he'd been ignorant before, he wouldn't be ignorant any longer. If he had trusted all the other people, from the EPA to the Sierra Club, to do something about it, now it would be up to him.

Chapter 8
Sarah

In the small-town high school everyone knew everyone else, and she was known to her friends and their parents as a good time girl but also reliable. She could hang out, smoke a little weed, and still help you with your math homework. If she was having sex (and she was, but not too often) you knew she wouldn't get pregnant or turn up with an STD; if she drank, she'd never drive afterward; and if your own kid was with her Sarah would try to put the brakes on anything really stupid.

To her parents, Sarah was a mystery. She made friends easily, socialized gracefully, did well but not brilliantly in school. When she suffered—a skiing accident that left her on crutches for months, a boyfriend's betrayal, a close friend moving to Colorado—she did so without making a fuss, taking only an occasional hug and the most banal of supports ("things will get better," "you're a good person," "this too shall pass") and would soon return to a basically sunny disposition. "Some kids," said a pediatrician family friend, "are just born on the right side of the bed. Who knows why?"

Her mother was tall, graceful, composed, moody, serious, intensely involved in Sarah's life except when she was working on a new poem, and then she hardly seemed to notice the walls or the floor, let alone her daughter. She would spend long minutes just staring at Sarah—doing her homework, in the bath when she was three or four, as she cleaned up her room. She would say something—"That shirt is too large." "Your neck is still dirty." "That's an excellent essay you've written." And then she would walk out of the room, not waiting for an answer. She touched Sarah rarely, kissed her almost never, and would retire to her undersized writing room for hours at a time, a room Sarah knew without being told never to enter when Mom was working.

The strange thing was, it didn't bother Sarah at all. The older she got the more she knew that her mother, in her own way, loved her. That the long looks and silences might have been her mother trying to find some way to create just the right metaphor to describe her hair or her skin; and that if her mother, a famous poet, got it right, well then Sarah's skin or hair would live forever in slender books with stark black and white covers and names like *Open Doors* or *Fog in the Early Morning*. And that if her mother might not love her as much as her writing, she loved her more than anyone else. That the long looks and the long silences were her mother's precious gifts. Love, at least Mom's love, was a kind of perfect, unwavering, attention.

Dad was another story. Where Mom was like a laser beam, severe, penetrating, perceptive, ultimately self-absorbed—a poet before she was a mother, wife, friend or citizen—Dad was all over the place. He made jokes and laughed at them more than anyone else, dressed in flamboyant oranges and reds that looked faintly ridiculous on pale white skin and washed out blond hair, and carried much more weight on his six feet than he needed. When he was "doing well," he would rush around the house cleaning the grime Cynthia never noticed, over shopping for food, starting a garden in the long late spring evenings after dinner, all the while talking business on the phone. When things weren't "going well," when another one of his businesses—a tourist magazine for the ski resort area they lived in year round, an alpine slide to bring folks to the slopes in the summer, a new shop with specialty dog foods and pet supplies—had gone into the toilet, he would mope around the house, looking for sympathy, staying in his pajamas for days, eating pasta and cake for breakfast.

If Cynthia was either right inside your head or unreachable, Doug was almost always there, even if he was kind of a mess. He'd talk to Sarah about school while fussing with yet another home project that would probably never be finished; about her friends while cooking a five course gourmet meal that, surprisingly, almost always tasted great; take her shopping for new clothes in the fall if Cynthia was off giving readings or too involved with writing to leave the house. When Sarah got older, each time his latest business crashed he would turn to her for the sympathy and attention Cynthia didn't provide. "It's o.k., Dad," she'd say, "the next one will work out." With Doug, love was need in the face of a near crushing insecurity, and the lesson that what she, Sarah, had to offer mattered.

Ludlow had its limits. Winter weekends when the two-lane road that ran through the center of town turned into a massive traffic jam as skiers first went up, and then came down the mountain. Three months of a kind of persistent cold and dark that made more than a few turn to alcohol or drugs or serial affairs. A too brief spring often marked by clouds of maddening black flies that would find the smallest opening in your clothes, car windows, or screens.

But in the fall, even with the hordes of leaf peepers who came up from New York or Boston, the trees were magic. And summer—Vermont in summer (her father often said when trying to raise a little money for another off-season investment) was paradise. There was a small swimming pond a half mile off main street, set against the mountain, surrounded by fields on one side and forest on the other, with a view of Mt. Ascutney twenty miles away. There were dozens of trails through Vermont's serene Green Mountains, and a series of larger lakes made by dams built decades ago. Most people, most of the time, were kind and generous. And if a few of them were jerks, what could you expect?

If Cynthia was withdrawn and Doug was lost in a too high or too low place, there were always the woods, summer butterflies, the sky endlessly changing its balance of blue and white and gray, rain and snow and occasional searing heat. The series of waterfalls two miles outside of town created rock rimmed pools, and if it was warm enough you could put your body under a thundering cascade that drowned out the noises in your head and washed away tension, fear, or loss. With the trees and the daily sunset, the birds and the stars on winter nights, Sarah never felt alone. They were her constant companions, the ones you could always count on, who had always been there and always would be.

She had decent enough grades to make it to a pretty good engineering school, where her interest in nature and her ability to handle math would push her, she thought, towards something in biology or biochemistry or engineering with a biology twist. She didn't mind all the science and calculus the school required, all of which she much preferred to reading novels or poetry (her mother's terrain, not hers), or studying history (which had always seemed pretty depressing). The university was very interested in getting more women to make campus more attractive to male students so a fat scholarship sealed the deal. And as a two hour drive from home, it wouldn't be hard to get back to see her father, who hadn't been doing well lately.

***

It was the first day of Sarah's sophomore year at Wilson

Polytechnic Institute, and she was headed towards her required humanities class. She had wanted to take the one about history of science and technology, figuring that she'd be interested in at least half of it, but that was filled and time constraints left her with few choices. So it would be "Philosophy and the Environment," which might have some science in it. She was leaning towards some kind of bio science major, having had a dynamic professor freshman year. The interplay of elements of an ecosystem were like magic, each part doing its bit without any direction, sustaining the whole, and then responding to some kind of change—climate, invasive species, human presence—to do something new and unexpected. Maybe a little in this course would be of use. And if not, well, the professor had a reputation of being a little odd, but not a terribly hard grader. She had to do something in the humanities to graduate. It might as well be this.

Professor Gradenstein looked like he was in his sixties, thick glasses with gold colored wire frames, only the barest memory of hair on his large, round skull, curly beard, prominent nose, and large blue eyes. Old khakis that hung off a skinny frame, faded red corduroy shirt and, "What the heck is that?" thought Sarah, some kind of green rock on a leather thong around his neck. As Sarah and the other students settled into their seats, he took an odd assortment of stuff out of an old backpack: a square of embroidered red and black cloth, two large stones, a feather, a sea shell.

She picked up her favorite note taking ball point, opened the term's new notebook, and prepared to do her thing. If this guy wanted to be a little, well, different, that was fine with her. She'd get her solid B and put her attention on the science, the part that mattered.

"I am Professor Gradenstein," he began, "and this is philosophy and the environment. Let us begin by noticing that there is something we are all, each one of us, doing now. I know I'm doing it and I sincerely hope that you are as well." He waited. They wondered what the hell this was about. "I mean, of course, breathing. And let us observe that with each breath we are connected to the rest of life on this planet: to several billion years of cosmic history, to uncounted generations of evolution, to organisms that produce oxygen, to the creation of the atmosphere. No breath. No connection. No life. This is our first lesson, and perhaps, really, the only lesson. We are, each of us, connected. Whether we realize it or not. There is, however, no need to write this down. I doubt that even without detailed notes that you will forget to breathe."

Gradenstein waited for a few moments, hands clasped behind his back, slowly letting his eyes move from student to student. Sarah knew the general feeling about humanities in a tech school: nothing they'll learn from this guy will help them get the great jobs they expect after graduation. So, no matter what he does, they won't be impressed. Sarah wasn't concerned about money that much, but she knew this wasn't real knowledge. It was just a lot of opinions. But when his gaze turned to her she was struck by a strange openness, a seeming refusal to accept the familiar boundaries and conventions of the classroom. She looked away, studying first the wall, and then her pen.

"I wish," he began slowly, "that I knew what to say to you. But I don't. Not really." There is a long pause. Sarah saw a few students start to write something in their notebooks. What could it be? Gradenstein made a dismissive gesture with his right hand. "Please, please, for today anyway, put away all the notebooks, and let's see if we can just talk together, like reasonable people." Shuffling sounds as the notebooks are closed, returned to backpacks. Many students leaned back in their chairs. If they don't have to take notes, it can't be that important. Sarah remained focused. But another part of her mind was suddenly and unusually distrustful.

"I suppose there is no easy way to put it. We are in the midst of an unprecedented threat to human life, and to the life support systems of countless other organisms. This threat I call the environmental crisis. It is the subject of this course. But the course, you see, is really not that important. Imagine you were a student of, oh let's say mechanical engineering, doing an off-campus project on metallic stress, and the site of your little project was, just by analogy of course, the Titanic. God knows you would be learning a great deal as you studied the structure of the hull, heard the scraping sound as it hit the iceberg, and observed the water slowly flooding the ship. You could write one hell of a paper on the process. An A for sure. The only problem, you see, is that there is a really good chance you wouldn't survive the learning experience.

"What could be more important than asking yourself: what is the meaning of my life when I and everyone else I know is living in a way that's liable to make the earth increasingly uninhabitable for human beings?"

Gradenstein walked back and forth in front of the long desk that fronted the blackboard, then stopped to take a sip from a dark green water bottle. Sarah glanced at the other students. Some seemed bored, some were smiling, a few looked a little uneasy. Sarah found his pompous style a drag, his theatrics too obvious. She'd heard all this before, and knew there were some real issues, but he was overdoing it. The air had always been clear in Ludlow; there were people in the government to take care of it and private groups like Sierra Club or Greenpeace or whatever. It was manageable.

"I don't know how to make this clear right now," Gradenstein started up again. "Take a look around the room, at the other students. If you're a woman, there's a one in three chance you'll get cancer. If you're a man, one in two." Now he has their attention. "Do you think it was always like this? Do you think we're winning the fucking *war on cancer*?" A few students gasp at the profanity. He continued. "You female students," he gestured at Sarah, at the few other women in the predominantly male class, typical of the predominantly male university. "Any of you expect to have children someday?" A few of them, Sarah included, tentatively raised their hands. "Then you should expect that they'll be born with a hundred to two hundred toxic chemicals already in their bloodstreams. And there's a chance, a good chance, that your own breast milk will be carrying the same stuff. Carcinogens. Endocrine disrupters. Things that mess with the immune system and the brain. Before they are born. In the womb. Where it is supposed to be safe."

Sarah was stunned. This can't be right. He must be exaggerating. It cannot be this bad. Then she turned to anger. Who is he to lay all this stuff on them, to make up such frightening ideas? This is not what a professor is supposed to do. Where's the syllabus and the course requirements and the first homework assignment? Who did he think he was to put her through something like this on a beautiful, if unusually warm, late August day in New England, at this pretty campus with its small trees and shrubs and tastefully arranged flower beds?

For the rest of the hour, Sarah alternated between fear and anger. The class ended with another instruction to pay attention to their breath. Gradenstein sat back against the desk, nodding at the students as they left—some seemingly upset like Sarah, others chatting happily about the upcoming football game, or digging in their pockets for a snack as they rushed to their next class.

Sarah dawdled at the door, not knowing what she was doing. Gradenstein gathered up his things, catching her eye as he set to leave.

"Can I help you, Ms.?"

"Sarah."

"Last names here."

"Oh, yes, Carson. Sarah Carson."

"Ah. Quite the name for all this. Well, Ms. Carson, what can I do for you?"

Sarah stumbled, words caught in her mouth. No teacher had ever called her Ms. anything before.

"This stuff you said. You were just saying it to get our attention, right? It's not all true, is it?" She saw Gradenstein studying her. Not angry.

"True? Yes, it's all true. Or let me put it this way. You find one major point in which I'm wrong, I'll give you an A for the course and you won't have to do any other work. Fair enough?"

"But. If it's true..." She suddenly felt a little faint, her stomach in an unexpected and rigid knot, her palms clammy, her fingers shaking a little. She can't get the words out.

She looked at him. His eyes hadn't moved, they were still focused on hers.

"It's. Kind of. Upsetting." She felt a bit like a fool using such a silly word.

"Yes, Ms. Carson, it is."

"But. But." This is not the right answer. It can't be. He may be a bit pompous and like to make an effect, but he's also obviously pretty smart and knows a lot. Isn't he supposed to tell her it will be all right, that the experts know what to do and that if she listens to the experts and follows along, she can feel secure and safe?

"I'm sorry, Ms. Carson. Truly I am. I know that I have taken something away from you today. But I cannot help but believe that knowing the truth is better than living a lie.

"It's not every day one learns the world is at risk. That might even be worth a few tears and sleepless nights."

He nodded to her, offered a sad smile, and made his way

out of the room.

***

It wasn't easy being Gradenstein's student. Sarah would make appointments to talk to him and he wouldn't show up. They would be talking about one thing—how global warming acidifies the oceans and disrupts oyster cultivation—and he would slide into something about the Russian revolution and some obscure old Marxist philosophers that Sarah had never heard of and had no desire to discuss. Every once in a while, he would just trail off in the middle of a sentence, and there would be an awkward minute or two of dead silence before he resumed. It was striking to Sarah that his lectures in class were coherent and challenging—and all that without a single note card or outline. But an hour or two a day seemed like the most the man could keep it together.

It all became clear when she realized that he was an alcoholic. He didn't slur his words or stumble. Never got completely wasted. The liquor seemed more like something he needed as a constant source of comfort for his daily round of teaching, student conferences, and the small amount of scholarly writing he still did.

One late afternoon they were discussing the idea that nature has moral value—that it was unethical to treat a living tree with the same cavalier disregard that we use on spoons, tires, or earrings. Gradenstein was in the middle of a medium sized rant, ranging over the way trees could communicate threats in their neighborhood to other trees and how monkeys had a primitive sense of fairness. Then a too vigorous hand movement knocked over the large, dark green plastic water bottle he always carried with him, the same one Sarah had seen him use during every lecture. He hadn't fully closed its top after his last sip, and what looked like orange juice spilled over a few half open books and splashed onto Sarah's well-worn Asics jogging shoes. Gradenstein stopped in the middle of his sentence and looked at the spilled liquid with a slightly stupefied expression, as if he didn't know where it had come from.

Sarah ran to the Ladies room, grabbed some paper towels and did her neat girl best to clean up. Suddenly she realized that the strange smell from the liquid indicated that this was not just juice. She'd been to enough parties, helped out with her parents' rare social events, and dealt with enough other people's drunken messes to realize that the juice was heavily laced with vodka. The smell was unmistakable.

"I don't understand," she said later to her roommate, a pleasant Chem Eng major with whom she would occasionally go for coffee, compare notes on professors, or lament the typically crude behavior of male students.

"Don't understand what?" answered Olivia, fishing out a huge chemistry text from her overstuffed backpack. "He's a drunk. Isn't that kind of standard for professors who do stuff like philosophy?" Olivia had told Sarah a few times that she saw humanities as, at best, a pleasant relief from real learning.

"No," said Sarah, "he's not like that. Oh, he's definitely a little strange at times. But," she didn't know how to put this so that Olivia would understand. "He knows things."

Glancing up from the text, Olivia switched gears. "He hit on you yet?"

"God no," Sarah answered, with a slight shudder. She respected Gradenstein, at times found his temporary mental vacations irritating, but sex? Not for a second.

"What I don't understand." Pause. She spoke slowly. When things weren't clear to her she didn't speed up to pretend she had it all together. She had learned her mother's patient, focused gaze—to give your full attention until you truly understand, and not to stop looking until then. "Is how he can be." What was it that made him so strange? "How he can be so smart and so strong. And so weak."

"What's strong about a philosophy professor," Olivia laughed. "All he does is read, talk, and write."

Sarah went on. A little faster now, because she was seeing it. "He has taught himself just how *bad* it is. And he's not afraid. Or, no, he is; but it doesn't stop him. Do you know anyone else doing that?"

Olivia turned back to her book, leaving the question unanswered. Sarah could see the conversation didn't agree with her. Then Olivia looked up to add one more thought.

"Well, if he does hit on you, don't be too surprised. A lot of them do that."

"Thanks for the moral support," Sarah laughed, once again seeing, quite easily this time, the limits of her relationship with people like Olivia.

So the vodka didn't keep her away from her teacher. She was used to this sort of thing. Dad didn't drink much, but he so often needed so much support, and reassurance, and general hand holding, his dependence on something outside his own sense of life was completely clear. She had learned from her mother to look, and from her father what to expect from older men.

Still, she wondered, what was bothering Gradenstein? What ate at his soul so much that he couldn't come to Wilson without the green bottle?

***

There they were, a rag-tag army of radical students, hippies, orthodox socialists and even a few old-time communists. Far out cultural rebels like beat poet Allen Ginsberg joined with famous baby doctor Benjamin Spock and novelist Norman Mailer, women's groups, veterans against the war, and some of the new psychedelic left. Hard core experienced civil rights organizers—who had been tested by hatred and violence in Mississippi and Alabama—protested alongside well-dressed suburban moms and nationalists seeking independence for Puerto Rico. They were there to stop the war—the endless Vietnam war that was making everyone crazy, that was America's use of fighter planes and thousands upon thousands of bombs and napalm that burned children while parents watched helplessly and G.I.'s, stoned on heroin or weed, fragged their own officers.

So they came to D.C. in the fall of 1967, signs, leaflets and ideals in hand.

At first it was kind of a lark. After the speeches at the Lincoln Memorial the hippies and yippies and hard core types converged on the Pentagon, joined hands around the building and tried to levitate it. Ginsberg sat there chanting some Tibetan Buddhist mantra, others danced or played incoherent music. They wore torn jeans and long skirts and t-shirts and Indian bedspreads made into pants and tunics, strange hats, dirty sneakers, hiking boots, weird sandals with no heels, tailored shirts with ties, miniskirts and see through blouses. Their signs and t-shirts and chants announced themselves: "Mothers against the war, veterans against the war, give peace a chance, no Vietnamese ever called me nigger, hey hey LBJ, how many kids did you kill today? Ho Ho Ho Chi Minh, NLF is gonna win."

And so on.

The Pentagon refused to cooperate, staying firmly in place and continuing, it would seem, with business as usual. As it got dark, most people drifted away, but a small, serious group of about two thousand remained.

They gradually moved closer and closer to the building, sitting down on the steps. "Take over the Pentagon," went the chant. "Stop the war, stop the war, STOP THE WAR!"

Gradenstein chanted along with everyone else. It hadn't taken much for him to see that the war was wrong. At somebody's wedding a second cousin from California, a few years older and a history major, explained what was going on: the nationalist movement for freedom from colonialism, the savage suppression, the broken agreements, the imposed separation of north and south, and just what the U.S. seemed to want from a war 11,000 miles away: control of Asian markets, protection for Japan, and a place to test new weapons. So his progressive suburban liberalism slid, with not much to stop it, towards the radicalism of the day.

There he was, on the steps of the Pentagon, as night fell and a few thousand die hards remained. National TV crews, sensing that something important was going on, surrounded them with glaring lights, which they turned towards the edges of the crowd when what the last speaker had called the "forces of repression" arrived. Hundreds of soldiers, quickly identified as the army's elite 101st Airborne, marching in neat ranks and carrying rifles fitted with bayonets. They were soon joined by large, aggressive looking men in suits and ties—"federal marshals" Gradenstein heard someone say—holding large and frightening clubs.

Had they been told to leave? If so, Gradenstein didn't hear the order. What he heard was a new chant, "The whole world is watching, the whole world is watching," as the reporters urged their crews to keep lights on so they could film what was looking to be a major confrontation. It was stand-off city for a while, until the lights dimmed. Then it all changed. "Turn on the lights," screamed the protestors, and then the screams had no words at all, as the federal marshals and soldiers charged into the crowd, clubs and rifle butts swinging. On went the lights, the charge stopped, and then the pattern was repeated. Gradenstein watched with horror as the clubs flailed around him, shouts and moans of people with whom he had just been sharing a bold moment of social protest turning his stomach sick with fear. His hands were shaking, his feet seemed frozen in place, and he found himself wondering how many minutes—or seconds—would pass before the clubs would be turned on him. Suddenly, about fifteen feet away, he saw a protestor knocked to the cement steps; and then, to his horror, he could see a marshal raise his baton high over his head and bring it down full force on the protestor's head, smashing it into the edge of the steps.

Gradenstein fell to his knees, fighting the urge to vomit, or urinate, or charge at the marshal with his fists, or lie down on the pavement and put his hands over his head. The moment passed, and he did none of those things. Slowly, carefully, he got to his feet, saw where the soldiers and marshals were thickest and where their charge was aimed, and backed away. The flashpoint of violence and confrontation wasn't really that large, and in a minute of brisk walking he was out of danger, leaving the struggle behind him. He would never forget the image of the club striking the protestor's head. And he would never get over the bitter self-loathing he felt as he protected himself and left his comrades to face the onslaught.

***

It was late in the afternoon when Gradenstein finished the story, looking to Sarah as if he once might have asked for absolution, but that would have been a very long time ago. He gestured at the green bottle—after the incident with the spill, and the face she'd involuntarily made as she cleaned it up, he knew that she knew.

"You see, my dear," he said, "it wasn't just that moment. That moment, as it were, set the stage for what followed." He stopped. Did he want her to ask him what followed? But no, by now she'd learned he would hesitate for slightly dramatic effect and then temporarily forget where he'd been going. But this time she wouldn't let that happen.

"Yes," she prompted him, feeling a little impatient but keeping her tone gentle.

"When I graduated from college, and my student draft exemption ran out, I could have gone to jail in resistance, or filed for conscientious objector. But those were risky, and besides, what would I have done in jail? And the company I'd be keeping might not have appreciated my stellar qualities."

Sarah could tell today's vodka was finally having an effect. The slightly more formal quality to his language, sort of pseudo-Oxford, always indicated that he was putting an effort into being coherent.

"And so it went. You see, my politics never changed. I hate all this"-waving a bony hand at a world dominated by Exxon and the Pentagon and corrupt governments and an unrelenting voracious capitalism that would eat everything, and then probably devour itself. "My vision is still clear, my mind, more or less, still knows what's going on."

His face turned to a grimace, then he shut his eyes and shivered. This was no attempt at an effect, Sarah realized, this was real. "It's my character that's defective. I was scared then, and I'm scared now. I have never, never, been willing to put it all on the line—go to jail, get fired for standing up to the administration here, or all those larger forces that make this place just a finishing school for destroying the world. I hate them for doing it; I hate all those normal, well-adjusted, neurotic, Visa-card carrying Americans. And because I know what it is, and how wrong it is, and I'm too attached to my job and my crummy salary and my little house and my little car and my own precious life to do anything, really do anything, to stop it—I hate myself most of all."

He stared at her for a long moment. Then put his head down into his hands and started to cry, his shoulders shaking with each muffled sob, his body soft and utterly defeated.

***

Despite all the differences, Gradenstein reminded her so much of her father. Another man defeated by life. Desperately wanting to be something he wasn't. For Doug, making a lot of money that neither Cynthia nor Sarah cared about.

And for Gradenstein? What could he have done all those year ago—punch a federal marshal and gotten his head broken? She guessed it would have been better, more politically correct (a term she didn't use as a put down, Gradenstein had explained where it came from and what it meant) to resist the draft in a more public way. But even so, Gradenstein had told her about some of the political work he *had* done: a public confrontation with a famous homophobic humanist therapist about gay rights in 1976, demonstrations against neo-Nazis in 1978, support for Greenpeace and, way back in what seemed like the Dark Ages, standing around supermarket parking lots asking people to support the struggling young farmworkers union by boycotting grapes and lettuce.

He laughed as he told the story, a rare pleasure to see Gradenstein enjoying anything. "They would pull into that parking lot, and I'd be standing there, not quite blocking the lane, but almost. I'd hand them a leaflet and say, in my most polite voice, 'We're asking for your support sir or ma'am, please don't buy grapes or lettuce, help the migrant workers who are just trying to get the barest of decent wages, and the right to go to the bathroom, and get a lunch break.'

"This was a fairly progressive town, and people were generally polite, so most of them just nodded, took the leaflet, and ignored what we asked. But a few got angry. It wasn't that they didn't like farmworkers, though maybe a few were racist against Hispanics. No, it was the idea that something might interfere with their choices. They figured they were entitled to absolutely *anything* that was on the shelves. And who was I, a complete stranger, to ask them to think about anything else?

"'I will buy whatever I want,'' they would say, raising their voices. 'Yes sir,' I'd answer, polite to a fault, even though I hated them, 'of course you can, I just hope you can *want* something different. Because,' and I'd point to the leaflet. That would usually stop them, except for some narrowed eyes, hard stares, or the sound that's not really a word, but everybody knows what it means." He cleared his throat, narrowed his eyes and said "harrumph" with such a convincing tone that Sarah almost fell off her chair laughing.

And then there was his teaching. He might be stoned on vodka half the time, have the world's messiest office and do a lousy job grading papers. But his lectures were close to brilliant, day after day, term after term. Sarah took all his classes, and did independent studies with him as well. From her bio courses, she got the details of what was happening to ecosystems, vulnerable species, water resources, the phytoplankton at the bottom of the ocean's food chain, and the monarch butterflies threatened by genetically engineered corn. From Gradenstein, she got the political and ethical perspective to see how it all fit together. How capitalism had to grow, how people were conditioned to consumerism, the way corporations controlled the government and the media. And for one painful term she got an introduction to all the movements that tried to change things: socialists, communists, labor movement, feminists, civil rights. Their successes and failures; their insights and their self-destructive stupidities.

By the time she graduated she knew who she was and what the world was like. Gradenstein had always made it clear what he thought, but never imposed. "I'll lay it out for you, my dear, with my reasons. See what you can find, if anything, that helps."

"Helps with what?" she'd asked, suppressing a smile.

He harrumphed at her as she looked at him, feigning innocence. Then he leaned forward in his old, rather shabby, desk chair. "Remember how you felt that first day? You will need to figure out what to do about the world that makes you feel like that. And whether or not you can make a difference, the kind I never did."

She closed her eyes, slowed her breathing and tried to bring in some courage. She leaned forward and for the first time in three years of almost daily contact, put her hand on his arm. "Professor. Why?" She pointed at the green bottle. "Why? You're a terrific teacher. You've helped me so much. And I know that you've done that for lots of other students. Why isn't that enough?"

"Thank you for your kind words. And I assure you the pleasure of teaching you has been all mine. But. Why. This, you ask?" He slowly unscrewed the bottle top, took a long drink, and replaced the cap carefully.

"Because I know what greatness is, and I never had the courage to be it. Because I understand, better than most, what's wrong, and I never could make it right. Because I am an extremely smart, at times almost brilliant, coward."

A single tear formed at the corner of his eye. And Sarah, whose clear headed, balanced, tolerant, and confident relation to life rarely led her to cry, felt a deep sadness reach from her heart to her eyes. Her mouth compressed, trying to hold it back. She reached out with both hands, grasping Gradenstein's one hand that wasn't on the bottle and gently stroked it.

"I'm so sorry," was the best she could do, her mind searching for words none of which, she knew, would make the slightest difference.

That was the last time Sarah saw him. He never went to commencement. And shortly afterward he developed a fatal cancer of the liver. As Sarah stood at the cemetery, thinking about their last encounter, she wondered if Gradenstein had really understood himself.

"You know," she said later in a rare phone call to her father, "I'm not sure it was really that he was scared to do what he thought he should. I think," she stopped, could this really be it? "I think the pain scared him. He looked, and kept looking, until that was all he could see. And after a while he just didn't know there was anything but pain in the world."

"Sad," said Doug, who would never know that Sarah saw it in him as well.

"I mean," Sarah went on, "It's just what life is? Anything else, that's sort of a fairy tale, right, Dad? Doesn't mean we can't have a good time."

"Oh, you are so right, Sarah. Why just yesterday," and he launched into a tale of a project that would never get off the ground. Never realizing, she thought, the beauty of what he already had.

She'd soon be interning with the best environmental magazine in the country. Her writing and analytic skills, honed by Gradenstein and combined with her knowledge of eco-biology, had given her a decisive edge. She would find out what was going on, and let people, the ones who were getting cancer and asthma and everything else, know. And then, hopefully, do something about it.

As for herself? She was just Sarah Carson. Nobody's hero—which was fine because she didn't want to be. Whatever she was, she'd only be Sarah Carson once. And she intended to have a good time being her, despite everything.

***

Twenty years later, Sarah was walking back from an early morning yoga class, saving a miniscule but meaningful bit of greenhouse gases and getting another thirty-two minutes of exercise, which on her self-devised system would allow her to put a little 'w' with a circle around it in her diary. Along with a double Y, which stood for extra-long yoga. She had fifteen years of records of every yoga session, every longish walk, and every time she jogged or lifted weights. In a series of Sierra Club year books that held the days of each week on one page, and on the left an exquisite picture of a beach, a mountain range or an endangered species of mountain goat. She'd draw a straight line down the right side of the page, about an inch in, and put in her little symbols to tell her that on such and such a day she'd run for thirty minutes and done a short yoga, or ridden her bike for an hour and lifted weights.

On the rest of the page she wrote about the world. "Massive oil spill in Gulf of Mexico today," was one entry. "The well keeps gushing into the ocean, you can see it on the web in real time." Or "400,000 gallon spill at Standing Rock, where we all tried to stop the pipeline. Cried for twenty minutes."

At home she showered and put on her work clothes: plain black corduroys, running shoes that were no longer good enough to run in but fine for short walks to her office, and a faded long sleeve pullover top with a picture of three wolves howling at the moon. The yoga class had been particularly challenging, with balancing poses that made her stumble and a series of quasi sit-ups that left her abs sore. "Staved off sloth for one more day, that's good," she mumbled as collected her keys, phone and small handbag, her one concession to femininity along with an occasional dab of lipstick,

It wasn't a particularly nice day, but she could never understand how people failed to find something beautiful—rain or no rain, blizzard or heat wave. Today it was the last of the season's leaves swirling through the air, swept from the almost bare trees by gusts of a sharp cold breeze that let everyone know winter would be here soon. The leaves did a kind of dance with the wind, almost as if they sensed that these were their last moments of separate life. Soon they would be trampled underfoot, gathered in huge paper bags, swept into storm drains, or slowly dissolved into Jamaica Pond, the neighborhood source of natural beauty that Sarah passed on her way to the office. From her house to the gray, stone, three story building would have been less than a half-mile, but she always walked the extra blocks that took her to the Pond. Today the wind stirred up tiny waves, made patterns in the sunlight that would come out for a few seconds, reflect in the water and, and then be hidden by fast moving dark gray clouds.

The loud honks of Canadian geese flying low and fast startled Sarah from her reverie about dancing leaves. They circled the center of the pond then slowly and gracefully descended. Sarah loved to watch them land, magically moving from air to water, coming back to the human level after visiting the place where people couldn't go without noisy, ozone destroying, polluting machines. There were far too many geese—people *would* feed them, destroying their need to migrate in winter, unsettling God knew how many natural balances; and Sarah herself had recently argued, to no avail, that if they just brought in a few coyotes that would solve the geese overpopulation problem pretty quick (a solution that in the midst of a densely populated urban setting filled with small kids, doting parents, and pampered pets, was clearly *way* ahead of its time.) Well, even if they ate too much grass and left too much goose poop on the paved sidewalk that bordered the water, they were beautiful.

Then a sudden flash of light took her breath away. Far across the pond, a beam of light from a small part of the sun uncovered by clouds had brightened the white wing of a seagull. The wing reflected that light back to Sarah—containing a message that other folks might have missed but that she could decipher with ease.

Murmuring her gratitude for it all to the unknown source—rarely she thought of God, sometimes of the Goddess, usually forces of evolution or just blind luck that there was a universe and she was in it—she turned back towards her office. There was work to be done. And later, well, it might be interesting and might not, dinner with Daniel Aiken.

Chapter 9
Patricia and Lily and Anne

Where Lily had been hard, Anne was easy. She had the usual number of ear aches and scraped knees, a strep throat here and chicken pox there. But if Lily had never really seemed to belong, and if the poor fit between her and reality started to get a lot worse as she approached puberty, Anne seemed to fit right in. She laughed a lot, made friends easily, hugged her mother and, for a time at least, even seemed to charm Joffrey. For a few minutes during the increasingly rare times he was home, he would slow down on the near constant sarcasm aimed at Patricia, and the flow of negative judgments he laid on Lily. He would stroke Anne's hair, toss a ball with her for a few minutes, ask mock serious questions about her dolls, and even sit for a few minutes in front of Sesame Street, pretending to need Anne's help to spell and count.

So for a time, things were, if not grand, at least tolerable. Patricia had given her body over, again, to reproduction; and now felt that it was up to someone else to deal with the result: nannies, teachers, doctors, therapists, whatever. As easy as the pregnancy and birth had been, now several years after Lily, recovery was not. She'd torn again, even worse this time, the extra weight stubbornly resisted getting lost, and Patricia—who'd never been one to have excess energy—found that she needed to sleep for ten hours a day, take a nap every afternoon, and still found herself longing for bed soon after dinner.

Yet her weakness seemed not to matter to Anne, who delighted in every new garden flower, every thrush or robin at the bird feeder, every time she learned a new skill like multiplying threes or paddling in the pool. Everyone liked her, and she liked everyone. And what was there not to like, at least for a while? The huge house on the hill was her personal playground. The fancy swing set was big enough for at least four kids to play on at once. As she got older the woods just beyond her yard became a second home. There were deer and squirrels and a feral cat that she semi-tamed with slices of turkey and little bowls of cream taken from a fridge that was always overflowing with food. Her friends from school were welcome, at least when Joffrey wasn't around, which was most of the time. Patricia tended to hire competent but relaxed helpers. With their wealth there was no reason, she believed, that Anne shouldn't have a good time. And the more pleasant it all was, the more there might be a chance that Lily would finally come round.

But Lily didn't. Initially fascinated by the new baby, then revolted by the seemingly endless amounts of piss and shit that had to be cleaned up, the baby food spilled on the kitchen table and the toys spread out in the playroom. She would play with Anne occasionally, making up silly songs, watching a video aimed at the under-five set and acting as if she enjoyed it. As Anne got older, she saw Lily as a kind of goddess, worthy of unquestioning worship. But outside of a few times when Patricia would see them laughing together, enjoying the rich and pampered lives they both had, Lily became ever more hidden, morose, and sullen. She got by at school, had almost no friends, and spent most of her time in her room, with the door closed. Patricia studied them closely, exulting in the few times when Lily showed some pleasure, or at least some interest, in Anne, trying to discount Lily's downturned mouth, squinted displeasure at so much of the world as "growing pains" and "sibling adjustment."

It all changed when Anne, now five, wandered into Lily's usually closed room while Lily was showering. Opening drawers, pulling out sweaters, picking up a small notebook quasi-hidden beneath Lily's underwear, she made a small but quite real, quite normal, five-year-old mess.

Lily came in from her bathroom, wrapped in a huge blue bath towel decorated with pictures of orange and red fish. She saw Anne, cheerfully oblivious to the desecration she was committing, standing on the bed, throwing the notebook up in the air and inspired by the carefully drawn thrush on the cover yelling at it to "Fly, fly, Mr. Bird."

Lily's eyes narrowed, taking in the carnage, then she saw the notebook in Anne's hands, and they widened to a size that seemed impossible for a slight and quite short eleven-year-old girl who wouldn't reach five feet tall for some time.

She screamed, a breathtakingly loud, horrified scream beyond all words or reason. Then the words came, and as scary as the scream had been, the words were more shocking. "You fucking piece of shit put that notebook down get out of my room if you ever come in here again I'll KILL YOU." The scream alerted Patricia, who raced in from the patio, up the stairs, and into Lily's room. By the time she got there, the screaming and cursing had stopped, the bath towel had dropped off, and Lily, naked and dripping, had dragged Anne off the bed and onto the floor, wrapped both hands around her throat, squeezing as hard as she could. Anne was trying to scream, trying to sob, but just able to gasp in tiny breaths.

Patricia stood stock still for the briefest of moments, then in two quick strides reached Lily, grabbed her forearms and started to squeeze, hard. "You will let go of your sister. Right. This. Instant." Harder and harder she squeezed, using her nails for added emphasis and pain. In that moment she felt she might have really hurt her, even killed. All the years of worry, the effort put into trying to make her happy. The second pregnancy, the work of managing another child. The constant sarcasm from Joffrey and his snide hints about what it cost him. And what did they have? This golden child, who could have made Lily's life so much better, if only she for once felt the way she was supposed to.

Suddenly Lily let go and just stood there. She didn't tell her mother to stop squeezing, didn't complain when Patricia let go, bending down to scoop up Anne in her arms. As Patricia headed out the doorway, murmuring as much comfort she could manage despite her racing heart, the rage that still coursed through and arms and fingers, her suppressed desire to scream out all the frustration and failure Lily had caused her, the worst happened.

"Mother," said Lily softly. It had always been "Mother" with her; never Mommy or Ma or Mom, just "Mother," as if they were characters in some old time British novel or people whose connection was defined by a census form: "mother"-and you fill in a name.

"Mother," she repeated, after Patricia stopped, and then turned, expecting some heartbroken apology.

"Yes, Lily."

Her voice flat, her arms by her sides, just the ends of her fingers curled up and still twitching. "I'll kill you too, you fucking cunt."

Patricia gasped, feeling as if someone had punched her in the stomach. And then she saw it, what she had known for years but wouldn't let herself know. This wasn't just an unhappy child, a selfish child, who was simply a little lost or shy or confused, or going through something she would grow out of. There was something very wrong here, something beyond good schools and a sibling to play with and the most beautiful house on the block.

***

"We have to talk." Joffrey looked up from his whiskey and the financial section of the New England edition of the *Times.* There was something about Patricia's tone that surprised him—flat, no supplication, no insecurity. None of the studied good manners and tentativeness that had been bred into her. He didn't like it.

"What?" And what indeed could she want? They had more money than ever, he left her alone to manage the house and children, and he'd stopped bothering her for sex years ago. It had been a successful week, indeed a successful year, very successful. But he was tired now, more tired than usual. Not as young as he used to be, and so forth, he often laughed to himself. And no matter how much money he made, no matter how beautiful the house, there was a kind of pall here. He could feel it when he walked in after a trip. He didn't know what it was, but he knew he couldn't fix it. And the weight of that failure dragged him down and made him disappear into his whiskey, his newspaper, or some escapist television when he was home. And now he'd just set himself down with a drink and the paper, and she wanted to talk.

"It's Lily. There's something very wrong with her. "

"I'll say there is. Haven't I been telling you all this time? She needs a firm hand. All these moods, disrespect. If I was in charge of her, she'd..."

"No, Joffrey, no. I've heard all this before." Patricia's tone was harsh and it stopped him. Had she ever, in all these years, used such a tone with him? His eyes narrowed, he prepared for a counterattack. He saw Patricia close her eyes, breathe deeply, a few tears forming slowly work their way down her smooth, impeccably made up face. She reached out to touch his hand, stroking it gently, silent. Joffrey waited, off balance, confused. Was this to be a time when he showed her, again, who was boss? Or was it time for his masculine ability to solve problems she couldn't handle.

Patricia looked at him, took another breath and began.

"I think she's sick, really sick, in her mind."

A sudden hole appeared in Joffrey's belly. Could this be it? The near constant unease the child projected. Each time he returned from a trip to hear of the small or occasionally large things she'd done wrong. But even more, the way she was never happy. She got no pleasure from doing forbidden things, and he couldn't figure out why she did them.

He listened to Patricia describe the incident with Anne, about what Lily had said and done.

"No normal child does that Joffrey. Who knows what else she might do? This time it was her hands, what if she grabbed a knife? Or had a fit in the car while I was driving? I'm frightened." Something hard was coming, he could tell. "I want to find a child psychiatrist for her."

Joffrey had waited through the story, his hand clenching and unclenching on the beautiful cut glass whiskey tumbler, his eyes taking in the exquisite furniture, the sunset colors in the sky through the huge plate glass windows, the simply tailored but very fine clothes his wife was wearing. He felt his mind moving towards Patricia, and then away. Towards the obvious truth of what he'd heard—that his daughter, *his* daughter, was mentally ill. And in a flash, he knew what it would mean. He and Patricia struggling with their baffling, now frightening child. Sitting in office waiting rooms. Begging for help. He could see the looks of pseudo-sympathy but really pity in the eyes of his business associates, the whispered comments about "Joffrey's crazy kid," the questioning look in their eyes as they would wonder if it was his fault, his wife's fault, something in the genes.

And that he would not allow. Never. He stood up, took a last long swig of whiskey, and hurled the glass against the six-foot-high stone fireplace, where it shattered in countless fragments onto the Berber rug.

"NO! And I mean *NO!* She is not crazy; she will not see a psychiatrist. She is just a spoiled, rotten kid. And it's your fault. You are a bad mother: weak, careless, useless."

He waited for her to fight back, so that he could redouble his assault. She simply bowed her head. Part of him knew he was dead wrong. But he felt like he could kill it, that part of himself, or anyone who said so.

"Joffrey, please. If you don't want to, I understand. I'll do it. I'll find the doctor, go to the appointments, do what he recommends."

"You will *not!*" he shouted. Then more slowly, calmly, in command. "There will be no psychiatrist. No one is crazy in this house."

"Joffrey, she needs this. I want to take her."

Briefly ashamed of his needlessly dramatic glass smashing, he became the ruthless businessman, the negotiator who always won in the end because he could control his feelings—and he believed, no, he *knew*, that he was stronger than the other person in the room.

"Yes, you've made that clear. But what will you use for money to pay the bill?"

Patricia gasped, her eyes widening in shock. Her tone softened even more. "No, Joffrey, you can't mean what you're saying. It's our money, after all. She's sick; please, let me find her some help."

Joffrey spoke slowly, using the tone of a self-assured grownup to a slow child. "The only help she needs is discipline, a firm hand, a few rules she'll be too scared to break. As for the money? I make it. I get to say where it's spent. You want a house and clothes and vacations and cars? Fine, have all you want. But for this? Not a cent. Not one. Single. Cent."

***

So Joffrey set up a "program": goals, rules, consequences. Respect your elders, do your homework and chores—and you have money and your favorite foods and new clothes. Skimp on your homework, let some foul language out of your mouth, disobey your parents—and the money would disappear, there'd be no social life, phone would be forbidden, you could have bread and butter for dinner.

To Joffrey, it made perfect sense. After all, didn't people grow, like plants, towards what they wanted, and away from what they didn't like? He laid it out to Lily, told her that he was in charge and that her mother, who was a nice person, was just a bit too soft and forgiving. He wasn't. Did she have any questions?

Lily stared at her father as if he was some strange crawling sea creature—a giant crab, a lobster in a tank at a seafood restaurant, something nameless that was supposed to live only at great depths—and said nothing. "Well," Joffrey fumed, "I'm waiting. Do you have any questions? Answer me."

Lily just looked up at her father and smiled. There was no love in her face and no amusement either. It was the coldest, most hate-filled expression Joffrey had ever seen—and it chilled him to the bone. "I understand, father, do you?"

"Of course I understand, I made the program myself."

"Oh, that's what you thought I meant?" And then, running the words together so that her contempt for him, his program, and his threats was crystal clear, she finished with: "yes-I-understand-responsibilities-consequences-oh-yes-are-we-done-now-can-I-go?"

The smile was gone, her eyes downcast, the fingernails of her right hand insistently scratching her left wrist.

To everyone's surprise it seemed to work until Lily was nearly fourteen. She presented completed homework, talked civilly to her family, dutifully set the table, made her bed, and kept her room reasonably neat. She didn't exactly smile at everyone but there were no more horrific incidents, no more seething expressions of implacable hostility.

And then Joffrey began to notice that his wallet seemed a little short of what he thought should be in it, the wallet he always left in a little brass bowl in the front hall along with his keys and his dark glasses. The first time he just thought he'd misremembered what was there. A while later he berated Patricia for taking cash without letting him know, even though she swore she hadn't. And then by the third time, when it was fifty dollars, two twenties and a ten missing, that he absolutely knew had been there, he finally got it.

***

It was then that Joffrey admitted to himself that Lily scared him. How could you control someone who didn't behave like a *normal* person? He knew how to get people to do what he wanted them to do. Offer enough money, and they would sell their property; make it worth their while and they'd give him a permit to build; make the area attractive enough and tourists would come to ski, vacation, relax, and spend money. Offer a child a bigger allowance and more privilege, they would behave. It all made sense.

But with Lily nothing worked. He confronted her about the stealing, and she screamed and told him he was crazy. "What do I want with your money? I would *never, never* be so low as to steal from *you*. You probably spent it in a bar, or on some woman. You disgust me. I hate you. Maybe *she*," pointing toward the kitchen, where Patricia was overseeing dinner preparations, "took it to buy another *fa shion a ble*" she dragged out the word in imitation of Patricia's careful speech, "new dress, or something for your stupid art collection." She pointed at the walls, offered a phony, bitter smile, and started to walk upstairs.

"I'm not finished with you yet," Joffrey said, doing his best imitation of parental power.

Lily turned, stared for a moment, and then laughed. "Let me guess," and then she deepened her voice, slowed down her speech, emphasized every word and did a surprisingly good imitation of his tone: "This behavior is unacceptable you know the rules I've established. Therefore. You are sentenced to a lifetime of being locked in your room. Or having your head cut off. Your choice.

"You know what, Daaadddyy," she drawled out the word in a mocking imitation of normal childish love, "just leave me a memo, on business stationary of course, of what my punishment—oh no, it's not a punishment, how could I have been so dumb—my *consequence* will be. Push it under my door, but don't forget to sign it first, so I'm sure it's. You know. Official."

***

Six months later, when the frustration of trying to make something work became intolerable, he ransacked her room one day when she was at school. There were hundreds of dollars, a half-empty bottle of vodka, and a diary filled with quite beautiful drawings of tropical birds and orchids, And there were detailed plans set fire to the house, run away to Brazil, and kill her hated parents. Shuddering at the magnitude of it all, Joffrey barely noticed that there was nothing, not a single word, about Anne.

The money, the diary, the liquor—she wasn't even fifteen for God's sake. He sat down on her bed, looked around her room, now something of a shamble from his search, but still a little girl's room in a lovely house in a great neighborhood. Posters of Avril Lavigne and Mariah Carey, My Little Pony dolls she had played with Anne, a huge teddy bear that Patricia had bought her at a school fair. There was a closet filled with skirts and dresses and kids sweat pants and jeans, and cute pajamas decorated with pictures of fish. A few school books neatly piled on her little desk, next to the new computer she'd gotten to help make her homework easier. Little kid slippers—furry with rabbit ears and plastic eyes—next to a chair that was a kind of big lumpy bag of hard beads, an old back pack colored pink and blue.

It was just a normal kid's room, wasn't it? If he took the money and the diary and the bottle, wouldn't everything just go back to normal? If he explained to her, really explained, that you couldn't live like this, couldn't lie to your parents and steal and hate your family. Because, after all, what would come of it? That this wasn't what life was all about—it was hard work, and planning, and doing your job to make sure everything came out right.

And then a small voice inside his head began to laugh. Come out right? You fool, stop kidding yourself? You barely talk to your wife, and your daughter, *your* daughter, is crazy. You think all you have to do is work hard and everything comes out right?

Joffrey was stunned by the contents of his own mind. He watched with horror as his right hand, the one that signed the papers, shook hands at the close of a deal, passed along the platinum American Express Card, started to tremble. This wouldn't do. He would not allow it. He stood up and in a gesture that resembled nothing so much as a pitcher try to deliver the perfect strike, threw his right hand in a violent, sweeping circular motion away from his body; then he repeated the gesture on his left side. Right, left, right, left.

Sweat formed on his forehead, his chest, staining his imported English dress shirt, while his silk tie flew to one side of his face and then the other. Soon he was puffing, panting, gasping for breath. He stopped the pitching motion, stood stock still, and saw with cold satisfaction that his hand had was perfectly still.

***

The long war between Joffrey and Lily continued. Anne could see Patricia trying to placate, soothe, and calm first one, then the other, and then, finally, giving up and receding into a depressed, self-medicated vagueness.

Though the war made little sense to her, from a young age Anne did know that her family was suffering. And that it was up to her to make it better. It was as if Patricia's motivation for having her had somehow filtered into the deepest recesses of her mind. Joffrey would come to her room, sit on the floor and play with her and her toys, but then start muttering about "damn kid" and "what the hell" and "what can I do?" She would lean her head against his chest and say "I love you, daddy." That seemed to soothe him for a few moments. And then he would mumble more confused and angry words to her dolls, and stomp off to confront Lily about ditching school or another missing bottle of liquor.

For Patricia, Anne did her best to be the world's best daughter. There were never clothes strewn on the floor, every dish she used went into the dishwasher, any rare spill she did her very best to clean up. From pre-school on, every teachers' report commented on how "Anne is just a wonderful, pleasant, good child. So cooperative. And helpful." She would sing Patricia her child's songs—"Inch by Inch" and "Frog in the Hollow"—over and over, because for a few moments they would change her mother's sad, lost expression to a small smile.

Few people noticed the gradually deepening shadows under her eyes, the way her mouth would twist in fear if she thought there might be a chance she'd made a mistake or done something wrong. She would lie in bed at night, dreading the next angry shouts, frozen in sleepless panic. Wasn't there something she could do? Couldn't she make it better? She had dreams of taking them all by the hand, bringing them to a spot in the woods, where they would sit down, and wait for some deer to come, or a cardinal to start singing, so that they would all stop being mean and love each other.

And a few times, not many, late at night, as the memories of the day's or week's struggles echoed in her mind, she would see herself bigger, so much bigger. And she would look down from a great height, above Mom and Dad and Lily, and grab their arms, lift them up, and shake them, not really that hard, but hard enough. So that they would understand. And they would learn.

By twelve, Lily developed breasts and hips to match her lustrous blond hair, perfect features, and huge, staring eyes. People often laughingly told her parents that they could get rich off having her model for Abercrombie or The Gap. Overwhelmed by her appearance, her endless bravado, and the reckless courage she showed in facing down the parents, Anne simply believed that the rules didn't apply to Lily, that she was beyond judgment or understanding. If Lily would go days, even weeks, without seeming to notice Anne; and then often grab something—a sandwich, a toy—out of her hand—it seemed to be acceptable, because that was just Lily. Anne had never known anything else and maybe this was just the way older sisters were.

Anne would look up at Lily and know that her own dull brown hair, skinny body, and plain face would never look beautiful or mysterious; that she would never make fun of her father, laugh contemptuously at her mother, flout the rules, and ignore whatever consequences they threw at her. Everything that had come to mean so much to Anne—being good, helping out, never causing anyone the slightest trouble—meant nothing to Lily. And while she knew she could never do what her sister did, sometimes, in the back of her mind, she enjoyed watching Lily make Patricia cry or Joffrey rage. But surely, surely she could never act the way Lily did, for she wanted, more than anything she believed, for them all to be happy.

A few times, after a particularly brutal confrontation with Joffrey, when Lily was trembling with anger, eyes wide, teeth clenched, Anne would silently walk into her room, sit next to her and gently, timorously, hold her hand. And sometimes Lily would accept Anne's comfort. Her breathing would slow, her hands unclench, her eyes soften. Rarely, but in times Anne always remembered, a few silent tears would roll down Lily's cheeks. She would reach out one arm and place it awkwardly around Anne's shoulders and stiffly, as if unsure how to perform this intimacy, connect her tortured soul to Anne's.

***

It began years, many years, before.

"I do my job, that's why we have this house," he'd say to Patricia. "And just what is your excuse for not doing yours?" Lily would sit at the table, eyes lowered, feeling Joffrey's bristling irritation, the deep anger underneath. What it was from, she couldn't figure out, any more than she could understand why her mother was so scared on top, but underneath, just a kind of sad and then nothing. Lily would pick at her food until Joffrey reminded her that food was for eating, not playing with. Then she would eat it, carefully, slowly, not wanting another reprimand for "stuffing your face like a pig, for God's sake."

The anger and sadness that came weren't hers but she felt them in her stomach, in her forehead, at the center of her chest. It was like somebody jabbing her with needles, only the needles were inside.

At school it was the same. She could see that Jamie was scared, that trying to read even the simplest thing made him so nervous he was terrified he might pee his pants. And then she would feel the fear, and the need to go. She saw how Howard, who threatened kids in the playground, was really sad about something. But she didn't know what. The teachers' pets kids who just seemed to bloom when an adult looked at them would kind of fade away when the adults looked at another child. She felt their need, like a hunger but in the heart instead of her belly. And then she could feel herself fading as well.

Even when Joffrey's anger was directed elsewhere, she felt it was aimed at her. Even when Patricia's sadness had nothing to do with her, she felt it pulling her down. To escape she hid in her room, staring into space much of the time, or drawing first with crayons and later with fancier craypas or pen and ink. She would do fine copies of pictures of frogs, or flowering bushes, or a panther draped on a tree branch. With a few stuffed animals, inside the quiet of the house on the hill, there was, for some of the time at least, a little peace.

Each year it got worse. Anger, fear, anxiety, grief—they came crashing through like she was made of cardboard and they were angry bulls. As then her breasts emerged, her hips widened, in the mirror she could see the hair between legs and under her arms. Whose body was this? And wasn't there something, anything, she could do with the way she felt?

Gradually, she saw it. You didn't have to keep it in; you could just let it out. Like her father, like the school bullies, like all the people in the world who made war or blew things up for no reason, you could just let it out. If you were a ten-year-old girl, living in a fancy house, you could take it out in small, mean ways on your sister, your mother, the occasional teacher or classmate. You could scream at your father when you didn't get what you wanted. Or, even better, make fun of him and watch him boil over. You could see the anger and fear in the eyes of other people when you turned up the volume. And for a little while it was them feeling that pain, not you.

But pinching another kid when no one was looking, or yelling at Anne, or even disobeying Father, only gave her a few moments relief. The bulls would return, stronger than ever, especially after she began menstruating. She needed something that would make all these feelings go away, that would make her as protected and unfeeling as all the normal people who weren't her.

She'd seen enough movies and TV to know what adults did when they were scared or unhappy, so she did it too. It started with quick sips of wine left over from dinner or half-finished cocktails the rare times her parents entertained. Then the vodka, which had little taste. It never made her sick; never left her with a headache the next day. The alcohol blunted the needles that had been torturing her insides for years. It made a wall that the bulls couldn't get through, or at least not nearly so much. It seemed so right that the thought of telling anyone what she was doing never crossed her mind.

***

And so it went, until one Sunday morning when the house rang with Joffrey's angry shouts and Patricia's hysterical crying. Lily was gone. It wasn't the first time she'd stayed out all night, to come home sullen and resentful the next morning; or to call, with studied politeness, for a ride from Cambridge or even the seedy downtown of Framingham. She'd always have an excuse—"Lost my wallet some asshole gave me a hard time and I had to split the party lost track of the time Susie got drunk and couldn't drive you wouldn't want me in a car with a drunk would you? Didn't have money for a phone call"—and after a while Patricia, glad that she was alive at least, stopped trying to get her to tell the truth.

But this was different. Her few favorite clothes were missing, along with her precious diary. Worst of all, she'd figured out how to break into the safe in Joffrey's study and lifted eleven hundred dollars, two credit cards, and a book of checks.

Anne stood in the hallway, seeing Joffrey in his office, the broken box in his hand, staring at Patricia. "The police, that's all, she's a runaway and a thief. I'm calling the police."

Patricia, sitting in his office chair, her head held in her hands, peach colored plush bathrobe half untied over an elegant but modest white negligee, jumped to her feet.

'NO, Joffrey, NO. You cannot. She is your daughter. She's sick, she needs help. The police? Are you crazy? We have money. Just cancel the checks and the credit cards. She'll come back; she'll be sorry. We'll try again."

Joffrey's voice turned calm and cold, only his left hand, compulsively rubbing the side of his gray slacks—up down up down—betrayed his anger and, below that, a kind of primal fear. "Patricia, we have to. This is not a few dollars. This is a lot of money. And what is she doing with it do you think?"

"Doing?" Patricia hesitated, retied her robe, and pushed her hair out of her eyes. "Why. Girls. They like to shop, all girls. I mean. And probably she eats in restaurants. And now maybe she has some idea about..."

"Patricia," Joffrey's voice was sharp, "She doesn't care about clothes or food. You know that. She's run away. She's probably using the money for drugs."

Patricia raised her hands to her throat, as if stopping the scream before it could get out, and just moaned. "No, no, no."

But she knew. “If you do all the right things with your child, and nothing works, it’s probably because of drugs or mental illness. Or both.” That’s what the psychiatrist had said last year, the one she’d gone to with money she’d siphoned out of the housekeeping accounts. “Your daughter needs extreme treatment, right away. Here is information on some excellent residential facilities.” Patricia had taken the brochures numbly, glanced at them in the street, and thrown them into the first trash can she could find. A mental institution? For drug addicts and crazy people? Even with lovely grounds and all sorts of New Agey treatments, it was a place for those who had gone over some line she couldn’t believe Lily had crossed. Lily couldn’t be that bad. She needed some treatment, some therapy, more than Joffrey would allow. Maybe some pills to make her feel better, then things would work out.

“I’ve tried everything I know,” said Joffrey. “Let someone else try.”

So they went, the two of them, down to the police station, gave a picture, told them she had disappeared, described her erratic, frightening, near uncontrollable behavior. To Patricia’s silent shock, the police were not surprised that this could happen to people like them, and that they should be standing there next to illegal immigrants who couldn’t speak English, African American women arrested for prostitution, white street thugs who gotten into drunken bar fights. The dirty linoleum, peeling green paint on poorly plastered walls, the endless notices in hard-to-read print on bulletin boards, the smell of cigarettes and unwashed clothes and sweat and, in the lady’s room she visited when she thought she might throw up, a penetrating stink of urine.

“You should know,” the surprisingly kind detective said, a gray-faced 30ish man in faded chinos and a tailored shirt with sweat stains at the neck and armpits. He had receding, straight black hair, a pockmarked face, and a deep voice that made him sound like an African. "You're not the first, that's for sure, and you won't be the last. Stealing from parents, that's a hard one, right? I'm sorry for your trouble. What you've said about her—it could be drugs. Or just, they think they have to get away.

"My hunch is, she'll be back. Only, you won't like what you'll see. She won't come to you until everything runs out—her money, the kinds of clothes you've bought her, maybe even—I'm sorry to say this—her body. She'll come back broke, desperate, with all kinds of scars. And probably she'll be mad, really mad, at you all. Even though she's the one who left. Because that's what the life does to them. And if she's been using, that'll make her crazy too. She'll need you then, bad; but she'll do everything she can to drive you away.

"But don't worry, almost all the time, they find out that however bad it is at home—no disrespect, it's just these kids, the way they think—no matter how bad home is, the street—that's ten times, a hundred times, worse. We'll put out a notice on her right away. And don't worry, we'll get her back for you."

As they walked back through the garbage strewn parking lot, Patricia started to chuckle, and then giggle. When she got in the car she was laughing: hysterical, racking guffaws that frightened Joffrey. "Stop it," he hissed. "Have you gone completely mad?"

"Oh Joffrey, like the nice policeman said, don't worry. Your daughter is a thief and maybe a drug addict. You can't control her; I can't reach her. Our family is a disaster." Suddenly the laughing stopped, replaced by tears. And, thinking of the treacly pop song of the day, "Don't worry, be happy!" she pulled up the bottom of her long tunic shirt she wore and buried her face in it, the sobs muffled by the expensive fabric.

Joffrey waited, sitting behind the steering wheel of the late model, beautifully equipped, top-of-the-line Cadillac. A few tears began in his own eyes, but he shook his head, almost violently, and they stopped. Through her sobs, Patricia knew what he wanted to say. "Irrelevant, all this grief. Tears. Hysterics. We must do something." But she knew, and knew he could see it too. There was nothing to be done.

PART III

Chapter 10
Daniel and Sarah

"How can you not hate them?" asked Daniel, genuinely confused, but maybe a little judgmental as well. Did this woman live in some land of spiritual by pass, where everything was milk, cookies, and love?

"Hate them?" Sarah answered. "Not really. I mean, sure, I get angry sometimes. It's so. Foolish. The short-term gains are so small, what's being lost is so big. And when I talk to them, it's a bit like talking to someone from another time, another culture. You could explain about the internet to somebody from a rainforest tribe. 'Oh yes,' they might say, 'a box with pictures on it, and the pictures are from far away, and writing from people as well.' And they wouldn't know what the hell you were talking about. And if you showed them a laptop, and they'd never seen one before, never used one, they might reach in to see if there was a Golden Retriever behind the dog themed screen saver. Any more than we could understand what they mean when they tell us they communicate with the spirit of the river or the hawk."

"But that's not right," he pursued her. "The tribals don't live in a computer world, and we don't go into mystic trances. But those people in that little town in Pennsylvania, where you worked on fracking, they have some idea what science is, what polluted water can do. All these," he nodded towards the people walking on the sidewalks of JP outside her office, where he often came to share information, talk about the newest depressing outrage, or—if he'd been honest—just to be in her presence. "They probably all know someone with cancer. If they're over thirty-five, they can see how the weather has changed. They don't have to read *E Magazine* or *The Times* for God's sake. Even the spaced-out kids tweeting on their cell phones had to do something about Earth Day in kindergarten."

"So?" Sarah smiled back at him. "When have human beings ever been particularly rational? Or even smart? Go back to feudal times. A tiny class of aristocrats, lording over countless peasants, taking their labor, a lot of what they produced—giving it to the church and their own luxuries. Why would anybody go along with that?"

"Well, superstition, fear, no sense of the kind of basic self-respect that you get from a modern democracy, being threatened with hell if they don't obey the priests. Stuff like that."

"So, you think people are that much different now?" She pointed to the chronograph on her wrist, the large computer monitor, her much smaller laptop, and finally at her extremely smart phone. "You think because we can do this stuff we know any more about what life is all about? Think we're kinder or more self-aware? Perhaps," Daniel smiled as she arched her eyebrows, deepened her voice and did her Gradenstein imitation, "your expectations are unrealistic."

"Sorry, wise one." He ducked his head in a fake bow. "But I don't buy it. I don't want to understand or to forgive. Or to be tolerant. Not when I see that." He pointed to large wall where Sarah kept an ever-changing series of photos of horror stories. There were smog-choked streets of a Chinese city; dead seabirds whose insides contained cigarette lighters, bottle tops, and fishing line; a sea turtle whose shell had been deformed into an insane tiny waisted figure eight by a plastic ring.

"Somebody is making that happen. Somebody knows it's happening and doing nothing. I wouldn't, I mean, of course I wouldn't. But sometimes I just feel like killing them." Instead of a shout, his voice had dropped, almost to a whisper; his fingers made claws on the top of his thighs as he leaned toward her.

"Sorry, sorry," he quickly added, hoping she didn't think he was a lunatic.

"It's o.k.," Sarah reassured him. "I understand. You know I do. It's just—well, someone once asked the Dalai Lama how he felt about the Chinese—after fifty years of trying to talk to them, and getting nowhere, and watching them turn his country into part home to overflow Chinese nationals and part dump for nuclear waste. After all this, wasn't he angry at them?

"I really like his answer. 'The Chinese have taken so much from me, I will not give them my peace of mind.'" She smiled at Daniel, and he knew she understood, but he also knew he didn't, not really. He hated them—the ones in power and the pathetic masses who just sat there, glued to their TVs and their iPhones and their Budweiser, while the world burned and the seabirds ate the plastic. And when he thought of what they were all doing, he included, there was a depth of grief that he was afraid to touch. He knew that if he started to cry, he'd never stop.

***

They had started to work together. Nothing dramatic, just sharing information, putting their heads together, giving each other lists of people to call, publications to consult, websites to monitor. Last week a small notice in the local paper of

Charleston reported thousands of dead fish floating in an estuary in eastern North Carolina, reminding Daniel of the reports he'd seen before they'd met.

Sarah had called the paper, tried to locate the reporter who'd written the story. "Beats me, Miss," he'd said to her questions. "I heard about it from a buddy of mine who fishes on the weekends. Drove over, took a look. There they were, floatin' upside down, coverin' the river from side to side, just awful. And some of them had horrible sores running the length of their bodies. And oh yeah, one other thing. I'd walked out on a small dock, where some folks tie up their boats, and I felt the dock kinda shakin' a little. There was no wind, and the river was still as a sleepin' baby, so I looked down to see if maybe some kids or a dog were playin' around. Would've told them to get the hell out of the water, what with all these weird fish deaths. And wouldn't you know, it wasn't kids and it wasn't a dog. The piles holdin' up the dock were covered with crabs. Hundreds of them. I've never seen anything like that, I tell you. And I've lived here all my life. It looked they were doin' anything they could to get the hell out of that river."

Today they had started in on the public health angle. Calling local hospitals and group practices, trying to fight their way through the confidentiality rules, explaining over and over why someone from Boston, who "No, I'm not a reporter, just someone trying to figure out about the environmental situation" would want to know about their town, their river, their health. They hadn't gotten far. Most people simply wouldn't offer any information, or they'd claim not to know anything and suggested calling Ms. X or Mr. Y, who would tell them it was none of their business and he or she didn't know anything anyway.

But after hours of this tedious frustration, Sarah shut down her phone, stood up, stretched her arms over her head in a "God I'm sick of sitting around doing this crap" gesture but then surprisingly smiled at Daniel and said, "I may have gotten something."

He looked up from his detailed records of useless calls. "And?"

"Finally, one med tech. Her boss, the GP, had the flu, and she had to take all his patients for three days. Six different guys came in. All fishermen. All with bad coughs and headaches. She was going to say it was just more flu, but then she saw they all had some weird kind of rash on their hands and forearms. Sores that just stayed there, wouldn't heal with antibiotic ointment or skin cream or stuff you put on for allergies. Nothing touched it. And yeah, they all said it had started when the cough did. And yeah, they'd all been fishing within a mile of the fish kill and the crazy climbing crabs. Something is going on down there. I can smell it. I bet you can too. Maybe we should go and check it out."

Daniel tried to contain his excitement. To face something like this, *with someone else*. Oh, no, he thought. Not 'someone else,' but Sarah. He was crazy about her. It was as simple as that. Woke up with a painful erection after doing unspeakable things to her in his dreams. Thought of her constantly—and almost as constantly cursed himself for a pathetic, childish fool.

"Let's grab something vegan from the Thai place. I've got a reasonable bottle of red, and a mildly neurotic one of white. Any more phone calling and I'll go batty. We'll eat and think about this and plan a trip and find out what the hell is going on."

After the Pad Thai and overly sweet tofu and vegetables and vegetarian spring rolls, Sarah brought out a pint of coconut milk ice cream, chocolate flavored, that they passed back and forth, not bothering with bowls. They drained the last of the bottle of white and having planned a four day trip to coincide with his upcoming term break, their conversation turned to the world—in a "see if you can top this one" and "I'll see you pulmonary damage from air pollution in L.A. and raise you the dying frogs and the Republican attack on environmentalists."

Coal dust on beaches in Columbia, mercury poisoning from oil extraction in Nigerian villagers, miscarriages on Indian reservations, probably from by-products of uranium mining. Corporate greed and power, and political dishonesty and greed. And the endless consumers who only seemed to care about things being faster, fancier, sweeter, easier, more amusing *today*–or at worst tomorrow. Who gave no thought about what might happen the day, or year, after that.

Daniel was amazed at her endurance. That anyone—especially a beautiful woman with so much going for her—could listen to him. It was talk like this that had driven Amy away, dried up his social life, made colleagues clear their throats and shuffle their notes and walk backwards towards their offices when they saw him in the hall. And here was Sarah, matching each of his sad, brutal tales with one of her own.

Suddenly she stops. She has had enough. She rises to the corner bookcase and takes out a cd mix she's created from the music stored on her hard drive, puts it on a small but surprisingly good sounding system. The mix begins with something soft and new age, no dissonance, a kind of melancholic Celtic sweetness of guitar and flute and wordless voice. She stands up and starts to move to the melody, holds out a hand to Daniel. He shakes his head, I don't dance, you go ahead, I'm fine. She smiles and continues to move to the music, swaying side to side, reaching with her arms overhead, rotating her head so that her soft brown hair flows towards one shoulder and then the other. She begins to move her hips in a manner frankly sexual but not a come on. She is just enjoying the music, her body, the fact that she can move, hear, see the flickering light from the four soy candles she's placed around the room, the pictures of hawks and trees and mountains that decorate her walls, her friend sitting at the small dining table, which is covered with food containers and dirty dishes and wine bottles. The music changes, something much faster, a kind semi-jazz, semi-flamenco. There's a persistent beat from drums and bass, a beat that compels movement. And brilliant, impossibly fast, runs from the guitar.

Surprising himself, Daniel rises and starts to move. He is awkward, self-conscious. But Sarah just smiles at him, turns up the music very loud, closes her eyes and seems to get lost in her own space. Daniel moves faster and faster—twirling, giving little jumps, bending his knees, spinning left and right with his breath coming hard in his throat and his heart pounding and the unfamiliar movements making his ankles ache. Faster and faster he drives himself, flinging his arms out to the side, leaping forward and back, then making fists and shaking them at the sky. As the music reaches its last crescendo, the sobs burst from him. He sinks to his knees, and in half a shriek and half a whisper his hoarse voice pleads over and over, "Please, please, please. make it stop." Then it's just tears, the salty liquid coursing down his cheeks into his beard, snot dripping from his nose, his body uncontrollably shaking. And then Sarah is next to him wrapping her arms around him from behind, her own soft weeping joining his.

The music stops; the tears cease. Sarah moves in front of Daniel, taking in the world of hurt in his eyes, reflected in her own, but she has something else as well. She lifts his chin in her hand. "Look at me," she says, "here, now. Here."

"Bu. uu. ut," he is still shaking, the word comes out in a stutter.

"No," she says it so gently it sounds like a bird cooing or a mother to an infant. 'Now, here. Nothing else." She takes his face in her two hands, pulls it to her own, and gently kisses him. "Nothing else. Just us." She takes his hand, places it on her breast. "This is real, my friend, as real as anything else." Then there is only the sweetness of the flesh under his hand, the sound of her voice, and the rare and blessed permission to be what he is and be with someone who doesn't seem so afraid.

***

The researcher and her assistant worked in a small trailer they'd rented from the local RV place, using funds her university set aside for community concerns. "Not really my field," she told Sarah, as they sipped some coffee in the tiny space, surrounded by microscopes, fish tanks filled with river water, containers of various obscure chemicals, research texts, and a large computer monitor connected to a powerful looking laptop. "I work mainly on" and she named something in a phrase so technical Sarah instantly forgot it. "But I heard about all those dead fish and the sick fishermen and I thought I'd give it a shot." She was a small woman, with brown hair and clear brown eyes, dressed in plain jeans and a plain black t-shirt under a soiled white lab coat. Her hands moved quickly over the instruments, the computer, the chemical containers. Occasionally, she would stop and cough, "Some kind of mild bronchitis I've got, can't get rid of it. Makes it a little hard to concentrate sometimes. Need some antibiotics. When I get a chance."

She pointed to one of the tanks, cloudy water being gently circulated and aerated. "I think I may have something." She gestured towards the monitor, pushed a few buttons on the laptop keyboard, and a slide show began on the screen. The first was of an indeterminate spherical something, with ropelike appendages (tentacles? thinks Sarah). The second has a shape that resembles a starfish, a concentrated center and five straight arm-like appendages sticking out. In a third, the sphere seems almost divided in half, like a hamburger, and the tentacles are wrapped around the middle.

Gillian pointed, "That's the little bugger that I think is making all the trouble. Those are three of the forms it can take. We think there's more. And here," she pushes a button, the slide show continues, and Sarah gasps at images of fish with gaping sores, one with all the skin shredded off the last four inches of its body, the muscles, blood vessels, and bones completely exposed. Then one of a human leg with a quarter-sized lesion that looks much like the ones on the fish: skin dissolved, red and swollen tissue around a gaping sore. Finally, a fish kill: countless fish covering the side of the river, a solid mass of death stretching over a hundred feet on each side.

"And the waters turned to blood," Daniel murmured. They stared at him. "Oh. It's a line from the bible. When the Jews were trying to get out of Egypt. Moses used his rod, given extra force by God, and tried to show the Egyptians the power of the Lord. So he turned the water to blood. And then the Egyptian magicians did the same."

"Waters turned to blood?" replied Gillian. "You bet."

"But why," asks Sarah, "why now?"

"Not sure, but I suspect," Gillian coughs again. Shakes her head in dismay at the sound she is making, "it's runoff. From the hog and chicken farms. Chemical composition of animal waste changes the water. Usually these guys pretty much just sleep at the bottom of the river. But the nitrates in the runoff, that wakes them up. I think. Not sure yet. But Edward, my assistant and me, we're tracking it down. He's out today, got a cough worse than mine, and feeling a little out of sorts. Too bad. He does great work."

She reached over for a bottle of water, took a small drink,

closed her eyes and seemed to be fighting down another cough.

"I'll tell you one more thing. These buggers are tough. See that tank," she points to the largest one, with its cloudy water. Sarah imagines the little buggers in the tank, then shivers at the idea of having her arm in the same water. "We took out the water," Gillian continued, "replaced it with sulfuric acid. The stuff that'll kill just about anything." She stops, reaches over for more water. Gives a slight cough.

"And," said Sarah, hoping, in what she knew as a crazy response, that the little buggers had been killed.

"And a third of them survived.

"These guys are *dangerous*. God knows the effects of any extended exposure. Next week I'm going to the state government to let them know. This river is not, repeat *not*, the world's best tourist destination right at the moment."

***

"All right, let's look at a farm."

"Are you sure," Daniel asked, noticing that Sarah had picked up Gillian's cough.

"Oh, I'm fine. Maybe if I start smoking it'll stop. How about you?" Daniel had complained of being tired and of a kind of brain fog since their visit with Gillian the day before.

"Probably just a little jet lag. Make me ten years younger and I'll be all right." They looked at each other, neither mentioning that a flight from Boston to North Carolina was not likely to produce jet lag; or that they'd both felt fine the day before, or that Sarah almost never got sick.

"So," Sarah went on, "the farms." She held her phone up, "there's one only about 42 miles from here. Operated by, you'll love this, Magnificent Chicken." She closed her eyes, grimaced, and shivered in mock disgust. "We'll have to stretch the truth a bit. Tell them. Let's see. Doing research on how these facilities contribute to the North Carolina economy? I mean, that's sort of true, right?" And she laughed.

Daniel smiled back at her, noticing how doing this awful work with Sarah was—not exactly fun, but not the torment it always was for him. He could only think of the horrors they faced, while she seemed to enjoy the people they met and know how to turn it all off at the end of the day. And if there was something to laugh at, like the fib they would tell to see firsthand the pollution from an industrial farm, she wouldn't just smile, but laugh long and hard.

***

It was a vast warehouse filled with life. But life cramped into thousands of small wire cages, a dozen chickens to a cage, each with the space of a piece of typing paper, too small, Daniel could see, for them to turn around or spread their wings. There were three shelves along the walls of the two-hundred-foot-long building, and he could see feces dropping from the higher rows onto the lower ones. The whole building had an ammonia-like stink, overladen with the smell of chickenshit. As they passed the cages, the chickens thrust their heads between the bars, their beaks having been agonizingly blunted to prevent them from attacking each other, maddened as they were by the crowding. They weakly cawed and moved their heads from side to side. Were they asking for help? Daniel wondered. No, couldn't be. They were just. Chickens. But he had a sudden memory of pictures of concentration camp barracks, with their three rows of bunks, and their starved and hollow-eyed inmates.

"Waste," said their guide, a large man wearing a filthy rubber apron over jeans and a sweatshirt, his mouth, like theirs, covered in a surgical mask to filter out the haze of dust, bits of feather, and odors that hung in the air, "goes there." He pointed to grooved channels in the cement floor, covered in a brown sludge. "Chicks comin' in," he added, pointing to the end of the shed, where buckets of newborns were tossed onto the floor of an open section, a few casually stepped on by the worker herding them into the corners.

"Only takes seven weeks to get 'em up to size," he said. Daniel thought he sensed a bit of pride in the man's voice. "Scientists did that—messed around with their genes. More meat, faster growth. Course," he went on, his voice colored, perhaps, with slight regret, "makes 'em a little too big for their own good. Muscles can't handle the weight, some of them. Organs neither. Just keel over before slaughter. Kind of a waste."

"How often do you clean?" asked Sarah, her voice bright and innocent, hiding the fact that she had known all this, and cried over it, for years.

"Oh, pretty often. Every year or so, we move all the crates out, wash the whole thing down with giant hoses and stuff that'll kill anything. Then back come the crates. Can't do it too often, costs too much to move all the gear. Something else I can show you folks?"

Given all the bad publicity factory farms had suffered, it had been surprisingly easy to get in. Sarah had astonished Daniel with bright smiles, almost girlish laughter, and, Really? he thought? an extra button undone on her shirt. They had agreed not to take pictures of any kind, promised, laughingly, to keep their hands empty at all times, and were admitted for what could be, the manager said, only a short tour.

"Yes, please," Sarah answered, and she pointed past the doorway. "What happens to the waste? I mean, it can't just build up here, right?"

The man nodded, gestured for them to follow him, where they gratefully removed the masks, now coated with bits of feathers and the stink of chicken manure. He pointed to pipes connected to the channels they'd seen in the sheds, leading down to an enormous open lagoon. "That's where she goes. Sometimes it goes on fields in the county."

"And when it rains," asked Sarah brightly, "do they ever overflow?" At the moment the lagoon was high, nearly at the top of the pit it rested in.

"Oh, not too often, we take good care. But if it's too much rain, well, down the hill there, is somethin' leads right to the Neuse." They stared at him blankly. "Neuse River, goes to the Atlantic, you know?" They nodded, smiled, nodded. Thanked him for his time. When they got back to the car, there really wasn't very much to say. The fish kills had been on the Neuse, forty-two miles from the farm. As they headed back down the highway, Daniel tried to focus on the size of it all. Just one farm among hundreds, in just one of the dozen or so states in which all this animal death took place, with all the waste, in all the waterways. He couldn't take it in, and in any case his mind was feeling fuzzy. Sarah coughed, loud and long. There was no laughter from her now, no smile, just a muted sound of breath scraping against irritated airways and a slight squint to her eyes, as if she were trying to see something she hoped wasn't there.

***

A week later they got a call from Gillian.

"Got it. Did the tests. We're sure. It's the outflow. From the farms. I was right." A little pride colored her voice. "That's what unbalances the water, wakes up the fishkillers. Damn those guys are tough. Remind me of the thing in the *Alien* movies. Turns out they've got at least a dozen forms they can change into." Sarah could see that despite everything, Gillian admired them. "I've got an appointment to see some folks in the state government. They have to do something to those farms." She let out a huge racking cough.

"You don't sound so good," Sarah said, concern in her tone.

"Yeah," Gillian answered. "Damn cough. Don't know what the hell it is. Anyway, I'll send you a copy of my report and let you know how it goes."

Three weeks later she called again. She spoke in halting tones, a mix of depression and fatigue coloring her speech.

"State government? Oh my God. That's why I went into science. Just want to deal with stuff you can put under a microscope. Leave the people out of it. They kept me waiting three times. Passed me around from office to office. Finally got in to the tourism office, not even the science side. I told the guy what I knew. He was pretty clear: Don't panic, don't go public. Probably overstating the case. Lots of people dependent on tourist revenue."

Sarah waited while Gillian coughed violently.

"I said that as long as the outflow was going into the river, it wasn't safe.

"He just stared. Then told me that Magnificent Chicken was a fine, upstanding part of the North Carolina economy. That he was sure they followed all relevant rules and regulations. That it was irresponsible of me to make unfounded, inflammatory charges against pillars of the community. Was I a troublemaker? Did I have a connection to some big time liberal environmental group? Did I have— he made it sound like a sexual disease—an agenda? Expect him to sacrifice this important economic and nutritional resource for some reckless speculation?

"I told him yeah, my agenda was people's health. And the fish, and the birds that ate the fish. Then I left.

"Look Sarah, I can't stay on. I'm not well. I can't get rid of this cough. And tired, all the time. And my assistant. It's terrible, he's having trouble remembering things, even finding the words to talk sometimes. I think it was the gas, the gas the fishkillers put out. In the trailer. It's toxic. We didn't realize. Thought you had to touch them to get hurt. But you just had to breathe where they were. I hope, oh God, I hope we get over it and I can go back to my life. I had no idea I might have to sacrifice my health for this."

***

With part of its magnificent profits, Magnificent Chicken, the country's second largest producer of poultry, was a leading contributor to the campaign coffers of North Carolina's governor and state legislators. So it wasn't very likely that they would be interested in whatever two out-of-staters, representing nobody very powerful, would have to say. But the fishkillers were clearly so dangerous, maybe the firm would listen.

Daniel didn't know if they would or not, but he felt like he could smash something if they didn't. His own brain fog had been bad enough. Thankfully, after the first few days it had lifted. But watching Sarah cough had been close to unbearable. Her small body, usually an emanation of grace and slender strength, had been shaken by breath that seemed broken. He had offered her herbal tea, repeatedly suggested she see a doctor, and told her to rest—until she had reminded him, in a slightly irritated tone, that her mother had passed away many years before and she didn't need another one.

Given how dangerous the little buggers were already, and who knew what could come next, they simply couldn't wait for some other, larger group to make a fuss or for public health officials to fight through the company's wall of lobbying and contributions. They had to try, even if they had about as little hope anything good would happen as you can have and still put one foot in front of another. So he cancelled his classes for a day, and they flew back down for the meeting they had finally been offered.

The sign over the large, plain office building held the picture of an oversized, robust chicken in a standard issue American-type barn, and the message: “I’m glad to be a Magnificent Chicken. You can boil me, fry me, grill me or put me in chicken salad. I’ll always be *MAGNIFICENT*!!!!” They saw the sign, grunted to each other, and walked in.

Sandra Smith was tall, elegant and, if you liked the almost but not quite anorexic look, very attractive. A B.A. in business from a large state university, thought Daniel. Upwardly mobile, using her looks but not her body, trying to get into middle management and away from pests like us. But maybe a little easier to talk to than some defensive, stuffed shirt man. A little, probably not much.

“Yes, please come into my office,” she said, leading them from the ground floor waiting area through an inner door that required a security code, and down a long corridor to a small, windowless room decorated pictures of various Magnificent Chicken facilities.

“Sorry about the security setup,” she said with a smile. “But there have been. Incidents. You understand. Extremists who want to impose their views on other people.” She smiled at them, her dark brown eyes flat and unfriendly.

Oh, we understand completely, thought Daniel. You murder animals. You sell the corpses. You lie about the pollution you cause and pay off politicians to leave you alone and employ undocumented immigrants who can’t complain about the horrible working conditions and dirt-poor farmers whom you pressure and threaten.

“Ms. Smith,” Sarah began, “we’ve come because we haven’t gotten any response to a series of emails and letters that we sent concerning the extremely grave consequences of effluent from your facilities in North Carolina." She reached into her bag, took out a large folder. "Please, if you will, just look at these pictures."

Ms. Smith, her lips flattened into a perfectly straight, perfectly expressionless line, looked at the photos: sores on fisherman, thousands of bloody fish floating in the water, a graph of estimated discharge of phosphorus and nitrogen from chicken wastes, the conclusion of Gillian's report linking them all together.

"Yes," she said, putting the ugly evidence back into the folder and pushing it back at Sarah across her desk. "And?"

"And?" said Daniel, his voice raising in disbelief, "what do you mean 'and'? What in hell are you, is this *company*," (he spat out the word), "going to do about it?"

Sarah reached over to put a restraining hand on Daniel's arm. She'd explained her strategy to him before. Shouts and accusations rarely got you anywhere. Why get someone's back up unnecessarily? Talk slowly and pleasantly, let them try to wiggle out of the obvious, close the loop until it rested on their throats just short of choking them, hanging on their own words.

"I see," Smith said slowly. "You want us to *do something*. Right?" She emphasized the two words, in a thinly veiled mockery.

"Ms. Smith, don't you think that provoking these organisms, killing millions of fish, infecting these fishermen, putting a toxic gas in the air—that these are things worth taking seriously?"

"Oh now," Smith's smile returned, thin, phony and perhaps even meant to be seen that way. "I'm not sure. You say it's from the farms. Someone else might say it's from something else. We know about Gillian's findings. Our scientists, who take a very close look at everything we are doing, don't agree. At least not yet. And the state government, always serious and reliable, don't you see, is investigating. Carefully. Not rushing to judgment. Our safety record is second to none. The EPA hasn't sited us for a violation in years."

Which EPA is that, Daniel wanted to yell, the one crippled by cuts? Or staffed by anti-environmental appointments who believed that ecological troubles were God's punishment on the wicked? Who were practically employees of the oil and gas industry?

"And in any event," Smith went on, clearly enjoying how angry she was making them, "the last thing we at Magnificent Chicken want to do is upset the supply line of food that America wants, America needs, and America, let's face it, loves.

"Chicken?" asked Daniel quietly, "America loves chicken?"

"Surely," Smith answered. "Go into any home, any restaurant, what do you think they are eating? For lunch, for dinner, for Sunday barbecue—Chinese, Indian, or Thai. African Americans or illegal immigrants or good old boys in Louisiana and Mississippi. We even have a one hundred percent kosher division for our traditional Jewish customers—that one went up forty-seven percent in the last ten years. Everybody loves Magnificent."

Sarah wouldn't give up just yet. "So you're saying, I just want to be quite clear about this, even with all this information, you won't do a thing?"

"Oh no. Not at all. We'll keep up our scrupulous attention to following regulations, our extra care in all our facilities, our commitment to America's health and well-being and happiness. Just like our chicken, we try our best to be magnificent." Then she burst out laughing, loud and, unlike her smiles, obviously heartfelt. Daniel and Sarah stared at her, wondering if she was a little out of whack.

"You've got phones?" she demanded, her eyes narrowing,

her fingers tapping on the desk in an insistent rhythm. They nodded. "Put them on the desk, now," her voice sharp and commanding. Stupefied, wondering what could possibly come next, they obeyed.

She held each one up, looking at the active apps. "I really don't think it would be too great if what comes next got recorded." They waited. Was she going to threaten them? Let them in on some secret? Offer to help?

Smith laughed again, shaking her head from side to side, her mouth twisted in a condescending smirk. She looked into Sarah's eyes, then turned her head to stare at Daniel. "Could you be any more stupid, the two of you? You think this company, which grossed four billion last year, which produces twelve million chickens. *A week*. And employs sixty-five thousand workers, doesn't know what it's doing?

"Of *course* we pollute. Of *course* the chickens aren't very healthy—not for your belly or your neighborhood or your water supply.

"And you know something." She waited. Here was the point and she clearly wanted to make sure they got it.

"We. Just. Don't. Care.

"Our sales have gone up eight years in a row, in nineteen of the last twenty-two. The people who run things here make a lot of money; the investors make even more. So," and here her voice turned harsh and vulgar and mean, and Sarah could see how far she'd come from where she had grown up.

"Fuck the chickens, and the workers, and the farmers we cheat and the rivers and all the rest. If they all get sacrificed, *we don't care*. We don't have to. Not as long as everybody thinks cheap chicken is just grand and nobody gives a shit about anything else."

She stopped, put her phony professional smile back on. Gently handed them their phones.

"So nice of you to drop by. Very much enjoyed meeting

you. I'm sure you do wonderful work, both of you. This way. Out."

Chapter 11
Sarah

Back in Boston, recovering from the physical and emotional strain of their efforts to deal with the fishkillers, Daniel asked her how she could take it all so well.

"Don't you ever feel like, I don't know, killing somebody? I don't mean doing it," He waited. They exchanged little smiles and an ironic "gee, it might be nice but we can't" look.

It was the end of a long day of reading, phone calls, and fruitless inquiries about legislative support for cutting pesticide use on public school athletic fields.

Sarah leaned back in her chair, stretched both arms over her head and gave a contented sigh as some of the tension in her upper back melted away.

"It's a long story, sure you want to hear it?"

"I'm sure." He leaned back in his chair, folded his fingers together on his chest and waited.

"There was a time, six years after I finished at Wilson. I was working for an NGO focused on water pollution. Just seemed tired, and then I'd snap at people for no reason. Didn't realize how bad it had gotten. Then the wheels finally came off.

"Hey, you wouldn't have recognized me. Nice gray slacks, perfect light blue blouse and," she laughed, shaking her head at the memory, then batted her eyelashes in mock display "black leather pumps with wedge heels. I even borrowed my boss's briefcase, didn't think the Jan Sport backpack would go too well with the spiffy clothes."

***

It had taken weeks to get the appointment with Peter Caralin, a third-tier EPA staffer, to discuss problems with the water quality in Kansas and some surrounding areas. To give him her findings of cancer clusters, respiratory ailments, and birth defects. Before getting to him she had been shuttled and shuffled between local, state, and federal departments, all of which seemed to have several possible relevant agencies. Was it water quality? Department of agriculture? Industrial regulation? Interstate commerce? Local zoning? She had filled out countless forms, sat in gray toned waiting rooms with bored or hostile or chatty secretaries, even once fallen asleep after being told for the fourth time "Just a bit longer, sorry for the delay, he's very busy."

After brief hellos, she started in, offering a slight smile to try to offset the rage she'd been carrying ever since she'd seen the figures. "As I'm sure you know, Mr. Caralin, the water quality in the U.S. is very bad. Forty percent of the rivers, streams, and lakes can't support aquatic life. Yet here, here," she repeated, jabbing at the small map indicating which counties were worst hit, "it's nearly twice as bad. We've found a staggering variety of toxic chemicals. Often in concentrations dozens of times higher than EPA regulations." She waited, hoping that Mr. Caralin—perhaps a few years older than her, dressed in worn chinos, corduroy sport jacket, and black shirt with a gray tie, top shirt button loose, a bland face topped by short black hair, eyes seeming to focus about three feet to the right and above her head—would register some emotion.

"Yes," he answered, "too bad. Probably, oh I can't be sure, of course, some combination of agricultural runoffs, non-source point pollution, and maybe particulates from power plants upwind. Local people and their outboard motors, dumping wastes in creeks, tossing in tires and letting motor oil seep into ground."

Then he yawned. Looked at his watch. He'd either heard about this particular area already or was hearing it for the first time and didn't care all that much.

She leaned in, trying to keep from standing up and throwing the report at his face. "What will the EPA do? How can we stop this?" seeing the dead waterfowl, trout with tumors, and four year olds with brain cancer.

Caralin just pointed to a large pile of folders on his desk. Then at three tall, four drawer gray metal filing cabinets, three feet deep, packed so tight that the two top drawers couldn't close, pushed open by gray hanging files.

"That, Ms. Carson, is my in-box. This here," he tapped with two fingers on a small pile of perhaps five or six folders, neatly arranged in a plastic desk top tray, "is what I've done this week. Since it's Thursday, at," he consulted his plastic running style watch, "almost four, you get an idea of how fast this is all going. So. Here. " He reached into a drawer under his desk, pulled out a gray hanging folder, attached the little plastic slot that held a label, carefully wrote "Water quality, Midwest, Preliminary studies" in red marker and pushed the folder over to Sarah. "Put all your information in here. And I'll get around to it just as soon," he stopped, nodded briefly at the pile on his desk, and then the bulging file cabinets, "as I can. Thanks so much."

Sarah stood up, leaned over Caralin's desk, her voice nearly a yell. "Not on your life. This," she shook the folder which now held her information, "goes to the *top of the pile.* Get it?" She leaned further towards him, clear now that she had his full attention, enjoying the growing fear in his eyes as she reached into her large square briefcase to pull out, not the gun or knife that had probably flashed through his mind, but a large, lined pad. Clipped to the pad were pictures she had taken after interviewing mothers of desperately sick children. She pushed the pictures towards Caralin: bald headed little boys and girls, trying to smile for the camera, holding teddy bears or Get Well balloons or the family cat.

As she repeated her demand Caralin stood up, and she suddenly noticed that he was several inches and probably at least sixty pounds bigger. Part of her wondered what the hell she thought she was doing, but another part, the part that had been ground down by loss after brush-off after loss, didn't care.

"Well?" she demanded, her eyes narrowing, her mouth a thin line of rage, her hands clenched in fists, and her shoulders slightly twisted, as if the wrong answer might set her off to slugging him.

"Well what?" said Caralin, a bit more relaxed that she hadn't pulled a gun out. "Talk to the head of my department, who can go to the head of the agency, who can go the Congressional committee, who can go to the chemical and gas and oil and meat packing industries who give them campaign contributions. In case you haven't noticed, environmentalists didn't win the last election. It was the guys who'd like to abolish"—he stopped, pointed with both hands at his office and all the other ones—"the EPA completely. Who only think about job creation and how bureaucrats like me just fuck things up. So you can yell and pound all you want, it won't change a thing."

Sarah felt the rage fade, the despair sweep down from her eyes to her hands, like a missile hurled into the air falling back to earth. At that moment she knew it was hopeless. There was nothing to be done. She sat back down, leaned her head in her hands and began to cry. But then, suddenly as a stroke of lightening or an unexpected heart attack, the rage came back.

Her tone turned flatly menacing, "Rules, is it? Files?" and then in a scream she repeated the single syllable, the one she'd heard from too many officials, assistant vice-presidents, and mayors of medium sized cities for the last six years:

No, we can't pass that law.

No to that proposed regulation.

No, you can't have access to those files.

No, you can't inspect our facility.

No, you can't speak to him, he's talking to a representative of (fill in the blank) *corporation.*

"No." she repeated it, louder each time, and suddenly her right arm extended violently and she swept everything on his desk onto the floor. Then she whirled to face the cabinets, yanked open the drawers scooped up handfuls of files and dumped them on the floor, screaming, "No No NO."

***

"Crazy, right?" laughed Sarah. They'd shared a large fruit salad and a bottle of white wine as she'd told the story, stopping occasionally to eat and drink, while he waited to see what was next.

"And," he demanded, "then?" He couldn't put it together. Calm, cool Sarah? Had this ended with her smashing Caralin's head against the file cabinet or some federal marshal breaking her arm?

"Oh, Caralin called in security. Didn't hear what he said, I was making so much noise, though I did catch something about 'crazy bitch.' So in they came—a really big guy and, as luck would have it, a woman about my size. They had clubs and guns, but the woman could sense, I guess, that I really wasn't a threat to life and limb. She just slid in between me and the files, put her hand in the middle of my chest and said, 'Won't help dear, and you know it.'

"I stopped, still mad as hell but kind of in shock at what I'd done. Judge gave me six months in prison for destruction of federal property, then suspended it, winking at me as he mentioned he was a life-long Sierra Club member. My boss gave me a little unpaid leave, and when that was over, told me my services, as wonderful as they'd been, were no longer needed. NGOs and crazy women, he said, just don't mix.

"So there I was. Late 20s. Unemployed, committed to the great cause. I'd saved some money and didn't need to work for a time. Used to take long walks, looking up at some of the bigger office buildings—and I'd think, what gives them the right, *the right*, to sit in their offices and do what they do? I even started to look into homemade bombs, thinking that maybe I should just blow something up—because, after all, why not? They were killing a lot more people every day, every year.

"So it went like that for a while. Mad all the time. But one day I took a walk by a river, and I was dead tired. Could hardly lift up my feet. So I sat down next to this big tree. What kind was it? Oh God, haven't the faintest. Never could keep most plant names straight in my head. I put my hand on a place where someone had carved a heart and some initials, deep, cut all the way through the bark and into the softer tree flesh underneath, and I started to cry. I sat there, bawling like a kid, for, who knows, some really long time. I could feel underneath all that rage, throwing poor Caralin's files around, fantasies of bombing some building, underneath I was just so sad.

"And then the strangest thing. I leaned even more into the trunk, and looked up, and I mumbled a kind of apology for all the awful things my species was doing. And it was like I heard a voice, or not a voice, just some thought in my head, but not really a thought, not with words, anyway. I know this makes no sense, but it's what happened. I just noticed all the bright leaves soaking up the sun, the thinnest branches dancing with the wind, the places where birds had nested, and felt how solid and strong the roots were, holding onto the earth, pulling up the water and the minerals. And I realized: the tree would do what it had to do to survive, as long as it could. But it wouldn't waste a minute, not a hundredth of a second, being angry at people who cut their names into it, or picked its leaves, or cut it down. And it wouldn't be sad when it died. All the energy into life and not a bit for resentment or regret. And I saw it, clear as day: I could be the same. And besides," she smiled, widened her eyes and raised her eyebrows in a 'get it?' expression, "I just didn't want to give the bastards the satisfaction of seeing me go down."

She waited. Smiled some more. Was there a tiny tear in each eye?

"Took me awhile to find my feet again, but I did, and with a little luck ended up more or less where I am now.

"One thing I was sure of then, and still am. There's every reason in the world to be angry. But there's no reason to take it out on other people—or file cabinets. And it can keep you going late at night, through the boredom and the waiting. Gets you past being intimidated by fancy lawyers, paid off scientists, even the bully boys they hire to scare us. But I don't turn it on myself anymore."

She waited. Daniel waited. He'd been with her long enough now to know that something else was coming.

Her calm, reflective face turned into another smile, then broke into full mouth grin. "But I'll tell you one more thing." She leaned over towards him, ran her tongue around the inside of his ear. "Getting that angry felt. Just. Great. Better than sex. Almost. I never had to do it again, but I'm not sorry, not a bit, I did it once."

And she pointed to a small frame hanging on the wall just

to the right side of her desk, a frame Daniel hadn't noticed before. In it was a gray, hanging folder, its identifying tag marked with the neatly written words "Water quality, Midwest, Preliminary studies." And under that, in a large, untidy, scrawl: *Crazy bitch*.

PART IV

Chapter 12
Anne

It had been blisteringly hot for the last week in June, but now, just before dawn, a slight breeze moved the pink and orange rhododendron blossoms that lined the long driveway. Chickadees, cardinals, and thrushes greeted the first light on the horizon, that long view to Boston that had made the house such a find. A thin, glowing crescent moon still hung low in the west.

The front door bell rang, and then, longer this time, rang again. Anne, who had slept badly all night, stirred at the first bell and then hurried down stairs after the second. She barely beat Patricia and Joffrey, all of them somehow knowing.

There she was, sitting slumped on her side against the stone steps. Anne heard Patricia gasp and start to cry, saw Joffrey grind his teeth together and shut his eyes, as if squeezing them together to erase his own tears. She stepped between her parents, knelt down beside Lily, put her hand on her sister's shoulder and whispered: "Oh Lily, I'm so glad to see you," and kissed her, very gently, on her forehead.

Anne was shocked by how Lily's large, beautiful eyes were nearly freakish in an emaciated face, her cheekbones emerging from the scant flesh of her cheeks. Her clothes were filthy, her hands nearly black with dirt. She wore a thin Red Sox t-shirt over her bare skin, jeans that were far too big, ripped in the cuff and the knee, held up by a thin black plastic belt. Old sneakers, not the expensive Nike cross trainers she left with, had broken shoe laces and holes in the sides. Her forearms were covered with small, round sores and dark blue bruises.

"Hello, family," she said, and gave a brief, harsh chuckle. Anne saw the fear in her eyes, tried and failed to get out some more phrases of reassurance, and desperately wanted her parents to. She saw that behind the fear was relentless despair. But how could Lily, the rebel, the goddess of smooth skin, who had the kind of body and hair every girl wanted, look like this? And seem so beaten? Anne waited for Joffrey and Patricia to respond as she had. But they seemed frozen in space. So she just sat down on the flagstone walk next to Lily, wrapped her own slender frame around her withered sister, and waited.

Joffrey finally broke the spell. "Come in, come in, this is no place." He reached down and grabbed Lily's arm, moving her with a suddenly gentle strength. They all went to the living room. Lily sank back onto the couch and closed her eyes. The effort of looking at her parents seemed more than she could manage. Patricia sat next to her, looked up briefly at Joffrey with narrowed eyes and compressed lips.

Patricia reached out to stroke Lily's hair, her body moving in a slight shudder. "We love you Lily, so much more than you know. Tell me what you need."

Lily looked up at her mother and smiled. Her smile was still so warm, so tender, that Anne felt a shudder of relief pass through belly and back. Part of her, a part that had grown bigger week by week, had thought she might never see that smile again.

"Mom, Dad," said Lily, looking first and Patricia and then Joffrey, "I'm really sorry for what I did. The money and, just taking off like that."

"We know, dear, we know. We're not mad. You need help, some kind of treatment."

Instantly Lily's eyes narrowed, her lips pressed together, her hands, which had been gently resting on her mother's forearms, tightened in a sudden spasm.

"What I need. What I need. What I need. "-- with each repetition her voice got louder, on and on until it was a shriek—"IS SOME DOPE!" She looked around at all of them fiercely, now desperate and unashamed, the beaten girl crumpled in front of their door, the exhausted, starved teenager, replaced by an insatiable monster. Patricia flinched, drew back. Joffrey clenched a fist and pushed it against his mouth. Anne started to cry, silently, pushing herself back against the wall, so hard she felt a scrape against her shoulder blades, as if with enough pushing she could move through the wall and not have to hear or see any of this.

They calmed Lily down with some of Patricia's Prozac and made it clear that was the best she would get from them. Then she told them where she'd been.

"There were a bunch of us, all running. Started out, I don't know, o.k. I guess. We shared food and smoked dope and told stories of, you know, why we were there. First Boston, you know, then I don't even remember why, to Brooklyn. But that got too rough, and one of the kids I'd hooked up with knew some people in Baltimore.

"Then I met Henry, and don't worry, Dad, he was white." She looked up at Joffrey, who grimaced but said nothing. "He told me he loved me, turned me on to dope, real dope. It was. It was." Anne stared in horror. What would come next? "It was. So good." Anne dug her fingernails into her palms, looked at Patricia, who slumped back against the couch with a gasp, her eyes completely closed. Joffrey clenched his fists and dug his chin into his chest. Then he looked up, his eyes widening further than Anne had even seen them.

"Next, we kinda ran out of money. Real fast. So. This is the rough part." She looked at each of them, waiting.

"Go on, dear," Patricia finally said, dabbing at her face with a handkerchief.

"The pig, *the pig!* He wanted me out in the street, to make money, get some more dope like that. Told me he loved me. It was so we could be together. Pig. So I got up in the middle of the night, got high one more time on a little I'd kept safe, walked over to the highway and stuck out my thumb.

"But, you don't, you can't. Know. I'm dying here, I really am." She looked around. Anne could see the effort she was putting in, trying to get them to understand. "Everything hurts. I got chills. I can't eat. I just need something to feel. Like. I don't know. Like. I. Belong." She squinted, bit down on her lower lip. "Took me eighteen hours, had to wait out a big storm under an overpass in New Jersey. Then this guy, I don't know why, stopped. Told him where I was going. Said I had the flu. Turns out he was going to Westborough, just past here. Took me right to the driveway." A small smile. "Wished me good luck, he did. Nice guy." She looked at each of them in turn, her voice turning bitter. "Bet he went off thanking God I'm not his daughter. Right, Dad?" She slumped further back onto the couch. The speech, one of the longest she'd made in years, seemed to have exhausted her.

Anne's mind raced—drugs, heroin, no, not possible, but can't you do something? What will this do to Mom, and Dad? They don't look so good. Drugs, I don't know I don't know. She had to help, to soothe them. But she didn't know what to do and somewhere in her twelve-year-old mind she knew, just knew, that someone was supposed to soothe her, but that no one would. She thought for the briefest moment that she could just kill Lily for all this pain that made her feel so helpless, and then her mind would race off again. Drugs? Not possible. What to do?

Patricia asked a few embarrassing questions about sex and protection and diseases, and then gently led Lily back to her bedroom, watching her continue to scratch the marks on her forearms even as she drifted off. Meanwhile Joffrey waited until 8:30 and then spent three hours on the phone, calling doctors, hospitals, and social service agencies. By noon he had a bed for Lily at a detox center, and after that, in a drug and alcohol treatment center in rural Connecticut, two hours away. "Yes, by all means," the intake director of Trailside Treatment had assured him, "we've got all types of people here; and many, if not most, have backgrounds not that different than your own family. This is a disease that needs serious treatment—for us, in our program, the 12 steps. But really the most important thing is fellowship—being with other people struggling with the same problems, fighting the same fight. It gives them hope and courage. You'd be amazed, simply amazed, at how they change."

Lily slept uneasily for a few hours, woke up begging, threatening, and crying hysterically. "Just $40, that's all I need. Just drop me off in Boston, on Blue Hill Ave. I'll be back, I swear, just let me get well." When nothing worked, her will suddenly collapsed. She allowed Patricia to lead her through a long bath, put on some clean clothes, even tried to eat some crackers and a banana. She looked at Anne, who offered the crackers, cut up the banana in pieces, a few tears in the corners of her eyes. "I can't," she said, her lips trembling, her eyes soft and defeated. Did she mean that withdrawal from heroin left her sick and uninterested in eating? But Anne heard something else as well. She couldn't, she just couldn't. Be happy. Be normal. Live.

Three weeks later Anne, picking up a receiver in another room, overheard a midnight phone call from Trailside telling Joffrey that Lily, in the company of two other "clients," had broken a window in the bathroom and run away from the facility. "I'm sorry to tell you this, and no, we don't go after them. There's no use forcing someone into treatment. She is, sad to say, still in love with heroin. She was very clear when she talked to me: she feels it is her best friend, the one thing that never lets her down. Until she stops feeling that way, no treatment will help. I am sorry, really. Do let us know what happens."

***

Anne watched what happened, over and over again. Running, coming back; fighting with Joffrey and Patricia, promising to do better so that they would take her back into the house; lying about where she'd been, where she was going, how she spent her time; where the sores on her forearms or ankles came from, who that man was she'd been talking to. They would find needles under her mattress, and she would scream they were from "before" or she hadn't used them, was just thinking about it, or that yes, she'd used them but they were just for water, because "You see, addicts have this crazy thing about needles but it wasn't dope believe me for once why don't you." Doors slamming, once a basement window broken so she could come back into the house after being locked out. There were endless lists of rules, counselors who specialized in substance abuse, and 12 step meetings that didn't seem to do her the slightest good.

Anne saw how much her father was drinking, and how old and gray her mother had gotten in three years. She grieved for Lily, whose rages would subside to jags of crying, or long hours of simply staring out of a window.

Yet when Lily stole money from her the fourth time, money she'd saved for months to buy a special series of expensive books, the grief was overtaken by anger. She stormed into Lily's room without knocking, just after Lily had returned from the bathroom and hadn't had time to lock it yet (it was before Joffrey had simply taken out the lock). "How could you do this to me? I have been a good sister to you. You *thief*. I hate you, I never want to talk to you again, never never never." And she bit her tongue before the forbidden words of what a forbidden part of herself wanted to add.

To Anne's amazement, Lily just sat there and took it. Her face creased in pain, she slumped back against the rumpled bedclothes, picked at the scabs on her arms, and her mouth twisted. "It's just who I am. I'd like to say I'm sorry, but I needed the money, bad. I hope to God you never need anything that bad." And she turned her face to the wall. Anne stood there, wilting. Was that it? Couldn't she at least get some anger in return? Or a promise, soon to be broken, never to do it again? Where had Lily gone, and left this shell, this leech on all of them, in her place?

Finally, Anne, who never stopped trying to help, and almost never asked for anything for herself (because, she very occasionally thought, who would give it to me?), went off to college. A solid record in high school, combined with no need of financial assistance, got her into an excellent liberal arts school in Ohio. Joffrey and Patricia grumbled about how far it was, but Anne patiently explained that she'd write and call every week. Lily didn't pay much attention, going through her twelfth relapse. She had been working at a cheap Italian restaurant and would eventually be fired, the owner red faced and shaking, for stealing from the register and lifting other waitresses' tips. But the day before Anne left Lily took her aside. She pushed her up against the wall of her bedroom, put her face next to Anne's and hissed at her. "This place, this family, all of us. There's nothing, nothing you can do. I'm telling you. Get out."

So Anne went, guilt ridden over what she was leaving behind, carrying images of her mother's sagging, defeated face; her father's rages and the helplessness behind it; and her sister, her still beloved sister, living endless rounds of torturer and victim.

***

Each month, each year, it seemed to get a little easier. There were whirlwind visits at Christmas and Thanksgiving, brief times at home between end of semester and summer programs in Venice and London. She kept her word with short informative letters about classes and friends. And there was the weekly Sunday evening phone call. Yes she was fine no she didn't need any money and how were they? and gee that's too bad maybe this time the treatment will work hope you and dad are getting some. Relief? Rest? A new life?

Still, Anne would always shudder a bit as she put the phone down, a brief shake of the head and shoulders, to throw off the lurking depression that her mother's defeated tone—another relapse, more lies about using, something stolen again—brought near. And then she would lower her shoulders, take a few deep breaths, and brighten like a just watered plant. For now, she had her own life.

She was majoring in European history, specializing in the medieval period, reveling in tales of monasteries, dukedoms, plagues, serfs, guilds, spice routes, wars between princes and kings, and the effects of Islamic culture. She relished the austere discipline of study, the way things actually worked if you did what you were supposed to. Get the syllabus, buy the books, take good notes in class, ask questions, do the reading, prep for the exam or do a few drafts of a paper—and it all worked out. If only in this term's study of the breakdown of feudalism and the rise of agrarian paid labor, with special emphasis on Polish wheat imports, life made sense. She had a few friends, low profile people who ate meals together, went to films, and compared notes on professors. That was enough.

She would go through a day: up early, classes, long hours in the library, casual chats with friends, perhaps a little TV or music before bed. And then just after she'd brushed her teeth and put on her pajamas, just before laying down in her own preciously peaceful room with its rows of books, her computer and printer, her neatly stacked belongings and clothes, she would flinch, a sudden jerky movement of shoulders raised and tightened, eyes rapidly flicking back and forth, peering at her surroundings. What was she looking for? What had she forgotten? What had she left undone?

Oh yes. She knew. She could still hear the voices, as she'd heard them so many times; still remember waiting in bed—for the last door slammed, perhaps a glass smashed against a wall, the final screamed threat or insult or lament—so that she could try to get back to sleep. But she would remind herself, that was far away and there was nothing, literally nothing, she could do about it. She would go to sleep, have few dreams and not too many nightmares, and get up the next morning.

Neither pretty nor plain, thin rather than chubby, and given to the simplest of clean, neat, and nondescript clothes, not a joiner of any particular group—the heavy druggies, the theater crowd, poetry crowd, philosophy crowd, grade grubbers or screw-ups, spoiled rich kids or social activists—she was rarely asked out on dates. Straight men and lesbians would look her over and sense a complete lack of sexual response. Even worse, she didn't drink or smoke weed, let alone fool around with the heavier stuff that some other students did. Somebody completely straight at a college party? The diet coke drinker at the bar? An anomaly, to be sure, and for almost all college students an unattractive one. She was, essentially, alone; and deeply grateful to be in a place where nobody needed her.

***

One night, at the end of her senior year's first semester, she decided that for once she would try to live like other people. Her difficult work was completed. Second semester would be a walk in the park. She had done well, with no mistakes, no problems, no trouble. She had earned, she told herself, the right to let go just a little. So she went to one of the many parties that dotted the campus. Semester-end celebrations with enough alcohol and pot to wreck several hundred more students than actually attended the small school. She filled a tall glass with diet coke, pretended to herself and anyone who asked that it was heavily laced with rum, and stood by the side of the smoky room, swaying gently to the heavy beat of ear splitting rock.

The thirty or so other students smoked and drank, engaged each other in brief shouted exchanges over the deafening hi-fi, and looked each other over to see what the night might hold. A college noted for its easygoing and broadly accepting sexual mores, there were almost as many women cruising women as men doing the same. Anne danced with a few strangers, surprised herself by enjoying it, and then decided, flatly and without plan or forethought, that she would have sex with someone that night. She was tired of being a virgin, tired of living a second hand life, tired of having her mind dominated by images from home. She had no clear career plans, and knew that in a few months she would be back there, with her sister's lies, her parents' desperation, and her own inability to make anything better for anyone.

When a rather sweet and shy sophomore, noticing her standing by herself, started a conversation with her, she knew he would be as good as anyone else. They danced a few fast songs, and then when a slow song came on, she surprised herself, and him, by leaning into him, letting her pelvis touch his, suggestively caressing his neck with her hands. After the dance she brought his face down to hers and gently kissed him, her lips moving back and forth on his, and then she slowly opened those lips and let her tongue play over his mouth.

As the embrace ended, she noticed that mixed look of surprise and deep gratitude on his face. Stifling a laugh—who was doing who a favor here anyway?—she leaned her lips next to his ear. "Let's go to my room. I want to sleep with you."

The surprise quickly turned to delight. "You're sure?" he whispered back, "I mean, you're great, but this is all kind of sudden. You really want me?"

"I do, I do," she answered, conscious of the lie but knowing this was hardly the place for the truth. Back in her room, she felt like two different people. One of them was sure of herself: lighting scented candles, arranging the bed, slowly, gracefully taking her clothes off, adjusting herself on the bed in an inviting pose. She had seen enough movies to know this was how it was done. If she wasn't the most beautiful woman in the world—her hair too plain, her breasts too small—she could tell by the astonished and increasingly excited look in his face that he felt like he'd just won the lottery. The room was overheated, so she took the heavy quilt off the bed and lay, completely naked, on the rose-colored sheets. She smiled reassuringly, as if saying, "No, I don't need any convincing. Come and get me."

He embraced her, kissed her neck and her lips, ran his hands with a kind of sweet, awe-struck gentleness over her back, her thighs, her armpits. And gradually, to her gratified surprise, she started to respond. Light moans escaped her lips, her hips rocked in a gentle rhythm against his thigh.

And then the other part, the part that was always there, became louder and louder in her head. This feels nice, doesn't it, just like it does for everyone else. What is it like for Lily?

When she's out there broke and needs a fix? Is it some drunk with a twenty in an alleyway, or some dealer who puts a knife at her throat for kicks? And while she's out there, what's happening to Mom and Dad? Do they have sex? Really?

Anne continued to move against the boy, trying to quiet the voice in her head, trying to concentrate, but the more pleasure she felt, the louder the voice got, the more she tried to let go the more images of the sores on Lily's arms, or the faded depression of Patricia's face, or the bitter set to Joffrey's mouth, came before her eyes. More sexual pleasure—he was kissing her nipples now, unexpectedly skilled, and she felt a tingle between her legs as her sex slowly awakened, and even became eager for his touch. Still the voice got louder, as if two instruments were competing for the audience's attention at a bizarre concert in which only one was supposed to be heard.

Here you are, all alone, but what about them? She shook her head, trying to stifle the voice, and her partner looked up to see if he was doing something wrong. "Go on," she murmured. "It feels nice."

But then it stopped feeling like anything. She was back in her old bedroom, desperately trying to think of something to do or say to get them to stop shouting at each other. She lay still with the boy, her moans silenced, her body's response lost. By this time, he was too aroused to notice her withdrawal. She let him go through the motions, caress her clitoris, put on a condom, and enter her and come almost immediately.

"Are you all right, I'm sorry I finished so fast, you're just so. You know. Sexy."

"No, that was fine, I enjoyed it. But I'm really tired now and I need to sleep. Why don't you go and maybe we'll talk tomorrow."

He looked stunned. But clearly wasn't going to argue with the lovely stranger who'd just let him have sex with her.

After he left, Anne lay on the bed, still naked, her body

slightly moist in unusual places, her mind a thousand miles away. It was there. It always would be.

***

It wasn't fair. Those last years at home had been so bad; she'd felt so abandoned, needed to help but unable to help, wanting something, anything, for herself, and getting practically nothing outside of the occasional "thank you" and "you like nice today, Anne."

And now, when she had escaped, or thought she had, to this place so far away, she realized that she hadn't escaped at all.

And it was getting worse. Ever since the brief, disastrous foray into sex, the nightmares returned. And the daymares as well. She would try to bury herself in a discussion of medieval theology or the effects of the Black Plague, and the voices of Patricia or an image of Joffrey, would crowd in, jostling the Bishops of France or the dying peasants of Germany. She would be having tea with someone, and emerge from a reverie to a persistent, "Anne, Anne, where are you?" from a concerned, or slightly annoyed, friend.

She was becoming more and more frightened of her thoughts. Dreaded trying to get to sleep. And where could she turn for help? The few times she had gone with her parents to family support groups, she hadn't seen them do anything but make everyone more miserable. People huddled in grimy basements listening to each other sob and whine. Counseling? Share this awful story with somebody in a suit and tie, who would hem and haw and ask embarrassing questions? And then say what? What could anyone say?

One day she even walked to the small nearby hospital, wondering if they had some medicine that would help. Some Prozac, or whatever it was her mother had taken. She stood on the steps, trying to push herself into the building to get some help. But she couldn't. Take drugs to help with the drug problems in her family? End up like her mother stoned on pills and vodka? Or the people who told stories of how they had turned to shrinks and ended up worse than when they started?

Over and over. Nothing to be done.

***

It was a rainy Saturday, a bit warm for January in Ohio, but still bleak and chill. Anne had stumbled into the college bookstore and was drifting aimlessly through the racks. History. Biography. Short Stories. Philosophy. Religion. Nothing interested her. Nothing would help, except as a kind of temporary distraction.

Not knowing why, her hand reached up at the Buddhism section, and she twisted her head to the side to read the titles of the texts. Some had words in them that meant nothing to her: mantra, sutra, Mahayana, Jataka. But then there were some that drew her in. *Freedom from the Known*, that sounded pretty good. She would give anything to be free of what she knew. *The Miracle of Mindfulness* was another one. Though she would have switched it around—the miracle would be shutting off her tormented mind.

And then, *Let yourself Be: Buddhist Meditation and the Quiet Mind*. She reached up and pulled the book down, and just stared at it. There was a woman on the cover, dressed in a dark brown wraparound tunic that looked foreign, her hair shorn to a brief, black half-inch. The woman's large, expressionless eyes seemed to be looking right at hers. It was as if a completely calm, infinitely large and perfectly quiet voice were whispering, directly to her. "Let yourself be. Let yourself be." A brief tear formed in the corner of each eye. Let herself be? If only she could. Just the thought of it, like a small boat being dropped off the side of a sinking ship, cutting the rope that connected them, and drifting away. She would do anything for that.

***

The meditation instructions were simple. "Sit up with your back comfortably straight, your body supported by the floor or a chair, close your eyes, and focus on your breath. The rise and fall of your chest or the place at the base of the nose where breath enters the body. Beliefs, memories, physical sensations, emotions, wishes—will come and go. As you develop an awareness of the way they come and go, how they are essentially transient, something else may happen. As it does, observe what that is. And continue."

Anne had no ideas about meditation, though she knew it had attracted people since the Beatles. No one she knew did it. She'd never been interested. But the thought of *Let Yourself Be* was enough to get her going. And at least, at least, it was something to do. And private. And wouldn't bother anyone else.

At first it was a simple fifteen minutes, twice a day. Back straight, watch the breath. In. Out. In. Out. Over and over. And at first all it did was make her sleepy. She had to fight to keep from nodding off, breaking her concentration to yawn widely. She read through the book, skimming through the essentials of Buddhist philosophy, none of which made sense to her, until she found a story about a novice monk with the same problem who had been told to meditate on the edge of a well. If he fell asleep, he would fall and drown.

"Pretty dangerous, wouldn't that be?" Anne thought, wishing she had the book's author to ask. And then, as if the author had read her mind, on the next page she found: "While sitting on the edge of a well might seem dangerous to some, from a Buddhist point of view nothing is more dangerous than not meditating." There weren't a lot of wells around, so before she sat, she'd jump up and down a few times to get her heart pumping, or douse her face with ice water.

The next problem was her legs. No matter how she sat—cross legged on a pillow, in a straight-backed chair, even sitting up in bed, her legs would start twitching.

As if the author were in the room, and knew her in advance, there was a section on physical problems of the novice meditator. "Physical sensations come and go as you meditate. Observe them the way you might observe anything else, in as much detail as possible. Do not cling to the good, do not avoid the bad. Just observe."

Her next practice began before bed. Closing her eyes, she took a few long breaths, then settled into the easy rhythm of meditative in and out, in and out. Sooner than usual her left leg felt tight, then painful, and then it started to twitch, her left foot jerking against the thigh it rested on. She remembered the book's advice and instead of squirming around to find a more comfortable position, she just let the twitching happen, as if it were happening to someone else, in another room, in another universe. She took note of the sensation—was it a burning or an itching? Constant or intermittent? Hot or cold or no particular temperature? Did it stay in one place or radiate? The more she inquired, the less threatened she felt. Instead of some monolithic block of discomfort, it dissolved into a whole host of sensations, constantly changing. She compared the twitching leg to the non-twitching one, found elements of each in the other, and then to her arms, resting comfortably on her knees. Then suddenly, out of nowhere, like magic, the twitching and discomfort simply stopped. Anne sat stunned, disbelieving. Just like that, just by looking at it, and not fearing it, the pain could go away.

So meditation became her medicine. And if a little helped a tiny bit, maybe a lot would soothe the ever-present ache in her heart. She would get up in pre-dawn darkness and sit for an hour, have a brief salad for lunch and sit again before her late afternoon classes, and then once more before bed. The meditation cushion became as familiar as her bed. Her hands would trace the classic Gayan Mudra—which according to certain Buddhist traditions sharpened the mind and soothed the emotions: index fingers curved under the thumbs, other fingers gracefully extended, hands resting on the back of her knees. She would keep her spine straight for as long as she could remember, and then gently curve in fatigue only to be raised again as her sternum would pull her back up and ever so slightly forward. Her eyes were gently closed, her tongue resting easily on the roof of the mouth. Above all, her mind, her mind, her mind: eager, bored, frustrated, anxious, angry, calm, sleepy, and sometimes—mercifully—turning off.

She read everything she could, using the research skills she'd developed in history classes. She no longer thought Buddhism made no sense; it was becoming the only thing that did. The original Buddhist teachings translated from Sanskrit and Pali, the crazy riddles of Chinese Zen, the unthreatening American-style Buddhism more than half of the authors of which seemed to be Jews. "For a time," said a monk 2500 years ago, "I had no thought of 'I am this, this is mine, this is myself.' 'Trying to turn yourself into something else?' asked a contemporary Japanese Zen master, 'you might as well try to make a bathroom tile into a diamond by polishing it. Your ordinary mind is all you have.'" Ordinary mind? thought Anne. Really? Laughing to herself. Right. Just my ordinary mind in the non-ordinary state of not being completely miserable. "Whatever the pain is," wrote an American, someone who had studied in Burma and now ran a little

Buddhist center in Massachusetts, "look at it, study it closely, and investigate it with openness and patience. What happens to the pain if you look at it like that?"

***

The more she meditated, the more the memories surfaced: vivid, filled with pain and hopelessness, boring into her mind's eye as she pored over them.

Here is Lily, a gaping sore on her leg weeping with blood and pus, a sore she'd brought on by shooting in her ankle because all her other veins were blown out. She wore a dirty black Gap t-shirt, cut-off jeans with holes where the back pocket should have been, tattered running shoes with the laces untied. It was an August evening, at the end of a long heat wave. The air conditioning in the house had broken that morning and would take a day to fix. The sweat dripped into Lily's eyes, and she would squint and curse but not bother to wipe it off her face. She was too occupied scratching the sores on her upper arms—first the right hand scratching the left arm, the then left scratching her right. And she was screaming at Joffrey. "Just give me a few dollars, will you? I just want to go into town by myself, like a normal person, and have some coffee. No, I don't want you to make me coffee on your fucking four-hundred-dollar uptight yuppie espresso machine. No, I don't want to go with you. I want to be alone, get it, fucking ALONE."

Joffrey stared at Lily, and Anne could see him trying, yet again, to figure her out. Anne knew how proud he was of how well his mind worked, the way he was always one step ahead of adversaries in business deals, how he could plan a hotel or condo complex or pricey restaurant and almost always make a good profit. "Why," he said to Anne once, in a rare moment when his anger and rigid control were replaced by genuine puzzlement tinged with defeat, "why doesn't anything work with her, with my own daughter?" Anne had murmured some encouragement and sympathy. But she was beginning to believe that there was no understanding Lily, not in any way that helped. There was just enduring her.

Patricia was upstairs in her room, sleeping through the screaming with the aid of the little yellow pills that got her through the days and nights. The pills and the vodka. If she overdosed on the two of them together, Anne knew, she could die. But Patricia had made it clear, without saying a word, that she'd rather take that chance than have no way to escape from Lily at least some of the time.

Sometimes Anne would go to her mother, desperately trying to think of something to say. "Look, she hasn't used in a few days, maybe this time." Or "Is there anything I can do for you mom?" or "Maybe you and Dad should go away for a few days, and I'll look after Lily."

Patricia would try to offer a weak smile, but manage at best a slight twitch of the corners of her mouth. "Oh, Anne," she would say, and reach out to touch her hand. "You're such a good girl. So pretty." And she would touch Anne's hair. "I'm so glad you are." And her voice would drift off. Anne could hear her mother's mind, as she'd heard her voice so many times, going over it yet again: how different Anne was than Lily, and what had happened to Lily, and why couldn't she get better. And why didn't anything work. And.

Once or twice she had wanted to scream at her mother, "Listen to me, damn it. I'm right in front of you." But what could she have said? And so they sat, together in silence, the only thing they could offer each other.

A few times the three went to support meetings for relatives of addicts. They would be told to "detach with love," to take care of themselves, not to enable, to be careful with their stuff because all addicts were thieves, to give unconditional love—but hide their checkbooks. They heard endless stories of the war. Other people, families magically untouched by the plague of heroin and cocaine and alcohol, were civilians. They heard about the magic of recovery, about addicts who relapsed twenty times, about the great treatment centers that did nothing and the therapists who started out confident and then threw up their hands in abject failure.

One evening, in a dirty, basement room in downtown Framingham, a short ride from the women's prison, with tired wooden chairs, a broken coffee maker, and seven other parents or spouses or sisters of addicts, they heard "Susan" (no last names here, all confidential, said the rules) tell her story. How seven months ago her husband had cleaned out their bank accounts, sold her car and taken his with him, and now was waiting trial for armed robbery, trying desperately to support his habit. And before that he had been a lawyer, specializing in getting rich teenagers off from drug busts. Susan talked in a low, calm voice, with very precise punctuation, as if she were a professor trying to figure out a problem on which she could write an article for her tenure file.

"I can't figure it out. Over and over, I can't get it, but I can't stop asking. Can you hate someone for being sick? Can you refuse to feel sorry for someone who is sick if their sickness is their own fault? Are they suffering any less—or is it more—because they make themselves sick over and over? Isn't being an addict like being mentally ill? Do people who are mentally ill have any free will? Is being mentally ill like being paralyzed, or blind, only it's what you think and what you want that are sick? Isn't that why we call it *mental* illness? And so we accept and forgive—but no, if they can't help themselves, then there's really nothing to forgive. But then I think this is wrong. Is refusing ever to get angry at someone who is mentally ill the final degradation? They are not even worth getting angry at? They just aren't really human anymore, and blaming them is like blaming the rain that soaks you on a cold March morning when you walk the dog."

***

Anne had tried to offer silent support to all of them or timidly make suggestions that no one wanted. Her breath would constrict, becoming shallower. Her appetite simply disappeared. In the calm periods between the explosive confrontations, she would lie on her bed, a damp washcloth pressed over her eyes. She would notice red marks on her arms where she had been scratching, in unconscious imitation of Lily. She would pace back and forth in her room, stumbling over shoes and socks she'd left on the floor, cursing under her breath.

At other times, and never out loud, but only in silent imagination, she would confront Lily and tell her to shape up, get her act together, stop being such a selfish bitch and a baby, think of someone else, take on some responsibility, be an adult, learn to do her job. And then, with a shudder, she would realize that none of these words or thoughts were hers. They were Joffrey's. Then the angry speeches would evaporate, and she would simply stare into space, her mouth compressed into a tight, even line, her shoulders hunched up around her ears.

And then she would think, and think and think. What would work? Would anything help? The endlessness of the questions and the absence of any answers, would turn her numb after a while. And sometimes, not very often for by now all drugs frightened her terribly, she would go the double sized elegant fridge, get some ice from the spout that you pushed against, with its settings for "water, cube, or crush," walk to the living room liquor cabinet, and pour some of her mother's high quality Finnish vodka into the glass. Grimacing, hating it, feeling like she was a character in a movie or a bad dream, she would finish the drink in three or four long swallows. Then she would go back to her room, put a damp washcloth over her face, and hope that the liquor would help her sleep.

***

The last months of senior year passed in a haze of meditation. She would go from brutally intense memories to hours of seemingly wasted fidgeting, fighting everything from back pain to adolescent sexual fantasies to pieces of the daily news to relentless hunger for an ice cream soda, chocolate ice cream and sauce, with whipped cream slopping over the sides of the tall glass with a lovely scalloped top. Countless times she had to fight off her own desire to stretch out her legs, stand up, put on some music, watch TV, read a book, or talk to a friend. Anything to escape her own relentless mind. She approached the cushion as a relief from suffering, but sometimes it hurt.

The more she practiced the more she knew she had a very long way to go. That first time she had felt the pain dissipate—such experiences were very rare, maybe ten minutes out of a hundred. Otherwise the memories and twitches and thought patterns just kept on coming. She had read enough to know she wasn't supposed to fight with her mind, but to let it be. Like clouds in a sky, like the chatter of squirrels, like a monkey on a hot tin roof with epilepsy being stung by bees. Return to the breath. In. Out. In. Out. You can't breathe in the future or the past. If you focus on the breath you will be in the present and all the fears for tomorrow and grief for yesterday will just fade away. In. Out. In. Out. Scan the body through the lens of the breath. Where is there holding? Tension? Slackness? Numbness? That pain at the base of the neck—is it sharp or dull, spreading or still, throbbing or unchanging? Hot or cold? Constriction or weakness? Is there an emotion connected to it? Grief or fear or anger? Are there thoughts? Images? Joffrey in a rage holding a syringe Lily had hidden behind her bed. Patricia whimpering to herself because she thought no one would hear. Lily scratching at her scabs, too junk sick to sleep or eat or even sit down. Anne frozen in the hallway, riddled with fear. Just watch them.

Meditation could also be, to say the least, incredibly boring. How much was there to do sitting in one spot, your eyes closed or just slightly open, doing nothing. But the instructions were all too clear. Just look at the boredom the way you might look at anxiety or the wish that you had a new sweater. "No one would ever be bored," said one book, "if we paid attention, really paid attention, to what is going on." There were always the miniscule variations of the breath, the way her spine sagged ever so slightly though she tried to keep it straight, even the fatigue that sometimes seemed about to overwhelm her. She could just look at it, experience it—and not have to change anything one little bit.

She caught an early spring flu, sat shivering with fever, noticing how hard it was to watch her breath when she couldn't breathe through a stuffed nose; or to resist the temptation to wipe the mucous away that dripped down over her lips and onto her Lands' End sweatshirt. If the body ached and pained, well, that's just what it did. "Don't move the body," said another book, "simply don't move. If we promised you a million dollars, or a cure for cancer, or world peace for not moving, think you could do it then? Well, that shows it's possible. We're offering you something just as valuable: knowledge of your true self. So don't move your body and maybe, just maybe, you'll get the point: Don't move your mind."

She dozed off after a late-night preparation for an Economics final, sliding from the pillow and bruising her shoulder. Remembering her teacher's words about how they dealt with sleepy students in the old days, she borrowed some paints from a friend who majored in art, smeared them on pieces of paper, surrounded her cushion with them and put on her most beautiful, delicate blouse. If she snoozed and keeled over, the blouse would be ruined. Giggling to herself at the thought that her oh-so-serious meditation practice might be motivated by sartorial vanity, she remembered a comment by a Tibetan teacher who'd become famous in the U.S.: "The Buddha compared his teaching to helping someone escape a burning building. Whatever gets you to practice, as long as you aren't hurting someone, that's just fine. Vanity, pride, curiosity, escapism—they all work. Because it's the practice that counts, not the motive. Eventually the practice itself will change your motivation—or you'll stop practicing. It's an iron law."

Her friends began with inquisitive questions, followed with pointed jokes, and then tried serious talks about whether or not three, or four or (on otherwise uneventful weekends) five hours of this were really, well, *normal*. Wasn't it a little crazy? She was an American college student, for God's sake, not a monk in Thailand.

The few times she was asked, she tried to be clear and unpretentious. The meditation made her feel better, even though it was hard. The mind was just, well, practically impossible to control. It's just, she lied, really relaxing. "So don't worry," she smiled back at them, "this is, you know, awesome." What she didn't say, what she wouldn't have the nerve to say for some time, was that if you looked at the malls and the armies and the polluting smokestacks and the people running for heroin or whisky or money or sex—what was so great about normal?

Chapter 13
Daniel

"Can I talk to you?" Daniel asked, his voice hesitant and low.

"Aren't we talking now?" Amy answered. Then reached over and patted his hand. She smiled, encouragingly he thought. Since the separation, and then the no-fault divorce, things had been surprisingly easy between them. The divorce hadn't cast her into poverty, his tenured position gave him more than enough to live on. Paying for Sharon's college wasn't easy, but she'd gotten a huge scholarship, and they'd saved for it for years. He saw that since Amy no longer depended on him emotionally, she could, as she said, appreciate all his wonderful qualities. She would chuckle a bit at the trite phrase. And he would grimace. But he could tell she meant it. And since she was no longer pressuring him to give up his obsession, he didn't have to convince her of anything, or even, in a response he probably would never have admitted, resent her for not being as anxious, angry, and grieving as he was.

They would come together for coffee or a small meal from time to time, usually to discuss Sharon. Did she need anything? Was she headed in the right direction? How was she doing with her courses, her social life? And, always a loaded question for Daniel, always something that made his lips pinch together, and his fingers clench into tight fists, fingernails jabbing into the skin, how was her health? And each time Amy would report that as far as she could tell, Sharon was fine. Maybe a little thinner than Amy would like, but girls today, they were so damn paranoid about weight; it wasn't surprising that a daughter would be heavy or thin, dieting or exercising too much.

"But she's happy, Daniel. I think, even, really happy. Sophomore year can be a killer, but she loves her professors, especially one old guy who's her advisor. She's got friends."

Stand in for me, thought Daniel, hope he doesn't put her in danger like I did. The thought was so quick and then so quickly repressed, that he barely noticed it. But even barely noticing, he knew, was a kind of noticing. And he knew he would never be free of those thoughts, even as he also knew they were crazy.

Yet, what Amy told him squared with his own sense of Sharon's life, his own phone calls and visits. Along with the never-ending guilt, there was also a kind of temporary reprieve of relief. Sharon was all right.

"I've been..." He stopped. What could he say? Seeing somebody? Starting a relationship? Fucking someone else? Banal, corny, stupid. And what made him think that the few times he'd been in bed with Sarah would continue, would amount to anything. She was younger, smarter, and a hell of lot less neurotic. It couldn't last. And he'd bet she'd never done what he had.

"You've been?" Amy asked.

He looked away, at the ceiling of the small coffee shop, nestled into a residential block that led down to the pond. He wanted to jump up, run out the door, and just look at the water and the trees. It was so much easier than saying this. But he needed Amy to know, and to tell him something.

He opted for understatement. "I've developed a friendship. With a woman. Sarah. She's," he stumbled over the words, looking for something that moved from trite to trite on steroids, and that wouldn't hurt Amy. "She's like me, works on environmental issues. We've done some stuff together. And."

Amy's smile broadened. It was, he knew, her "Men are such babies" smile.

"And we kind of have been, you know." He couldn't get it out.

"You've slept with her, right?"

"Right." His eyes looked down at the table. He knew he probably looked like a dog expecting to be kicked, but he couldn't help it.

"Daniel, Daniel." Amy's voice was rich with delight. He looked up, a little shocked. "That's great. Really. Did you think I'd be upset? Of course you did. You know I've seen a few people over the last years, I haven't hid it. I only hope," and here her tone changed. Was there a thin thread of regret in it? "I hope she can give you what you need."

What I need? What I want? What I don't deserve? The last thought flew by, then he drew a circle around it and crossed it out, like a street sign. But it would always be there. Always.

This time he reached across the table, clutched her hand, tried not to burst out crying. "Thanks, Amy. Thanks a lot."

***

It was just a week after the disaster at Magnificent Chicken. Sarah and Daniel had drunk a little too much wine after a long drive to a regional meeting of climate activists, a meeting that had begun with great promise and ended with some pointless arguments over phrasing of a joint statement, arguments that didn't get resolved and left both of them feeling that working with other people was vastly overrated. And then frustrated by the familiar realization that it had to be done anyway. They didn't quite stagger into the motel room, a perfect copy of highway motel rooms on the outskirts of any medium to large size city in America: the oversized bed, bathroom with a small sink and just a light scratch on the porcelain under the only slightly dirty mirror, huge lamps on the night tables, and tiny armchair in the corner next to the oversized television.

Now what? Daniel thought. They'd slept together three other times after the first encounter. There hadn't been any great protestations of love or devotion, nothing about the future. He'd never met a woman who was less into, what? Talking about how she felt about him or how he felt about her.

It wasn't that she was cold. She would hug him, hold his hand, be passionate in bed, commiserate about the state of the world, and he'd seen her, from time to time, tear up at the latest atrocity. And she just flowed into sex as if it was the easiest, most natural thing in the world. Touching his penis, kissing and sucking it until he came, groaning with delight. Climbing on top of him, barely moving at first and then speeding up towards her own orgasm, occasionally reaching down to caress her clitoris. And then she would hug him, murmur something like "lovely, just lovely, sleep well" curl up into a little ball and fall asleep in about a minute.

Each time he was left with a mixture of disbelief and wonder. He was so. Damaged. His obsessions. His guilt. But they didn't seem to bother her. She was so preoccupied herself—with the latest facts and policy decisions and environmental successes and failures—she just didn't seem to need what other women, what Amy, really, had needed. Did he need it too?

They each finished in the bathroom, met in bed. She looked him over and laughed. "What," he asked, "something wrong?"

"No sweetie, nothing wrong. Just look at what we're wearing." And indeed, they both wore the exact same Sierra

Club t-shirt, hers an extra-large that went down to mid-thigh, his the same size that struggled over his belly, and then met the boxer shorts he'd left on.

She turned to face him, leaned over and kissed him gently on the mouth. Her lips played over his, and then her hand came up to stroke the side of his head and then his neck.

Really? thought Daniel. Oh, yes. He hugged her close, his hand smoothing out the fabric covering her back, and then drifting down to her ass.

Her lips left his mouth, and she kissed her way across his cheek to his ear, and the down the line of his neck. As her hips moved in towards his, he could feel his penis stirring.

Oh my God, he couldn't help thinking. How is this happening? And then something else began. In the back of his mind, far away from the feeling of her breasts pushing into his chest, the subtle movement of her groin against his, even the warmth and fullness pulsing through his sex, was the face and voice of Smith.

"Could you be any stupider?" she had said. He heard it, heard it louder, more insistent. He didn't mind anyone putting him down, but Sarah, that was different. She was one of the smartest people he'd ever met. But that wasn't what Smith meant, and he knew it. No, the whole thing. Fighting back, trying to stop them, trying to win, losing over and over and over again.

Wasn't that stupid?

"Hello, hello?" Sarah had stopped moving against him, stopped kissing his neck.

"I'm sorry, I'm sorry, it's just that."

She smiled, looked at him tenderly. "Something you'd like? Something you want me to do? Just so you know up front, I don't do anal." Her smile broadened. Was she enjoying this? Why wasn't she mad? Hurt? "But I'm up for most other things." She raised up off the bed, put on a mock frown and a ridiculous German accent, "Vud yuu like me to tie yu up? And tell you vat bad boy yu arrrre?" Then collapsed into giggles.

He couldn't help smiling too.

"Nothing like that, Oh God. Really. It's just. I'm sorry."

Sarah stroked his cheek. "Daniel, don't worry. It's just sex, you know? People do it, or they don't. So do spiders and trout and elephants and seals. In their own way, plants too. So we do it. And it's fun. Or we don't."

Here goes, the thought. "I can't stop thinking about Smith. About what she said. About being stupid. Is it true? Is everything we do just a waste?"

"Oh, that. Well, I suppose that's a higher-class distraction than wanting me in a French maid outfit or my tits to be bigger." She hushed his hasty denial. "I know, I know. Just a little joke."

She rolled back onto her side of the bed, interlacing her fingers behind her head, stretched out her legs. The long t-shirt rode up, almost exposing her crotch. Her nipples, aroused from the earlier contact, were visible through the thin cotton. Yet the image and sound of Smith were like a gauze screen between them, unfolding from his brain to obscure the presence of Sarah's body.

"I've tried. But it doesn't seem to make any difference." His voice was strained, getting louder. Sarah sighed. It was late. They'd been drinking a bit. She must be tired. But he couldn't stop. "What's the point, I think. But then, how can we not care, not try to do something. Do you know? Can you tell me?" his voice was plea now, a touch of desperation." God she must think I'm crazy, or just a drag. Stop it, Daniel, now. But he didn't know how.

"You're the pro, I'm just the amateur. You must know something. Help me," and the slightest tinge of anger colored his voice.

Sarah reached out and touched him, very gently, on the

side of his face, and he felt, as he always did when a woman touched him like that, like a child. "Dear friend, I don't know anything you don't. Sorry, there isn't any secret that us pros keep to ourselves. It's just..." She waited. Did she doubt that he could understand? He couldn't blame her if she did. Probably he couldn't.

She spoke very slowly, emphasizing each word. "Imagine someone you loved was on life support in a hospital. You bring flowers, you hold their hand, you sing to them, rub their feet, whisper I love you into their ears. Are you thinking if you're doing any good?"

She waited. His mind turned the image over and over. Found a dozen ways in which it was a crummy analogy. Thought maybe there was something, a little something in it for him.

She leaned over and kissed him again, gently. What was she offering?

"Well, that took the last of what I've got. Would have been nice. But tomorrow is another day. Sleep well."

She would, he thought. And he wouldn't. He groaned silently, thinking of what he had just thrown away, of what he'd done to Sharon, and of the crisis he couldn't cure. And then, in a jolt, his erection came back in full force. Next time, he promised himself, Smith can go fuck herself, and I will fuck Sarah, or die trying.

Chapter 14
Anne and Patricia

The car turned off. Unmoving, both tried to find some strength for whatever was coming.

Patricia looked over at Anne. Such a good girl. Pretty. The clothes were too simple, not stylish and a little lipstick would have helped her pale face. But at least her blouse and slacks were clean and unwrinkled, her face was washed, her hair neatly gathered in a ponytail with two heart shaped barrettes holding it off her face. At least when she spoke, she told the truth, never mumbled or screamed, and pronounced every syllable clearly.

Why couldn't she take more pleasure in Anne? Spend more time with her, even if Lily was destroying herself, doing God knows what on the street, and when back at home once more would lie and steal, steal and lie until they had to throw her out yet again.

Now that she had finished college, time with Anne could be something to treasure. Maybe a concert in Boston, or a quiet afternoon walking around the Museum of Fine Arts. She could take her shopping at the store of her choice. Yes, that was it. Buy her some clothes. And, and—have her get her hair done. More fashionable, stylish. She was pretty now. Too thin, maybe, but with the right accessories that could be all right. Mother-daughter time. Isn't that what they called it? Just the two of them. Almost like sisters. Sharing something, nothing special, just regular, normal, plain fun that other families, other mothers and daughters, had and didn't know, hadn't the faintest idea, how precious it was.

Oh, the fools, the blind fools. They worried about what college their kids got into, whether they would make partner in a law firm, marry the right boy or girl, go to the right church or vote for the right party. They had no idea. If only their kids are healthy; if only they are not drug addicts. Nothing else matters. Nothing.

Her mind drifted off, forgetting Anne, forgetting the blessed normal families, and back to Lily. Why? Why? And why was there nothing to be done?

***

They crossed the pot-hole strewn street and approached the tattered two-story wooden house, with its first floor Hispanic convenience store. Rusted auto parts and used tires littered the back yard; the front had been grass once, now turned to mud and garbage. A man came out of the store, blocking their approach, and looked them over. He was several inches taller than either of them, with broad shoulders, unlaced work boots, oversized jeans, and a tight t-shirt advertising "UMASS Basketball." He had a large gold earring in his left ear, shaped like a heart, two thick chains around his neck, a large ring with a blood red stone on his left index finger, and a long thin scar running down his neck. He just stood there, as if considering what to do, then offered a slightly ingratiating smile. "Maybe you need something? I can help you out. You don't feel right I can make you a little better. Hmmm?"

Anne stared, her mind stumbling in confusion, thoughts tumbling after each other. What to do? Don't make him angry. Would he try to steal something? But they were here to see Lily. Was this her dealer? Would he take their car? Frozen in place, unable to respond, she watched her mind, just like the books had told her to do,

Patricia's body slumped into itself, her graceful face contorted into a grimace of revulsion, her chin sagging into her chest. Anne reached over to take her hand, when suddenly Patricia jerked her hand loose, raised her head and walked closer to the man. She squared her shoulders, raised her voice loud enough for people to hear across the street and turned up the corners of her mouth into a small, brittle smile. "I'll tell you what," she said, reaching out her hand to rest ever-so-gently on his heavily muscled forearm, "I'm here to see my daughter, who lives up there." She pointed to the second story window. "White girl, mid-twenties, blond hair, medium build before she started using, now looks like a fucking ghost. Know her?"

The man stepped back, his salesman's smooth tone replaced by instant distrust and hostility. "What if I do?" he snapped.

"Well, like I said, she's my daughter. So I'm here for her and not you. But I work for the state, the police are my friends. If you give her any problems, or me, I'll be back with my friends. You can repeat your kind offer to them. Otherwise, you go your way and I'll go mine." She waited, staring straight into his eyes.

Disbelief, anger, and behind that, the usual fear of the petty businessman who above all wants to keep on selling, swept over the man's face. Then he smiled back at Patricia, the deadest, least appealing smile Anne had ever seen.

"Yeah lady, whatever you say." He gave a mock bow and walked away.

Anne was stunned. How had the vague, sensible, ineffectual Patricia stared down a drug dealer?

Patricia nodded towards the rusted-out doorbell. "Broken," she said to Anne. "Like everything else." They pushed open the front door, noticing that the door frame looked to have been forced aside a few times, as if someone had forgotten their keys and wasn't about to wait for a locksmith; or a person who didn't live there wanted very much to have a conversation with someone who did. The banister shook as they climbed the stairs, stepping over empty coke cans, cigarette butts, burnt matches, candy wrappers, three cheap spoons blackened with soot, and several of the small, ribbed orange tops that came with store bought syringes. Anne and Patricia stopped midway, exchanged the familiar haunted look that Members of the Immediate Family knew all too well. Someone, probably Lily, had been using on these stairs, too desperate to wait to get inside the apartment.

Home after graduation, Anne hadn't seen Lily since Christmas vacation. Soon after Lily had relapsed and left, on a run, supporting herself doing whatever it was that addicts did with their bodies and souls to survive.

They knocked, waited, knocked, then Patricia called out "Lily, Lily dear, it's me, Mom, and a nice surprise, Anne is here too." They tried the door. This one was locked. Maybe she wasn't home. But they'd agreed on this time. Lily had used a pay phone down the block and said, "Yeah, please, come around eleven. That will be good. I need to see you. Please." What if she had overdosed? Was lying there barely breathing? Should they call an ambulance? What to do?

They knocked again, louder. Patricia smacked the door with the flat of her hand, sending tremors through the building. Anne's mind raced from thought to thought, image to image, and then stumbled and caught, like an old car engine finally turning on: Is she dead? Is it over? At last? And now the horror turned on herself. How could she have such a thought? And how could it offer her such pleasure?

Suddenly the door opened, and there she was. The yellow t-shirt, a once-stylish Abercrombie that Patricia had bought "to cheer you up dear" now covered in dark brown stains (food? blood?) with a few small, round burn holes just under her breasts. Lily turned aside and steered them in, slammed the door shut and threw a heavy bolt lock. "Gotta have a good lock here. Assholes come all day and night. Wantin. Everybody wantin' somethin."

"Hi, Mom," she said, with a phony cheerfulness that made Anne blink, hugging her mother. And turning to Anne: "And my one true sis, Annie." Anne wanted to move over, hug her, ask questions, offer support; but she was overwhelmed by their encounter with the small-time dealer, by the drug works on the staircase, Lily's stained shirt, the haunted look behind her false joviality, and the crushing smell of garbage that came from the cramped kitchen the front door led to. She managed to reach out one arm and Lily closed the distance between them, whispering, "Not so easy, being here. I understand. But if you want messed up, trying livin' here. Know what I mean?"

Anne felt a surprising strength in Lily's hug, the way her hands pushed in against Anne's shoulder blades, her face against the side of Anne's neck. Was there some veiled hostility in the near overwhelming physical closeness? And beneath that, desperation, someone hanging on for dear life? Anne didn't trust herself to speak. And she could not understand how her sister had lost the ability to say 'ing' instead of 'in'? Was Lily truly and completely gone, replaced by this grimy stranger who probably hoped to get some money from them for old times' sake?

Patricia looked for some place to sit. A gray couch, its cushions filthy with food stains and more cigarette burns, sat along the wall of the other room, a space that passed for bedroom, living room, dining room and family room, all in one twelve by twelve area with barred windows at one end, overlooking the street where they had parked. Patricia marched over to the couch, gently pushed the candy wrappers and an old pizza box aside, picked up two used needles and without comment put them on top of the pizza box, brushed off the flattened cushion with her hands, and sat. Anne noticed that Patricia's hands trembled ever so slightly as she picked up the box and moved the used needles. Was it fear? Premature aging? The liquor and the pills?

"Come dear," she said to Lily, "come and sit by me. And Anne, I'm sorry dear, perhaps you can just sit on the floor. You meditate so much, it won't be hard for you."

"Tell me, Lily, tell *us*, how are you? Why did you want to see us?" Then silence. Anne knew it wouldn't be good, whatever it was. One look at Lily, at the sores on her arms, the state of the apartment, and she knew. Nothing good could ever come of this.

Lily began, "I'm thinking." she paused, clearly having a hard time getting the words out. "Of a change."

Anne waited. What could this be? Suddenly Lily stood up, "Back in a sec," walked into the kitchen and returned with half a cigarette. Her hands shook just the smallest amount as she lit it with a pack of matches she took from the corner of the couch. Two long drags and she turned back to Patricia.

"Methadone."

"What?"

"Methadone," Lily repeated, nearly shouting. "It's the only thing that will stop the craving. And it's legal. I just. Can't. Do this anymore." She pointed at the rooms, then ran her hands up each arm. "I was stopped by a cop the other day, after I'd done a little drop. Not much, I'm not a drug kingpin yet," she laughed at Patricia and Anne's appalled expression. "But the guy could have busted me if he'd wanted. So I gave him a blowjob instead."

Anne heard Patricia gave a sharp intake of breath, saw her mother close her eyes, as if a too bright light was shining in her face. "No, you couldn't. He couldn't." Anne herself slumped down, her back muscles struck with a sudden, overwhelming fatigue. And then felt as if a small, sharp stake had just penetrated her abdomen. Of course she had known, or imagined, that this sort of thing happened. And Lily—how could this be?—didn't even seem that bothered. Was it just business as usual?

Lily almost laughed at their reactions. "Oh yeah, Mom. He could and I could and he did and I did. And it wasn't the first time." Her voice rose. "Get it?" Then, calmer: "He even let me keep the money from the drop. So I'm set for now. But tomorrow? Or the day after? The next time they get me, I could get sent away. And there won't be anything in jail, not like Detox where they give you tranquilizers to tide you over. I'd just be sick for real."

She turned to Anne, leaning over her, a spot of saliva forming at the corner of her mouth, her fingers rippling in the air as she opened and closed her hands. "Take the flu, the worst flu you ever had, and multiply it by, like, a hundred. Fever, body aches, sick in your gut, your skin twitching, cramps all over, and like all of your nervous system wants to run out of your body and wrap itself around dope, morphine, oxy-pill or oxy-powder. Crack? That stuff is shit. But you'll take that too. Anything."

She stopped, closed her eyes, light shiver running across her head and shoulders.

"I've done sick. Too many times. I can't do it again."

She turned back to Patricia. "There's a clinic, Mom, in Framingham. Right near the women's prison. Where I'll end up if I don't stop using. You have to get it from the clinic. It's not some pill in a bottle. I'd have to live at home so I can get there every day. But I've learned my lesson. I've talked to people. Once you're on the clinic, you don't crave, you're not crazy."

She smiled her most ingratiating smile. "You know me,

Mom, I'm not bad, am I? It's just when I'm using, right?" A bit of quaver in her voice: asking for reassurance or just playing them? When had she ever cared what they thought of her?

"So. I want to come home. Try again, but this time with help. I gotta tell you," her voice lowered, this time clearly trembling, "I'm scared here, Mom. It isn't safe. I sleep, you gotta know, you gotta help me, I sleep with this." She reached under the couch pillow, pulled out a long, thin switchblade with a pearl white handle. She opened it, made cutting gestures by waving it in the air. Anne flinched, saw Patricia shrink back into the couch. Lily put the knife down, leaving the blade extended. "You saw the front door, right? I did a drop and paid a guy to put a better lock on my door. The landlord, he's gone, way gone. Died or something. Maybe busted for dealing. So nobody collects the rent. But last week somebody from the city was here, told me they might condemn this place.

"I don't have long. And I got no place to go. Take me home. I'll be good. I promise. I promise. I promise." Her reserve broke, and the little girl came back. She sobbed and sobbed, throwing herself on Patricia for comfort.

The talk petered out. Patricia holding Lily, patting her hair. Anne frozen in place. Lily home again? The screaming, the lying, the thefts. Joffrey in a rage, Patricia drinking even more. And then the hope. Maybe this would work. Something that would make her less crazy. She tried to remember Lily as someone you could talk to, play games with, eat a sandwich with on the porch, looking at the view, talking about music or boys or nothing at all. She tried, but she couldn't.

Chapter 15
Joffrey, Lily, Anne

Joffrey hadn't been to the apartment over the Hispanic grocery, had never met the dealer on the street, or seen the broken door and the littered stairs. But he came to collect her, feeling sure that his newest luxury Mercedes would have enough room for the two of them and whatever junk she dragged along. He walked quickly in past the broken bell, through the outer door, which was now off one of its hinges. But the littered, filthy staircase defeated him. How could he be the father of someone who lived here? Forcing himself not to sink down on the bottom steps and let his expensive slacks, his hand-made tailored shirt, be touched by the grime of whoever had left two used needles there, he shouted up to Lily, using the voice that carried over drills and saws at the construction sites of his projects.

"Lily, I'm here. Let's go. I'll be in the car."

Back in the car, the motor idling, the radio playing his favorite classical station, he tried to calm the trembling in his hands, the pain, more frequent each month, in his stomach. He could feel the fear seeping outward from the pain, up to his chest, dragging his eyelids down, stealing the strength from his legs. Along with the pain, another feeling rose up in from his belly to his throat. It was a fury so vital and pure it could have smashed the windshield and let in the overcast sky. He would kill her, yes, he would, if she betrayed them again, lied again, stole again. He played it over again and again like the scene from a movie. He would take his still much stronger hands and wrap them around her filthy throat and squeeze until she would stop, just stop, making his life a ruin. She would gasp, and cry, and beg. But it would be too late.

And then it all went away, replaced by an exhaustion so overwhelming he felt he might just recline the driver's seat and sleep. If he could sleep deeply enough, he wouldn't have a daughter, wouldn't have anything. That would be better.

And then another thought, one he'd never let himself think. He sat up, gave a small smile, flicked his eyes from side to side to see if anyone was looking at him, noticing what he was doing. He would start driving—and not stop. The car was comfortable, powerful, and fast. He could buy anything he needed. He could go wherever he wanted. Away from Lily, from the struggles with Patricia over Lily, from another daughter he'd never wanted and never had the emotional reserves to really love. Whatever happened here wouldn't be his job anymore. He would just quit.

Refreshed by images of escape, he settled back in the seat, laughing to himself over the crazy ideas. "Joffrey," he told himself, "you're not done yet. Little tired, little indigestion. Not surprising, given what you're putting up with. But you'll do it this time. Her last chance. Make it work by God."

Lily soon appeared. She had one small bag over her shoulder, and a few large plastic shopping bags in her hands. She wore black chino pants, a sleeveless shirt that exposed a tattered black bra when she raised her hands to light a cigarette, and plastic sandals. Joffrey worked his mouth to keep from starting in about her clothes, the bags she used instead of a decent suitcase, the filth on the stairs. She thanked him for coming, no she didn't need any help, this was all there was.

***

The clinic was a concrete box with a small parking lot in front, a security guard monitoring the clients going in and out. Joffrey looked at them—tattered clothes, cigarettes dangling from dirty fingers, raised voices of "what the fuck" and "you asshole"—and he felt a despair like an iron weight on his chest. Because he knew that this—*this*—was where Lily belonged. She wore the same dirty clothes marked with cigarette burns, had the same disheveled hair, wore hooded sweatshirts with broken zippers and holes in the pockets, mouthed the same reckless curses and had the same rage brimming just under the surface.

He was parked on the street to avoid the racing last minute arrivals for a clinic that shut tight at eleven a.m. A tall man came over, studying the expensive car, knocked on his window and in a whiny, placating voice, asked, "Could you help me out? Real quick, I mean. A few dollars. Something to eat. Really." Joffrey looked up at him, unshaven stubble, pupils dilated, shirt missing two buttons, eyes that shift away and then back in desperation.

Joffrey was silent, merely shaking his head in clear denial. "C'mon, man, just a little help. What's it gonna cost ya?" the man's tone had changed to impatience and bitter need. Joffrey shook his head again, started the car and pointed to the man's hands gripping the side of the car door.

"Get. Off. My. Car." And then pulled away without noticing what happened, remembering how many times Lily had begged like that, been turned down, and changed from whining to rage. And then he wondered how many times she'd done it to strangers, and how many had felt the same hatred and contempt he felt.

But suddenly he remembered a science fiction novel he

had read as a kid—where extraterrestrials in the form of worm-like creatures perch on humans' shoulders, take over their brains and ultimately get control of Earth. It was as if he saw them on the shoulders of these desperate, lost addicts at the clinic. The opiates were the worms, controlling their every move. Going from heroin to methadone, he had learned, simply substituted one highly addictive drug for another, with a lot less pleasure. Because going off methadone was even more painful than going off heroin, these were "chemical chains." So these poor bastards had tried to get better, and this was the only thing that worked. Go off everything? Not possible. The worm is there, digging its claws deeper and deeper into your flesh, causing unbearable pain. "Stick around," it said, "Heroin or methadone, or something else—stick around, or you'll regret it."

Then he smiled a bitter, private smile. Was there a worm on his shoulder too? No matter how strong the desire to walk away and not look back, he knew he wouldn't. Maybe he didn't *know* it, really. He just hoped to God he wouldn't. He'd die first.

***

Getting on the clinic had been easy. A quick physical, four insurance forms, a long list of clinic rules—and she was in. Each morning between six and eleven, after rattling off her name and special i.d. number, she would get the small cup of yellow liquid. Sometimes she would be in and out in three minutes, and sometimes—she could never tell why—there would be a line out the door and into the sides of the littered parking lot. She had her own counselor, an ex-addict who had taken some evening classes at the local state college and now fancied herself an expert. And once a week she had a group. She and eleven other trying-to-recover addicts would talk about their lives, their hopes, how things never worked out, and complain about toothaches, backaches, insomnia, and heartache.

At first Lily took it all in. She said over and over how grateful she was to Joffrey and Patricia, kept her mouth shut waiting on line, and mostly slept. Often, she would barely make it up on time for Joffrey or Patricia to take her to the clinic, sometimes just staggering out of the house in the sweatpants and t-shirt she slept in. "I'm sorry, I'm sorry," she would repeat over and over to whoever had knocked on her door, yelled her name, begged her to get up and get into the car. "You gotta understand, for the last month I just haven't slept. I was so scared. I had that knife under my pillow."

Three days in Joffrey sat her down in the living room after clinic. She knew her tattered clothes were a blight against the huge leather couch with its embroidered Persian pillows. The scene through the sliders was lovely: high clouds muting the light, the oak and birch trees at the edge of the conservation land they abutted quivering in an afternoon breeze, sounds of thrush, nuthatch, red-winged blackbird and one exotic mockingbird audible through the screened sliders that lead to the terrace. If she could just dissolve into those trees, fly away like the birds did, it would be all right, finally. But she couldn't.

"This is it, Lily," said Joffrey. To her surprise his tone was soft. Would he actually skip his usual "I'm the general you're the private" tone that just made her crazy mad? Was he trying something different?

"No more chances. None. I'm sorry, I know it's not easy for you." Lily's eyes widened as she looked up from studying her hands. Did he really know how unbearably hard it was? When every other minute, sometimes every other second, all she could think of was getting her hands on the little plastic package, ripping it open, cooking it up in the spoon, adjusting the needle, finding a vein, and then relief and peace. Did he get that? Or was he just talking?

"To tell you the truth, I wasn't sure about this time. I'm worried about your mother. She can't take all this." Joffrey waved his hand and Lily knew what he was waving at: the lies, the fights, the endless ways she hurt them. But, thankfully, he didn't explain. "So you go to the clinic. You stay off anything else. We'll help you. I know you're still recovering from that place," he shuddered, "and you'll be decent to us.

"That's it, that's the deal. Otherwise? You're on your own."

She looked up, studying his face. Was this one more empty threat? She had heard it all before, and each time they had relented or forgotten. But she also knew too many people whose parents had threatened and threatened and then, after one last horror, had finally followed through. Stopped helping, stopped letting them come home, stopped talking to them. A lot of the addicts died. And the parents, who had "detached with love," "taken care of themselves," "moved on with their lives," who had gotten to the point where they just couldn't stand it anymore, would get a phone call asking if they knew John Jones, and then hearing the dry voice on the other end say how sorry it was for their loss.

Lily tried to make herself sound sincere, confident. "I know, Dad, I get it. The last time. I'll do it. I promise." She tried to believe it. She wanted to so badly. But she had tried and failed too many times. Deep inside there was the lurking, ever present fear that something—physical pain, endless shame, the crushing boredom of having nothing to do but think about dope all the time—would lead her back.

***

The days wore on, into the heat of July. Anne would get up early and meditate, take a long walk and swim in the pool. She, or occasionally one of her parents, would drive Lily to the clinic. They would try to get her to eat something afterward, but she complained of nausea and would just pick at a salad, yogurt, or toast. Anne had a long reading list of Buddhist sutras, original teachings that went on and on. And some of the more serious western commentaries. Her parents asked a few skeptical questions about the meditation, seemed glad that Anne was neither following some long-haired guru in orange robes, nor interested in telling them they should do it too, and then ignored it. She would shop for food for the house, help Patricia cook, and meditate again, and again, and again. What was going to happen next month or in six months? She had no idea. None of them did. Through the meditation, Anne learned to watch her own reactions without judgment and what she saw in herself was a kind of frozen fear. All of the books told her just to focus on the now, that past and future were illusions that only bred pain, that the breath was in the present and her mind could follow her breath. When she remembered, her anxiety lessened a bit. But part of her still knew that she lived in a war zone and that at any minute a rocket could shatter them all.

And to everyone's surprise, the first month and half went surprisingly well. Lily was mainly unobtrusive around the house, occasionally trying to be politely interested in her parents or sister, in a way that was so awkward that it was more painful than her rages or lies. Where had she been living, and with whom, Anne kept wondering, that she could barely keep up a conversation with normal, non-high, non-addicted adults for more than a few minutes before she would start scratching her arms, running her hands through her close cropped, dirty hair, fiddling with the small brass owl she kept on a thin silver chain around her neck and never, it seemed, took off? And then, after a few false starts of "Well, Dad, how's it going at work" to which he would narrow his eyes and make a perfunctory reply; and some "Gee, Mom, this dinner is good" when she'd barely had a mouthful, and had pushed the lamb or roast beef or salmon or scalloped potatoes around her plate, only to attack the freezer's selection of ice cream when the rest of the house was sleeping.

After yet another interminable, tormented dinner, they'd retire to their respective hiding places: Patricia with a headache and some more vodka to her bedroom; Joffrey to the now ironically named "family room" to a news program or a PBS drama; Anne and Lily to their rooms. This night, walking towards the kitchen to make some tea, Anne passed Lily's unusually open door. Typically, Lily locked herself in, occupying herself with sketching women with large, bloody wounds, surrounded by jagged rocks and men with guns; or listening, at earsplitting volume in her headphones, to what seemed to be organized shouting, cursing, percussion, and endlessly repeated bass.

Tonight, the door was open. Anne looked in, wondering if the slumped figure, chin on chest, in oversized sweat pants and a man's slightly ripped flannel shirt, was asleep. Then she noticed that Lily's shoulders were shaking, her head moving up and down slightly, and that she was sobbing. Anne stood at the door, waiting, her normal impulse to go in and offer comfort slowed by the many times that what she'd offered—a hug, a reassuring word, sane advice, a sympathetic ear—had been turned away.

Lily looked up, her face a mask of dirt, tears, and sorrow. Anne noticed small crescent moon shaped indentations on Lily's left forearm, and just below her elbow raised welts with smears of blood next to them. Had she been digging her nails into her own flesh? Was it to distract herself from her cravings? Or was it to punish herself for what she had done to her own life and the family?

And then a memory: an experiment from a middle school science class. She had chilled one hand by holding an ice pack, and warmed the other with a heating pad, then plunged both into the same bowl of water. To one hand, the water was warm, to the other, cold. Yet, she had marveled, it's just one bowl, one temperature, how could it feel so different?

And back in the house on the hill, it was the same thing. There was Lily's wretched face—the eyes wide and beseeching, the lips mumbling something about "Can't you help me, just a little." And Lily's face was like the bowl of water, for Anne looked at it and felt herself divided in two, having opposite reactions.

Part of her felt ripped open, as if something that had been broken over and over was somehow breaking yet again. Lily just lying there, in a hole so deep she had dug herself, looking like the loneliest person in the world. Yes, of course, she had dug the hole herself. But did that mean it hurt any less? If your suffering is your own fault; and if for some godforsaken reason, you just can't reach for the fearless honesty of the self-help groups, the chemicals science aims at the brain's recalcitrant opiate receptors, the advice from highly trained professionals, or from poorly paid ex-addicts with their Mickey Mouse counseling degrees who are sure, just sure, that if *they* did it ("and no one, *no one*, could be more messed up than I was, let me tell you") then *you can too*.

If you'd just make up your mind.

"But I can't," moaned Lily, "I can't. And God, Anne, I'm so tired of feeling wrong. If only I could sleep, forever, than I wouldn't have to feel this way anymore." She bit her lip, a few tears, which she didn't bother to wipe away, fell from each eye. She was a lost child, begging for help, and willing only to take poison instead of everything else she'd been offered.

Anne stiffened, felt her heart speed up and her breath stop for a moment. This was a traveler on a bleak road who looked ahead, and looked behind, and couldn't see any difference. So, suicide. They all knew it was possible. Anne felt her sister's absolute misery, the implacability of the prison she'd built for herself. And at that moment she would have done anything to make it go away.

At the very same time another part of her could see with absolute clarity that there was nothing to be done. Lily had put herself where she was. Only Lily could get herself out. Of course, each addict always looked like they'd never recover. Yet, some did. Through God or psychiatry or relentless body-building, organic farming in the country or counseling other addicts in the city, three twelve-step meetings a day or a not too unreasonable supply of legally prescribed brain-soothing pills. Why couldn't Lily be one of these wonderful, God be praised, success stories? The choice was hers, not anyone else's.

If Lily didn't or couldn't, then all of Anne's and Patricia's and Joffrey's efforts were a waste of time. As the character said at the beginning of what had become Anne's favorite piece of literature, there was "Nothing to be done."

If this was true, then Anne could just cry her tears of grief over Lily and get on with her life. And it was true of Joffrey and Patricia as well. They, too, could see that there was nothing to be done. And if this was true, then she, Anne, was free. She could give up all her efforts to say what Lily needed to hear, be supportive to her mother's thickening alcoholic haze, find just the right kind word to offer her father. She could just let them be—and herself as well.

It was a moment's peace, and it didn't last long. Not until the years of meditation cemented it in place.

***

Then Joffrey went away—a new project in western New York, possibilities of a casino complex in the Finger Lakes region. "Beautiful spot, that," he said to Patricia. "This could be very big."

"But do you really have to go?" Anne heard Patricia ask in a frightened tone. "I know things have been good here, but I'm scared Joffrey. I don't know how long. " Her voice faltered, her hands, palms towards the ceiling, floated up and out from her body—as if she didn't know what would come down on her next.

"Nonsense, nonsense," Joffrey scoffed. "You have Anne here; and Lily? Well, she's got her medicine. That will be enough. She knows, she *knows*, that this is the last time."

Then on a blisteringly hot Thursday morning, Lily came down a few minutes early, an unusual smile on her face, her clothes untypically neat and clean. "You don't have to wait at the clinic for me, Mom," she said to Patricia. "There's this girl, she's nice, in my group there. She's been clean for two years and she's going to give me some help, you know, some pointers on how to stay clean. Good ideas. You know? She's got a car, she can bring me back."

Patricia asked some vague questions—who was the girl? What did she do? Was she a good companion at this stage? Lily gave all the right answers. Laughing a little at Patricia's concern, acting like a basically together teenage daughter comforting the loving but overprotective Mom, as if she hadn't associated with anyone but addicts and dealers for years.

Making some mint tea in the kitchen, Anne overheard the exchange and didn't believe a word. This was not Lily. This was some stranger imitating a trustworthy daughter to manipulate the exhausted and easily suckered mother. A chill went up Anne's back, her hand started to tremble so violently she dropped the tea mug onto the beautifully tiled floor, and gave a little shriek as it smashed into large jagged pieces.

"Hey, what's that?" Lily called out.

"Just clumsy me," laughing a bit to cover the terror which had taken over, Anne answered. "Broken mug."

"Well, don't tell Dad, he'll take it out of your allowance." A joke, from Lily. Why was she in such a good mood? Could the methadone be working? Not likely, not like this. A week ago, Lily had been lying around, drained and lifeless, complaining that if something else didn't happen she'd go nuts.

And then Anne remembered something one of Lily's first counselors had told them. Addicts were always at their best when they started using again, or were about to. "You see, the heroin addict, they'd like to be back in the womb where everything is safe and dark. I mean, I sure did." He had been clean for twelve years, a thick bodied man with a cropped black beard, long black hair, deep-set eyes that looked you over hard and long. "So if they think they're going to get high, then it's like the last day of school before vacation, Christmas morning, and your birthday all rolled into one. So for a little while, and I do mean a little, you feel good and you want to treat other folks nice."

Anne had seen this before, but never recognized it. This time it was clear. Lily was on the edge of using.

"I just need a few dollars, Mom," she said, her tone light and brisk, as if she weren't an addict and giving her money weren't fraught with endless conflict and fear, "you know, for coffee with Sheila, and maybe a sandwich. And then some dessert. This coffee shop makes all that stuff, and she says the chocolate cake is something else. So I don't know, maybe a twenty, in case I get a really good sandwich and some cake. And an iced latte."

Patricia reached for her wallet. Hesitated. Reached again. Hesitated. Anne had overheard all this and joined them in the vestibule where they were standing. She saw the look in Lily's eyes, yearning, desperate, pleading, with more emotion in it than she'd seen in the month since coming home. "Hey, mom," she called, "it's o.k., I can drive today. I have to get a book at Barnes and Noble in the mall anyway." Patricia looked from one daughter to the next, confused, disoriented.

Anne could almost hear what Patricia was thinking; they'd been through it so many times. What would Joffrey say? Give her money? Of course not. Don't be a fool, Patricia. But she was doing so well. And could she really get drugs for that little? And look how nicely she was asking. And didn't she need to have some friends? Someone besides the family? If this girl had been clean for that long, maybe she could help Lily? Wouldn't that be good? Didn't recovering addicts need their family to have faith in them? But giving money to an addict, that's crazy.

Lily and Anne stood, waiting, while Patricia's eye's flicked from one to the other. "But dear, that's a lot of money just to have coffee, and I'm concerned."

"Oh, mom," Lily reached out, put her hand on top of Patricia's, reassuring silly, lovable old Mom. "It's just iced coffee and a sandwich and maybe some cake. You know how much things cost these days? A lot more than when you were my age, I'll bet." She gently stroked her mother's hand. "And trust me, if you're worried I'm going out to cop some dope, you can't get *anything* for $20. So what's the problem?"

Patricia looked at Anne, who was praying she would stand firm against this tide of phony normality. And then Anne went back to watching her breaths. In. Out. In. Out. The future is not real, neither is the past. In. Out. In. Out.

Slowly, gently, as if she might change her mind at any moment, Patricia took out the bill, slowly extended it to Lily. "Please dear, just. Just. Promise me."

Lily seemed surprisingly calm. Could this be on the level? No, she almost started crying, it couldn't. She tried to get the words out, but they wouldn't come. Breathe in. Breathe out. "I promise." Lily gently took the bill out of Patricia's hand. "Just coffee and maybe lunch with a friend. That's all, I promise."

Patricia turned to Anne. "Well, dear, if you wouldn't mind

driving. I think I'm developing a little bit of a headache."

Anne nodded, dashed up to her room for her bag and keys, and in two minutes they were on their way. Anne didn't know what to say, how to ask, no, to beg Lily not to do it. She had to say something. Change her mind. Make her see how wrong it was. But she knew nothing she could say would make a difference. All she could do was to watch her breath. In. Out. In. Out. Until they got to the clinic.

"You sure your friend will be here? You don't need me to stay?"

"Yeah, I'm sure. In fact, there she is now. Bye, sis. Thanks for the ride. See you later."

Lily walked over to a tattered white Ford just beyond the edge of the lot, a large woman in a white shirt wearing enormous sunglasses in the front seat. Lily leaned over to talk to her.

Anne didn't know what to do. After a moment Lily turned around to see if she was still there. She waved goodbye, then made "o.k., that's the way out" gestures.

Soon it was Sheila, the woman in the tattered Ford, who was picking up Lily to go to the clinic. Sheila would arrive too late for Lily to make the eleven o'clock deadline, and Lily would run shrieking out of the house when she saw Sheila pull up, calling out to Anne or Patricia, "Don't worry, they stay open later today." Sometimes she would come back very late, complain "Oh God, I'm so tired," and stumble up the stairs. She started wearing long-sleeve t-shirts, even in the heat, no more tank tops that exposed her arms.

Then one day Patricia woke up with unbearable tooth pain. She got an emergency appointment, asked Anne to drive her since Lily had sworn that "Sheila will get here on time, Goddamit, she promised" and off they went to wait as her dentist had to deal with another emergency before Patricia's. When he got to her, it turned out to be a rare and extremely painful double root canal. She staggered out into the waiting room to greet Anne with a whimper, where Anne had alternated meditating, pacing the hallways and, this was a new one, biting her fingernails in a crunch of anxiety over what might be happening at the house.

When they returned, there was a small pickup truck parked by the front door, already filled with their wide screen TVs, stereo equipment, and computers. They just stared at the truck, the unreality too stark to take in, then stumbled into the house, Anne thinking, "No, this is all wrong, we have to get the police," but something drew them in, past the front door, the coat closet, the disordered living room with overturned furniture and the drawers of the sideboard on the floor, up the stairs to the master bedroom where Lily was cursing at a tall, powerfully built man in a UMASS t-shirt who was stuffing Patricia's jewelry into a large backpack. "I told you to hurry up you asshole," she shrieked as Patricia and Anne came in.

"What, what. What is all this," mumbled Patricia, her speech still sludgy from the dental anesthetic. She looked up at the man, suddenly pointed her finger. "I know you. I do. Lowell. You offered me..." Her voice trailed off. She walked slowly towards the phone. "I have friends. I told you, I have friends."

The man walked swiftly to the phone, tore it out of the wall and threw it into the hall. "Friends is it?" he smiled at Patricia—and then swiveled his upper body to launch a sudden, vicious punch at her jaw. "No," shrieked Lily and Anne together, rushing to Patricia, their minds hearing the terrible crunching sound her jaw had made. Patricia collapsed.

Lily turned to the man, "You fuck," she screamed, "that's my fucking *mother*."

"Yeah," he answered flatly, "and this is your fucking house, which I'm fucking ripping off."

Anne got to her feet. There was only one thing to do, get

him out. Before he killed somebody. The jewelry was insured; they had enough money. Just get him out.

She nodded at the dresser, a sudden calmness holding back the terror. In, out. In, out. "Take the small black box, that's the only one with real stuff in it. The rest is fake. Take it and go. There are people coming over, the weekly cleaners. There are too many of us for you to kill. Go. Now."

The man narrowed his eyes, sneering at the three women, daring them to challenge him in any way. As he left, he turned back them. "Don't go anywhere for fifteen minutes. I've got friends too, and we know where you live. It can get a lot worse than this."

To Lily: "You know where to find me if you want your share. Like last time."

They heard his footsteps on the stairs, the front door open and close, the truck engine stumble and then catch, and the sound of the engine slowly diminishing as he drove down the long driveway.

Anne didn't scream at Lily, didn't cry. The present. The only moment. In. Out. In. Out. There would be time for the police, but she couldn't deal with that now. "We have to get Mom to a hospital. I think he broke her jaw. Help me get her to the car." After that, silence. In. Out. In. Out. They drove Patricia to the hospital, sat with her in the emergency room, walked up to the room that the doctor suggested she stay in overnight, heavily sedated for pain and shock. "She's had quite a blow, and we've wired her jaw. Too bad it was on top of the root canal, I think it will be all right, but let's just be sure the wiring works, and anyway here we can give her more meds that will help with the pain. She will sleep through the night."

They went back to the car, Anne put the keys in the ignition, turned it on. Then after a sharp inhale and a long slow breath out, she turned it off. In, out. In, out. She watched her mind. Watched her thoughts. And then couldn't watch anymore. In a sudden lunge she caught Lily by the throat. The flesh under her hands was encrusted with dirt, Lily's eyes wide with shock. "You, you, you, you," she kept repeating, squeezing as hard as she could, a red haze of rage coating Lily's hateful face, all her caution and suppressed fear exploding in one violent demand that the world be different, that Lily not be in it anymore. More than she'd ever wanted anything, she wanted her sister to stop breathing. She could see fear in Lily's eyes, and that gave her more strength. If only she were strong enough to finish it, now.

Lily pawed at Anne's hand, forcing the words through the pressure on her throat, "Let go, you bitch." And when Anne didn't, Lily reached back and punched her in the throat. Anne let go, the anger oozing out of her like jelly from a broken jar. She put her head down on the steering wheel, crying silently.

"All right, all right. I know. But I needed a fix bad, and he said he would just take a few things and what the fuck, it's all insured, right? So let's just go home and I'll go to the clinic tomorrow and fuck him and fuck Sheila; he's her boyfriend. But could you just help me out and real quick drop me down over on Prince and Maple I could get a little of what he got and get taken care of. I didn't get to the clinic today and I'm feeling rough, real rough. O.k.? And then I'll be back later, I promise. I'm sorry. O.k.? Just get me there."

Anne started the car, drove carefully to the place—known for small gangs fighting over turf and places to score for addicts who couldn't make it to Boston's much better selection. Silently she let Lily go, drove back to the house on the hill, went to one of the working phones and made four calls. The first was to Joffrey, leaving him a message that he had to come home, now, not later, no matter what, *now*. His wife was in the hospital because a thief, brought into the house by Lily, had broken her jaw. The second was to the police. The third to the insurance company.

The fourth was to a telephone number she'd called before.

"Yes. Thailand. Three months," she replied to the cautionary questions, "I'm sure. No, three months isn't too long. It's what I want. Passport, yes, and shots. Just as soon as I can. Thank you. No, I can't." And that was that.

Lily didn't come home. Perhaps still hanging with Sheila and the thief, dealing or stealing or selling her body. Patricia stayed in her room, on double doses of tranquilizers, eating through a straw, her once beautiful face crumpled around her broken jaw.

"I simply can't do it anymore," Anne said to Joffrey, who fumed, and yelled, and forbade, and then just sat down on the couch and held his head in his hands. Anne never raised her voice, never argued. She spoke slowly. "If I had had a weapon, Dad, I would have killed her. I cannot live. Like this. Anymore. There must be something else."

He looked up. Was that a silent plea in his eyes, her father who never asked for help? The defeat in his face made her stomach clench, her eyes begin to water. In, out. In, out. Watch the breath. The feelings come and go, like clouds.

Chapter 16
Sarah and Daniel

The scruffy basement room had a dirty linoleum floor, cinder block walls painted a bizarre shade of teal, and about twenty chair and desk combinations, most of which had been scratched, written on with indelible ink, or had their aging wood splintered by generations of nervous, bored, and neurologically twitchy undergraduates. The front of the room held a large metal table, bolted to the floor, and the front wall was covered by an enormous blackboard, much of which was scraped and unusable. "Sorry, professor," said Northern University's overworked and underpaid master of room use, "But at the last minute it's about all we have. The last few years we upped our enrollment, started the business school intensive night courses, and the business-technology center, and the bio-research hub. So all the rooms with carpeting and new furniture and built in computers and sound systems—they're all taken."

Daniel didn't care that much about the room. Activists in Brazil defending the rainforest, or in China trying to do something about the urban air pollution that put half the people in hospitals for a few weeks each year—they probably didn't have the loveliest of accommodations. So it was a small sacrifice to be in this crummy room, and only a slightly larger one to get to meetings, listen to people drone on and say not much, and even try to accomplish something breathtakingly small and not even succeed at that. Dashed hopes hurt, for sure, but not nearly as much as having your local river poisoned or losing a species every eleven minutes.

Still, he wondered if there was something richly symbolic here. Surely the people he was fighting—business consultants for coal companies, pesticide salesmen, lobbyists defending fracking—didn't work in grungy basement rooms. And they sure as hell, in this day and age, had a wired room with all the internet could offer at their fingertips.

But grunge or no, he would do what he could. And with Sarah here as well, maybe something good could happen. His last group had fallen apart. Not with anything dramatic, just a series of whimpers: this member moving to New York, this one getting some kind of immune system breakdown that left her too exhausted to do political work, another dropping out of college, and one having a monumental fight with her lover, and becoming "like, just overwhelmed, Daniel, get it? It's all too much. Sorry, really sorry, but no, no more meetings." With the already small group cut almost in half, everything else just melted away to nothing.

It had been some time since he'd tried to do some organizing and while he would have much preferred simply to do research, keep putting up posts on his website, and—by far the best of all—spending time with Sarah, he knew that group action was the key. And Sarah, bless her, had agreed to come along for the ride, at least in the beginning. She had all the work she could handle, consulting with groups in North Dakota about toxins from oil and gas extraction, and in California about the effects of the drought. But she was in between trips and knew, as he did, that every once in a great while a group would come together and, in the words of the activists most overused cliché, "make a difference."

"I'd love to be there at the beginning, to see that," she had said to him on the phone, after he'd called and apologetically told her he was trying to organize a student environmental group at Northern, it probably wouldn't happen, and he knew how busy she was, and of course she shouldn't feel obliged, she did so much already, and nothing would happen in the first meeting and. "Daniel," she'd laughed, with a kind of affectionate tone that made it all right no matter what she said to him, "don't be so negative. I'll be glad to come, offer moral support from the sidelines, and watch the birth of the new Greenpeace."

So here they were: 7:20 for a meeting called for 7:30, he with notes for what he would do and what he wanted to come out, Sarah kissing him supportively on the cheek, taking a chair in the back and immediately pulling a copy of NRDC's *OnEarth* Magazine to resume reading the cover story on the overused and probably soon-to-disappear Colorado River.

Daniel found a small piece of yellow chalk and wrote on the blackboard. NATIONAL STUDENT ENVIRONMENTAL COALITION—NSEC. And then, a little less boldly: "1. Who are we? 2. Why are we here? 3. What can we do?" Then he sat down to wait, too nervous to read, crossing and then uncrossing his legs, shuffling his notes, trying to remember to breathe, as Amy had once tried to teach him, to calm his racing heart and sweaty palms. Why all this should make him so nervous, he didn't really understand. He was a tenured professor in his fifties for Christ's sake, why should he feel anxious about being in front of some undergraduates, or feel like a failure if no one came?

Unbidden and certainly unwelcome, he suddenly remembered waiting in what felt like just this same way for other kids to come to his birthday parties. Born in late September, it was always early in the school year when his day came around, and friendships, which always loosened, broke and re-formed between summer vacation and October, were far from solidified. Had he invited the right kids? Missed anyone? Asked some who really didn't like him? What if no one came? Surprise, surprise, it had always worked out, more or less. Maybe a few got sick at the last minute or their parents screwed up the dates, but most of them came, liked him well enough, had a fine time playing softball in the big yard across the street and then eating hot dogs and chocolate cake. No matter how good it was, the memory didn't stay, and the next year, or, as an adult during the rare times he had entertained, he still would wait around at the beginning, wondering if he'd done it right and if anyone would come.

Once again, they came. Not a lot of them, but enough. A tall, nervous looking boy, with a baby face, long uncombed brown hair, and a Led Zeppelin t-shirt half tucked in to jeans that looked like he hadn't taken them off for a week; a well-dressed African American man in gray slacks and a green turtle neck, with what looked like a knock-off Gucci briefcase and a receding hairline; a strikingly beautiful coed, with long black hair, luminous brown eyes, wearing a long skirt, sandals, a simple tunic styled shirt and a large blue stone on a silver chain around her neck; a stocky woman in an old Northern University sweatshirt, sleeves cut off at the shoulders, a close haircut, a pug nose, arms like a weight lifter and a fierce look in her narrow gray eyes. Those were the first, another half-dozen came in so quickly afterwards that they all blurred in Daniel's mind. But they were, Daniel thought to himself, the usual suspects you'd find in any grimy basement room trying to overthrow the environmental regime that was destroying ecosystems. Underpaid, under-supported, understaffed, and nearly without hope. But still, they were here. For a fleeting moment, he could feel a little less alone.

He had sent out a simple notice: "Bothered by pollution, global warming, species loss, toxins in your food? Then come along: A New Campus Environmental Group is forming.

Tuesday, in Blair 06, 7:30. Meet others who want to save the planet. We'll talk, share ideas, and find something to do that matters."

And here they were. His ragged army. Of course, with his own wrinkled, ill-fitting clothes (that Sarah had tried in vain to get him to spruce up a bit), he was just as ragged as they were. But he was here as well. And that was something.

***

They all knew a little about how bad things were. And a few, the African American, who turned out to be a second year law student, and the uptight skinny white kid—even though he looked like a combination of skate-boarder and computer geek—had done some rather remarkable work in high school.

The others were vaguely interested, vaguely sympathetic, and not quite sure what they were here for, except for the beautiful young woman, whose name was Faith.

"I'm here," she said during the first go around, when they all were to say a little bit about themselves and why they were here, "for my mother," she waited, a shy smile coming over her face, fingers wrapped around her necklace for security, "Mother Nature I mean." She smiled a little more broadly, looked around for response, got it from Daniel and Sarah and no one else, and sank back in her seat looking at her hands.

"Great, just great," said Daniel, wondering if he sounded like an idiot, "So, let's see what's up." Asked about their interests, several had mentioned global warming, a few had talked about toxic chemicals, and Diane—the short woman with the bulging biceps—had talked about the destruction of the rainforest. He listed their interests on the board. He really didn't care what they did, as long, he'd made this clear in his introduction, as they did something. To him it was all of a piece: kill the rainforest, kill the climate, kill people with carcinogenic chemicals—if you were going to stop any one of them, you'd have to stop them all. And if you didn't stop them all, the others would just rise up somewhere else. It was all or nothing. And from where he sat, it looked almost certain that they—all the environmentalists everywhere—would be incredibly lucky to do a very small something. And that was why he was so depressed, a depression lifted by the miracle of Sarah in his life, but not eliminated, not by a long shot. What was his personal happiness, his *pleasure,* in a world filled with so much suffering?

They all studied the list on the board, then turned to the black man who had cleared his throat and raised his hand. "Yes, Steven," Daniel asked, pleased that he had for once written down everyone's first name as they spoke so he could actually remember who was speaking. "You have a thought?"

"What I want to know," Steven spoke slowly, with a kind of stark seriousness, "is what we are doing all this for? *Whom,*" he paused, seeming to enjoy the subtle correctness of his grammar, "are we trying to save? And why?"

"Could you be a little more specific," asked Daniel, wondering where this was going.

Steven turned to Diane, leaning forward in his chair, eyes narrowed, something clearly on his mind. "I'm not here for the rainforest, and not the polar bears, and not the bees." No one had mentioned the last two, but their threatened survival was common currency in environmental talk: the first dying from global warming, the second, no one was certain, but probably from pesticides.

"I'm here for people. My people, yeah, that's the center, but other people as well. I'm here because people of color get it in the neck—or in this case, in the water, the air, the bloodstream. Environmental racism," he ended, "maybe you heard of it?" Daniel saw Sarah look up from her magazine and focus on Steven. She had introduced herself merely as a "sympathetic friend of Daniel and I hope this all works out" and left it at that. Everyone shuffled in their seats, a little nervous to be confronted by an "angry black man." Then Faith, clutching her necklace again, raised her hand and looked Steven.

"I'm sorry, I really don't know what you mean. All I know is that, well, when I'm in the woods, or on the river in my kayak, that's when I feel, well, safe. Whole. Home. I want to protect the trees and the water. Is that bad?"

"Of course not," Daniel answered, trying to be soothing. "We've all got."

"Bad?" Steven almost shouted, "Who said anything about bad? But if you want bad, I'll give it to you. Bad is what the white power structure is doing to people of color."

"White power structure?" thought Daniel. Where is this guy coming from? The last thing they needed was some heavy-duty racial guilt trip.

"Where we live, that's where they put the toxic waste dumps; where our kids go to school, there's asbestos. The water in our communities? A little high in lead, in case you haven't noticed. All this stuff that white folks are making a profit on, buying in malls, plugging into the grid, all that stuff *pollutes*. And who do you think gets to live among the garbage? And get killed by it?"

He stood up and turned to Daniel, his eyes wide, fists clenched. "You, *professor*," a thinly veiled contempt in the typically respectful term, "don't tell me you call yourself an *environmentalist*"–more contempt–"and you don't know about all this?"

Daniel looked back at Steven, his initial reaction of fear settling into gratitude that here was a person of color who cared, who wasn't lost in the grind of daily life, or the struggle for benefits, or the day-to-day crap that white people dished out in a hundred casual, unthinking ways.

"I do. I do. I know about the struggle in Warren County, about how John Lewis, the civil rights guy, went to jail fighting for some justice there. About how the United Church of Christ helped bring a lot of minority environmental activists together. And all the rest. I've read the history, Steven, I'm on your side." Steven stared, the tension in his arms dissipating, then sat down.

"People, yeah, people." They turned to Diane, who'd looked singularly unimpressed by Steven's angry black man routine. "Always comes back to us, doesn't it? What is it that people want? More, better, easier, faster. Who cares what it does to the trees or the—yeah, buddy," staring hard at Steven, daring him to interrupt—"to the bees and the polar bears. I mean, yeah, you guys have it rough, that's for sure. But that's probably as much because you're poor as anything else. Think we can end wealth inequality, and power inequality, and influence inequality, and all the rest? Doubt it. But maybe we could take care of a few trees, or help clean up Boston Harbor so the fish don't have to choke on sewage or get stoned on all the medications that come out in the pee. How about that? "

"Yes, yes," said Faith. "The Harbor could be so beautiful. The waterfowl could come back. Kids could learn to kayak there and get to see it, and learn to love it."

"What planet do you two live on," fumed Steven. "Almost every inner-city kid has lead in his blood. Not a great basis for *career advancement,"* he spat out the stock phrase, "if you get my drift. And you want to take them kayaking? You'll provide the kayaks, no doubt. Or do you think the kids from the projects have lots of extra cash around to spend the next time they ride their 18-speeds over to REI?"

Slowly, suddenly losing steam. "I'm sorry, I'm sorry. I don't mean to shout. I'm sure you are all well-intentioned, good people. It's just that." He stopped, looked around at their white faces, then unclenched his fists and let his chin sink to his chest.

"Steven. I..." Daniel didn't know what to say, but knew he had to say something. He looked over at Sarah, who was calmly studying Diane, and Faith, and Steven, and him. He made a "What the hell do I do now?" face but she simply smiled, and in a quick, private gesture rotated her wrists so her open hands signaled back "It's your show."

"Let's just try talking," Daniel said slowly, not really knowing where he was going with this. "Look, ultimately I'm here because." he waited, would this sound ridiculous? Would it just scream "white privilege" to Steven? But suddenly he didn't care. His pain was real, just as real as Steven's. What would they all get from some Olympics of suffering where only the biggest victims won?

"I'm here because I didn't test the soil in my little garden. And it had lead in it. And my daughter—well, she ended up with lead levels too high. She had to take special pills for two years to get it down. They didn't think the damage was lasting. But we could never be sure. And I did that, *me*. And so I'm here. And you, Steven?"

"Pancreatic cancer. Not me, but my aunt, and seven other women in my neighborhood. My aunt, who raised me after my father stepped on a land mine in Iraq, and my Mom, who was working two jobs to support the family, stumbled in the street because she was so damn tired from working all the time, and got hit by a bus. But the cancer, we know just what chemical caused it, and where it came from, and how it got into the water we drank, and what big law firms defended the corporations that put it there, and just who the corporations paid off with campaign contributions. And we knew all that, but we were a black community, and nobody cared. Eight years in the courts, and the company just dissolved and there was no one left to sue. And would they ever, *ever*," voice raising again, the pain gripping his eyes and his mouth, "put some of those guys in jail for *murder*—even though that's what it was? Long distance, slow-motion, murder. Like throwing a bomb into a crowd, a bomb that takes ten years to go off. Only if the bomber is white and crowd is black, who gives a shit?"

Daniel noticed Steven's hands were shaking, had heard a suppressed choking sound, as if he were holding back sobs. But nothing came. He turned to Diane.

She looked over at Daniel. "I'll follow your lead professor."

"Daniel, please, just Daniel."

"O.k., Daniel. I mean, I don't like to bleed all over the place with other people, but you and," she nodded respectfully, acknowledging something, not exactly clear what—"Steven—well, you guys laid it out, so I will too."

She turned to Steven. "Look man, you got a sad story there, no doubt about it. Repeated all over this country, I bet." Steven looked up, surprised at the recognition, and nodded.

"Well, I do too. I may not look like much now," she gestured at the cutoff jeans, the stained t-shirt, the butch haircut, even the strange, hard to decipher tattoo circling her left forearm, but my *father*, my fucking piece of shit *father*"—she kept a flat monotone on everything but "father," and that came out in a bitter whisper—"thought that I was really hot. O. So. Hot. Mom was a little busy being a patron of the arts—symphony, museums, experimental theatre. Dad would cruise around the world setting up deals, then come back for a little family time. Dinner with mom, sex with me. He made it clear, really clear, that if I said anything, he'd kill me, and then Mom, and then himself. It almost would have been worth it, that last bit.

"So who took care of little Diane? Nobody. I took care of myself. And I'd go out to the grounds of our estate, all seven exurban acres with its own stream and fish ponds and flower gardens. And the trees, who listened to me cry and shake, day after day, night after night. And that's where I felt safe, loved even. If I hadn't had that, I'd never have made it. And that's why I want to give back."

No response. Silence. Daniel saw Faith wiping her eyes, and even Steven just stared at the ground.

Daniel looked up helplessly at Sarah, hoping she would intervene. She was biting her lip but when he caught her eye, she just shook her head slowly. It would still be up to him.

"Diane. Steven," they turned to him, a world of hurt joined by suspicion. He was a much older white man, could he begin to understand? "I don't know what to say, except that I'm sorry for all of you, and,"—turning to Steven—"those you love, have suffered. It's a shame, a damn shame."

He waited. Somewhere he'd read that the most effective trick in public speaking was the pregnant pause. Don't bury them with your riveting eloquence. Make them wait.

"Together," he turned to the others, "maybe we can listen to each other's suffering, and what has brought us to the point, for real. Give up our fear of each other, so we can help take back what they made us lose. And find some way to change this madness." He slowly raised both arms, fingers spread, to take in all the vicious crap that was being inflicted on innocents everywhere. Then he gestured to Faith—"Tell us why you are here, why you care. And then we will hear from everyone else. What is it that hurts? And what do you want to do?"

***

Well, at least it hadn't been a complete failure. They'd heard some more from the others. Nothing as painful as Steven's or Diane's tales. Mostly about people who'd seen some favorite meadow turned into a parking lot; or who had asthma that they associated with soot from power plants; or who had just been shocked, dead shocked, when they'd stumbled on a TV special about the Great Pacific Garbage Patch.

It bothered Daniel, and he couldn't let go, the struggle that had arisen between Diane and Faith on the one hand, and Steven on the other. How could they be so blind not to realize that everything was connected, that the dying shore birds and the lead in black kids' schools, the ocean and the inner city—well, if one was poisoned, what did they think would happen to the other? Was there supposed to be some magic line that said: "Keep out—no pollution allowed—we're rich and white here, or at least, we're human." And was it so different, what had happened to Diane and what some faceless corporate polluter like Magnificent Chicken had done to Steven's aunt? Why didn't Steven and Diane walk into that meeting ready, eager, just jumping up and down, to support each other? It put him in a rage, and then sank him in a depression.

"But don't you see," Sarah tried to comfort him, "how great that meeting was?"

He just stared at her. They had told some stories, vaguely indicated an interest in doing something. Would meet again. No formal structure. No defined goal. Just a vague sympathy replacing a much more focused initial antipathy.

"But that's a tremendous accomplishment. That woman, Diane, imagine how strong she had to be to survive that monstrous father, and tell her story to strangers, and want to do something with her pain. And the same for Steven, in front of a bunch of whites. Oh, I'm telling you Daniel, that was wonderful.

"And you! How cool you were. You didn't get uptight when Steven challenged you. And you told them about Sharon. And you listened. Really listened." With only the slightest irony, she added: "You're my environmental hero!"

She laughed and hugged him and kissed him passionately, scraping her teeth gently on his lower lip and the twirling her tongue on the inside of his mouth.

Daniel gasped with pleasure from her kiss, and from her words. Everything she touched, everything she saw, she made better. How did she do it? Of course he didn't believe what she was saying. How could he?

Chapter 17
Anne

The strangest thing was, Anne didn't mind any of it—not getting up at four and going to bed at 9:30, sleeping on a straw mat on a concrete floor, two small, strangely cooked vegetarian meals a day, the second one of which ended by twelve thirty in the afternoon, having dinner in the form of weak green tea at six, the crude, sometimes overflowing toilets, the ferocious buzz and flapping of mosquitos and moths and beetles trying to get through her mosquito net, the suspicious looks she got from the older monks and the few male westerners, plainly none of whom had expected a slight, white American woman to be part of their heroic journey towards enlightenment. She had no desire to talk to anyone, so the imposition of complete silence save a five-minute interview every other day with an elderly monk who spoke little English was no sacrifice at all. Even the ban on books, including Buddhist books, didn't bother her. Reading was fine, no doubt, but at this point all those words were more than a little redundant.

And above all, she didn't mind, in fact she came back to it again and again with an almost erotic attraction, eleven hours of meditation each day. She still used a small pillow, her hips flexible for an American but far from the way the Thai monks simply sat there in a full or half-lotus, their hips and ankles unstrained, their backs held straight for an hour at a time seemingly with no effort.

She had bought the pillow at a small gift shop in Bangkok, having heard from the Agency rep in the U.S. that there might not be anything like that where she was going. "Traditional, orthodox, serious. This is the real thing. You might get a few irritated stares if you sit on a pillow, but I don't think they'll chuck you out. Better to have a little support and do the sitting, then not be able to think about anything but how much it hurts."

Well, it hurt anyway. Sometimes right before the little bell would ring that began and ended the sessions; sometimes five or ten minutes later. Then Anne would smile ruefully to herself, thinking, "Now I'm in for it," and know that the spasm in her hip, the burning buzz just to the left of her thoracic spine, or—given how little she was eating—the monstrous hunger headache would be her company for the next fifty-five minutes.

Unless it didn't—there just was no telling. The pain might be throbbing, vicious, a few short steps below intolerable. And it might stay there for the whole session—or it might disappear, giving way to relaxed focus in five minutes. It might start awful, disappear, re-appear, change location and tone. It might be one way at ten a.m. and another at eleven and one, or the exact same experience throughout the day.

Best of all, this almost made her laugh out loud it was so wonderful, there was no knowing what would happen and nothing she could do about it in any case. There was discomfort, irritation, pain, that was for sure. But since there was nothing to be done, she had no responsibility for it. It was just pain, but without any compulsion to make it go away. In a sense, it wasn't hers.

And wasn't that what all the books she had read that last year in college, and jammed into her flight bag along with an expensive rain jacket her mother had pressed on her a few hours before her flight, isn't that what the books had said: *The self is an illusion, a construction of the mind. The more you look at it, really look at it, the more it dissolves.*

And that was what was happening. The self that oh-so-desperately tried to anticipate what her mother or sister might need and try to get it for them—that self was drying up, like a plant without water, like a pervasive mist that kept you from seeing the road, and the downed trees and rocks and potholes that made the road so dangerous, blown away by a relentless wind. Her past began to seem like an old movie—she could remember how intense it had been, but now that she'd left the theater, it was a memory, not a reality.

Eventually, she sensed, the physical discomfort and the emotional anguish would just blend into each other, neither of them very important no matter how much they hurt. As the monk had said when she'd mentioned how intense but also variable the physical pain was, "Pain come, pain go. Sometimes lot, sometimes little, sometime nothing. But we," he'd stopped, pointed one thin finger almost into the center of Anne's forehead, "we always here. So?"

The bus had left her off at the Temple's turnoff, a quarter mile down a dusty dirt road from the Temple's entrance. Two other passengers, typically short, fit-looking, and handsome Thai teenagers in t-shirts, shorts and plastic sandals, had made sure she was let off where she wanted to go. She stood on the paved "highway"—just a two-lane road with small shoulders to let trucks pass each other—as the bus pulled away. She stared carefully at the sign, which being in Thai meant nothing to her, and trusted that the boys on the bus knew that this was the Suan Mokkh monastery. "Oh yes, Miss, this place we know, you go to study Lord Buddha, to meditate, yes we know, we go there too sometime to meditate." Her small suitcase bumping on the dirt, canvas carryon bag over her shoulder, she walked toward the gate.

In the office, the monk had looked her over, frowning in either concentration or disapproval, she couldn't tell. He was a man of indeterminate age, his hair cut down to his scalp, his body swathed in the brilliant orange robes that Thai monks wore: one shoulder uncovered, gathered slightly at the waste and then skirted around the lower body.

In passable but halting English, emphasizing each word, he had sought to make sure that between her inherently limited female mind and his limited English the point was getting across: "This. Will. Be. Most. Difficult. Thing. Comforts. Rich foods. You have. America. Here, no. Just rules. American? Woman? Nothing." And he'd flicked his right hand up into the air, dismissing as unheard of, impossible, that the rigid rules of the retreat would be lessened for anyone.

Anne had nodded, repeated almost word for word what he had said, reassured him that it was all fine; this was what she had come for. What she hadn't done, what she'd almost done but kept herself from doing, was laugh in his face. For it was at that exact moment, one she would never forget, that she first heard The Voice.

Up to then she'd had nothing but respect, bordering on reverence, for everything she was learning. From the first time the meditation had stilled the pain in her legs, through the books, the endless hours watching her mind, she was all the grateful student. But now there would be this inner voice of resistance and cynicism standing against the daily background of obedience and discipline.

The most difficult thing?—the unspoken words in her mind began, *are you kidding me? Try to beg Lily out of one shot of heroin. Or listen to her rant about how it wasn't her fault she'd stolen money. Take in the bombed out look in your parents' eyes, knowing that there is no choice except to throw Lily back onto the street and wait for the phone call that would be some cop asking, a little catch in his voice, if they knew Lily Sattvic, and he was very sorry, so sorry, to tell them she was dead.*

Sitting on your ass doing nothing? With a little back pain and crummy food and a shitty bed? That isn't hard; it's a vacation.

***

And it was beautiful. The four a.m. sessions always began in the dark, with a sky full of stars softened by a slight fog or heavy cumulous clouds. At five, when she went for the breakfast of rice porridge or soup and bananas, the sky was just beginning to brighten, the stars or moon fading, the dawn chorus of tree frogs ending and insects beginning. Out of the pre-dawn darkness the shapes of palms trees and yellow ratchaphruek flowers crowded into the forest trails that led from her tiny sleeping room to the dining room and back to the meditation hall: a roof over concrete floor without walls, supported by wooden pillars.

Each student or monk would put down a three-foot square cloth to mark their spot. Lily had purchased one in the nearby village the afternoon after she had registered. That and her round meditation pillow—stuffed hard with flax seeds, colored a modest black—were all she had and all she needed. At the front of the hall was a raised dais, with two large and not very good wooden statues of the Buddha: seated in a graceful half lotus, right leg over the left. Left hand resting palm up on his left knee and right had raised with palm out—all this to indicate a teaching mode.

Anne couldn't imagine what it had been like to have heard him, twenty-five centuries ago; or, really, whether the man had ever existed. Eight months of intensive study had gotten the basic point across to her and the mystique of Buddha as a man or kind of God didn't seem particularly important. It was the ideas, the prescription for the illness everyone shared, that she was after. Do not attach, do not resist. Everything changes, arises, perishes. There is nothing that is not made from countless other things, each reflecting all the other realities, like jewels at the nodes of an infinite net. A virtuous life is the only source of contentment. Above all, the mind: learn its tricks, its endless tricks, and don't be taken in.

The days were hot—heavy, sweating, squinting into a brutal sun that in the mid-afternoon simply poured its power into every nook and cranny of the temple. By four in the morning, it relaxed enough to be in the low-60s. She'd heard it would stay like this more or less until monsoon, when the flash storms would cool things off a bit for a few hours on some afternoons and you might, just might, need two layers of clothing instead of one in the early morning.

She had no idea what she looked like anymore, nor did she care. The simple white drawstring pants and thin white cotton shirts over the plain white underwear and bra she'd been told to bring had no belt notches to indicate how much weight the Spartan meals were causing her to lose. But after five weeks she did inadvertently notice how much her hip bones stuck out, sometimes painfully jutting into the concrete floor of her room when she turned over in the night. The few nuns that lived here, residing in a small structure on the edge of the thirty-four-acre campus, had completely shaven heads. She hadn't gone that far, less from an attachment to her hair than fearing to seem pretentious. But before going up to the retreat center she had found a barber on a side street in Bangkok.

The barber smiled, almost but not quite obsequiously, when she walked in, repeating "hello" over and over until it became clear that was the only English he knew. Anne's Thai was non-existent, but she made her point with hand gestures: "Cut hair," she said, making scissors out of her second and third fingers, and pushing them through her hair. "Short, very short," and she spread her thumb and index finger an inch apart, resting her thumb on her scalp.

"Shot. Shot," said the barber, furrowing his brow. Something here wasn't right. Then he turned to the pictures of hair styles lining the walls, pointing to women with long, straight, lustrous, black or brunette hair, the kind almost all Thai women had, arranged in various graceful shapes. He looked back at Anne, "Hello?" he said, pointing to her and then back to the pictures.

"No," said Anne, and to herself, "Not anymore." And then she saw a picture of a young Thai man with a crew cut, obviously an imitation of something he'd seen in a Western movie, his own dark hair a bare half-inch long. "Hello," she said, and repeated, "Hello, hello," moving her pointing finger back and forth between her head and the picture of the man.

Twenty minutes later she emerged from the shop, feeling the sun strike her scalp before putting on her hat. She had the directions, and the bus ticket, and the permission. She would get a little pillow to sit on, and she'd watched her femininity—looking good, thoughts of boyfriends, sex, marriage, children—fall to the floor of this tiny shop where the barber's only English was "hello." Somehow that was perfect. Hello to her new life, and goodbye to everything she couldn't fix.

***

She had signed on for a ninety-day course, the most intense experience offered to someone who hadn't taken formal vows. As the weeks wore on, she could see, and had enough ego left to quite enjoy, the grudging respect she had earned. She hadn't flaunted her femaleness or Americanness, had asked for nothing, and had not missed a single session in the meditation hall. She had talked to no one except Sirichai, the

English-speaking monk, and then kept her questions simple, often just brief descriptions of what she was experiencing. "Sometimes I am very sleepy." "The pain moves around." "Today I forgot what I was doing and it seemed like the hour was only a few minutes." "Yesterday I had a very bad headache all day."

She was content, and let the monk know she was, with his small stock of basic, Buddhist answers. "Return to breath." "Desires come and go. Not important." "Continue with your practice." "Remember Lord Buddha's teaching." This was not a place for the complexities of Buddhist philosophy—how they could believe that there was no self, yet there was reincarnation. Like a match transferring flame to another match and going out in the process, one author had suggested, admitting it was a pretty lame analogy and a pretty confusing doctrine.

Anne could see that all this talk was like the Zen story of the man who'd spent his whole life looking for the moon, not realizing it was in the sky and not on the ground. Finally, he saw it reflected in the water he'd cupped in his hands to drink and looked up, dropped the water and finally beheld the moon. The reflection—all the words and teaching and theories—was the discarded water. The moon, well that was what all this was about: enlightenment, true equanimity, boundless, undriven compassion, and having a life that didn't hurt so much.

***

During the tenth week there was a holiday: Buddha's birthday. The gateway to the Temple complex was decorated with flags with Buddhist sutras printed on them. Outside the gates, men and women set up small stalls, or simply laid out large cloths, and took out their wares: sweets and small colored toys for kids, used or cheap clothes for grownups, candles and incense to offer at the alter in the meditation hall, and Buddhist talismans for good luck. These were small amulets with images of Buddha on them that many villagers wore around their necks, or miniature statues of the Buddha—teaching, or meditating, or reclining in deep trance—that the faithful used to adorn their home alters.

Anne stood by the Temple gate and looked at the many sellers, the kids carrying balloons, the parents who'd come to pay their respects and also to make donations of food or money to the Temple monks. Because of the holiday, the most important one of the year, she actually had a few hours off from the rigid daily schedule. The morning session had started an hour later than usual; there had been more food; and an actual dessert following the usual rice, soup, vegetables, and fruit.

"Holiday," the head teacher had said to her, the day before. "You enjoy, o.k.?" And he had actually smiled at her. She smiled back, looking forward to a slight change in routine. And even more, she realized, enjoying the fact that he—that anyone—would smile at her. The seamless edge of seriousness of the place, almost but not quite self-importance, was the only thing that grated on her. She accepted the austerity, but she didn't feel she was doing anything all that important. Oh, it was important to her, virtually saving her life, she knew that. But it wasn't important to anyone else, nothing that justified pride or arrogance. And sometimes she felt that kind of pride from the monks, and even more from the westerners who seemed to be saying to themselves: "Look at me, meditating. My friends and family and the ordinary people back home, they are just living their regular lives, trapped in illusion." Every once in a while, The Voice would mock their pretensions, wondering *if they know just how stupid they look, playing at Buddhism when in the end they'll roll on back to the land of malls, air conditioning, and a job in daddy's law firm.*

As the neighboring villagers arrived for the festival, their first action was always to proceed to a place near the Temple where the head teacher and few other monks sat on cheap folding lawn chairs, waiting. Old men, middle-aged householders with small children, women who might have been widows, slender teenagers brimming with adolescent energy—they all bowed and kneeled and placed offerings in the hands of the monks, many of whom were strong young men who could have worked in the fields or in the small local machine shop to make money to buy their own food. *Look familiar?* The Voice mused. *Remind you of anything you read about in medieval Europe? Who works and who doesn't?*

At her next interview she asked Sirichai, making it as simple as she could: "The villagers, why do you take food and money from them?"

He sat back, just slightly, and reached up to straighten his robe, which didn't really need straightening.

"Always. This way. Since Lord Buddha."

"But why," she asked again, genuinely confused. This wasn't Catholicism, where the monks could somehow do something to improve the spiritual condition of laypeople. In this kind of Buddhism, everyone was out for themselves—stranded on the wrong side of the river of samsara, the endlessness of desire, seeking to make it across to the "other shore" of Enlightenment. The monks were trying to get there, just as she was; that was all.

"Why not grow your own food; earn your own money?" she persisted.

The Teacher's eyes narrowed slightly.

"Always. This. Way. Will no change." And with a flick of his hand indicated that the interview was over. She bowed respectfully, knowing by now that The Voice would have a field day with this one, then calculated that she had time to take her brief daily bath before the next meditation session and moved off swiftly and silently down the well-trod packed dirt path.

***

Soon after that Anne started to sit without the pillow. Nearly twelve weeks had passed, and she was so used to the discomfort of sitting for eleven hours a day that more discomfort didn't seem to matter. She simply didn't care if it hurt. And that was what she wanted. Not to care anymore. Even about The Voice. She would reach a moment of perfect peace in her meditation, and she might simply hear the sound of laughter that mocked, taking obvious pleasure in another's folly and self-deception. As her eyes casually took in the monks moving out of the hall, The Voice would murmur, *Fine looking bunch, too bad they live off the peasants, right?*

But she dismissed The Voice—answering back with her own inner laughter, her own gentle mockery. You are just a phantom, a nothingness made of memory and desire and the pain in my left hip. In a minute, in a moment, you will be gone.

Sirichai narrowed his eyes when she approached him outside of the allotted time and asked to speak to him.

He nodded curtly, and they walked in silence back to the office where she'd registered, the one place in the compound where she was entitled to talk.

"Gracious elder," she began, it was the formula that she had been instructed to use, even though she never knew if it was really correct, or if he even knew what the English words meant. But she kept her eyes modestly downcast, had made sure that her simple white garments were freshly washed, and that except for her neck, wrists, and ankles, none of her female flesh was on display.

"I am grateful, so grateful," she repeated, speaking as

slowly and clearly as she could. Usually he seemed to get what she said, but he said so little in return that she could never be sure. She slowly took out her wallet, put the amount of money she'd given at the start on the floor between them, placed her palms together, and bowed her head. "I want to stay another three months." And waited.

"Hmmm," came from the monk, a sound surprisingly like someone hemming and hawing in English.

"You. American. Go back. Easier life. Why be. Here?" To her surprise he leaned forward, and reached out with one thin finger, placed it under her chin, and lifted, so that her eyes had to meet his. This was not a stock answer. He'd understood what she said and known what to ask.

Her mind, medicated by hours of meditation, months of almost total silence, started to race. Why indeed? Why wasn't she with Lily and Patricia? Getting a job? Having love affairs? Seeing the latest movies? Spending a week on a beach in Jamaica or Mexico? Drinking heavily or smoking marijuana? Sleeping in a bed and watching TV? *Doing something for someone else*, The Voice added.

In a moment all that flashed through her mind, all that she didn't have here; and, she knew, would have very little of if she continued on this path. She was turning her back on what everyone she had ever known valued.

"Because," she spoke as slowly as she could, feeling like the simple thing she was about to say was a little like jumping off a cliff into thin air; or carefully stepping into a small boat, pushing off from shore, and not knowing where the current would take her.

"Because," she repeated, savoring the last moment of decision, the last moment in which part of her was in the old reality and part in the new, the last moment before she would abandon her old self, her old life, forever.

"Because here, I have known peace."

He stared into her eyes. What was he looking for? "Yes. You stay long. If want. And if want. Shave head."

Anne bowed once more—the slightest tear forming in each eye, feeling the boat oh so slowly pull away from the shore. She got to her feet, glanced at her watch to see that there were seventeen minutes until the next sitting. She would wash her face before. And afterwards find out where she could remove the last of her hair.

As she took a step towards the doorway the monk cleared his throat and called out to her.

"Miss Anne." She turned. What now?

"Do. No. Cling. To this. Peace. Cling. Nothing."

She bowed a last time. The Voice was silent.

***

From Framingham to Thailand, from Thailand to River of Compassion Buddhist Center of Northern California, where they'd needed an aspiring Buddhist student willing to work in the kitchen for virtually no wages. There had been no stopover at the house on the hill. Phone calls less often, simply silence when one of her parents asked her to come home and help. If they pressed, she would simply say, trying to fulfill the precept of honesty: "I simply cannot; I am too involved, too committed to the practice. I hope you are at peace and happy," borrowing from a traditional Buddhist invocation wishing that all beings "be at peace, be happy, be free from suffering."

And when it had all collapsed, she still stayed away. Her father desperately ill. Her mother's stroke. "Of course, for your family," the head teacher at the River of Compassion Center had reassured her both times, "you can go. Your place will be safe. When would you like to leave?" She hadn't answered; just thanked him and walked back to the kitchen. At the next meditation session, she had sobbed, for how long she didn't know—not a completely unusual occurrence in a hard-core Buddhist center, where people confronted, without relief, the pains of past and present. But then the tears stopped, she did her work in the kitchen, she meditated. When the head teacher asked her what she had decided, she tried not to see the surprise—was it disapproval?—in his eyes. But he had just nodded, and bowed ever so slightly. And that was that.

After five years, Anne progressed from cook to assistant teacher when a noted visiting dignitary, who was slated to take over teaching duties for a week, broke his ankle at the last minute and couldn't make his flight. The center's two main teachers had arranged to leave the center during that week for important family affairs or needed surgery.

"Anne," the tall, skinny, balding man, stroking his well-trimmed beard, asked. "Can you run the meditation sessions while we are gone? And the talks? I mean, you don't have to give a talk, not like we do" (their talks were always well received, and they'd both written several books about meditation and life and death and grief and the present moment) "of course. I mean, you could just read from one of our books, or from the sutras."

Anne spoke directly, with few words, as she always did. "Yes, I can." Nearly seven years of intense practice, thousands of hours looking inward. Extensive study of traditional materials and recent Buddhist writings. Even the beginnings of Pali and Sanskrit to help with the old texts, though so much had been translated into English it really wasn't necessary. Unless, of course, you wanted to be that much closer to what these people had originally thought.

"Do you have any questions for us? I mean, can we help you prepare something?" they asked, with a slight emphasis on "help."

"No, thank you," Anne answered. "It will be all right."

Anne's presentations were simple, clear, and irrefutable.

She answered questions directly, without going into rambling illustrations from her own life or recommending that students buy her books or DVDs. In the calm, even, unexpressive tone that would be her hallmark, she told the seventeen weekend meditators her vision of the truth. "You do not need to become something different. You do not need to save yourself or anyone else. You do not need to change. Except, to change the pattern of trying to change. Do not pursue. Do not avoid. Do not control. You will feel desire, fear, hatred. Of course. But you do not need to act on them. You merely need to let yourself be. And with constant practice the fires of desire and fear will slowly fade."

Several visitors during the week she taught left long evaluation forms praising her to the skies. And so at twenty-eight Anne became assistant teacher at one of the largest Buddhist centers on the West Coast. Four years later, two serious lay followers of the path, who also happened to have made a great deal of money creating a website for gay singles, asked her to come to Vermont as head teacher at a new center they were starting. All sorts of practical details, from lousy plumbing to emotionally needy students, would crop up. None of them bothered her. Her short book, *Nothing to be Done,* with its cover of her calm, unsmiling, accepting face, now completely shorn of hair, attracted enough students. She was content, at peace, purified from desire. Let The Voice say whatever it wanted. She would listen and ignore, as she had ignored so many other things.

Chapter 18
Anne

But now, so many years later, she could not ignore. She lay on the old mattress, with no pillow to support the increasingly tense muscles of her neck. She straightened the old woolen blanket over the cotton pants and t-shirt she slept in. She closed her eyes, focused on her breath, and waited for sleep to come. In. Out. In. Out. Thoughts are like clouds. They come and go. Sensations will pass. Beliefs and wishes are just composites, made of the skandas, meaning nothing, empty.

But sleep wouldn't come. Instead, once again, the memories.

Lily at the door of the house, wearing filthy cutoff jeans, and old red t-shirt with a picture of some anorexic male star who looked to be screaming. On her feet were tattered flip-flops, with blood from blisters oozing between her toes. She was cursing Joffrey, to be let in, given some food, some money, "At least a place where I can rest, Dad, you know, your daughter, yeah, yeah, your bad daughter, but still your daughter needs a place to put her head. You think you can manage that?"

Over and over the scene played itself out in her mind.

After the sleepless night, a vestige of awareness allowed her to notice the slight tremor in her hands, the uncalled-for irritation in her voice when a volunteer spilled a cup of tea on the dining room table and some splashed on her pants. Walking the grounds, she looked with distaste at the ragged edges of the window frames, the bare patches of earth in the middle of the small front lawn, how the third wooden step going up to the main building was rotting out. She had taken, not pleasure, but satisfaction, in this protected haven of mindfulness and acceptance, and now it just seemed small and broken and pathetic. A hiding place.

At the beginning of the afternoon meditation period, watching herself as if from a great distance, she walked over to the pile of meditation cushions, took one that was colored a deep purple, carried it to the slightly raised dais that was her place, and sat down on it. *Comfy?* The Voice asked. *What made you wait so long?* Wrong, wrong, wrong, she nearly screamed aloud. Comfort, self-care, greed, need. One after another, always, the iron law.

Could an internal voice smile without saying anything? It seemed this one could.

In the late afternoon discussion session, there were the all too familiar queries. How long should I meditate? When will I feel better? What are the best books to read on Buddhism? And she gave the usual answers: As long as you can. Is feeling better what you want? Whatever book you actually read, that's the best book.

And then a short, heavy set woman, perhaps in her late forties, with long brown hair, wearing dark blue active wear and a gray fleece top burst into tears. "I'm so sorry, so sorry," she kept repeating, as the sobs continued, and the other students sat in awkward uncertainty. "It's my daughter. She got hurt in an accident. The doctor gave her painkillers. And now. She can't get any more pills. She goes downtown. She acts crazy sometimes. And I found, Oh I'm so ashamed, how could I have let this happen? I found needles and a black spoon in her room." The sobs subsided. She blew her nose. Looked up at Anne, who was sitting, unmoving, her mouth a thin straight line, on her cushion. “Please, please tell me. What should I do?”

Anne didn’t answer. But the vision was clear in her mind. She would stand up, slowly walk over to this woman, wrap her hands around her fat neck, and squeeze the life out of her. All the while screaming: The answer is right in front of you. Here. Now. Sit. Watch your mind. Let yourself be. There’s nothing to be done.

Stunned by the clarity of the vision, and the way the desire to act it out left her muscles cramped and aching for action, her breathing ragged, the fingernails of her thumbs digging into her index fingers in the frustrated impulse to grip something and cause some pain, she rang the small bell by her side, indicating, some twelve minutes early, that the session was over. She walked out swiftly without uttering a word, hiding in her office for the rest of the day behind a locked door and an “In conference, please do not disturb” sign.

That night she lay in bed wondering if she was losing her mind—the mind she had watched, cultivated, and, she’d thought, virtually perfected. A mind that could serve her best interests in running the center, remembering to brush her teeth, get to sessions on time, and make sure her old car got yearly inspection stickers. Of course her mind still offered up its lusts and terrors, that’s just what minds did. But they had no power over her.

And they hadn’t, not for years. But now it seemed her mind had always been there, just waiting.

***

Let yourself be. Let yourself be. But who in God’s name was she now? Fantasies of attacking students, craving sugar and grabbing pillows. This was not her, couldn’t be her. But it was. She returned, again and again, to her breath. In. Out. In. Out.

The rise and fall of her chest. The spot at the base of the nose where breath enters the body. How many times had she repeated those phrases, first to herself, and then to students? How many times? In. Out. In. Out. The breath. The breath. The breath. But then the focus would fade, like a loud voice slowly becoming hushed and indistinct. Replaced by sounds of Lily, and Joffrey, and Patricia. And then images of chocolates, a thick woolen sweater to give her a bit of warmth in the early morning, and even a brief and vivid recollection of the one time she'd attempted sex.

Finally, at three in the morning, her body stiff from the nighttime chill, exhausted from the fruitless struggle to stop her mind, she wrapped the worn woolen blanket around her shivering shoulders and walked outside. A slight moon was hovering in the west, playing off some high thin clouds. Stars swept across the sky. A wood pigeon called out, and slight rustling sounds in the dead leaves indicated that she wasn't the only one awake. She tried to start over, as if she were not a revered teacher whom many thought wise, but a novice, a beginner. "Know nothing," one of the first books had advised, "knowledge is a limit, like a prison wall. If you know nothing, you can be free of the prison, and simply look at what is."

So if she didn't know anything, except, perhaps, that there was nothing to be done, why had she spent, by her rough calculation, around fifteen thousand hours meditating? But if she really knew *nothing*, maybe there *was* something to be done. Maybe the belief that there was nothing to be done, maybe that was just another prison. But that was crazy, they had tried everything to help, and nothing had worked.

And then The Voice, insistent, *What have you lost?*

Her thoughts stopped, stunned by an idea that seemed so alien, it was as if someone else's mind had accidentally leaked into hers.

Nonsense, she thought. Whatever I've given up, I've

gained the most important thing: peace of mind. This put her back on secure ground. "First of all," she began, in a calm, quiet voice, as if explaining something to a novice, "surely peace of mind is worth any sacrifice. Nothing could be more important. Second," she went on, a part of her wondering why she was stumbling around in the dark, on the edge of the center's dozen acres of woods, talking to herself, "I married the teaching, the practice, and then this place. I don't get up in the morning wishing for a better bed, or to be taking a daughter to soccer practice, or talking over family finances with a husband. When I sailed away from normal life, I never looked back."

What have you lost? The Voice persisted. It had mocked The Teacher for years. But now its questions were simple, direct, and more brutal than any sarcasm.

Pacing the forest path, seeking an answer that wouldn't come, she tripped over the jutting root of an old maple tree and sprawled on the ground, her forehead striking bare earth. And a plain, heartbreakingly unexpected realization told her that something else was possible.

***

A few days later she was in the nearby town, buying some needed supplies for the center's carpenter, depositing tuition checks from students. Next to the bank she noticed for the first time, even though no doubt she'd passed it countless times, a small store called, of all things, "True Love." Its brightly lit window was decorated with large vividly colored posters of ice cream: in small, silver dishes, smothered in fudge and crushed almonds, slopping out of tall scallop edged glasses, floating in a sea of seltzer and chocolate sauce. And suddenly a memory came to her, so vivid she had to stop walking and put her hand to her throat.

She was young, maybe seven, and Lily perhaps twelve. There had been a power outage from a violent summer storm: high winds, ferocious downpour, and fallen trees knocking down electric lines. As darkness fell, they gathered in a rare moment of solidarity in the kitchen, each of them sweating in the unmoving, humid July night while the soft candlelight covered their hurts and resentments. Then Joffrey walked over to the huge freezer and brought out two gallons of ice cream, both less than half eaten. A chocolate that they all loved, and a black raspberry that Patricia had a special fondness for.

"It's still damn hot," Joffrey said, "What the hell, this stuff will melt anyway." He walked over to the cutlery drawer, took out four of the expensive plate silver tablespoons, the kind you eat soup with, almost big enough to use as servers. "I'll get bowls," Patricia stood. Gently, with a smile, Joffrey pushed her back in her seat. "Who needs more dishes to wash?" he laughed. "Just make sure," and he furrowed his brow in mock severity, "You all keep passing the stuff."

And they did. They moved the gallon containers around, spilling some on the table, dripping off their chins, getting sticky fingers and lips. Joffrey and Patricia are laughing as a small chunk of raspberry slides down his chin and onto his neatly pressed short sleeve dress shirt. Then he reached over and kissed her, just a short peck really, on her lips, pretending to push some chocolate from his mouth into hers. They burst out laughing. Lily was smiling, actually smiling, as she shoveled in the melting sweetness.

Anne was giggling, part sheer joy and part relief that for once no one is angry, yelling, doing something that hurts. Then she took her spoon and flicked a bit of black raspberry at Lily, hitting her on the collar of her Backstreet Boys t-shirt. Lily swiveled and stared Anne down, and for a moment they all wondered if this would set her off. But she just gave a loud,

"Ha! More for me," and used her spoon to lift the bit to her mouth. She picked up a little of the chocolate and flicked it back at Anne, hitting her in the center of her forehead. Then, affecting an English accent, "And mawh, deah sistuh, for you." Anne looked at Patricia, who looked at Joffrey, who looked at Lily, and they all, yes all, succumbed to helpless giggles.

Anne could remember, as if it were yesterday, the creamy chocolate in her mouth and the precious feeling of knowing, for these few moments, that they were all happy.

***

So she enters True Love, noticing to her dismay that her hands are shaking slightly. This is wrong, this is desire, this will only breed unhappiness, she thinks, years of discipline rebelling at the very idea of unnecessary, self-indulgent food. She pretends to be studying the menu on the wall, with special flavors and endless possibilities handwritten in a smooth cursive script in different colors. Would a small bowl of chocolate make her sick with wanting at some future time? Wasn't this what she had been avoiding all these years? And just then, at that endless, elusive, precious present moment that so many of the books had talked about, her fear of desire is gone. A small dish of ice cream was not the incarnation of limitless desire, it was just a small helping of chocolate with—and here she almost bursts into hysterical laughter as she orders it—some hot fudge sauce as well. She holds off on the whipped cream. Must keep some limits, she smiles to herself, giggling like a schoolgirl, wondering if the few other people in the shop notice a small, mousy looking woman with a shaved head laughing into her sundae. And then, as if a wind has driven away the last of a lingering fog, she doesn't care about that either.

Driving slowly, the taste of the small dish still lingering, her smile lingering as well, Anne threads her way through the small country road's twists and turns. When twenty minutes later she reaches the small parking lot, at the end of the narrow pebble path that leads to the center, she turns off her engine and sits, unmoving, at the wheel.

Her mind keeps returning to the scene in the kitchen, the night of the blackout, the taste of the ice cream they had shared. She holds the memory up to the light of her mind, like an experienced jeweler studying a gem she's never seen before, but whose years of training ensure she would come to understand. What did those few moments mean? Lily was already deeply troubled, surely flirting with alcohol, if not fully engaged already. Before too long, Patricia and Joffrey would be terribly distant, even more than they were at that point, whatever feelings they had for each other erased by the never-ending ache of trying to deal with an illness that had no cure. And Anne? Like a shipwreck victim, she would cling to the only thing that seemed to float—her attempt to make someone, anyone, in the family happy. To help cure Lily, cure her parents, as the only way to cure herself. And then she would let go of the family ship and sail off on her one-person vehicle of meditation.

And suddenly she sees how wrong she has been. Nothing to be done? That was just a story she told herself. She could have told herself a different one. It was a prison, but maybe there was a way out. She gasps, shivers, screws her eyes shut as if to blot out a vision she cannot live with, then opens them as wide as possible to take it in. There was, yes, there was something to be done. She thinks she will cry, and then does—nearly retching as the sobs break through the last shreds of her carefully constructed composure. The sobs subside, she blows her nose on a paper napkin left over from the ice cream, then wipes the tears from her face with the sleeve of her old brown shirt—momentarily wondering why, for God's sake, she is wearing these drab, boring rags.

And then, surprise upon surprise, an enormous weight that she has been carrying since before she could remember, something she has taken as basic and inescapable as gravity, slowly leaves her. The relentless constriction of her arms, legs, belly, and above all her chest is gone. Slowly she gets out of the car, feeling as if she doesn't need to walk up the path, she can simply float, maybe even fly. Her lips curl up into a broad smile she couldn't have stopped even if she'd tried, which she doesn't. Each pebble on the path, the last yellow and white chrysanthemums of the fall, even the red brick of the center's chimney seem to glow with an ethereal, heartbreaking beauty. She is alive, and so is the world, every particle of it.

She enters the Center, nods to the three students who bow at her, goes into her office and closes the door. She picks up the phone and, one after another, makes two calls. They aren't long, but she says, and hears, what she needs. Once again she is in the boat, pushing off. But this time what she is leaving is her solitary battle with desire and grief; where she is headed, she has no idea, but it is not solitary, and not cloaked with fear, not anymore.

Chapter 19
Daniel and Sarah

"This must be what they mean by sacred." She pointed, and Daniel looked: the incredibly solid old maple and oak and beech trees on a little rise of land near the pond, bare branches reaching up, the rough bark unmoved by wind or rain, heat or cold, branches that in sixty days or so would be covered with thousands of leaves. But now it was all skeleton, the naked bones of the tree people. Some went almost at right angles to the trunk, then put shoots straight up, evenly spaced but getting smaller and smaller; others began at a forty-five degree angle, then changed directions to negotiate rival branches, or the way the sun's rays happen to fall, dividing into twigs smaller then her fingers, having started from a trunk that was far larger than she could put her arms around.

"Look. Each tree gripping the ground for dear life, and pleading to the sun for more energy—energy that these flimsy, two-dimensional nothings," she picked up a few dead leaves from the ground—"turn into sugar, and build trees out of. Could anything be more wonderful?"

She smiled at Daniel, looking supremely satisfied with herself, with him, with the trees in this small urban space, as they listened to ambulance sirens, the occasional motorcycle, and a large moving truck laboring on the Jamaicaway. "This is the only religion I'll ever have. Who wants a god without a body, who lives forever, who is everywhere and nowhere?" Her bold grin turned into a laugh as she spun on her toes, and seemed to drink in the sky, the water whipped by the wind, the geese floating in the corner of the pond where the shoreline of rocks gave way to dirt. She took Daniel's hand as they strolled the gentle curves that marked the northeast corner of the pond. The late March day had turned surprisingly warm, and though at 5:00 the sun was close to setting, it was still mild enough for a sweater and a light jacket. But now the late winter clouds masked the sun, and it reflected off the few parts of the pond that were still snow covered and frozen, looking almost like a full moon.

Two cormorants, small, gray water birds with webbed feet, dark lines on their brown wings, sharp yellow beaks and tiny green eyes, dove under the surface of the open water, coming up twenty seconds and thirty feet away. Sarah stopped, her face lit up with delight, and hugged Daniel as tight as she could.

Daniel returned the hug, but when she was like this, he just didn't know what to do. Where she saw arms reaching to the sky, he could see only the effects of acid rain and the way pesticides built up in the fat of the cormorants. Part of him wanted to get down on his knees, and beg her to teach him. But another part wondered if she was a little nuts. How could you know everything she knew and not be filled with anguish? How did she have the right—the right!—to be happy in this world of pain and loss?

Once he had asked her, straight out, a little afraid that her answer would be some weak spiritual pabulum about God or the Cosmic meaning of it all. "Look at the trees," she'd answered. "One dies, and one lives. Do the healthy ones mourn? Sit around grieving? Or just grab as much soil, sun, and water as they can?"

"But we are not trees," he'd fumed back at her, frustrated

that she seemed to just run away from the human responsibility to suffer with all those who suffer and are anxious about a darkening future.

"Why not learn from them?" she'd replied quietly. Then smiled and changed the subject.

Right now, he was stuck in the encounter they had just had with a man named Martin.

It had happened earlier that morning, when they arrived together at Sarah's office to find a large, bearded man, with dark gray eyes, long, straight, black hair, a prominent nose, dressed in blue jeans and a work shirt and a heavy cloth coat and work boots, sitting on the steps in front.

Sarah smiled at him, said good morning, and was about to pass him on the steps when he reached out and put a large, not very clean hand on her arm. Daniels's heart started to race immediately. Was this to be another threat—or worse—from people Sarah's work threatened?

"You Sarah Carson?" the man asked.

Sarah smiled again, and put her hand on top of his. "Yes, that's me."

The man stood, towering over her and Daniel both. He was well over six feet, his broad shoulders, long, flat face, and large forehead looming above them. "My name's Martin. Martin Brower. I come to you. I..." the power of his imposing physical being suddenly seemed to fade. Was that a catch in his throat? And his accent—surely this man had not grown up anywhere near Jamaica Plain. "I. We. Need some help. I heard, that's what you do. You help."

Sarah kept her hand on Martin's hand, looked up at him, her green eyes focused directly on his. "That's what I do. At least, I try." Then she removed the hand, stepped back and extended it. "Sarah Carson, pleased to meet you." They shook; her tiny hand and thin fingers easily swallowed up in his. "And this is Daniel Aiken, my friend and co-worker. He also tries to help." Martin looked Daniel up and down, his face unexpressive, his grip thankfully soft on Daniel's hand.

"Come in, Martin, and tell us what's going on."

They entered the small office with its large desk, neatly arranged manila folders, substantial desktop computer and slender notebook, and attachments for Sarah's smartphone, the large bulletin board covering one wall, to which more than twenty newspaper articles had been pinned, the small mobile of interestingly shaped driftwood that hung over the desk, and the serious looking, silver colored coffee maker that took pride of place along with a large bag of shade grown organic Costa Rican French roasted beans, with various organic sweeteners, sitting on top of a tiny fridge.

"I take it we'll all have some coffee?" Sarah asked, still smiling, moving towards the supplies. Daniel sat to the side in a wooden armchair, and Martin on the soft, well-worn tan couch that served when Sarah had visitors. They waited while the coffee was brewed and served, Martin's hands clasped in front of his stomach, Sarah fiddling with the coffee, Daniel hoping this wasn't the start of something that would threaten his precious time with Sarah. To him the long silence was awkward and nearly painful. But Sarah just hummed under her breath; and Martin seemed content to wait, his unmoving eyes fixed on his interlaced fingers. As they all gripped the steaming mugs and the fresh smell seemed to soften everyone's nerves, Sarah nodded encouragingly to Martin.

"I'm from West Virginia, small town, in the hills. Things, they've gotten real bad. See, we were poor, that's for sure, but we had each other, and the church. There was some farming, and a coal mine forty miles away, and the state park in the summer. Then that mine closed, and another one opened, right over us on the hilltop."

"On the hilltop, not in the ground," Daniel said softly. He knew where this was going.

"Yeah," Martin declared, his dark eyes burning, his body leaning forward on the coach, his fingers now held rigidly in front of his body. "They just take the top off the damn mountain. Rip it to pieces, take the coal and leave all the junk behind. Falling down the hillsides, poisoning the streams, killing everything.

"Before, well, before. Oh, I don't know." He stopped, his head lowering to study the coffee in his mug, then the floor. Daniel waited, sensing that this couldn't be easy. A big man, tough and probably used to things being hard and taking it, spilling his guts in front of strangers.

"There was this one spot next to a stream, where a dogwood tree always flowered in early April. It was," Daniel had a sense there might be some word he wanted to use but couldn't. "Kinda. Special. Well, the refuse from the mine blew out the stream, killed the trees." His voice softened, a kind of wonder, mixed with horror, shaping it. "On hot days the air would turn yellow, yellow air!—who can breathe that?" He stopped again. His voice lowered, but the ache that came through got louder. "My sister used to cough, and cough, and cough." His big hands twisted on each other, and suddenly he stood up.

"I went to the church leaders for help. 'We've got to fight this,' I told them. The pastor, the deacons, they didn't buy any of it. They called me a tree hugger, an environmentalist. 'Pray for patience, pray for a forgiving heart, that's the Christian way. Then you will get your reward in heaven.' *Heaven*," he made a face like someone had told him to kiss a rat, "that was going to be my *true* home."

"Later, a friend of mine told me he saw the deacon with a car, much better than the heap he'd been driving. And I heard the pastor got a church in some other town, one with no damn mine."

He looked around, clearly unaware he'd stood up, then sat

down, drank from his mug, and stared hard at Sarah, then at Daniel, waiting. Sarah gestured at the bulletin board, with its stories of island nations flooded by rising seas, tens of thousands of deaths from air pollution, mountains of garbage everywhere. “This is what we do, Martin. How can we help you?”

“I didn’t sell. Just about everyone else did. My place, it’s nothing special. Not like,” He gestured at the comfortable office, the well-kept homes with small, tidy, urban backyards, the smooth, paved streets with sidewalks, the slender young women carrying yoga mats on their way to fifty dollar haircuts, the shops filled with organic produce, micro brewed beer, and hybrid bicycles.

“But it’s mine. And it was my father’s. I’ll be goddamned if I’m going to let it go so those sons of bitches can eat more of the mountain. The blasting comes day and night. They can do it, it’s legal. But God I’m tellin’ you, no one should live like this, eight hundred feet away. In the house, no way to keep the dust out. In your eyes. In your mouth. All the trees they took out, so when it rains we get water on the road, in the yards, sweeping away some houses even. My well is no good anymore. Tasted awful. Dirty. Then the water just stopped. Some friends in the next town, twelve miles away, let me use their well, sometimes, at night. They don’t want anyone from the company seein’ them.

“Company goons come round, laughin’ at me, threatenin.’ Fancy lawyers shove papers at me, offer to buy; tell me they’ll sue me for obstructing business, and tell me they don’t need the land they just want to do me a favor. Every few weeks a new face. Sometimes warnin’, sometimes askin’.” He stopped, raised his palms in a “what do you know” gesture, and—for the first time since they had met him—smiled. “I figure if I ain’t so important, if they don’t need the land, well. They wouldn’t be coming ‘round quite so often.” The smiled broadened, then hardened into something closer to a snarl. "And if it hurts them, one hundredth, one millionth, of what they hurt me, well. That might be worth somethin'."

His face returned to what was probably its impassive norm. "You," he gestured at Sarah, "I got a cousin had a friend from the service in some town in Pennsylvania. Said you came in and did something about fracking. Helped it stop.

"So here I am."

"What you want. Tell me if I've got this right," Sarah began. "You want to be able to live in your house, in your place. That's number one." She stopped. Martin nodded. Daniel saw what she was doing. Move slow. Make sure you've understood. He wondered how often, if ever, Martin had gone to a woman for help.

"Number two, you want the blasting to stop. It's impossible to live with dynamite going off so close to your house." Again she waited. Another nod from Martin.

"Number three, you want your well back, if that's at all possible." Martin looked sharply at her. "I know it's probably not possible," Sarah added. "I just need to know what you want." He nodded again, slowly, letting her have her say. "And," she went on, "if it's not, you want some kind of recompense—some money—to make up for such a significant loss, due, no doubt, to the criminal negligence of the mining company." Martin nodded vigorously.

"Ultimately, I suppose, you'd like the mining stopped and the land put back, as much as possible, to what it was."

Martin just stared at her.

"Martin, let's be clear." Sarah leaned forward and put her hands, palms down, on the desk. She looked directly into his eyes, her gesture saying, I'm putting all my cards on the table.

"I don't know what we can do for you, and for the land and water. But I need to know what you want. That's where we start. I have no idea where we'll end up. Sometimes incredible things, wonderful things, happen. And too often it's not enough, or hardly anything. I can't promise any results; only that I'll try.

"Is there anything else you want?"

"Yeah. I'd like to hear somebody tell me, and the few folks that are left in my town, that God didn't create the world so we could piss on it—sorry for the language ma'am."

"Don't worry about your language with me, Martin," Sarah smiled at him. "Believe me I've heard—and said myself—a lot worse. And anyway," her smile faded, replaced by a set mouth, narrowed eyes, and hands that came up in small, determined fists, holding them as if she is ready to have a fist fight with the people who have hurt him so. "The truth is, you got trampled on; and mountaintop removal is a crime against life.

"If we can help you, we will."

After Martin left, Sarah set Daniel to research, and started making phone calls: to lawyers, researchers, friends in nearby states who might know something. Four hours later she pushed back from her desk, stretched her arms over her head and said that if she didn't get out of this office and away from this phone, she'd kill someone. "To the pond!" she commanded, and they grabbed their coats and walked the two blocks over.

And now, after the difficult interview with Martin, all the information she'd gotten—none of it particularly hopeful—now she was practically dancing around the pond, in love again, still, with the bare trees, the sun struggling through the clouds, the breeze making tiny waves on the water, the geese, and ducks and cormorants. Had she forgotten about Martin? Didn't she care? Of course she did, look at her work. But how could she be dancing when Martin was so beaten down?

***

"It's hopeless, isn't' it." Daniel's face was serious, but also a little childlike, as if he was hoping she could make it all better.

"Probably, but we'll see. You can't tell." They were at 30,000 feet, cruising towards Martin's home. "Sometimes you can get something from the EPA, sometimes from a local politician who hasn't been bought off."

"That's not what I'm talking about. I mean. Everything. We win a little, but the big things," he hesitated; they both knew what the big things were. "We won't stop them, we just won't."

Sarah smiled, patted his hand. He gently bent over and kissed the back of her wrist.

"You know, I've been doing this for almost twenty years now. God knows how many campaigns I've been on—how many losses. And we've won a few. We slowed down that awful dam complex in India, beat back the nut jobs when they tried to abolish the EPA. Hell, we've doubled fuel efficiency in U.S. cars. And we're not alone. Japan and Germany are going crazy putting solar energy in offices and homes."

Daniel sighed, started to answer. She could see him thinking of ten bad things for every good one. And how even the good ones were too little too late and easily overturned.

"But..." he started. She put a finger to his lips.

"It doesn't really matter, does it?"

He stared at her, clearly dumbfounded.

"Suppose you had a crystal ball and could see, oh, thirty years down the pike. And suppose all the terrible things happening now had only gotten worse. Drought and storms, wars over water shortages, the ocean even more fished out. And the cultural pollution worse—though that one is hard to imagine.

"Would you stop doing what we're doing? Stop caring? Stop trying?"

Daniel couldn't know that Gradenstein had posed the same question to her a few months before she'd graduated. She had come to him, distraught, in tears, about, of all things, the fate of Lake Aral —the world's fourth largest lake destroyed by upstream water taken to irrigate cotton, the consequent pollution from pesticides and fertilizers, the ruined economies and terrible illnesses of the neighboring villages, the eliminated species of fish and plants and insects.

And she had used almost the same words as Daniel. "We won't win, will we Professor?" Gradenstein had sighed and taken some sips from his vodka and orange juice and reminded her of the lame joke he'd used often enough in class.

"Look, Ms. Carson, you remember how I often say philosophy is like pornography?"

Oh God, she thought, not that one again. "Yes, yes. Lots of unrealistic examples. But what has that..."

And then he had described the crystal ball, and asked her what she would do. She didn't get it then. She didn't for some time. But somewhere along the line, after about six years of the work, she did. So now she could share it with Daniel. Dear, sweet Daniel. So kind, so devoted to the work, so broken by what he saw, and so infatuated with her. She quite liked him: the passion and hard work and intellectual sharpness buried under the caustic comments and the sloppy old professor's wardrobe. It was certainly a relief to be with someone who wasn't going to tell her "for Christ's sake Sarah, enough already." But this last thing, what Gradenstein had tried to teach her and she'd only learned six years later, she suspected Daniel didn't get. And that he never would.

***

Daniel took her hand again, kissed it. She was right, of course she was right. But sometimes he didn't care about being right.

He just wanted to be in some other world, where all this was gone. And if his rage, which he sometimes knew was a waste of energy, and only stole, yes, his peace of mind, would bring that other world a fraction of a fraction of an inch closer, he would feel it as deeply as he could. And if it was useless, well, all the more reason to feel it, just out of spite at the world for being what it was.

***

Later that day they were in Richwood, West Virginia, Martin's hometown, or what was left of it. The hills were so steep, and so close to the road, that the sun was only up for a few hours a day—the rest of the time everything was in shadow. Run down houses, small, tired-looking stores, beaten up cars and pickup trucks and beaten down people collected in tiny towns usually next to a small river or a large creek—population a hundred, or three hundred or, if it was the largest city around, maybe three thousand. As they'd flown into Charlotte, Sarah and Daniel had seen the beauty, and then the wreckage, of Appalachia. Green hill after green hill, separated by small valleys shaped by twisting waterways. Not really mountains, not like the Rockies, or even the Whites or the Greens, just an endless series of raised humps, maybe six, seven, eight hundred feet higher than the roads that wound through them, topped with small trees and thick underbrush, graced with streams and the occasional tiny pond.

And then, naked and violently exposed, rent by bulldozers the size of houses with tires twenty feet tall, and surface clearing drag lines the length of a city block, the planet's bare skin without the green—a series of pits and holes, where the life and fertile earth had been ripped off. Daniel reached over and grabbed Sarah's hand as they stared out of the plane window. He saw her close her eyes and whisper something under her breath, then lean closer to take in the sweep of devastation. Just from her side of the plane through the tiny window they could see more than twenty sites, brooding scars upon the land.

They met Martin at the last remaining store in Richwood, still in shadow at nearly ten in the morning, a combination service station and tiny general store, where people came for gas and coffee, beef jerky, and the occasional candy treat for the kids. Martin was waiting for them outside, leaning against an outer door with a ripped screen.

He had told them to rent a four-wheel drive vehicle, and he sat in front as Sarah drove with Daniel, pensive and clearly out of his normal ecosystem, sitting uneasily in the back. He sympathized with Martin's brooding anger, but didn't trust that the big man had it under control not to turn on them if they did something he didn't like, or if they ended up being just another hopeless attempt to defeat the monster that had eaten the land he loved. A small woman and a useless university professor would be easier targets than a global corporation worth billions.

He realized that Martin's long silences made him uncomfortable; and his obvious lack of education made Daniel worried he might use words Martin wouldn't understand. It bothered him that Martin probably thought that an overweight, overeducated guy who let a woman call most of the shots wasn't much of a man. Then he silently cursed himself for the stupidity of the whole line of thought, and wondered how Sarah, who quietly joked with Martin, or sat contentedly during the long silences, just seemed at home with everyone.

They followed the main road for a few miles, then took a side road up into the hills, which soon became hard packed dirt, and then, as Sarah downshifted into the series of bumps, gullies, and ruts, hard packed dirt alternating with mud, sand, puddles, and rocks. Aspen, white ash, and birch lined the road, gradually giving way to hemlock and pine as they slowly climbed, the late March sun glaring off the occasional puddles, finally making it over the sharply angled horizon. Sarah drove calmly, never rushing, but seeming to sense when to let the forward momentum of the car carry them across the larger ruts and mud patches, knowing that sometimes going too slow was as liable to mess you up as going too fast.

The road angled up once more, steeply rising and covered in loose stones. Sarah gunned the engine just enough to handle the slope, then muttered something under her breath as they had to make a hairpin turn across a series of sudden muddy ruts.

Abruptly, painfully, the woods just stopped. As far as they could see the earth was bare, scored with dirt tracks on which the monstrous machines moved. In several places, pits, hundreds of yards across, impossible to tell how deep, made bowl shaped markers in the ravaged landscape: *Here,* they said, *here there used to be coal. But we've taken it out, and left this barren waste in its place. You don't like it? Stop buying the coal.*

They got out of the car, Martin pointing to where the forest had been, where springs had bubbled forth from rocks, where he'd seen deer, where there used to be a sudden, unexplained patch of dogwood that would flower in early spring.

"Gone, all gone." His face, his tone, flat, expressionless. What was underneath all that, Daniel wondered. Underneath the dust in his mouth, and the dishes knocked off the dining room table by the dynamite. How did it enable him to hold on like a pit bull that had to be beaten into unconsciousness before you could pry him off whatever he'd sunk his teeth into?

Sarah and Daniel walked into the mining area. "You're not supposed to be here," Martin cautioned them. "Where the woods end, that's it."

"Oh well," Sarah said, "let's just see." She took a small, extremely expensive, digital camera out of her lightweight windbreaker, set the telephoto to wide angle, and started shooting pictures: of the woods behind them, of the enormous pits, the thirty and forty foot high machines which, even in the distance, would showed up just fine when she changed the camera to telephoto. She kept walking at a brisk pace further and further into the area, stopping to aim the camera, then moving on, the two men following behind.

Daniel felt like a fool, trailing her, not having the faintest idea what to do. He was, he realized, way out of his league. He could do research, track stories on the web, look up government reports, collate statistics on lung disease from coal plant emissions. But this? Being on the site? What in God's name could he do that local groups, or the Sierra Club or Greenpeace or God knows who else, hadn't done already? He felt terrible for Martin, for everything erased by the coal company. But, really, there was nothing to be done.

Sarah kept moving, taking pictures, walking towards the giant pits. Then she draped the camera over her shoulder on its long strap and took a small digital recorder out of another pocket. As she walked, she spoke quietly, holding it up to her mouth. She spoke so quietly Daniel and Martin could only hear fragments: "Forested area. Effects. Water. Air quality. Mental health. Community. Loss. Destroyed. Destroyed. Destroyed."

Daniel was so focused on the pit, and on the way Sarah was swapping the recorder for the camera and back again, that he didn't notice the bright red pick-up truck bearing down on them, a late-model 4x4 with the Beta Coal Company logo—the sun rising over a field with cows and a happy family. Martin cursed under his breath. Sarah took pictures of the truck, and then of four very large men dressed in jeans, work boots, and denim jackets, with baseball caps pulled low over their eyes. Two of them carried baseball bats and a third had a large pistol hanging off a belt low slung on his hip. The fourth man left the truck last. He was a little smaller than the rest, but still as big as Martin. He carried a silver travel coffee mug in one hand. In the other was a smart phone, into which he quietly talked. He sighed, balanced the mug on the hood of the truck, swiped the phone to turn it off, and walked slowly up to them.

"Good morning folks, out for a little sight-seeing? And Martin, so nice to see you again. I trust you haven't changed your mind about our generous offer. Or have you? And you're just showing your friends around as a kind of farewell before you sell," the voice suddenly became harder, just a little threatening, and tightly controlled, "and get the hell out of our way."

"Not selling to you sons of bitches. Not to anyone. If I'm in your way, I'm damn glad."

"Not surprised. Some folks just don't know what's good for them." He turned to Sarah and Daniel. "Do you know you're trespassing? And," again the tone changed. He moved forward and leaned towards them, "we've got laws against this sort of thing." He gestured at their bodies, at Sarah's camera.

Sarah smiled at the man. Daniel knew she had been through this sort of things before. "First they are polite," she had told him, letting him know what could happen, "then they threaten, then they get angry, but then–if they don't punch me in the mouth like they did at the oil refinery in Baton Rouge, or take a tire iron to my rented car, like in a uranium mine in Utah–I take what I've come for and get out fast." He had listened, his jaw dropping a bit. "You up for this?" she'd asked. "Look, really," and she'd put her hand over his, "no shame if you're not. There's so much to do, if you don't want to do this, that's just fine." He had swallowed, twice, unwilling to play the coward in front of Sarah, putting memories of schoolboy fights out of his mind. "I'll come, wouldn't miss it," he'd said, smiling, while hoping to God he didn't pass out or piss his pants if someone took a swing at him.

"Sarah Carson," she said, holding out her hand. "Friend of Martin, but also representing a variety of environmental groups located in several states, including this one. Here to make sure everything fits in with West Virginia's well-constructed and carefully applied environmental regulations. I'm sure you can imagine how important that is for all of us, your employers included." She smiled again, waited for him to shake her hand. He didn't move. She lowered her arm, the expression on her face never changing. "What's your name?" she asked brightly, her tone friendly, as if they were having a casual encounter at a restaurant or a ball game. Then she turned and looked directly, still smiling, at the other three men. "What are all your names?" When no one answered she took out her recorder and held it up. "Come on guys, I gave you mine. How about you give me yours? Only fair, right?"

"I'll give you fair," the leader muttered under his breath, and faster than Daniel could have thought possible, he lunged forward and ripped the recorder out of Sarah's hand, opened the back, took out the batteries and threw them over his shoulder. Then, staring right at Sarah, he dropped it on a large rock by the side of the dirt track and ground it to pieces under his boot.

"Hey," said Daniel, moving up towards Sarah. His heart pounded in his chest, his hands started to shake, and he felt his stomach clench. For a split second, he had an image of his living room, with its books and CDs and worn, comfortable chair, and wished for nothing else than to be sitting there, reading yet another environmental magazine. But on top of that image was a single compelling thought: protect her if you can. He tried to put his body between Sarah and the man who'd destroyed the recorder. The man just stared at him. Then slowly raised his arm and snapped his fingers once. With practiced efficiency the three other men quickly moved forward. One of them faked a jab and Daniel's head, and when Daniel instinctively threw up his hands to defend, punched him low and hard in the stomach. Daniel bent in half, suddenly seeing only the ground and fighting the urge to throw up. Then a short, anguished scream burst from his throat as the man kicked the side of his knee. An all too familiar pain ripped through it, and he collapsed, feeling stones scrape his hands and face. Through the haze of pain, he could see the other two men surround Martin, one of them drawing his gun and pointing it straight at Martin's head.

"Be a shame," the leader said, walking over to Martin, "after all we've been through together, to see you die for threatening Beta's employees, bringing people to help you sabotage the mine. On the other hand, you piece of shit, make one move and I'll be real glad to have my associate here put one right between your eyes." Martin was silent and unmoving. Daniel prayed he would stay that way. He knew the two blows had finished him. But what would they do to Sarah? A tense silence built among the seven of them, until Sarah broke it.

"I take it," she began calmly, her hands thrust into the pockets of her windbreaker. Was that to keep them from shaking, Daniel wondered? "You'd like us to leave." The leader walked back to her, slowly moving closer until his body was almost touching hers. With a swift, smooth motion he swung a fist at Sarah's face, stopping just in front of her eyes. She didn't move.

"I don't like men who hit women," he said slowly, drawing out each word. "Not what a man should do. But I'll tell you somethin' else. I don't like women who mess around in men's business. Who try to stop something that puts food on my kids' table. And does that for a lot of us. Get out of here. Don't come back. Or I won't stop. Not my fist, not those bats, not his gun. Got it?"

Once again there was an extended silence, Daniel now praying to himself that Sarah wouldn't do anything foolish. Slowly, staring calmly and directly at him, Sarah raised her hand and gently pushed the man's fist away from her face. "We will leave. For now." Her voice quiet, neutral, without tremor or supplication. "You have fists and bats and guns. Good for you. We'll see what we have." She turned, slowly walked over to the man holding the gun on Martin. "Please put that away. He and I have to help Daniel back to the car."

And slowly, painfully, that is what they did. One arm over each of their shoulders, Daniel tried to muffle his groans that wrenched through him with every step. The only other sounds were Sarah's heavy breathing at the effort of supporting him and Martin's whispered curses, over and over, too low to hear the words.

***

Sarah drove slowly and carefully back down the mountain. Daniel was in the front seat, his leg stretched in front of him. He'd snapped it forward a few times to bring the knee cap back to where it was supposed to be, remembering Sarah's instruction from their first meeting; and it wasn't as bad as that time. He'd survive the pain, but for a time was sunk in the intensity of his shame at being so useless. The lingering vestiges of masculine pride made him feel like a failure. Can't take care of your woman? What kind of man are you? Just a puny intellectual. Then the absurdity of the whole train of thought became clear. Would it really have helped the world for him to get a baseball bat to the side of his head?

He reached over and patted her knee. "I'll be o.k.," he

whispered.

She turned her head, gave him a brief smile, "I know," she said. "You're my hero." And put her attention back on the road. "Oh my God," he thought once again, "how does she do it?" And a small part of him wondered, with a stab of annoyance, why she wasn't angrier at the men who'd done this to him.

Where the dirt road met the state highway, someone was waiting for them. He had parked his Porsche SUV across the road so that they couldn't pass, not without trying to jump a culvert, where they'd probably lose an axle. Sarah braked the car and turned to Martin. "Let me try, you stay in the car. Probably less likely to come after me if you stay here, o.k.?" Martin nodded, but Sarah could a storm of rage in his eyes and the way his teeth were biting down on his lower lip.

Out of the Porsche climbed a medium sized man in a dark blue business suit, wearing a sparkling white dress shirt and an expensive looking red and blue striped tie. Incongruously, his pants legs were tucked into the top of scuffed and muddy work books, making him look as if he'd changed his mind about where he was going to work; or that he had two jobs, one as a financial analyst and the other as a day laborer. He had a bland face, with a neat small nose and small brown eyes, wore expensive sunglasses, and had carefully trimmed hair cut close to his head.

"Ms. Carson, I presume," he said, smiling slightly as he advanced on Sarah and took off his glasses. My name is Henderson, Alexander Henderson. Feel free to call me Alex." His smile broadened as he reached into his inside jacket pocket and Sarah flinched slightly. "No, no, not to worry. Just," he extended his hand, "my business card."

Sarah took the card, reading aloud: "Alexander Henderson, Beta Corporation, West Virginia Division, chief of public relations." She looked up. "Well, Mr. Henderson, I'm a member of the public, and believe me we've got some problems with our relations. Four of your employees assaulted my party, attacking my colleague Daniel, and threatening my friend Martin at gunpoint. They stole and then destroyed some of my personal equipment. Luckily, I have photos," she gestured to her camera, "of their vehicle and their faces."

"Really. How terrible. You see," he waited, clearly enjoying what was to come, "right about now those four employees are completing affidavits that they politely asked you to leave property on which you were trespassing, that in response you threatened them; that your man Daniel here took a swing at the foreman in the group, and that you, yes you, Ms. Carson, threw your digital recorder at another. In self-defense, they had to restrain Daniel and keep Martin—a well-known opponent of our little hilltop enterprise—from the violence for which he's so well-known."

Sarah's eyes narrowed. Was this a bluff on Henderson's part? Would any local policeman really believe that people who looked like her and Daniel would have gone after four goons on the hilltop?

"All right, Mr. Henderson. Let's just see who the police believe. You file your affidavit, and I'll file mine."

"Very good, very good. That's only fair. I will just tell you one other thing. The foreman you met up there? The one who generally does the talking and gives the orders in the few unfortunate cases of trespass or other nuisance? He has several brothers in this area. One is the local police chief, another is the town clerk."

He stopped. Waited. Sarah thought for a moment, realized this was pretty much game over. If something really serious had happened, they could have gone to the state authorities or even the FBI. But a few body blows and a broken recorder wouldn't get anyone's attention.

"All right, Mr. Henderson, score one for your side. Now if

you could move your car, we can get on with our day."

"Ms. Carson, let me say that we, that I, know who you are and what you do."

"And why is that?"

"I should think that for someone in your line of work it would be obvious: For the same reason you study us. We know what you did in in Pennsylvania, in North Carolina, and what you tried—and failed—to do in Minnesota and Baton Rouge. After all, your work and ours makes us, in a strange way, partners. You try to stop what we do and vice versa. You have your lists of so-called polluting corporations—and we have ours of—forgive the clichés, it's just business,—we have our lists of tree huggers, extremists, environmentalist whackos, job-killers, and eco-terrorists."

"And?" Sarah waited. This guy was no dummy, no empty suit. That was certain. But she was tired of the verbal games. Maybe Beta had won this round, but the game wasn't finished. And if she lost this one, there were plenty of others.

"And?" Henderson replied, as if Sarah had begun the conversation and he was politely waiting to see what was on her mind.

Sarah sighed, wondering how long Daniel would hold out with the pain in his knee, wanting to get him to ice and something more comfortable than the front seat of a car; and hoping Martin wouldn't lose his patience, come out of the car and beat the hell out of Henderson.

"Mr. Henderson. You know what really happened up there. Now you've blocked the road and assured me that the police won't take what I say seriously because of personal connections to my assailants. Is there anything else? For if there isn't, I'd like to get my colleague a little relief for his badly bruised knee."

"Straight to the point. What we've heard about you is quite, quite true." He smiled again. "I'd just like to say that although we clearly have something of an adversarial relationship right here, that I'm a big admirer of your work."

Sarah opened her eyes, then pressed her lips together in a dismissive frown.

"Oh yes, that toxic waste dump you stopped in that suburb of Philadelphia, the one so clearly related to environmental racism. That was brilliant, just brilliant. And the uranium poisoning in Utah. Terrible situation. You made a difference there, to be sure. Though not quite the difference you aimed at.

"But forgive me for my little digression."

"Little digression?" thought Sarah. Where did he learn to talk like this? Here in a part of the U.S. that often looked, and whose people were often treated, like a third world country being ripped off for its minerals by corporate behemoths from the north.

"I thought perhaps we could have a little talk, in somewhere a little more" he gestured at the dirt road on one side, the twisting, pot hole filled state road on the other, "hospitable to a, let us say, meeting of the minds. Perhaps each of us could get something that they want."

***

Three hours later they were seated in Henderson's office in Beta's regional headquarters. Martin had gone back to his small, beleaguered home; Daniel had been dropped off at their cheap motel with several bags of ice, a small bottle of Tylenol, a medium sized bottle of the best mediocre Scotch the local package store had in stock, some local bread and cheese and a fresh apple pie.

"Don't let him sweet talk you," he'd murmured to Sarah, and he lay down on the bed and she put a pillow under his throbbing knee.

She batted her eyes at him and then leaned over to kiss his cheek. "Only you, lover, you're the only sweet talker I listen to." Then she walked over to the door, giving her hips an exaggerated swing, looking back over her shoulder and batting her eyes again, looking like a not very good imitation of a femme fatal from a cheap movie.

Daniel burst out laughing, which reassured Sarah that he would survive without her, and went out to the parking lot where Henderson waited.

Henderson had ordered food for the two of them, all of it vegetarian: fresh baked whole wheat bread, bean dip, humus, thick lentil soup, bowls of almonds and cashews, and a platter of fruit. To her surprise Sarah realized the stress of the day, not to mention that she hadn't eaten since breakfast, had left her famished. While she ate, she let Henderson make small talk: about his upbringing in a Tennessee town not all that different from Martin's little place, about doing well in school and not doing very well at anything else, feeling estranged from most of the people but close to the schoolteachers who'd encouraged him to go to university on a special scholarship for rural applicants. How he'd always been good with words but had hated being poor, which had led to a joint degree in communication and business, which had led to an MBA in corporate public relations, which had led, more or less, to Beta, and to this meeting with Ms. Carson.

Sarah sipped her coffee, taken black and sweet, resisting the post-food lassitude trying to take over her mind. The flight from Boston, driving on the torturous roads, the struggle this morning, concern for Daniel's injury and empathy for Martin's long-term suffering—they'd taken their toll. She'd enjoyed the food, found Henderson both vaguely amusing and vaguely annoying, but was more than ready to find out what he wanted.

"Mr. Henderson, thanks for the food. You seem like a

smart man, and I'm sure you have all sorts of reasons," she waved her hand at the large office, the large building it was in, even the very expensive car he drove and clothes he wore, "for what you do. But you know who I am and what I do—and you seem well informed enough to have some idea what *my* reasons are.

"So just what are we doing here?"

"First, I just want to show you some pictures. Before and after, if you will." He opened the largest screened laptop Sarah had ever seen, placed it on the small table where the food dishes had been, swiveled it around for her to look at. "Just hit the right arrow to get to the next slide."

The first ten slides were a mix of horrible close-ups and horrible wide-angle shots of mountaintop removal sites. A brutal repetition of what she'd seen from the air and what she'd experienced, close up, this morning. After the seventh she looked up at Henderson, opened her hands, palms up, in a "What for?" gesture.

"Just keep on, Ms. Carson. You're almost halfway there."

After the tenth picture there was a slide with words. "That was before. Now see what Beta leaves you with."

There was a lot of grass. There was even a golf course next to more of a ravaged landscape. There were no ponds or streams, no forests, no place for wildlife, or herb gathering, or dogwood trees that would flower in early spring. The gigantic mounds of refuse that had filled the valleys were covered. So were the ponds that held the liquid waste, billions of gallons of it, which sometimes broke and brought more devastation. And there was no record of the contaminants that had seeped into all the waterways, poisoning them for tens or even hundreds of miles.

But it didn't *look* bad. If it was a cemetery for everything that had lived there, the graves had been filled and the lawn planted. It was a restoration that might fool the casual onlooker, the ignorant bureaucrat asked to give a permit, the voter in a referendum.

But of course it didn't fool Sarah.

"Do you have any idea, Mr. Henderson, how disgusting I find all this? First you murder the land, then you put lipstick on the corpse. Some of these places had a thousand different types of plants. There were animals, and insects, and trails and hidden little nooks for people to get to know the other beings that live on this planet." Her voice had raised, she sat forward on the edge of the expensive padded chair, all trace of fatigue gone. "You'll *never* get back what you've destroyed. Oh maybe, but I doubt it, you could recover the stream ecosystem in a thousand years. Maybe. You want me to be happy with this bad joke?

"Ms. Carson, I am sorry. I didn't mean to upset you."

"Skip the paternalism, Henderson, the point is Beta and its mining practices, not my feelings."

"The point," his voice still held its smooth, practiced, public quality, but she thought she detected a bit of a strain. It was getting harder to keep his cool in the face of her relentless refusal to be charmed.

"The point," he repeated, after clearing his throat, "is that *this*," he gestured to the last slide, thousands of acres of yellowing grass, "is what we can present to the public. You can offer facts and figures and articles about sludge ponds. But to the broader public, it's just a huge golf course, a backyard. And we've got the awards from the wildlife organizations, and our corporate membership in a national environmental group, to prove what stewards of the earth we are."

"And that's why you're talking to me," she answered slowly. "Because you know I'm not part of any group that has a 'corporate membership' option; I don't make deals; I don't trade green street cred for money."

"But why not," Henderson almost shouted, then he

remembered what he was doing, and lowered his voice, the salesman's charm returning. "We know what kind of shoestring operation you are on. Think, just *think*, what a difference it would make if you could hire research assistants; if you had more resources to travel; if you could be in touch with sympathetic people of enormous means who could help you transition from that tiny office in Jamaica Plain to something more like this." He pointed to the elegant furniture, the world class computer and, though invisible, Sarah knew, to his expense account and retirement plan. "And think, just think, of all the good you could do."

Sarah just laughed, her anger at the propaganda photos receding, replaced by genuine amusement that this breathtakingly huge industrial giant was trying to buy her, little Sarah Carson, and her one-woman, or lately one-woman and one-man, operation.

"Henderson, you're probably not a bad guy to your wife and kids,"—she had seen pictures on his desk. "And I imagine that you're pretty good at what you do. But to tell you the truth, I'm not tempted. Not for one. Single. Second. Because I know you'd want something, something I wouldn't give you if you were the last corporation in the world and I was someone whose home you destroyed, whose landscape you blew out. Your cheap energy is just too expensive. Martin, and his little town, and millions of people who get lung disease, and the damage fossil fuels are doing everywhere—try paying *their* bills, and see how much of this,"—she pointed to what he had, and meant all the rest that wasn't right in front of them—"you'll have left."

Now it was Henderson's turn to sigh. Sarah could see him gathering for a final effort.

"Ms. Carson." He stopped. Sighed again. "Oh hell," he said loudly, taking off his jacket and tossing it (strategically, carefully, Sarah noted), onto a chair, undoing his top shirt button and dramatically loosening his tie. "Look, can I call you Sarah, and please, please, call me Alex."

"Why not?"

"I *know* what you're talking about—the effects of mining, of taking down these beautiful mountains, of burning coal for power. But *this* is what people, all of us, *need*. We *need* more energy—to keep our standard of living going, for progress, so our kids will have a better life. Where would you plug in your computer? How would you turn on your lights at night or call your aging mother in another city or cook dinner? How could we produce cars—even that old Corolla you drive—or build homes or educate our kids or run hospitals? And what about the military—they are out there protecting our freedom, willing to die for us, and without electricity, the kind *we* provide, it would all stop.

"Renewables? Absolutely. A solar collector on every roof? I'm for that. Conservation, insulation, efficiency?—we've got labs working hard on all of those.

"But what about today, and tomorrow, and the day after? None of those green things are ready, you know that. So what do we do? We mine coal, we help the country run.

"It's too bad about Martin and his town. It's too bad about the deer and foxes who used to live in the forest and the fish in the streams. It's too bad about the lung disease from coal fired power plant emissions.

"But what do you think? That we can have all *this*,"—his eyes widened, his arms extended, fingers rigidly pointing at Chevy pickup trucks, six hundred million televisions, countless recharging smart phones whose design changed every ten months, the lights on in the office buildings and hospitals and university lecture rooms, and all the factories in the U.S. and China and Mexico and everywhere else going full steam ahead, day after month after year—"without burning oil and gas and, yes, coal?

"No omelet without broken eggs, Sarah, surely you can see that? No military victory without collateral damage to civilians. Some places, some people, too, I'm afraid, have to be sacrificed. It's too bad about the ones that don't make it, who get lost along the way so that the rest of us can have what we need. But I know, Beta knows, we can do much better in the future. We're on your side. Believe me, we are.

"Let's work together. Let's help each other. Let's help make it right.

"What do you say?"

"What do I say?" repeated Sarah. She felt a flash of sympathy for Henderson, so terribly lost that he didn't know he was. For a moment she wanted to agree, just to make him feel better. "I say: are you out of your mind? Do you really think all this is *necessary*? Do you think because people *want* something that it's good for them? Take a look at the destruction, the sickness, the loneliness and fear not very well masked by all the pills we hand out like candy, the dead land and the dying people and all the dead animals. Do you think this is a way of life worth sacrificing for?"

"It's what people want," Henderson snapped, his patience finally run out, his anger showing through. "Who are you to tell them to want something else?"

"I'm a human being, with a mind and a heart. And if I saw my mother or my brother destroying their lives with drugs, you think I'd say, 'Oh well, it's what they want, who am I to judge?' No, I'd try to stop it. And for me, the human race and this little green planet we're on are my family. I'm not about to put a gun to anyone's head, but if I can help make the water and air a little cleaner; if I can stop one-half of one-half of one-half of one percent of your mountaintop atrocities, you can bet I'll do it." She stood up, gathered her things. Her brief anger at his folly replaced with a deep sympathy for what this poor man had done to deal with his wounds.

"Goodbye, Mr. Henderson. I'll leave you with one thought. It's exaggerated, it's overdramatic—and that's not my usual style. But a long time ago I had a professor in college who made me read this book about a Nazi, a functionary who ran some concentration camps. Not a bad guy, really, not a sadist, not even someone who hated Jews. No, he just liked the uniform and the money and the power and being somebody. But years later, sitting in prison for war crimes, he talked to a journalist about his life. And you know what he said? 'I should have died,' is what he said, 'before it all happened.'

"Take a good look at who you work for, Henderson, who gives you your uniform and your money and your sense that you're somebody. Take a really good look. And make sure you don't end up like him."

Chapter 20
Daniel and Sarah

Past midnight, his house darkened except for the single bed lamp, the other side of the old mattress littered with environmental magazines, Daniel heard the phone ring and quickly answered.

"You o.k.? How is it going?"

"Fine, I mean, as fine as could be expected," Sarah answered, her voice thin but clear.

"And Martin?"

"I think. I think he's hanging in there, but I don't know. God, it really is awful. Just being there for a few hours, when the blasting starts you can't think, the dust is so thick you can barely see. It feels like the earth is going to just break apart and something awful will come out of it, or you'll fall in and never come back. Everyone picked up a little cough, just from the afternoon. And Martin, I don't know how he stands it, and he looks awful. Huge dark circles under his eyes, says he doesn't sleep much, his face gets red with this hacking cough. He's thinner than when we were down here. Doesn't seem to eat much."

"Well, you tried. God knows you tried."

"For sure. This was the last thing and it's not much but maybe it'll mean something. If not for Martin, maybe for the next folks about to get rolled over."

"All those calls you made. Still nothing, right?"

"I talked to experts on mining law, on conservation, not just coal but copper, uranium, silver, aluminum. All of it. People from the EPA, from state environmental. Even rights groups for Native Americans. Not that Martin is native but they face the damn mining interests all the time. Nothing, nothing, and for variety," she laughed, a little bitterness in it, "some more nothing. Just like Magnificent. The corporations give people what they want and take their money; the money buys the politicians, who stay bought.

"And now?" There had been something else, and she was doing it.

"Seemed to go pretty well. I was at Martin's house before they came. It's a ramshackle thing. Three rooms, outhouse out back, shed for tools. But inside, wow, he's got some really beautiful wooden stuff he made himself. Big oak dining room table, with little designs carved in the legs supporting this solid slab stained a great color. And some rocking chairs—no cushions, just these incredibly delicate curved slats for backs, stained again, no paint.

"'Been workin' with wood, long time now,' he told me. 'Some folks think I could sell.' He'd almost whispered, looked away. As if he was scared I'd think he was bragging.

"I told him I agreed, the pieces were beautiful. He smiled at that, and you saw him, he doesn't smile too often. Then he said," Daniel marveled at Sarah's easy imitation of Martin's mid-south drawl, "Well, I'm sure glad folks like 'em but I wouldn't take money. Just wouldn't. Give 'em away, sometimes. Gifts. Christmas. Somebody's birthday. Can't afford nothin' much from the store. But way I figure it, trees didn't take any money for the wood they give me, I shouldn't take money either.

"And then, oh Daniel, wait until you see, I can't get over it, he reached up to this shelf over the fireplace and took down this carved hawk. I mean, it's not great art, but you get a sense of the white and red stripes on the feathers from the staining, and the curve of the beak, and the tiny, vicious claws, and the shape of the wings, and the eyes. And he just gave it to me.

"I was so touched, I wanted to offer him money. It's so lovely. But I was pretty sure he would have been offended. It was his way of saying what he probably couldn't say in words. That he knows we're on his side."

Daniel swallowed, squinted, keeping the tears at bay. On his side? They sure were. And the good that it did Martin, outside of feeling a little less alone? More nothing.

"So they came around noon in this seriously big SUV; miracle that the GPS got them to the house. There were six of them. They call it, oh God, you'll love this," Daniel can hear the smile in her voice, and he smiles too. Everything with Martin had been so bleak, it was a brief relief to find something to smile at.

"They call it Mountaintop Removal Tours," as if they are going around Colonial Williamsburg or the historic synagogues of Prague."

"Who was there?"

"The driver, and I guess the one who was sort of in charge, was this incredibly rich woman from Louisville. Not sure where her money is from. Banking? Liquor? Real Estate? Anyway, she's an environmental fanatic like us. Organizes some festival every year in Louisville where they do a lot of the religious environmentalism stuff—lectures, music, prayer services. Gets all sorts of people involved."

"And with her?"

"Two professors from northern colleges who work on environmental ethics. A rabbi from Richmond doing social justice stuff, and, fairly big time this, an Episcopal Bishop from California. And his wife."

"How'd they take it?"

"These are good folks, willing to drive six hundred miles to look at a dying mountain. They were what you'd expect, shocked, horrified, sad. The professor, it was kind of touching, just sat down on a rock and cried. I heard him whisper, I think he was saying, 'They have no soul. No soul. No soul.' Then he and the rabbi said some kind of Jewish prayer for the dead. The bishop had this big wooden cross hanging around his neck. I could see him gripping it hard, as if he might break it. And he seemed to be talking to himself. Or, I don't know, maybe to God," she laughed again. Gently. No malice.

"Will this go anywhere?"

"Could be. Don't know. The professors talked about doing an issue on mountaintop removal in some academic journal they run. The bishop will try for a resolution from his church. And the woman, Christy, said she had folks for at least two more tours next month."

"How'd you leave it with Martin?"

"He was pleased, I think. Maybe, by now, he realizes there isn't much he can do. Except stick it out and try to help people see the truth. That's all."

"More nothing?"

"It's not what we want. That's for sure. But nothing? No, I don't think so." A long wait, Daniel still unsure of how to end the call.

"I'll see you soon, I hope," he finally said.

"Be back next week," she answered, her typical brightness tinged with a touch of sadness. "Stopping in D.C. to check on a few things. Meet me in my office around nine on Tuesday?"

"Yes, yes, yes," he couldn't keep the excitement out of his voice. And didn't try.

***

The first flowers of spring had appeared: crocuses pushing

their way through what was left of the grim urban snow; then yellow forsythia bushes, which comforted Daniel by their familiar presence at particular intersections or the lawns of some of the elegant old Victorian mansions on the quiet streets running between the center of Jamaica Plain and the pond. And now the first brilliant daffodils and jonquils, taking the shape of the crocuses and the colors of the forsythia and making two- and three-inch explosions of yellow that lit up the brown lawns.

Walking to Sarah's office, Daniel's mind kept returning to the spring weather. It was wonderful to be wearing only a light jacket, without gloves or a hat, and to walk on sidewalks without worrying that he'd slip on the ice and blow out his knee yet again. Yet he also knew that temperatures this high, for this many days, typically came a month later. Everyone else was thrilled by the warmth, and he enjoyed it too. But alongside his enjoyment was the nagging fear of what this meant. Too little snow, leading to countless communities short of water; rising oceans wiping out island nations in the Pacific; disordered relations between predators and prey, so that birds would hatch before the insects they needed for food were ready, so that the hatchlings would starve. And here in Jamaica Plain, cherry trees, magnolias, and forsythia—a riot of unplanned, unscheduled colors soon to die when the cold came back in the first week of April. Everyone who had the slightest awareness of climate change felt a distracting combination of pleasure at the sweetness of the gentle breezes and the lurking realization that this was not how it was supposed to be.

He would be talking to colleagues, or neighbors, or someone in a doctor's office, listening to them relish the blue skies and balmy temperatures. And he would say something bleak about omens of global warming. A silence would descend, as if he'd committed an unspeakable rudeness that polite and reasonable people should just ignore. Or he would say nothing, maybe add in a few innocuous assents of his own—feeling like a coward and a hypocrite.

He knew that millions of people cared, and tried, and grieved. But he also knew, as he knew he breathed and walked and thought, that they were losing. Yes, millions of young people had skipped school and marched. Bless them. But hundreds of millions had not. And then the marchers went back to school, and the hundreds of millions, the billions, kept driving, cooking, plugging in, swiping their credit cards and phone screens, littering the earth, the ocean and the atmosphere with their garbage. And in the meantime, even now, today, investment banks continued to pour trillions into fossil fuels.

He would talk to Sarah about this. She would help him. "People," she'd say, laughing at how wonderfully amusing they were. "What do you expect? And you have to admit, spring just is great." And he'd wonder how she could do everything she did and not hate what blind, avoiding, denying fools people were. How they had created a whole civilization that was, just like the Titanic, billed as invincible and about to go down, way down, and they couldn't even talk about it over coffee in the faculty lounge. Meanwhile, here was this glorious spring morning, and he'd barely noticed it the last four blocks. He was too busy mulling over everyone else's denial, his own feelings of isolation, the end of the world, and his lover's strange penchant for compartmentalizing her work and her enjoyment of life.

"Arrgh," he groaned aloud, getting a slightly frightened look from an elegantly dressed, elderly gentleman walking two beagles. And then he remembered something else Sarah had said, on the plane back from West Virginia, after her talk with the public relations guy, Henderson.

"I've been wondering," she began, "for a long time now.

It's something I used to talk about with Gradenstein. It's about responsibility and freedom and, I guess the only way to put it, about sanity as well.

"We look at the world and what do we say? I mean, about what people are doing. We say it's crazy, mad, just plain nuts. To be inflicting all these illnesses and losses on ourselves. On the earth, the air, the ocean. And all for what? For consumer society? For armies? So my company can do better and I'll get a raise?

"But look, Daniel. If we mean what we say, how can we be angry at the people doing it? Can you get angry at a crazy person? For being crazy? Wouldn't that be like being angry at a blind person for not noticing your new dress? Isn't that what crazy *means*—that people can't help what they think? So if people are so attached, so addicted, to this way of life, surely that's a sign of some deep illness. Isn't it?"

She hesitated, trying to get the thought just right.

"And maybe this is the final loss. We can have compassion for all the Hendersons and Sandra Smiths fleeing whatever demons haunt them and trying to get to a little happiness; for the super-rich who are as addicted to wealth and power as any addict addicted to heroin; for ordinary folks who can't see the big picture, because they've lost a job, or Mom is sick, or Dad is hitting the bottle too much. For all the people who think getting their kids into a good college or buying a better house or having the right wine with dinner are the most important things in the world. We can feel sad for them, but maybe we can't give them the respect of anger—because we know they aren't responsible. Any more than the schizophrenic who hears voices.

"But, who knows? Maybe even crazy people, even the worst of the alcoholics and addicts do have *some* control, at least some of them and at least some of the time. Schizophrenics can choose whether or not to take their meds, depressives can learn to exercise and meditate, even Odysseus, who knew he would be crazy, had himself tied to the mast."

Daniel had smiled, taken her hand in his and kissed it. "Any chance of recovery?"

"Well, it sure doesn't look like it, does it? But the thing is, every addict always looks like he'll never recover. Never. And some of them do."

***

The office was dark and seemed empty when he arrived, using the key she'd given him months ago. But as he switched on the overhead light, he saw her, sitting in a corner, wearing running shoes and a sweat-stained t-shirt with a picture of two jaguars on it, her head in her hands. "The light," she said softly, "turn it off."

He did and then knelt down beside her, his heart thumping in his chest, his hands instantly sweaty. "Sarah, are you? What's wrong?" He wanted to take her in his arms, carefully examine every inch of her body, do an immediate x-ray, MRI, CT scan and anything else to see if she was hurt in some way, and if there was anything he could do to help.

"I'm. No. It's not me. It's just." She looked up and he could see tears streaming down her cheeks, and wet patches on the collar of her shirt indicating she'd been crying already. This was not the Sarah who fought the good fight and then danced around the pond delighting in oak trees and sea gulls.

"I heard this morning. It's Martin. Found dead in his house. Overdose of sleeping pills. The noise, the dust, the way he felt. Couldn't sleep. Did he take too many? Mix them with alcohol? Did someone do something to him? And there was a terrible rainstorm the next day, so any tire tracks leading up to his place would have been erased. Oh God, I don't know if he did it or they..." She broke then, sobbing softly on and on, reaching up to hold on to Daniel, this frail friend of hers.

Daniel held her, thinking of the big man's fierce attachment to his little house, his tiny town, the corpse of his mountain. Would he really have been willing to let all that go? Could he have been that depressed? Didn't seem like him, even though Daniel recognized they hadn't exactly been best buddies, and you could never tell for sure.

Sarah's tears subsided, she blew her nose, untangled from Daniel and murmured her thanks. "What do you think," he asked. "Did he do it?"

"Oh God, I don't know. I mean, he was pretty down when I told him there wasn't anything I could do. That the law wouldn't help. But the tour we set up seemed to help, a little, anyway. Told me he wanted to see if the Bishop could do something, appreciated an important Christian cared about the mountains. When I left, he raised his hand, didn't wave. Just held it up there, palm facing out. Was he thinking he couldn't take it anymore? Wanting to give up, finally?"

She stopped talking. Daniel searched for something to say. He felt lost in grief for the big brave man, another sacrificial offering to the way they all lived. But he couldn't think of anything that would make Sarah feel better, just as she really couldn't know if it had been an accident, suicide, or murder. Just as there were so many things they didn't know, and had to carry on anyway, lost in doubt and ignorance so much of the time.

Sarah hugged him tighter, then got up and stood in front of the window. "I don't think he did it. But there's no evidence. You heard who the police are down there. We'll just have to let this one go." She looked at Daniel, at the floor. At the ceiling. Out the window at the still bare maple trees that lined the street. She started to cry again. "Dammit," she whispered, closing her eyes, leaning her forehead against the glass, "dammit to hell."

***

Three weeks later they were strolling up one of Jamaica Plain's pretty side streets. Aptly named "Spring Park," it led from the subway line up to Centre Street a half mile away. It was early May, in the late afternoon. Suddenly the sun broke through low clouds and made the magical squall light of a brightening horizon and a still dark, threatening sky. The warmth of the sunlight illuminated the cold gray clouds, making the myriad colors of the flowering bushes reflect in the countless drops of rain which dotted their surfaces. There were Rhododendron, most of the lush buds in three different shades of purple, and a few in orange or red, the long stamens with their thick ends waving enticingly; the last of the pink and white Azaleas, the Rhodos' smaller, less dramatic cousin, almost but not quite beginning to wither; lilacs that you could smell from fifteen feet away, a dwarf Japanese maple positively glowing in deep red, low lying poppies bursting with energy; and three different types of irises, mostly purple and blue, but a few of the bearded hybrid with yellow and white petals and a pistil that looked like a tiny, furry caterpillar lying in the center. As they walked slowly towards Centre Street, bending to sniff, exclaiming to each other over the shape of this petal, the brilliance of that color, or the tiny details of one particular iris.

They had been to a meeting with some other environmentalists downtown, and were walking back to Sarah's office to check some records of legal actions used to require better handling of non-source point water pollution. "Oh lord," Sarah said, "the research will wait. I mean, even if we don't do it for a few days. Probably the environmental crisis will still be with us, right?" They both laughed. Daniel waited expectantly, having a pretty good idea of what she would suggest, what she almost always suggested when she was feeling good, and even more likely on those rare times when she just couldn't stand it anymore. In fact, this time he'd beat her to it. "To the pond!" he shouted, raising his hand over his head and pointing his finger like a general commanding the troops to charge a hilltop fort.

"Oh yes," Sarah practically purred, "to the pond." On they strolled, now arm in arm, crossing Centre Street and passing a small bakery which sold pretty much only bread that was driven down from Maine every day, a dairy free ice cream shop where everything was made from almonds, three gas stations, a dry cleaner, and a trendy restaurant tucked into two tiny rooms that offered dishes like artisanal spaghetti and borscht made with yellow beets. Turning from the main drag onto the street that led to the pond, they could see that there was about to be a world class sunset. Thin cirrus clouds were low to the ground, near but not blocking the sun. In the east, giant puffy cumulous took on the pink from the changing sky, and the whole sky, from west to east, celebrated the end of another day in this particular part of the planet.

"Quick," said Sarah, and started to run towards the pond, Daniel laughing and stumbling behind her, thinking for the hundredth time that she was too young for him, or he was too old for her, or that something this good couldn't possibly last.

Two small Elizabethan structures made what everyone called "The Boathouse," the only buildings on the sidewalk that bordered the pond. One was essentially a small room that had years ago sold ice cream and candy and hot dogs, and now was an office for the renting of sailboats and kayaks. Across a paved area with a fountain there was a Parks Department Office below, and above a kind of open, roofed terrace. Sarah sprinted up the steps to the terrace, Daniel following behind, his breath ragged in his chest. They went to the edge overlooking the water, and saw the reflection of luminous sunset colors in the water, the last of the sun sinking below the wooded hills, not formally part of the park, but which gave them the remarkable experience of watching a resplendent sunset over a forest and a not insignificant body of water—still within a major, modern city.

Sarah put her hands in front of her chest, palms together like a prayer or the gesture Hindus use to say hello. "Thank you, thank you, thank you," she whispered. "Thank you, sun, and clouds, and water; and people for protecting this place, and letting us be in it." She rubbed her palms together and placed them gently over her eyes. "Thank you, eyes," and, patting her arms and legs, "thank you, body, for carrying me here." Turning to Daniel, "And thank you, friend, for being here with me."

Daniel couldn't speak. He just took her hand and kissed it, over and over. How had she come to him? And what would he do if she ever went away? It was never a word he would have used before he met her; never a thought that would have entered his head; and if he'd said anything like this she would have laughed in his face and made a joke about the way she farted or pigged out on chocolate. But. There it was. If there were saints in the world, then she was one. An improbable saint wearing battered running shoes, loose-fitting light weight jeans, a long sleeve cotton shirt with a picture of an eagle, and a bright red windbreaker; her short brown hair swept off her forehead with a red headband, faded lipstick matching her jacket, and eyes that seemed to caress everything she saw.

PART V

Chapter 21
Daniel and Sarah, and the others

Six months later Jamaica Plain was covered with snow, and most of what was under the snow was frozen. An early December storm ("Where is global warming when we need it, ha ha" laughed the weathermen) had blanketed the city in nearly a foot of light, dry flakes, and afterwards the temperature had taken a real nose dive, leaving them several degrees under freezing for days. In the streets, there was a recurrent sound of tires spinning in drifts, people cursing when their batteries died, or yelling in pain as they slipped on patches of ice. Almost no one was out walking except those who had to take the bus to work, or the relentless dog walkers who knew that it really didn't matter how frozen or forbidding, Fido needed his time outside.

And now, the coldest night so far, Daniel and Sarah were at a meeting in the basement of Jamaica Plain's solid, stone Unitarian church. They weren't alone. Packed in beside them, sitting on hard wooden benches, standing along the wall, spilling out into the corridor because there just wasn't enough room, were over a hundred people who'd come to listen, speak, and above all protest something that was about to break their hearts.

It was the wooded hillside, the one just to the west of the pond, the one that gave them all a view of forest as they looked across the pond from its long eastern shore. The hills were owned by a Christian seminary located higher up the hill, and someone was thinking that the forested area would be just perfect for some upscale condos.

He was a medium sized man, with large brown eyes, a broad forehead, a small nose, and a perfect shave. Thin lips smiled often, but rarely broke into a full grin. His company, the Eastern Development Group, knew exactly what it wanted and how to make it happen, as Mr. Lawrence Pillington explained to the crowd: "Some of the trees—not too many, you understand, since we have to build, put in sewers and electricity and gas lines, and you have to have nice roads and garages, and enough units to make back our investment—will stay. And the view! My goodness, what a view these lucky owners of homes in the Peaceful Shores community will have. Sunrise over the pond. Several of the area's best parks a stone's throw away. And often just a fifteen-minute drive downtown.

"And don't forget the construction jobs. The real estate taxes to the local community. Lovely homes for solid, tax-paying, upstanding young couples and families. Smaller ones for empty nesters. Just the kind you want in your community. When right now, well, the woods are nice, for sure. But what good are they doing, really? Shouldn't they be used for people? Isn't that what they are for? And anyone who disagrees, remember: where *you* live, right this moment, used to be woods or something like it."

It wasn't flying, not a bit of it, not with this crowd. Leftover radicals from the sixties, with bald heads or gray hair, wearing flannel shirts and down vests and talking about civil disobedience to stop "Any development of the people's space." Lesbian couples who explained how they first met walking around the pond, how it was where they would bring their children—to sit on the terrace and look at the geese and learn to love the trees on the hillside. To Daniel's surprise, there were people from the suburbs, from ten or fifteen miles away, who regularly drove into Boston just to walk around the pond. There were joggers, poets who found inspiration in the view, and an attorney in a perfectly pressed pinstriped suit who said that after a day being a lawyer, an hour at the pond was the only thing that kept him sane.

A woman in a powered wheelchair said that the boathouse was a place for her. She would roll down to the edge of the sailboat dock and look across the water and that would be the highpoint of her week, since that was about all the outside time she could manage, what with the weakness, the headaches, the fevers, the body aches and the nausea. "The pond," she said quietly, but in a voice everyone could hear, almost but not quite apologetic about whatever illness had done this to her, "it's my medicine." She looked over at Pillington, who had sat in stony silence while everyone else talked. "Please," she begged, "please don't change it."

Finally, a gray-haired man with a short, scruffy beard, his down jacket draped over one arm, came to the mic. Sarah and Daniel had seen him many times—walking his dog, jogging slowly and panting heavily in the summer, sometimes pointing out a beautiful gray heron that stood in the shallow water to a passerby who no doubt initially wondered what the hell this guy wanted.

"I am going," he began, "to use a word that we don't usually hear at political meetings in this country. No, we don't." He waited. Looking around the room at the faces, milking the moment. Whatever this guy does, Daniel thought, he knows how to handle an audience. "The pond," he went on, "is sacred space." A shocked silence fell over the crowd. The man waited again. Daniel, his own professorial experience of judging the reaction of students in a large lecture kicking in, could see that the guy had hit a nerve, a big one.

"I am not talking," the man went on, "about who owns the land. About legal rights, economic development, or the glory of condo living in the big city. All that is true, but in this case, it is not important. What is important is that the pond is sacred, and it is sacred because of what it means to us all,"—his arms, which had been resting by his sides, raised and opened as if to embrace—"and what it means to the seagulls and geese and ducks and cormorants; to the fish and the flowers; and to whatever lives under the trees in those hills.

"How many times," he paused again, "How many times have you gone to the pond feeling awful and come back feeling better? Gone without hope and come back feeling life was worth living?"

Murmured assents ran through the crowd.

"That is why the pond is sacred. And that is why," he walked over to Pillington, stared at him long and hard, "that is why we will defend it: without violence, without hatred, but with whatever it takes to keep it the way it is for just as long as we can."

He returned to his seat, nodding a bit to the long and loud applause; and Daniel thought he saw him wipe his eyes.

***

Daniel and Sarah had applauded along with the rest of them, knowing that the man had captured something many, if not most, of the audience felt. And so along with another dozen audience members they'd started the Defend Our Pond Association, with the unfortunate acronym of DOPA. "What can you do," Sarah had laughed, "at least it's easy to remember."

There had been meetings, a good number of them. Discussions with lawyers, with members of various state commissions, even an attempted meeting with the governor.

Because condos were relatively clean, they couldn't push a pollution angle, and they could see the local pols already figuring out how to spend the increased tax revenue. The state boards, they heard over and over, were limited by the fact that this was, after all, "private property, not under the control of the government, limited to what we can do, certainly appreciate your concern, I've walked around the pond myself, beautiful spot, but don't worry, of course the pond itself is safe, nothing anyone can do to touch that, we must respect property rights, above all, I'm sure you agree, so sorry we couldn't be of more help, thanks so much for contacting us, is there anything else I can help you with?"

No, there wasn't.

The worst was when the governor's chief of staff, who was an old friend of an old friend of a member of DOPA, had them slated for a fifteen minute meeting in between an appearance at the funeral of a state cop who'd been hit by a drunk driver and a fundraiser for a buddy running for State Senate. But when the governor heard what it was about, and when the name of Pillington was checked against the list of the governor's fifty top contributors, the fifteen minutes suddenly evaporated, the governor being "much too busy, really sorry folks, do put everything in writing and I'll do my best to bring it to his attention, and I'm sure he'll get back to you just as soon as he can. I'm *sure* you appreciate how much he has on his plate right now."

They didn't appreciate, not one bit.

No legal case; no government help; no interested, sympathetic officials. Even the local newspapers hadn't been that concerned. A small article in the city section of the Boston *Globe* presented "both sides," but pitched it as a fight between "extreme environmental activists like Sarah Carson, who has thrown herself into every environmental fight one can think of, some meaningful and some, many would say, a bit frivolous"; and a responsible real estate developer out to create well-crafted, livable homes in an environmentally responsible way, and not incidentally raise the tax base and create dozens of construction jobs. The points of view of the trees, squirrels, chipmunks, skunks, occasional deer (Daniel had actually seen one, not twenty feet from the pond, one evening in late November), coyote, badgers, possum, at least seven bird species and countless worms and insects were not considered relevant.

They had worked through the winter, and spring was fast upon them. Groundbreaking would start at the beginning of May. It was to be a quiet beginning, no fuss or fanfare. A huge transfer truck would deposit a specially equipped bulldozer at the edge of the property. A path of trees to be demolished would have been marked with orange paint. The bulldozer would begin knocking the trees down, ripping their stumps out of the ground, clearing the land for people.

***

"Over my dead body," said Sarah, pulling a grim face and narrowing her eyes. Daniel and the other DOPA member turned to her. Then she laughed, and said quite calmly, "I really don't think that the bulldozer will run over a poor, defenseless little woman. Especially one,"—she struck a pose and moved her shoulders back and forth in an "aren't I cute" gesture—"as breathtakingly beautiful as I am." She laughed again. "I will bring my own chains—it's so much more convenient. I will be chained to a tree. Hopefully, so will some others. The more people we could have chained up like that, the better it will be. We will have a whole bunch of onlookers with their phones taking pictures and videos, tweeting, sending out Instagrams, doing Facebook Live. A little group like us in this room just asking questions, nobody cares. But think of the play on the evening news and social media, when you see five or ten or however many folks we can get, chained to the trees, facing down the bulldozer."

People hemmed and hawed, and in the end only a few were willing to go along with her, though all the rest vowed to help generate publicity, get a legal defense team ready, take pictures, and contact the press.

Later that evening, lying together in Daniel's bed, in one of the rare times she consented to sleep over at his house, Daniel had second thoughts.

"Are you sure, I mean, are you sure this is the right issue for something this extreme? It's not like the oil companies destroying the villages in Nigeria. It's just a few acres of forest and some condos. Who will take it all that seriously?" He didn't add, he didn't have to: "And what if something goes wrong?" Suddenly the fear swept over him. First the cough she'd had from the fishkillers. Then the scene on the mountaintop—men with clubs and guns, a brutal fist a fraction of an inch from her face. How many times would she expose herself? What would she have to sacrifice for this? What would he?

She rolled over on her side to look at him, her post-sex lassitude evaporating, her other passion, the one that guided her life day in and day out, returning in a rush. She reached out and ran her fingers down his face, lingering on his perennially stiff neck. Her tone was calm, almost a whisper, but Daniel could feel every ounce of her spirit behind it.

"I take it seriously, Daniel. I take it very seriously. That hillside, those trees, they are part of my community, part of the lives of all those people who came to the meeting and thousands, tens of thousands, of others. You're right, it's not as bad as a lot of other things. God knows it doesn't compare to what Martin went through. But this is *my* neighborhood, those trees are my friends, my family. I don't care how silly that would sound to most people—I don't know, maybe it sounds silly to you." Was there a hint of sadness in her tone?

She waited. He shook his head. "No, Sarah, nothing you've ever said has sounded silly to me. I just don't quite get it."

She leaned over and kissed him, passionately. He kissed back, marveling that a little gesture like that could make his sex stir so soon after.

"Then I'll try to explain. I'd really like you to understand." She stopped, collecting the words.

"We're here." She nodded at the room, the world beyond, maybe even the universe filled with galaxies. "And it's a miracle. Not a God miracle, not that kind. But a miracle. That anything exists, that there is an earth, that there's life, that there are people and houses and language and music and wine. And that all the other life is here with us. Does it hurt, when we lose something? When fish are wiped out, or the mountains get blown to bits, or someone like Martin dies? Sure, it hurts." She waited. He knew she felt the pain of the world. Sometimes he thought she felt every bit of it.

"Yet." Her voice lowered, now it really was a whisper, but somehow it was even more intense, an indomitable cry too strong to be shouted. "It's still a miracle. And that's why I have to defend it. And it really doesn't matter whether it's here or there, Martin's mountain or a kid choking on fumes or the babies born with a hundred toxins in their blood." She stopped. She was regular old Sarah again, who was far more likely to make a joke about how messy her clothes were or how dumb some government regulation was than to try to explain what Gradenstein would no doubt have called her "quasi-pagan world view combined with essentially reformist politics."

She laughed again, kissed him gently on his forehead, his chin, and the base of his neck, curled up into a small, fetal position, her head resting on her the back of her outstretched hands. Her breathing slowed, her body sank into the mattress, completely relaxed.

***

Kevin Marshall had always been big—a big baby, a big kid, a big tackle on the Dorchester High School football team, a big marine who'd help construct airbases in Iraq. Now the bigness was turning to fat as the stress built up and his idea of how to deal with it was coffee cake and Swiss chocolate at the end of each day. Having worked his way up from day laborer to foreman to highly skilled contractor he didn't have to dress in jeans and work boots anymore. He favored wash-and-wear gray slacks made to fit over his growing beer belly, black shirts with gray ties, a hard hat, and, when necessary, a lined woolen jacket. The wardrobe made him, he felt, look the part. And that was how he had created and sustained KM Builders over the last six years. It hadn't hurt that an old friend had become head of hiring construction workers for the local state university or that his neighborhood had enjoyed a surprising round of gentrification. But it was also true that he knew what he was doing and did it well.

Lately, however, the building trades were just, well, if "dead" wasn't the right word, in a "pretty bad coma" would capture it. The condo boom fell flat, money for new state buildings went into free fall, existing office space went begging so new offices were completely off the table.

On top of that, life in the Marshall household was way less than perfect. Kevin had two teenage daughters, both in the local parochial school, and both monumentally hostile to their teachers, the school's rules, and virtually anything out of Kevin's mouth. He suspected they drank, and probably smoked pot. Everyone said that almost all the kids did: whether in parochial school, private school, or just the dead-end public school that seemed to have as many policemen hanging around as gym teachers.

And he also suspected they were having sex with their boyfriends. He had tried to talk to them about protection, sexually transmitted diseases, the role of intimacy in love-making, waiting until you were sure, the sanctity of marriage—and he always got the same response. "Ewww, daddy, for-God's-sake-shut-up-I-don't-want-to-hear-it-that's-gross-how-can-you-talk-to-me-about-that-so-perverted leave me alone get *out* of my room."

And why was he, the father, talking about sex to his teenage daughters? Because his wife, their mother, had lost interest years ago. In him, in the kids, in the house. She was, said the family doctor, depressed, not uncommon in middle-aged women. Periodically she would rouse herself: register for a part time degree in business, try to get a license to sell real estate, get deeply involved in meditation or yoga. But it never lasted. She would return to her favored couch, endless cups of iced tea, and endless rounds of day time and prime time soap operas. From time to time, she would be placed on a new medication.

Then things turned around a bit. Eastern Development contacted KM, talked to Kevin directly, told him what the project was, mentioned the largest budget Kevin had seen in years and asked him if he was interested, then waited and mentioned: "Oh yeah, you should know, there's a chance, I mean, I don't think anything will happen, but there's a chance there might be some public opposition. You know, environmental cranks who love the trees more than people."

Kevin reassured Pillington he knew all about them, even though he didn't follow the news very much or really care about politics. "I will get the job done. No question. Check anyone I've worked for. Quality. On time. On budget. That's what we do. And if anyone gets in my way, they won't be there long."

***

Pillington was reasonably sure that Kevin Marshall was the right choice. Ties to the community—not the actual neighborhood where the project was to unfold, but fairly close. And that was what you wanted. Didn't want angry confrontations with real neighbors. And he liked Marshall's quiet, no-nonsense style. Clearly the man hadn't a clue about local attachment to the woods that were coming down and would simply do what he was told.

Pillington sighed a more or less contented sigh. Life had been quite good to him over the last fifteen years. Three huge malls and four condo developments had risen under his direction and ownership. He'd had a few other investors, made them all a tidy profit, but kept most of the winnings for himself. Now a millionaire several times over, he had a house in Dover, Boston's most exclusive suburb, a small, two-million-dollar condo in West Palm and pretty much anything else a person whose personal wealth had broken into eight figures wanted.

He checked tomorrow's appointments on his phone, made sure a few notes were synced with his home computer, his office computer, and his two secretaries, and poured himself a nightcap of single malt. His wife would be back soon from her museum benefit. And he looked forward to that. Unlike a lot of wealthy men who'd been married for decades, he didn't bother with prostitutes or mistresses—not that he hadn't been offered a fair amount of young and attractive female flesh along the way. There was no better aphrodisiac than money, a lot of it. No, he loved his wife, put so much energy into his business that having sex with a young woman felt intimidating, and was quite satisfied to have someone in his life who shared his values, enjoyed his company and would, when requested, perform some brief but pleasurable oral sex.

This new project held some challenges, he could see that. He had heard the neighborhood types with their talk of sacred space and what the pond area meant to them and what they would do to protect their friends the trees. Hell, he could see it was pretty, no doubt about it. But the world was filled with trees, and that neighborhood already had more parks that most any other urban area he could think of. So he understood their point of view, but what he didn't understand was how self-important and self-righteous they were. Did they live in caves or apartments and houses? Hadn't there been trees where their homes now stood? What right did they have to prevent somebody else from getting a nice place to live? What did they want to do, take over every piece of land in the country? There was a word for that, and it wasn't a nice one. It hadn't worked in other places and it sure as hell wasn't going to work here.

Pillington was confident about this project. The condos would probably sell before they were completed, maybe a lot of them when the ground was still being broken. So close to the city, with that amazing water view. And as for these clowns from Jamaica Plain—he would take care of them. A little force, a little sweet talking; give them input on the design of the condos, promise to save as many trees as possible—and then make whatever changes were necessary six months later. "Sorry, technical difficulties. We did our best. I'm sure you can appreciate how complicated a building project is. Oh, you've never managed a forty-million-dollar development? Well, let me tell you, it's not as easy as it looks. Why one time..."

And what he knew, and they didn't, was that one of their pals in DOPA worked for him. The quiet dirty blond who wore slightly too tight jeans and baggy sweaters, just happened to be the chronically out of work cousin of his secretary, happy to get paid for simply going to these dumb meetings, recording them on her cell phone, and emailing him the mp3 files. Simple as that, he knew everything they planned before they had finished planning. He'd handle DOPA alright, just like the political causes he supported usually did a pretty good job handling the environmental extremists who wanted to ban everything from useful pesticides to oil pipelines.

Life was good, Pillington thought, very good. Except for Gwendolyn. His youngest child. The others had been fine—two strong boys who went to good schools, good universities and were on their way to good lives. But Gwen, well, she had problems. Lots of them. Slow to walk, slow to talk, complicated, sometimes debilitating asthma, problems with intellectual focus. Not exactly retarded, thank God, but not right either. Physically weak, tended to break bones or get sick under the mildest stress. Had almost no friends, unclear if she could manage college, certainly not without still living at home.

And why? Who knew? Not the dozens of specialists to whom his wife had taken Gwen. First it was this, then it was that, then something else. Each idea led to a bunch of tests; the tests would be "suggestive, interesting. But not conclusive. Perhaps we should." That sort of thing had gone on for years, and wasn't about to stop anytime soon.

And the last specialist, the one had ruled out anything genetically inherited, but had seemed to find some abnormalities in Gwen's DNA, had suggested something else.

"It could be, I mean, we're seeing more and more of this: some kind of spontaneous genetic variation in response to environmental pollutants. There are, you know I'm sure, so many. Everywhere. Every," he hesitated, not unaware of how much money Gwen's parents had, "neighborhood. Very hard to tell, to be sure.

"Best of luck and very sorry I couldn't have been more

helpful."

***

If Jason didn't get a job soon, he would lose his apartment and have to move back in with his parents. And that would be really bad news. His father stumbling home drunk most nights, his mother's constant shrieking complaints, his own temptation to join in his father's drinking, after he'd managed, barely but he'd done it, to give up the booze himself for almost two years. He didn't need any family triggers, but his bank account had been running on fumes for some time.

It wasn't as if he hadn't looked for work when it seemed like all the construction sites had shut down. He was a talented bulldozer operator. The boss, Kevin, had told him so. And he'd appreciated that. And the money was great. During the good times, he'd moved out of his family's triple decker, gotten his own place, bought a used car, some decent clothes, some nice furniture. He'd even gone out to dinner in some fancy places. But one morning, when he'd come in an hour late, hung-over from a little too much fun, Kevin had taken him aside and told him, straight, that if he ever came in late again that would be it. Finished. And that he shouldn't look so shit-faced either. "Watch it," Kevin had said, "I know all about you guys and booze. Just watch it."

That had frightened Jason, because he'd seen what it had done to his father, and he would be damned if he was going down the same road. So he went to some AA meetings, finding, to his great surprise, some really nice folks, and kept going. If people from the job kidded him about drinking cokes or tomato juice instead of beer when they went out after work, he really didn't give a shit. He'd just smile, hold up his wallet, and say, "You keep the booze, buddy, I'll keep the money."

Then Kevin laid him off, telling him that he had been a

great worker, he was really sorry, there just weren't any jobs. He'd tried to get anything he could: fast food, supermarket, city park service. Anything. And there was zero. Every opening had thirty guys lined up ahead of him. And nobody needed a bulldozer right at the moment, not for months and months.

And then this morning he'd gotten the call from Kevin. New job, several weeks work, maybe more. Not too far away. Near that pond in Jamaica Plain. Be there May 1st, that was groundbreaking day. Be there early, six a.m. Need to get started early on that first day. Get it?

Jason had gotten it. He would be there anytime Kevin wanted. Hell, he'd be there a week early and sleep on the ground for this job.

***

Salvador Diaz had had a long, hard week. Or month. Or year, if you wanted to know the truth. But the last few nights had been particularly bad. Constanza, his five-year-old, had the flu: high fever, sweats, aches and pains all around. Even with that horrible tasting liquid stuff that promised you'd "Sleep all night! Wake up feeling better!" she'd woken up crying out for him at midnight and three-thirty. And then Velma, the baby, who'd never been much of a sleeper in any case, seemed to be finally getting into the heart of teething. She would scream for half an hour, doze for an hour, and then start up again. He didn't think he'd had more than three hours sleep all together in the last two days. His wife didn't have it so easy either. Her mother was slowly, painfully, being devoured by a brain tumor. The usual night nurse, Kathy, who had stuck with her through hospitalization after hospitalization, had fallen and broken her arm in two places—not the kind of injury that lets you do what night nurses have to do.

So that's where Salvador's wife had been. She'd be back

pretty soon. The day staff wasn't great, but they were o.k., not like some of the night ones who'd ignored his mother-in-law's cries for help one night, confused a medication dose, and "somehow not noticed" that one of the I.V.'s had gotten tangled up. Yes, Sophia would soon be back, and then Salvador would have to go to work, at the CAT plant, where he did quality control on medium sized bulldozers. They would wheel the huge beasts off the assembly line and out onto a vast park like area filled with mounds of dirt, excavated pits, and piles of rock. It was up to Salvador to put them through their paces. Did the engines put out the power? Was the steering tight and accurate? Were the brakes strong and sharp enough to slow down twenty-three tons of aggressive, dangerous metal, with a six hundred horsepower motor, even on a sharp incline?

He didn't mind his work; he was damn good at it. But lately that had gotten all screwed up as well. Somebody way up the corporate ladder had decided that not enough dozers had been produced per year; that too much was being spent on quality control; that if people like Salvador could be more efficient, thirty percent more units could be tested per year, saving the company X amount of dollars, leading to Y amount more profit and a very large Z amount of raise for the Efficiency Expert who'd made the recommendations.

So this filtered down to the plant manager making it very clear to Salvador: "Of course don't cut any corners safety first priority just make damn sure you get thirty percent more done per week or we'll all be in the shit and believe me you'll be in it a lot deeper than me."

So here was Salvador at work. This particular model had power to spare. They had done something new to the engine and the big cat climbed the test hill faster than he'd ever seen comparable models. It had fine lift capacity, easily handling piles of rocks. And the six-inch-thick wooden stakes? It just mowed them down like they were grass and it was a lawnmower. It turned on a dime, or at least what passed for a dime for something this large, heavy, and awkward. And the brakes? Felt just fine. Maybe there was a tiny bit of slippage, a little delay in responsiveness. But the decelerator pedal was primo, and maybe that brake slippage was just the mechanism wearing itself in. And after all, it's not like this thing needed to stop at traffic lights. On a construction site, clearing brush, flattening the landscape for a road, it didn't matter. This was the brand-new model that was the center of the company's fall sales campaign. The manager was on his back about fulfilling the quota. And from lack of sleep he felt like his head was going to fall off anyway. He'd be damned if he was going to slow things up. So Salvador gave that particular dozer, serial number XK346791, his stamp of approval.

***

It was the kind of spring morning that made Boston seem a little bit like paradise. At least, that what it seemed to Sarah. The full moon was just setting in the west. She had seen it high overhead, reflecting in the pond, when she had gone out to try to make herself tired enough to sleep. The sight of the white sphere reflected on the motionless water, the few calls of geese, the tiniest whisper of breeze moving the first of the new leaves, the smell of the earth coming back to life—all these captivated her, but didn't do much to quiet her nerves.

Of course she was nervous. This was The Big Day. Pillington was going to try to clear some of the forest on the hill. And she, along with a few others, was going to stop him. It had required a little more planning than your typical civil disobedience action because Pillington had placed a spy in her little group of activists. It hadn't been hard to tell that Monica really didn't belong. When asked to share her history of activism like the rest of the members, she offered only vague generalities, most of them couched in crude caricature descriptions of environmental groups, the kind one might have gotten off of Fox News or some hostile internet site. "Stuff about, you know, global warming," she had said when asked about other issues in which she'd been involved. "Because, well, you know, like, I really care about nature and people, you know, like, they just mess it up." Sarah didn't think activists needed to talk like a Gradenstein lecture when it came to explaining why they did the work they did. But even for a generation more known for texting than talking, this was a little thin and suspicious. So she had to create two plans—one discussed and set at meetings in which Monica was present; and the other, the real one, which she circulated on an email list that didn't include the spy.

So Monica believed, and had no doubt told Pillington, that before dawn on the morning of May 1st Sarah and a few others would chain themselves to the first trees to be taken out by the bulldozer. In response, Pillington had hired a private security detail of several heavy-set, experienced men and a few women. The chains would be cut, the tree lovers hustled away from Pillington's private property, and things would proceed as planned.

Except that wasn't going to be it, not at all. Sarah had called in all her local, and a few of her regional, chips; and she had commitments from nearly fifty people. Nobody was going to go early and chain themselves to the trees. Rather, they were going to arrive in twos and threes, posing as interested neighbors, just there for the spectacle. As the dozer started forward, Sarah and five others would stand directly in front of it. And each time it moved they would move as well. The fifty friends would simply keep shifting around, shielding the people blocking the dozer, delaying the inevitable actions of whatever security force Pillington had on the scene. When confronted by cops or private security, the five people blocking would lock arms and go limp. And maybe seeing all this would provoke some of those who had said, "Glad to help, Sarah, but getting arrested? No, sorry, can't do it." She hadn't pressured them, hadn't tried the old "What about Gandhi and King and don't you care about?" guilt routine. She considered everyone even vaguely sympathetic to the cause an ally. Let them do what they can, she had always felt. There's always plenty to be done.

For back-up, or maybe the most important resource they had, there would be several people conspicuously filming the whole event: old acquaintances who had been working for years on a documentary about environmental activism, stringers from the area PBS stations hoping to sell a little footage for local news, and two friends who just happened to own old style, large video cameras—who would only pretend to be filming but would thereby increase the threat of terrible publicity pressure on Pillington not to have his hired thugs do anything stupid.

"This is still Massachusetts," Sarah tried to reassure a hopelessly anxious Daniel. "Nobody is going to want their project looking like Tiananmen Square for God's sake—one lone heroic protestor against a tank." She laughed, clearly both relishing and finding faintly ridiculous the idea that she might become an icon of resistance. "This will slow him down, get some publicity out there, maybe activate some politicians when the emails and texts and calls from concerned folks start coming. Just talking about it—nobody notices. But if there's a confrontation, and people get arrested, and it's in the Globe or on the news or YouTube—well, then it gets bumped up to the front of the line. It's today's catastrophe, or at least," she deepened her voice and pronounced each word with emphasis, "Urgent Matter Requiring Instant Attention and Redress." She smiled at Daniel, ruffled his hair with her fingers. "At least, that's the grand plan. So, comrade, let us do what we can."

***

At 5:37 in the morning Sarah, and Daniel, and others from DOPA and her acquaintances park their cars around the pond and walk up the hill leading to the dirt track which is the entry to the area, having been given detailed instructions. It had been a cool night, and wouldn't warm up until the sun rose over the eastern horizon and flooded the hillside with light. Still, even in jeans, work shirt, and light down jacket, Daniel sweats as he walks the quarter mile from the pond to the construction site. He is scared, every inch of him. What if the cops get violent? What if there is some kind of mob scene, a brawl, between the protestors and the construction workers who are, he is sure, damn glad to be getting some work in this spirit-killing recession? He is scared for himself, and even more, for Sarah. She just doesn't seem afraid, and that seems crazy to him. It is one thing for her to dance around the pond, hug trees, and positively beam with delight practically every time she sees a goose landing on the water. But the way she had faced those creeps in West Virginia, and the devil may care attitude she has today—doesn't she know that people can get hurt; can, God forbid, get killed when they get in the way of The Machine that is eating the world? Surely she knows that, she has seen it up close, she is fully aware of Chico Mendes and Ken Saro-Wiwa and hundreds, thousands of other martyrs for life.

"Don't you know it could happen to you?"

"Daniel," she had answered softly, reaching out to stroke his hand, "Of course I know. And I'm scared. Sometimes, really scared. Not this time, but I know it's always a risk. But, you know, when I run sometimes my legs ache, or I get winded. I don't stop. Why should I? It's just a sensation that will pass.

"So is the fear. I'm not doing anything stupid—not riding a motorcycle drunk or drinking unfiltered tap water or antagonizing the Russian mob. I'm just doing my job. And if that gets a little dangerous, and I get scared, well—that's just part of it. I'm not going to stop because I'm scared. There's too much at stake."

***

He had to be content, or at least to shut up, with that. And he did his best to believe her. But he has all the signs of panic as they walk up the hill: sick feeling in his belly, shaking hands, a heartbeat so loud he is surprised no one notices it.

And then they are there: a wide dirt area off the side road; a half dozen pickup trucks parked along the edge of the space; and in pride of place, a huge bulldozer. It's carrying a special attachment designed to break down trees and remove brush, the kind Daniel has seen in pictures of machines clearing Brazilian rainforest to raise cows for America's fast food industry, land that in five years would turn barren and lifeless. By common agreement Sarah walks in the center of a larger group of protestors pretending to be onlookers. Pillington has probably seen pictures of her, and she wants to be inconspicuous.

Surely Pillington knows that it is unusual, to say the least, for a few dozen people to show up at a construction site before six in the morning. But all they are doing is standing on the edge of his property, not threatening, not carrying signs, not chanting about Gaia or the Circle of Life. So he is content to glare over at them briefly and continue his intense conversation with a large man in work boots, gray slacks, a dress shirt and tie, and a hard hat. Then the two of them wave at a third man—solidly built, in heavy work clothes and tall boots—point at the dozer and the first line of trees with splashes of orange paint on them, and the third man slowly, determinedly, climbs in the dozer and turns it on.

The early morning stillness, just before carrying only the low tones of the workers, the call of birds announcing themselves to the world, the gurgles of a tiny stream that carries water from the hillside to some culverts under the roads that border the pond—all are smothered by the deep, threatening rumble of the machine.

***

The directions were explicit. As soon as the bulldozer starts, Sarah and three others would move in front of it, the support staff surround them, unfurl their signs, and start their chants. People with cameras, which had been hidden in backpacks and under stylish, South American ponchos, would make a dramatic show of bringing them out and starting to film—even the ones whose camera hadn't worked in years.

They all follow their instructions; everything works like a charm.

Kevin is instantly in a rage. Who were these people to get in the way? It is Pillington's land, it is his trade, his occupation, his goddam *calling* someone might say, to build according to whatever plans Pillington hands him. He does his work; he stands behind it. Nobody is going to threaten that.

Jason is confused. He is a dozer operator, and a good one; but what the hell is this? Four people standing in front of the big blade he'll use to start taking out the densely packed trees at the edge of the property. What is he supposed to do about that? Would this stop the build? Put him back to trying to get work at McDonalds or a convenience store?

When there hadn't been anyone chained to the trees, Pillington figured the protest had been called off and everything would run smoothly. He doesn't remember the last time he's been this mad. It is a beautiful morning, with a perfectly clear blue sky, just the right amount of sunlight beginning to warm things up, perfect for the start of this new task in front of him—one that he knows would work out great if these environmental fools would get out of his way.

He calls Jason down from the dozer, huddles with him and Kevin, keeping his voice low so no one can hear them over the roar of the huge machine.

"Give it a little while. My people will wrap these guys up. But we have to be slow and we can't be rough, not with," he points to the cameras, "all that and God knows how many iPhones as well. We don't want to hit the front page tomorrow as the crew that beat the hell out of the environmental clowns. You," he points his finger at Jason, almost into his chest, "get up next to them, let them smell the oil from the engine, see how scary that thing is up close. But for God's sake, don't hurt anybody. Not a touch, just a good scare. We'll see how long they last with that big baby bearing down on them. Get it?"

"Yes sir, got it," answers Jason. He is good with a dozer. Real good. He could take out a wall or a bunch of trees, turn on a dime, and make the thing go just where he wanted. Whatever was bothering those people, he knew that they didn't deserve to threaten the first decent job he'd had in ages, didn't have the *right* to stop him from earning a living.

Jason climbs back into the cab of the dozer, revs the engine super loud, smiles as he sees a bunch of the demonstrators grimacing and covering their ears. Then, slowly and under tight control, he inches forward. The four people in front of him, fear lodged deep in their eyes, move back a few feet. Jason smiles again, keeps inching forward. Then the short woman on the left shouts something to the others. They all stop moving, put up their hands, palms out towards him in a "Stop" gesture, and squint with fear.

Jason jams on the brakes. The dozer grinds to a halt, less

than a foot from Sarah's outstretched hands. "Let's play a little," thinks Jason. Slowly he backs the dozer up a few feet, then jams the levers so that it lurches to the right. He guns the engine. If they don't move pretty quickly, he'll be around them. Then they'll have to run to get back in front before he hits the first of the orange marked trees. They'll look pretty stupid, he thinks. And he knows he can keep up this cat and mouse bit for a long time. Longer, he thinks, then they'll be able to deal with the fear of being in front of the dozer.

But they do move pretty fast, and once again, standing tall, hands facing him, they wait, some of their hands shaking. Waiting. Behind him, he can hear the chants, "Nature is not for sale." "Defend our pond area." "Protect creation."

He backs up, leaves the throttle low, waits, and then goes even further to the right. They move with him, but before they can get in place, he quickly reverses, then lurches sharply left. They are all a little stunned. Who knew a bulldozer could move that fast? Three of them are still moving right but one, the small woman on the end, the one who seems like she is in charge, has seen it coming. She is over to his left, almost before he realizes it.

***

For a few hours the night before, in one of those strange spring showers that seem to come from nowhere and then dissipate, rain had fallen in a medium strength downpour for a few minutes. There is mud, slippery mud, not that much of it, but some, underfoot. Sarah's low-cut hiking boots perform well on mud, but parts of them are worn, too worn, to hold very well today.

So with a quick turn to her right, trying to head off the dozer's sudden, unexpected move, she slips—skidding on the mud until she is down first on one knee, and then on both. She rests there for a moment, staring up at the six-foot-high tree cutting blade, and once again she holds up her hands, palms facing Jason. She mouths the words, "No. Stop. Please."

Jason slams on the brake. "Crazy bitch," he yells, the phrase carrying over the sound of the engine, "get out of my way."

Is it because Jason's boots too are a little slippery, and don't grip the brake pedal as they should? Is the pedal itself, from brand new machine XK346791, not yet worn in enough, and also a little slippery? Are the brakes themselves, as Salvador had found on the test, not quite right? A little slow to respond, giving the operator just the slightest lag, so that maybe the machine will lurch a little more forward then is wanted. Not far. Just a few feet. But at this point there is a slight decline, and the rumbling, oil smelling beast slides just the smallest bit on the muddy ground. And with Jason's sliding boot, and the lag in the brakes, and the little extra from the hillside, the machine goes a little too far.

The huge blade, made to prepare the land to hold condos and malls and factories and highways and office parks for businesses like Eastern Development and Beta Mining and Magnificent Chicken—the edge of that huge blade catches Sarah Carson on the side of her head.

Jason barely notices it. You can't feel the impact of a two-ton blade as it hits a human head, especially when you're barely moving, just about to stop. And the machine you're driving is so big, and the head of a short, compact woman, who is telling you not to do your job—is so small, compared to your machine, to all the machines everywhere.

Horrified screams tear from the throats of the protestors. The dozer halts a bare second after the impact. Daniel, who has been assigned legal and media oversight, races the forty feet from where he's standing and kneels by her side. Everything else fades from view, at first all he can see is her face. Her eyes are open, her hair, close cropped and freshly washed, gleams in the sunlight that has just risen above the trees, her mouth is open, as if she is saying "Oh," as if she is struck with sudden understanding of a question she'd known that someday her life would answer. Here is the answer. There won't be another.

An enormous gaping wound has opened up on the side of her head, blood flowing through her hair, down her neck and onto her shirt. Her head tilts towards her shoulder at an impossible angle. Daniel takes her hands, his face a mask of terror and pity.

Sarah's mouth forms into the slightest of smiles. "Look...Da...look." That is all she can get out, but her eyes, which have been fastened on his, move to the tallest branch of a small sapling on the edge of the clearing. A fiery scarlet cardinal with a small pointed beak surrounded by a quarter inch of black, a tuft of feathers for a pointed crown, and an astoundingly red breast and wings, has just landed there. His bright, brittle cry pierces the tumult of people shouting for doctors and ambulances, crying in shock, screaming in rage. He wants a mate, a nest, to father some eggs, to carry on.

Chapter 22
Anne

The neighborhood was pretty much what she had expected. Shabby, three story wooden houses, with small porches front and back, the well-known 'triple-deckers' of Boston's working-class neighborhoods. A few bare trees, none over twenty feet, cracked sidewalks littered with plastic bags, cigarette butts, bits of uneaten food, and old newspapers. Aging cars with broken fenders, gashes from old accidents, tires rubbed bald from too many trips to work, the doctor, or the grown children in the army or vocational school or jail. And, she noted with sadness but no longer terror, there were also used needles and the ribbed orange caps that kept them safe before they were used to destroy the minds and souls of addicts. No doubt there was plenty going on around here, just as there was in New York and L.A. and Chicago, in the small towns of bucolic, scenic, progressive Vermont, whose governor had recently declared a state of emergency over heroin use; and in rural Montana, where it was likely to be the even more lethal methamphetamines. Or in the places where it was legal anti-depressants, or alcoholic drinks in beautifully finished tumblers or champagne flutes or plastic cases of cheap wine or micro brewed beer with names like Ugly Bastard and Field of Dreams. There was no end to the ways in which people could obliterate their consciousness, change the way they felt for an hour or so, no matter what they had to sacrifice to get there.

"And I," she smiled quietly to herself, "know about all that about as well as anyone, don't I?" There was no anger in her self-reflection, no bitterness about the strange, solitary path she had chosen. An enormous compassion had risen up, taking her, and Lily, and Joffrey, and Patricia, and all the other tormented souls with it. She had no idea if it would last, but it was one of the gifts of her long years of training that worrying about shifts in her future mental state didn't arise very often. She was no longer tormented by trying to figure out what had happened to Lily, where and why the poor girl had gone so wrong.

She carried a half full medium sized cloth shopping bag. It bore the name of an American Buddhist publisher, and an image of Buddha's face taken from a Tibetan tonka that she quite liked. The bag was half full: a bouquet of irises, a box of chocolates, and a green, zippered fleece vest from a well-known maker of camping gear. She had thought long and hard over what to put in the bag. Would the chocolate seem condescending? Would the flowers be way past irrelevant and on into ridiculous? Would the vest fit? Or just demonstrate to its recipient how out of touch Anne had been for so long?

In the end, though, she had just gone back to the basics, to the fundamental insight with which this still breathtakingly new part of her life had begun. Who, after all, didn't like chocolate? Unless you were on some kind of rigid, weight-loss-at-all-costs diet, and she would have bet her modest but not nonexistent savings that that wasn't going on in this case. And the flowers? Well, the simple fact was that they were beautiful—the rich play of purple and yellow, the incredibly delicate center, the way the whole being seemed to invite the love that only the pollinating insect could offer, but people could surely, surely, marvel at. Finally, the vest just seemed right. Even in this beginning of spring, with crocuses pushing through the dirty snow in the littered front yards, mornings and evenings could be chill. And if not now, then in October and November, when the reality of summer heat gave way to the surprising briskness of a fifty-degree morning.

And if *she* didn't like the vest, well, Anne would take it back for herself. The green went well with her brown eyes; and it would match the yellow skirt and black blouse, which today was topped by heavy woolen sweater with a delicate lavender trim but which would be perfect when it got just a little warmer. And her brown hair, slowly growing out, would look good with it as well. She had never, not really, liked the bald look of the aspiring Buddhist student or the confirmed hairlessness of The Teacher. She enjoyed the rich brown of her naturally thick, healthy hair; hoped other people liked the way it looked as well. Soon enough it would be gray, she was sure, so why not enjoy—treasure, really—what she had today?

"Yes, by God, maybe a vest for myself." She chuckled aloud, then whispered, tenderly, "Desire, desire." And she felt a shocked delight in the feeling of attraction to something outside herself. Wasn't it wonderful to want? And not be afraid of wanting? She had been listening to music that she liked and turning the station or changing the CD if she didn't. It was all right to like, to want, and to be disappointed when you didn't get what you desired. It was just fine.

Still, there was Lily. That wasn't fine. But the simple truth was that anything else—a healthy sister, a loving father, a stronger mother—had never existed. They were just thoughts, as real as the mist that formed on the lake when a sudden warm front made a little fog. It would vanish with the rising sun. Reality wouldn't change just because she didn't like it. She had learned that from Buddhism, from meditation, from teaching. And she would always be grateful.

But there was more to life than not suffering.

Once again she consulted the piece of paper she'd gotten from the attorney, the younger partner of the now-retired man who had settled Joffrey's will and taken the role of trustee of the money that had been left for Lily.

"I'm not sure what to recommend to you," he'd said, looking up from a desk burdened with case files, depositions, note pads, and three cell phones. He had a broad forehead, small, perpetually squinting blue eyes, a tailored white shirt with a loosened blue tie and a gray suit, a long thin nose and clear, pale skin leading to a slender neck and narrow shoulders. "I see her, as per the requirements of the trust, every month. She comes with results from a small clinic, bearing the results of a test taken within the last three days. Sometimes she passes the test, sometimes she does not. If she passes, she gets a little spending money for the month. If not, well, there's always another chance in thirty days. The trust pays her rent and utilities, food bills from the nearby Market Basket go directly to me, limited to $80 per week and only if she gets the food herself. I made the arrangements with the management. She has medical coverage, and all the doctors know what she is. I make sure of that.

"How is she? I don't know. She doesn't have much to say. Nothing at all, really. She just arrives, hands me the paper, and waits for the money that I count out. Could she be using drugs? I'm sure she could, though not all that much and not all that often, I don't think."

He hesitated, brushed the mop of straight brown hair back over his forehead, bent over his desk to consult some record on his computer screen, humming tunelessly to himself.

"Yes. Yes. As a matter of fact, it has been some time, nearly two years, really, since she has failed a test. She has been, as they say, 'clean' for some time."

He looked again at the computer, and then at some papers, and then back at Anne. Clearing his throat, speaking slowly, hedging his bets the way any cautious legal mind would. "Or, of course, she could simply be finding a way to beat the tests. They are very smart these. People. At doing that. Shame they don't put their minds to better uses. Yes. Really. A shame."

Anne could see the question in his eyes. Did she, who clearly had been living a long way from the drug wars, really want to resume this relationship? She simply waited. She'd made it clear what she wanted, and that any threats of pain or loss or deterioration were simply not relevant.

"Very well," the man continued. "Here it is. She may actually have a phone. You can get them for a few dollars, and pay only by the minutes. But if she does, she's never given us the number. I hope things work out."

He handed Anne the paper with Lily's address. She thanked him quietly, looking him directly in the eyes for a moment, then smiling, and walked out to see her sister.

***

There is still a bit of dirty snow left between the sidewalk and front yard of the house, some of it black from air pollution, some yellow from dog pee, and some lumpy from dog shit. Still, there is some, Anne sees, that hasn't been stepped on or fouled. She bends down, looking closely at the white crystals forming the slightly frozen surface where thaws and overnight cold snaps have left a crust. Cautiously she extends the index finger from her right hand, touching the frigid surface, feeling its icy finish painfully chill her skin almost immediately. Then she pokes the finger through, into the virgin snow beneath. The snow surrounds her finger, turning the shock of cold to pain. She pushes further, until her whole hand is surrounded by an assault of cold, continuing until she reaches the ground beneath the snow pack. The ground is still in the grip of winter's immobilizing temperatures. It feels so hard that if one didn't understand New England's seasons, one might think it would always be the way it was at that moment: covered in dirty, freezing, lifeless crystals; hard to the touch, unyielding to the spirit. But she knows it won't always be like this. Things would change. There would be warmth, and something, she had no idea what, would soften, yield, and cause, for a while at least, less pain.

She stands there, staring at the house, reflecting on all she has learned and all she hasn't.

Buddhism, she now thought, was an escape, made for people who couldn't stand too much reality. But it was also the thing that had saved her life. She had continued meditating, the habit far too ingrained to break. But she didn't take it so seriously, wasn't afraid to use a solid pillow to cushion her hips and ease the pressure on her knees, and often stopped before the hour was up, when she just felt like stopping. Perhaps it was just a way to do something when God knows you need to do something, but there is just nothing to do.

There had been a third way, between having her spirit killed by her family and just disappearing into a haze of meditation. But she hadn't seen it. And if she had, she couldn't have done it. That, and not endless rounds of practice, was "the hardest" thing. The old monk, who was no fool and whose center had welcomed her when there seemed to be no place for her in the world, hadn't understood. Or, she wonders, maybe he had understood, but had been smart enough to realize that *she* wasn't ready, that she couldn't handle the truth.

For this third way came at a terrible cost—the pain of watching people you care about suffer, knowing you can't do much about it, and being content with just being there, and doing a little along the way. It meant finding some joy in life even though Lily was using, or Patricia was fading away, or Joffrey's veins were practically popping out of his head in useless fury. It meant acknowledging that her own pain was not just from watching theirs but from how little she could get from them. She had gotten so tired of waiting for someone to pay attention to anything she wanted that it had seemed so much easier just to stop wanting.

Ultimately, Buddhism was wrong, she *did* have a self. It wasn't what people thought of her, the size of bank account or her breasts or whether or not she was listed in some Sunday *New York Times* article on "rising American Buddhist teachers." No, the teachings were right about all that. They were illusions which simply bred pain.

But that didn't mean the self was an emptiness, an illusion, nothing. It was there, as real as the earth and sky, as powerful as sunlight, as important as anything God or evolution or the laws of physics had ever created. It was her ability to love. She could care for other people, and the world, and herself—or not. She could care even if it only meant giving someone else, giving Lily, a few minutes of happiness in an otherwise tortured and hopeless life. If only to offer a bowl of ice cream on a hot night.

She stands up and dries her hand on her skirt, taking one last look at the other houses. One has a split and tilted "for sale" sign in the yard, a front door that seems about to fall off its hinges, and some cracked windows. "Just for me," she thinks, on the edge of loud laughter, "the site of my new meditation center. Free instruction in the world's wisdom. Or at least a little company with some fellow sufferers."

Anne walks up the steps and rings the bell. To her surprise a clearly audible chime comes from within. She waits, then calls out. "Lily, it's me. It's Anne. I'm here."

Chapter 23
Daniel

It was the first bench you came to, after turning right where the two hundred yards of sidewalk led from the small rise of land down from the Jamaicaway to the Pond. There were fine old oak and maple trees lining the walk down, rising sixty to eighty feet high, seeming to revel in this unbroken string of blisteringly hot July days and long, clear nights of stars and moon.

Daniel barely made it from his house, a third of a mile away, down to the bench. Some days he wasn't sure if he could do it, this dawn walk of his, but he forced himself, cursing aloud at his weakness, the self-loathing a momentary respite from his pointless rage and grief.

Sarah was gone. As much as he had loved her while she was alive, he only felt now how deeply the loss cut into him. She had given him some joy in life. Something, he now knew, he had lost years ago. It was that loss that had poisoned his marriage, cut him off from his friends, and made him a poor organizer. Depressed? You bet, he thought to himself. And given the state of the world, is that really so surprising? How many different ways are there for human beings to be cruel and stupid? However many there are, we'll find them all—or die trying.

Or die anyway.

But Sarah just laughed, or danced, or smiled. She knew all about it, every bit. And she worked, God she worked hard: ten, twelve, fourteen hours a day. Success, failure, boring meetings, impossible bureaucrats, polluters with a thousand, ten thousand, a million times more resources. Average people who would not, could not be made to understand just how dangerous and destructive all these poisons were.

Sarah had breathed in all that pain and horror and stupidity; and breathed out love and care and good humor. A silly joke, a self-deprecating irony were her stock in trade, just as much as she would glow with appreciation at a goose in flight, a tree coming to life in the spring, a cute baby, or a couple of chatty nine-year old girls.

And now he couldn't face the computer, couldn't read the journals. He was stuck at the bottom of a pit. She had died, and he had lived. She had stood there, in front of that horrible machine, and he had watched it kill her. Why in God's name was he still alive? Why were any of them—Pillington, the big contractor, the stocky guy driving the bulldozer—not rotting in the ground instead of Sarah?

A week after the funeral he had driven to Pillington's mansion in Dover, sat in the car across the street, looking at the huge windows, the tastefully placed "Orbit Security" sign, the massive wooden front door. He wondered if he could get through the door, past whoever would answer at this hour. Whether or not Pillington would be home. Whether he could find the words he needed to tell him what he'd killed. And whether he, Daniel, could find it within himself to pick up something heavy lying around—an ornate plate, a small statue, a big lamp—and smash it into the side of the man's head so he would know what it felt like.

But he couldn't. He was just Daniel, the college professor, not someone who would take physical vengeance on another person, much as he might have liked to. He just drove away, fighting off the tears that now came a little less often, but still several times a day.

At least something had happened to soften the pain. The project, the development, was simply stopped in its tracks. An outpouring of sympathy for the dead woman, outrage at the brutality of her wounds, graphically displayed on all the usual internet sources; an eruption of public outrage that the few dozen acres of precious woodland were to be sacrificed for upscale dwellings. All sorts of zoning, environmental, and public interest regulations were discovered to put the whole thing on hold for years. Politicians made their opposition clear, glossing over questions of why they hadn't said much until someone died.

***

Pillington had considered aggressive legal action, but his lawyer had cautioned against it.

"Let this all die down; you should pardon the expression. Give it a few years, then we'll see. You don't want to get the reputation of someone callous, greedy, a ravager of all that natural beauty." Then gave an ironic chuckle. "But later, well, people forget, get involved in other things. Remember: they have to win every single time. But if we want that land to look the way we want it to: well, we only have to win once."

Kevin licked his wounds and waited for calls for some other jobs. After a few weeks the construction freeze lifted a bit, and he was asked to rehab some dilapidated triple deckers in Roslindale. It wasn't much, but it was something.

Jason hadn't recovered. He had jumped down from the bulldozer when he realized what had happened. He had seen the blood, the strange, sick angle of Sarah's head against her own shoulder. And he'd realized immediately that he had killed her. This wasn't him. He wouldn't, he couldn't, have done this. But he had. How? How? He kept asking himself over and over. Was there something hidden and dangerous in him? Was there something wrong with what he did for work? It wasn't like he was building atomic bombs, for God's sake. He wasn't shooting anyone, or selling drugs to children. He was just helping people get a nice place to live. How could that lead to death? He went over it in his mind, sinking further and further into an anxious, agitated depression, complicated with increasing numbers of vodka tonics each day.

***

Years ago, Daniel had heard about Jewish rituals of mourning, ideas from an identity and tradition that had meant virtually nothing to him since childhood. But he had learned from a widowed colleague about the practice of saying the same prayer, a special prayer for the dead that actually was only several paragraphs praising God, which observant Jews said every day for eleven months after a death. This was to be said in the synagogue, in the presence of other Jews, in part so that the mourner was reminded that *everyone* knew death and at some point would be a mourner. He had also heard that after the first week or so, a friend was supposed to come to the house of the mourner, and literally pull them up to their feet from where they sat or lay, separated from the flow of ordinary life. It's enough, the friend's pull was saying, you can come back now, even though the one you love is gone.

Daniel knew he wasn't about to start going to a synagogue, even one of the modernized, gay welcoming, guitar-playing rabbi ones that had sprung up in the last thirty years. But he needed something to do, every day, something besides stare into his computer screen, pick up and put down environmental magazines, lie on his couch trying to eat something other than the occasional chocolate bar or donut. He'd avoided alcohol, knowing without a doubt where that would lead. And the idea of taking anti-depressants just seemed silly. Amy and Sharon had called, come over, offered support. He could see them trying, but it hadn't helped.

Most of the time he turned his phone off, ignored his email, and just sat with his thoughts: memories of his time with Sarah, bitterness at his loss, rage at the forces that had killed her, even some rare, but incredibly intense, anger at her. He had warned her. He had. And *why*, for *what*, had she sacrificed herself? Her body was now just another piece of wreckage. Like the rivers in North Carolina, like Martin's tiny town and mountain, like Lake Aral, like the breasts of so many cancer victims and the minds of all the teenagers fried by the screens. Just another sacrifice zone that could never be recovered.

Why had she put herself in their path? Why hadn't she stayed with him for as long as they could be together?

But he also knew, and hated knowing, that this just was Sarah. Attachment to the life she so intensely loved would not keep her from putting it at risk. Her own life wasn't the point. Sooner or later, something like this would have happened. It was Sarah Carson vs. The Machine—the machine that made her look like an ant under an elephant's foot. She had studied it, criticized it, even given it a few small bruises. But sooner or later she was going to be crushed.

So Daniel stumbled out of bed each morning in the dark, slowly making his way down to the bench, a bench sheltered by a particularly beautiful old beech tree, whose main trunk went straight up for fifty feet, and which had a large secondary branch that gently curved over the paved path to droop small branches and leaves over the dirt beach next to the pond. The area under the tree had been one of Sarah's favorites. It was shaded from the glare of the July sun, protected from rain, and graced by a magical yellow canopy in late October.

***

Daniel sits on the bench, watching the sky slowly brighten. In the last two months, he has come to the bench every single morning: exhausted, emotionally broken, for a week sick with a vicious summer flu, his sinuses clogged, his throat aching, his forehead hot to the touch. He has seen dog walkers, solitary pedestrians, hard core runners speeding by; and, always a wonder within the city limits of a major metropolitan area, wildlife: blue herons, a single, arrogant coyote ("I'm not somebody's stupid pet, asshole," it seemed to say, looking him over, "so fuck off"), and even a deer, whom Daniel had tried to tell to go back to the wooded hillside, not towards the dangerous roads on which people were already speeding to work.

Once, as he was walking back to his house, two slender women of indeterminate age walking arm in arm passed him on the path leading back up towards his house. They were talking animatedly, and as they were next to him, both burst into laughter. To his surprise he thought he recognized one of them. But who was it? Minutes later he realized it was the Teacher, he'd forgotten her name, from the Buddhist center he'd gone to with Amy, in what now seemed like another lifetime.

He would sit, stare at the water, for how long he didn't really know. As the light grew, he could see the seagulls swooping low, cormorants hunting for fish, geese gliding in for a landing on the face of the water. Then he would drag himself back to his house, or to Sarah's office, on which for some reason, he still didn't know, he'd taken the lease.

But today. Today feels different. He doesn't drag himself out of bed, but jumps out, throws on his clothes, feels a need to hurry down here. Everything seems sharply outlined, even in the pre-dawn gray: the bark of the trees lining his street, the metal of the parked cars, the leaves on the trees and on the sidewalk, the grass on the fields that slope down to the pond.

He can feel his fingers and toes tingling, the early morning calls of birds and insects seem strangely loud, as if they are being amplified by microphones or as if something has been removed from his ears, something that has been blocking his hearing. His hands shake slightly, he keeps twisting and turning on the bench, looking behind him, then right and left, then leaning forward to stare across the pond at the boathouse, the wooded hillside, the far shore with its wider beach.

What is happening? Who or what is coming? The sense of expectation—like dogs who know when earthquakes are imminent, or birds know when to migrate, or some women can tell that birth labor will start *today*—fills every corner of his being. "Stand up," he hears a voice tell him. "Stand up and touch the tree." But who or what is speaking? There is no one here; it can't have been outside him. "I said STAND UP AND TOUCH THE TREE," the voice repeats.

So he does, reaching out with both hands first just to touch, and then, not caring what anyone who sees him might have thought, to embrace it. "So silly, so absurd," he thinks, "to make fun of people for hugging trees. Look at everything else we hold close—our phones and cars and bank accounts. And consider what the trees do for us and what they are." But then his mind, blessedly, turns off. He can feel the rough texture of the bark on his cheek and fingers, the slight dampness from the dew that has fallen overnight, the spot where a bit of moss has started to grow, even the smoothed over place where a branch was cut off years ago.

And then he feels something more, something that first stuns and then thrills him. He can sense the tree, the roots down into the soil, under the surface, starting out thick and terribly strong, getting smaller and smaller to become the slightest tendrils that take up nutrients, working with the bacteria that make it possible for vegetation to get life from dirt. Below and around the roots, that same dirt holds tight to the tree, gives it water and food, and gives the same things to every other tree and bush and tiny flower. All of them, connected, together, here.

And he can feel the leaves, filled with desire for the sun, reaching out to that huge fireball ninety-seven million miles away—the fireball which would have killed them all in an instant if they had been too close, but is, miraculously, just the right distance to enable them all to live. These leaves, here, waving to the sky, to the moon, the sun, to all the galaxies in the universe—to all the places where there is just rock and gas and flame and deadly cold.

Daniel rests his head on the tree, tightens the grip of his arms around it, and for the briefest of instants knows, as deeply and completely as he will ever know anything, that he and the roots, and the leaves, and the trunk which connect them, and all the dirt and stars and trees and all the rest, are all together, together in some strange incomprehensible magnificent and horrible and painful and splendid existence. That is all there is, this everything. And the rest, as someone had said long ago, is commentary.

He pats the tree, even presses his lips briefly to the bark, and turns back to the water. The early mist has dissipated, the same sun which lit up the hillside when Sarah died has risen today, fiercely bright in its summer power, illuminating the woods for which she'd sacrificed herself and catching, for just a moment, the white wings of a seagull on the far side of the pond.

The water, the trees, the sky, and now that instant flash of beauty of sun and bird. Daniel gasps in pleasure. He whispers, "Thank you, thank you."

About Atmosphere Press

Atmosphere Press is an independent, full-service publisher for excellent books in all genres and for all audiences. Learn more about what we do at atmospherepress.com.

We encourage you to check out some of Atmosphere's latest releases, which are available at Amazon.com and via order from your local bookstore:

Tree One, a novel by Fred Caron
Connie Undone, a novel by Kristine Brown
The Enemy of Everything, poetry by Michael Jones
A Cage Called Freedom, a novel by Paul P.S. Berg
Giving Up the Ghost, essays by Tina Cabrera
Family Legends, Family Lies, nonfiction by Wendy Hoke
Shining in Infinity, a novel by Charles McIntyre
Buildings Without Murders, a novel by Dan Gutstein
What?! You Don't Want Children?: Understanding Rejection in the Childfree Lifestyle, nonfiction by Marcia Drut-Davis
Katastrophe: The Dramatic Actions of Kat Morgan, a young adult novel by Sylvia M. DeSantis
Peaceful Meridian: Sailing into War, Protesting at Home, nonfiction by David Rogers Jr.
The Stargazers, poetry by James McKee
SEED: A Jack and Lake Creek Book, a novel by Chris S. McGee
The Pretend Life, poetry by Michelle Brooks
The Testament, a novel by S. Lee Glick
Minnesota and Other Poems, poetry by Daniel N. Nelson
Southern. Gay. Teacher., nonfiction by Randy Fair
Mondegreen Monk, a novel by Jonathan Kumar

About the Author

Roger S. Gottlieb is professor of philosophy at Worcester Polytechnic Institute and the author or editor of twenty-one books and more than 150 articles on environmentalism, religious life, contemporary spirituality, political philosophy, ethics, the Holocaust, feminism, and disability. He is internationally known for his work as a leading analyst and exponent of religious environmentalism, his passionate and moving account of spirituality in an age of environmental crisis, and his innovative and humane description of the role of religion in a democratic society. Two of his books received Nautilus Book Awards: *Engaging Voices* (for fiction) and *Spirituality: What it Is and Why it Matters*; and he was awarded the Prophetic Witness Award by Massachusetts Interfaith Power and Light.

He has edited six academic book series, serves on the editorial boards of several academic journals, is contributing editor to *Tikkun Magazine*, and has appeared online on *Patheos, Huffington, Grist, Wall Street Journal, Washington Post, Real Clear Religion, Stardust Review, E Magazine Online* and others. His writings have been endorsed by many luminaries, including Elie Wiesel, Harvey Cox, Bill McKibben, Holmes Rolston, Barbara Ehrenreich, and the heads of both the National Council of Churches and the Sierra Club.

As a public speaker Roger is a riveting presenter whose message resonates long after his formal presentation is done and can lead people to act as well as think and feel.

He lives in Jamaica Plain with his wife, the feminist psychotherapist, non-fiction author and poet, Miriam Greenspan. Roger can be reached at gottlieb@wpi.edu.

CPSIA information can be obtained
at www.ICGtesting.com
Printed in the USA
FSHW010803290121
78021FS